Grand Avenue

Also by Joy Fielding

The First Time

Missing Pieces

Don't Cry Now

Tell Me No Secrets

See Jane Run

Good Intentions

The Deep End

Life Penalty

The Other Woman

Kiss Mommy Goodbye

Grand Avenue

Joy Fielding

Pocket Books
New York London Toronto Sydney Singapore

This Large Print Book carries the Seal of Approval of N.A.V.H.

POCKET BOOKS, a division of Simon & Schuster, Inc.
1230 Avenue of the Americas, New York, NY 10020

ISBN: 0-7434-2269-4

First Pocket Books large-print hardcover edition November 2001

10 9 8 7 6 5 4 3 2 1

POCKET and colophon are registered trademarks of Simon & Schuster, Inc.

For information regarding special discounts for bulk purchases, please contact Simon & Schuster Special Sales at 1-800-456-6798 or business@simonandschuster.com

Designed by Jaime Putorti

Printed in the U.S.A

To Beverley Slopen,
a truly Grand Dame.

Acknowledgments

Firstly, I'd like to thank all the readers who wrote or e-mailed me after the publication of *The First Time*. It was wonderful hearing from all of you, and especially gratifying that you loved the novel. I hope you'll feel the same way about *Grand Avenue,* and that you'll take the time and trouble to let me know your thoughts. They are greatly appreciated.

A special thank you to Jan Evans, a wonderful and generous woman who escorted me through Cincinnati during one of my recent book tours, and who provided me with literally boxes of information about that beautiful city. I hope I got everything right.

A heartfelt thank you to my former editor, Linda Marrow, for her enthusiasm at the beginning of this project, and to my current editor, Emily Bestler, for taking such good care of it. Thanks also to all the terrific and talented people at Pocket—especially copy editor Steve Boldt—for being so helpful and supportive. A special thanks to Judith Curr for being every writer's dream publisher.

Love, as always, to my regular, and very special, crew—Owen Laster, Larry Mirkin, and Beverley Slopen, and to Warren, Shannon, and Annie. I'm deeply grateful to—and for—all of you.

Introduction

We called ourselves the Grand Dames: four women of varying height, weight, and age, with shockingly little in common, or so it seemed at the time of our initial meeting some twenty-three years ago, other than that we all lived on the same quiet, tree-lined street, were all married to ambitious and successful men, and each had a daughter around the age of two.

The street was named Grand Avenue, and despite the changes the years have brought to Mariemont, the upscale suburb of Cincinnati in which we lived, the street itself has remained remarkably the same: a series of neat wood-framed houses set well back from the road, the road itself winding lazily away from the busy main street it intersects toward the small park at its opposite end. It was in this park—the Grand Parkette, as the town council had christened the tiny triangle of land, unaware of the inherent irony—that we first met almost a quarter of a century ago, four grown women making a beeline for three children's swings, knowing the loser would be relegated to the sandbox, her disappointed youngster loudly wailing her displeasure for the rest of the world to hear. Not the first time a mother has failed to live up to her daughter's expectations. Certainly not the last.

I don't remember who lost that race, or who started talking to whom, or even what that initial conversation was about. I remember only how easily the words flowed amongst us, how seamlessly we moved from one topic to another, the familiar anecdotes, the understanding smiles, the welcome, if unexpected, intimacy of it all, all the more welcome precisely because it was so unexpected.

More than anything else, I remember the laughter. Even now, so many years later, so many tears later—and despite everything that has happened, the unforeseen, sometimes horrifying detours our lives took—I can still hear it, the undisciplined, yet curiously melodious collection of giggles and guffaws that shuffled between octaves with varying degrees of intensity, each laugh a signature, as different as we were ourselves. Yet, how well those diverse sounds blended together, how harmonious the end result. For years, I carried the sound of that early laughter with me wherever I went. I summoned it at will. It sustained me. Maybe because there was so little of it later on.

We stayed in the park that day until it started raining, a sudden summer shower no one was prepared for, and one of us suggested transferring the impromptu party to someone's house. It must have been me, because we ended up at my house. Or maybe it was just that my home was closest to the park. I don't remember. I do remember the four of us happily ensconced in the wood-paneled family room in my basement, shoes off, hair wet, clothes damp, drinking freshly brewed coffee and still laughing, as we watched our daughters parallel play at our feet, guiltily aware that we were having more fun than they were, that our children would just as soon be in their own homes, where they didn't have to share their toys or compete with strangers for their mothers' attention.

"We should form a club," one of the women suggested. "Do this on a regular basis."

"Great idea," the rest of us quickly agreed.

To commemorate the occasion, I dug out my husband's badly neglected Kodak Super 8 movie camera, at which I was as hopeless as I am with its modern counterpart, and the end result was something less than satisfactory, lots of quick, jerky movements and blurred women missing the tops of their heads. A few years ago, I had the film transferred to VHS, and strangely enough, it looks much better. Maybe it's the improved technology, or my wide-screen TV, ten feet by twelve, that descends from the ceiling with the mere push of a button. Or maybe it's that my vision has blurred just enough to compensate for my failure as a technician, because the women now seem clear, very much in focus.

Looking at this film today, what strikes me most, what, in fact, never fails to take my breath away, no matter how many times I view it, is not just how ineffably, unbearably young we all were, but how everything we were—and everything we were to become—was already present in those miraculously unlined faces. And yet, if you were to ask me to look into those seemingly happy faces and predict their futures, even now, twenty-three years later, when I know only too well how everything turned out, I couldn't do it. Even knowing what I know, it is impossible for me to reconcile these women with their fate. Is that the reason I return so often to this tape? Am I looking for answers? Maybe it's justice I'm seeking. Maybe peace.

Or resolution.

Maybe it's as simple—and as difficult—as that.

I only know that when I look at these four young women,

myself included, our youth captured, *imprisoned,* as it were, on videotape, I see four strangers. Not one feels more familiar to me than the rest. I am as foreign to myself as any of the others.

They say that the eyes are the mirror of the soul. Can anyone staring into the eyes of these four women really pretend to see so deep? And those sweet, innocent babies in their mothers' arms—is there even one among you who can see beyond those big, tender eyes, who can hear the heart of a monster beating below? I don't think so.

We see what we want to see.

So there we sit, in a kind of free-form semicircle, taking our turns smiling and waving for the camera, four beguilingly average women thrown together by random circumstance and a suddenly rainy afternoon. Our names are as ordinary as we were: Susan, Vicki, Barbara, and Chris. Common enough names for the women of our generation. Our daughters, of course, are a different story altogether. Children of the seventies, and products of our imaginative and privileged loins, our offspring were anything but ordinary, or so each of us was thoroughly convinced, and their names reflected that conviction: Ariel, Kirsten, Tracey, and Montana. Yes, Montana. That's her on the far right, the fair-haired, apple-cheeked cherub kicking angrily at her mother's ankles, huge navy-blue eyes filling with bitter tears, just before her chubby little legs carry her rigid little body out of the camera's range. No one is able to figure out the source of this sudden outburst, especially her mother, Chris, who does her best to placate the little girl, to coax her back into the safety of her outstretched arms. To no avail. Montana remains stubbornly outside the frame, unwilling to be cajoled or comforted. Chris holds this uneasy posture for some time, perched on the end of her high-backed chair, slim arms extended and empty. Her shoulder-length, blond hair is pulled back and away from her heart-shaped face into a high ponytail, so that she looks more like a well-scrubbed teenaged baby-sitter than a woman approaching thirty. The look on her face says she will wait forever for her daughter to forgive her these imagined transgressions and come back where she belongs.

It seems inconceivable to me now, and yet I know it to be true, that not one of us considered herself especially pretty, let alone beautiful. Even Barbara, who was a former Miss Cincinnati and a finalist for the title of Miss Ohio, and who never abandoned her fondness for big hair and stiletto heels, was constantly plagued by self-doubt, always worrying about her weight and agonizing over each tiny wrinkle that teased at the skin around her large brown eyes and full, almost obscenely lush, lips. That's her, beside Chris. Her tall helmet of dark hair has been somewhat flattened by the rain, and her stylish Ferragamo pumps lie abandoned by the front door amidst the other women's sandals and sneakers, but her posture is still beauty-pageant perfect. Barbara never wore flats, even to the park, and she didn't own a pair of blue jeans. She was never less than impeccably dressed, and from the time she was fifteen, no one had ever seen her without full makeup, and that included her husband, Ron. She confessed to the group that in the four years they'd been married, she'd been getting up at six o'clock every morning, a full half hour before her husband, to shower and do her hair and makeup. Ron had fallen in love with Miss Cincinnati, she proclaimed, as if addressing a panel of judges. Just because she was now a Mrs. didn't give her the right to fall down on the job. Even on weekends, she was out of bed early enough to make sure she was suitably presentable before her daughter, Tracey, woke up, demanding to be fed.

Not that Tracey was ever one to make demands. According to Barbara, her daughter was, in every respect, the perfect child. In fact, the only difficulty she'd ever had with Tracey had been in the hours before her birth, when the nine-pound-plus infant, securely settled in a breech position, and not particularly anxious to make an appearance, refused to drop or turn around and had to be taken by cesarean section, leaving a scar that ran from Barbara's belly button to her pubis. Today, of course, doctors generally opt for the less disfiguring, more cosmetically appealing crosscut, one that disturbs fewer muscles and lies hidden beneath the bikini line. Barbara's bikini days were behind her, she acknowledged ruefully. Something else to fret over. Something else that separated the Mrs.'s from the Miss Cincinnatis of this world.

Watch how regally Barbara slides off her chair and onto the floor, casually securing her skirt beneath her knees while showing her eighteen-month-old daughter the best way to stack the blocks she's been struggling with, patiently picking them up whenever they fall down, encouraging Tracey to try again, ultimately stacking them herself, then restacking them each time her daughter accidentally knocks them over. Any second now, Tracey will climb into her mother's protective arms, the dark curls she has inherited from Barbara surrounding her porcelain-doll face, and close her eyes in sleep.

"There was a little girl," I can still hear Barbara say, in that soothing, singsongy voice she always affected when talking to her daughter, as I watch her lips moving silently on the film, "who had a little curl, right in the middle of her forehead. And when she was good, she was very, very good. And when she was bad, she was—"

"A really bad girl!" Tracey shouted gleefully, chocolate brown eyes popping open. And we all laughed.

Barbara laughed the loudest, although her face moved the least. Terrified of those impending wrinkles, and, at 32, the oldest of the women present, she'd perfected the art of laughing without actually breaking into a smile. Her mouth would open and a loud, even raucous, sound would emerge, but her lips remained curiously static, refusing either to wiggle or curl. This was in marked contrast to Chris, whose every feature was engaged when she laughed, her mouth twisting this way and that in careless abandon, although the resulting sound was delicate, even tentative, as if she knew there was a price to pay for having too good a time.

Amazingly, Barbara and Chris had never even seen each other before that afternoon, despite the fact that we'd all lived on Grand Avenue for at least a year, but they instantly became the best of friends, proof positive of the old adage that opposites attract. Aside from the obvious physical differences—blond versus brunette, short versus tall, fresh-faced glow versus Day-Glo sheen—their inner natures were as different as their outer surfaces. Yet they complemented each other perfectly, Chris soft where Barbara was hard, strong where Barbara was weak, demure where Barbara was anything but. They quickly became inseparable.

That's Vicki, pushing herself into the frame, making her presence felt, the way she did with just about everything in her life. At twenty-eight, Vicki was the youngest of the women and easily the most accomplished. She was a lawyer, and, at the time, the only one of us who worked outside the home, although Susan was enrolled at the university, working toward a degree in English literature. Vicki had short reddish-brown hair, cut on the diagonal, a style that emphasized the sharp planes of her long, thin face. Her eyes were hazel and small, although almost alarmingly intense, even intimidating, no doubt a plus for an ambitious litigator with a prestigious downtown law firm. Vicki was shorter than Barbara, taller than Chris, and at 105 pounds, the thinnest of the group. Her small-boned frame made her look deceptively fragile, but she had hidden strength and boundless energy. Even when sitting still, as she is here, she seemed to be moving, her body vibrating, like a tuning fork.

Her daughter, Kirsten, at only twenty-two months, was already her mother's clone. She had the same delicate bone structure and clear hazel eyes, the same way of looking just past you when you spoke, as if there might be something more interesting, more engaging, more *important,* going on just behind you, that she couldn't chance missing. The toddler was forever up and down, down and up, back and forth, clamoring for her mother's attention and approval. Vicki gave her daughter an occasional, absent-minded pat on the head, but their eyes rarely connected. Maybe the child was blinded, as we all were initially, by the enormous diamond sparkler on the third finger of Vicki's left hand. Watch how it temporarily obliterates all other images, turning the screen a ghostly white.

Vicki was married to a man some twenty-five years her senior, whom she'd known since childhood. In fact, she and his eldest son had been high school classmates and budding sweethearts. Until, of course, Vicki decided she preferred the father to the son, and the resulting scandal tore the family apart. "You can't break up a happy marriage," Vicki assured us that afternoon, stealing a quote from Elizabeth Taylor's résumé, and the rest of the women nodded in unison, although they couldn't quite hide their shock.

Vicki liked to shock, the women quickly learned, just as they learned to secretly enjoy being shocked. For whatever her faults, and they were many, Vicki was rarely less than totally entertaining. She was the spark that ignited the flame, the presence who signaled the party could officially begin, the mover, the shaker, the one whom everyone clucked over and fussed about. Even if she wasn't the one who got the ball rolling—surprisingly, it was usually the more unassuming Susan who did that—Vicki was invariably the one who ran with it, who made sure her team scored the winning touchdown. And Vicki always played to win.

Next to Vicki's coiled intensity, Susan seems almost stately, sitting there with her hands clasped easily in her lap, light brown hair folding neatly under at her chin, the quintessential Breck girl, except that she was still carrying around fifteen of the thirty-five pounds she'd gained when pregnant and hadn't been able to shed since Ariel's birth. The extra pounds made her noticeably self-conscious and camera-shy, although she'd always preferred the sidelines to center stage. The other women offered their encouragement and advice, shared their diet and exercise regimes, and Susan listened, not out of politeness, but because she'd always enjoyed listening more than speaking, her mind a sponge, absorbing each proffered tidbit. She'd make note of their suggestions later in the journal she'd been keeping since Ariel was born. She'd once had dreams of being a writer, she admitted when pressed, and Vicki told her that she should speak to her husband, who owned a string of trade magazines and was thinking of expanding his growing empire.

Susan smiled, her daughter tickling her feet as she played happily with Susan's bare toes, and changed the subject, preferring to talk about her courses at the university. They were more tangible than dreams, and Susan was nothing if not practical. She'd quit school when she got married to help put her husband through medical school. Only now that his practice was established and going strong had she decided to return to school to finish her degree. Her husband was very supportive of her decision, she told the women, and her mother was helping out by looking after Ariel during the day.

"You're lucky," Chris told her. "My mother lives in California."

"My mother died just after Tracey was born," Barbara said, eyes instantly filling with tears.

"I haven't seen my mother since I was four years old," Vicki announced. "She ran off with my father's business partner. Haven't heard from the bitch since."

And then the room fell silent, as was so often the case after one of Vicki's calculated pronouncements.

Susan glanced at her watch. The others followed suit. Someone mentioned the lateness of the hour, that they should probably be getting home. We decided on a group picture to commemorate the afternoon, and together we managed to prop the camera on top of a stack of books at the far end of the room and arrange ourselves and our daughters so that we all fit inside the camera's scope.

So there we are, ladies and gentlemen.

In one corner, Susan, wearing blue jeans and a sloppy, loose-fitting shirt, balancing daughter Ariel on her lap, the child's wiry little body in marked contrast to her mother's quiet bulk.

In the other corner, Vicki, wearing white shorts and a polka-dot halter top, trying to extricate daughter Kirsten's arms from around her neck, small eyes mischievously ablaze as she mouths a silent obscenity directly into the lens of the camera.

In between, Barbara and Chris, Chris wearing white pants and a red-and-white-striped T-shirt, straining to prevent her daughter, Montana, from abandoning her yet again, while Tracey sits obediently on her mother's skirted lap, Barbara manipulating Tracey's hand up and down, as both mother and daughter wave as one.

The Grand Dames.

Friends for life.

Of course, one of us turned out not to be a friend at all, but we didn't know it then.

Nor could any of us have predicted that twenty-three years later, two of the women would be dead, one murdered in the cruelest of fashions.

Which, of course, leaves me.

I press another button, listen as the tape rewinds, shift expectantly on my chair, waiting for the film to start afresh. Perhaps, I think, as the women suddenly reappear, their babies in their laps, their futures in their faces, this will be the time it all makes sense. I will find the justice I seek, the peace I desire, the resolution I need.

I hear the women's laughter. The story begins.

Part One

1982–1985

CHRIS

One

Chris lay in her queen-size brass bed with her eyes closed. Crisp white cotton sheets pulled tight against her toes and stretched up across her body, stopping under her chin. Her arms lay stiff at her sides, as if secured by shackles. She imagined herself an Egyptian mummy entombed inside an ancient pyramid, as hoards of curious tourists flopped about in worn and dirty sandals above her head. That would explain the headache, she thought, and might have laughed, but for the incessant pounding at her temples, a pounding that echoed the dull thud of her heartbeat. When was the last time she'd felt so lost, so afraid?

No, *fear* was much too strong a word, Chris immediately amended, censoring her thoughts even before they were fully formed. It wasn't fear that was immobilizing her so much as dread, a vague disquiet trickling through her body like a poisoned stream. It was this ill-defined, perhaps indefinable, sensation that was keeping her eyes tightly closed, her arms pinned to her sides, her body rigid, as if she'd died in her sleep.

Did the dead feel this invasive, this *pervasive,* sense of unease? she wondered, growing impatient with such morbidity, allowing the sounds of morning to creep inside her head: her six-year-old daughter, Montana, singing down the hall; three-year-old Wyatt playing with the train set he got for Christmas; Tony opening and closing kitchen cupboards directly below. Within minutes, paralyzing fear had been reduced to mere unease, which was much more manageable, and ultimately much easier to dismiss. Another few minutes and Chris might actually be able to persuade herself that what had happened last night was all a bad dream, the product of her overheated—*overwrought,* as Tony might suggest—imagination.

"*It's a heartache!*" Montana belted out from her room at the end of the hall.

"Choo-choo-choo-choo, choo-choo-choo-choo," Wyatt whispered loudly, mimicking the whirring of the trains.

Somewhere beneath her, another cupboard door opened and closed. Dishes rattled.

"*Nothing but a heartache!*"

Chris opened her eyes.

I've got a secret, she thought.

Her eyes scanned the small master bedroom, although her head remained still in the center of the oversize, down-filled pillow. Sun was filtering through the heavy ivory curtains, bleaching the pale blue walls a ghostly white, throwing small spotlights on stray particles of dust dancing in the air above her head. The black turtleneck sweater Tony had worn to dinner last night was flung carelessly across the back of the small blue chair in the corner, one empty arm extended toward the worn blue broadloom, still sticky with long-ago-spilled apple juice. The door to their small en suite bathroom was open, as was the closet and the top drawer of the wicker dresser. The clock on the night table beside her said 9:04.

Probably she should get up, get dressed, see how Wyatt and Montana were making out. Tony had obviously fed them breakfast, which didn't surprise her. It was Sunday, his day to get up with the kids. Besides, he was always extra nice to her after a big fight. She'd felt him quietly slip out of bed at Wyatt's first audible rumblings, feigned sleep as he'd hurried into his clothes before bending over to kiss her forehead. "Sleep," she'd heard him whisper, his breath reassuringly gentle against her skin.

She'd tried to drift off, but she couldn't, and now, just when she felt sleep mercifully tugging at her eyelids, it was too late. Any minute, the kids would grow bored with their solitary pursuits and come charging through the bedroom door, demanding her attention. She had to get up, shower, prepare herself for the busy day ahead. Chris threw the covers off with a determined hand and slid her legs over the side of the bed, invisible cookie crumbs crunching beneath her bare toes as she padded toward the washroom. "Oh, God," she said, confronting the swollen face of her reflection in the mirror over the sink. "I know you're in there somewhere." Her fingers prodded the puffy flesh around her eyes. Wasn't she was getting too old to cry herself to sleep?

Except she hadn't slept. Not once all night. "Chris," she'd heard Tony whisper in her ear at repeated intervals throughout the night, withdrawing to his side of the bed when she failed to respond. "Chris, are you awake?"

So, he hadn't slept either, she thought with no small degree of satisfaction as she splashed cold water on her face, held a cold compress against her eyes, gradually feeling her tired skin shrink back to its normal size. "Who are you?" she asked wearily, not for the first time, pushing several strands of matted blond hair away from her cheeks. "Beats the shit out of me," her reflection answered in Vicki's voice, and Chris giggled, the sound scratching at her throat, like a cat at a screen door.

"*It's a heartache!*" Montana sang out from behind the bathroom wall.

You can say that again, Chris thought, stepping into the shower, turning on the tap, welcoming the assault of hot water on her arms and legs, feeling it whip across her back like thousands of sharp, tiny lashes. What had happened last night had been her fault as much as Tony's, she acknowledged, positioning herself directly under the shower's spray, the water roughly parting her hair in the center before cascading down over her face.

Had the kids heard them fighting? she wondered, hearing the distant echo of her parents shouting at one another beneath the steady onslaught of hot water. Three decades later, and their voices were still as loud, as potent, as ever. Chris remembered lying in her bed, listening as her parents argued downstairs, their angry words knocking against the walls of her room, as if determined to include her, impatiently circling the hallway, eventually slithering through the vents on the floor, filtering into the very air she breathed. She'd pressed her small pillow over her face, so as not to inhale the poison, covered her ears with her trembling hands, tried to muffle the unpleasant sounds. Once she'd even climbed out of bed, buried herself at the back of her closet, but the voices only got louder, until it seemed as if someone were in the closet with her. She'd felt invisible fingers poking at her from the hems of the dresses hanging above her head, alien tongues licking at her cheeks, and she'd run crying back to her bed, pulled the covers tightly around her, lying rigid, arms at her sides, eyes squeezed tightly closed, staying that way till morning.

Hadn't she done essentially the same thing last night?

Hadn't she grown up at all?

Chris turned off the water, stepped out of the shower, bundled her head in one soft blue-and-white-striped towel, her body in another, grateful for the steam that rendered the mirror opaque. She opened the bathroom door, felt the cold embrace of the surrounding air immediately wrap itself around her. How had she ended up here? she wondered, shuffling back into the bedroom. In the middle of her parents' nightmare.

"Hi, sweetheart," Tony said softly from beside the window.

Chris nodded, said nothing, her gaze directed at the floor, her nose twitching at the scent of freshly made pancakes.

"I brought you breakfast in bed," he said.

Chris sank down on the bed, leaned back against the pillows, watched as a stack of blueberry pancakes miraculously materialized on a tray in front of her, next to a glass of freshly squeezed orange juice and a pot of wonderful-smelling coffee. A stainless steel butter dish sat beside a small white ceramic pitcher of real maple syrup. A plastic, red daisy leaned against the side of a glass bud vase. "You didn't have to do this," Chris said, eyes still averted, voice low. She didn't deserve this, she thought.

Tony sat at the foot of the bed. She felt him watching her as she buttered the pancakes, smothered them in the warm syrup, carefully lifting one forkful, then another, into her mouth. Paradoxically, she grew hungrier with each bite, thirstier with each sip. In minutes, the pancakes were gone, the juice glass empty, the coffee finished. "Good?" Tony asked expectantly. She could hear the smile in his voice.

"Wonderful," she told him, determined not to look at him, knowing if she looked at him, it was game over.

"I'm so sorry, Chris."

"Don't."

"You know I didn't mean it."

"Please . . ."

"You know how much I love you."

Chris felt her eyes fill with tears. God, did she never stop crying? "Please, Tony . . ."

"Won't you even look at me? Do you hate me so much you can't even look at me?"

"I don't hate you." Chris lifted her gaze, swallowed her husband with one quick gulp of her eyes.

While Tony would never be described as gorgeous, like Barbara's husband, or distinguished, like Vicki's husband, or even kindly, the first word that came to mind when describing Susan's husband, once he trapped you in his gaze, there was no turning back. A man of mystery, Barbara had pronounced. A formidable presence, Susan offered. Sexy, Vicki summed up succinctly. A diamond in the rough, they all agreed.

More rough than sparkle, Chris thought now, watching as her husband inched forward on the bed, his hand grazing the damp skin of her legs, sending a current, like a wayward electrical charge, racing toward her heart. Up close, Tony was smaller, more compact, than he first appeared, barely five feet eight inches tall, although he was more muscular than his narrow shoulders would indicate. He was wearing jeans and the moss green sweater she'd bought him for his last birthday, the soft color of the wool underlining the harsher green of his eyes. His hair was thick and brown, except for a small patch of white near his right temple. Tony told everyone the patch was the result of a childhood trauma, although the precise trauma tended to shift with each telling, as did his explanation for the scar that scissored through his flesh from the base of his left ear to the curve of his jaw. Over the eleven years of their marriage, Chris had heard so many versions of how he got that scar that she was no longer able to recall whether it was the result of a near-fatal childhood fall, a death-defying car crash, or a barroom brawl. The answer, she was sure, was something infinitely more prosaic than any of these alternatives, although she would never think of questioning Tony's story. Tony had a need for the dramatic. He exaggerated life's mundane details, enlarged the ordinary, enhanced the everyday. It was part of his charm, part of what drove him, made him so creative. You couldn't open a newspaper without seeing one of his ads; you couldn't walk a city block without seeing a billboard he'd designed. The "Cat's Meow" campaign for VIP Cat Food, the "Really Cheese Them Off" campaign for Dairyvale cheeses, both were his. Hadn't he been promoted to senior art director faster than anyone else in the history of Warsh, Rubican? And wasn't this natural flair for hyperbole at least part of what had attracted her to him in the first place? In those early years, Tony had made everything seem so exciting, so limitless, so *possible.*

Chris smiled, all the encouragement he needed. She watched him immediately move forward on the bed. Tony lifted the tray, laid it gently on the floor, took her hands in his.

"Tony . . ."

"It'll never happen again, Chris. I promise."

"It can't."

"It won't."

"You scared me."

"I scared myself," he agreed. "I heard this voice yelling. I couldn't believe it was me. The awful things I was saying. . . . "

"That's not what I'm talking about."

"I know. Please forgive me."

Could she? Chris wondered. Could she forgive him? "Maybe we should go for counseling." Chris held her breath, braced herself for the outrage she was sure would follow. Hadn't Tony made his opinion of marriage counselors painfully clear? Hadn't he told her that there was no way he would ever allow some overeducated quack to interfere in his private life?

"Counseling won't help," he said quietly.

"It might. We could at least give it a try. Whatever problems we're having—"

"I got fired."

"What!" Chris was sure she'd heard him incorrectly. "What are you talking about?"

"They let me go," he said without further elaboration.

Chris saw the words bouncing around in front of her eyes, like the errant particles of dust hanging in the sunlight, and tried to grab hold of them, get them to stay still long enough for her to understand their implications, but they refused to be so easily corralled. "They let you go?" she repeated helplessly, the words making no more sense for her having said them out loud. "Why?"

Tony shrugged. "Dan Warsh said something about the need for fresh perspectives, new ideas."

"But they've always loved your ideas. The 'Cat's Meow,' the 'Really Cheese Them Off' campaigns, I thought they loved those."

"They did—last year. This is 1982, Chris. We're in the middle of a major recession. Everyone's running scared."

"But . . ." Chris stopped. Wasn't Tony always complaining she didn't know when to leave well enough alone? "When did this happen?"

"Friday morning."

"Friday! Why didn't you tell me?"

Tears filled Tony's eyes. He turned away. "I tried to tell you last night."

Chris took a deep breath, tried to recall the sequence of events of the night before, the precise order of everything that was said before things began spiraling out of control. But she'd worked so hard to suppress the angry words that they now refused to come forward, and she was left with snarled snatches of indistinct utterances, potentially potent images shooting toward her only to blur into passivity, like snow hitting a car windshield during a winter storm. Tony was always accusing her of not listening to him. My God, was he right?

"I'm so sorry," she told him now, taking his head in her hands, cradling it against the towel at her breasts.

"We'll be fine," he was quick to assure her. "It's not like I can't find another job."

"Of course you'll find another job."

"I don't want you to worry."

"I'm not worried. I just wish I'd known. Maybe last night wouldn't have. . . . "

"I'm not trying to make excuses for my behavior last night."

"I know you're not."

"I was way out of line."

"You were upset about losing your job."

"That doesn't give me the right to take it out on you."

"It was my fault as much as yours. Tony, I'm so sorry . . ."

"I love you, Chris. I love you so much. I don't care about the damn job. I can lose a million jobs. I can't lose you."

"You won't lose me. You won't. You won't."

And then they were in each other's arms, and he was kissing her the way he'd kissed her when she was nineteen years old and he was trying to convince her to run away with him, the way he'd kissed her the first time they'd made love, the way he always kissed her when they were making up after a fight, short, tender kisses that barely flirted with the outlines of her lips, that seemed almost afraid to overstay their welcome. And then suddenly she felt him releasing the towel around her head, felt it collapse and drop around her bare shoulders. Damp hair fell about her face in careless waves. Automatically Chris reached up to tuck the hair behind her ears, but Tony's hands were already pulling at the towel at her breast, throwing it open as he pushed her down on the bed.

"Mommy!" came the sudden cry from outside the closed bedroom door.

Immediately Chris felt Tony's body tense, and she held her breath, waiting for his reaction. But Tony only laughed, and in that unexpected, full-throated sound Chris heard all the reasons why she'd agreed to run off with him so many years ago. The sound promised both safety and permanence, qualities missing from her childhood.

"Mommy's a little busy right now, Montana," Tony called out, his hand on the zipper of his jeans.

"I want Mommy," the child persisted, jiggling the handle of the door.

"I'll be there in a minute, pumpkin," Chris told her, trying to sit up, feeling Tony's unexpectedly firm grip on her shoulder as Montana continued pushing at the bedroom door. Why had Tony locked it?

"Mommy! Mommy!" Wyatt's small voice joined his sister's in the hall.

"Remember what we talked about at breakfast, kids?" Tony asked, his noticeable erection pushing at the front of his jeans. "How Mommy wasn't feeling too well, and you were going to let her sleep real late? Remember that?"

"But she's up now," Montana persisted. "I heard you guys talking."

"Yeah, but she's still not feeling very well."

"What's *wrong* with her?" Montana's voice carried more accusation than concern.

"Mommy! Mommy!" Wyatt cried.

"Tony," Chris whispered, kissing his chin. "We can do this later."

Tony's grip on her shoulder tightened. "Go back to your rooms, kids. Mommy'll be there real soon."

"Now!" Montana insisted.

"Tony, please," Chris said. "There's no way I'm going to be able to relax."

"This won't take long." Tony pushed his jeans down his thighs, drew her head toward him. "Come on, Chris. You can't just leave me like this."

"Mommy! Let me in."

"Please, Chris."

"Mommmmmy!"

"Why don't you sing Mommy a song?" Tony suggested, guiding Chris's mouth around him, his hand moving her head slowly back and forth.

"What'll I sing?"

"Whatever your little heart desires," Tony said, his fingers digging into Chris's scalp.

"It's a heartache!" Montana began singing at the top of her lungs. *"Nothing but a heartache!"*

Dear God, Chris thought. Was this really happening?

"Gets you if you're too late. Feels just like a clown."

Was she really going down on her husband while her six-year-old child sang about heartache outside their bedroom door? No, she couldn't do this. It was too ludicrous, too bizarre.

As if sensing her growing discomfort, Tony picked up his pace. Chris grabbed the side of the bed to keep from losing her balance.

"Oh, it's a heartache . . ."

"God, Chris, that's so good. I love you so much."

"Nothing but a heartache . . ."

"Tony . . ."

"Now, Chris. Now!"

Chris felt Tony's body shudder around her, his hand in her hair relaxing as he withdrew. He quickly pulled his jeans back up over his hips. Chris swallowed, wiped her mouth, massaged her jaw as Tony went to the bedroom door and opened it. Immediately, Montana and Wyatt flew inside, jumped on the bed and into Chris's lap, jockeying for position.

"You smell funny," Montana said.

"Morning breath," Tony said with a wink, lifting Wyatt into the air, holding him high above his head as the boy shrieked his approval.

"Yuck," Montana said, sliding out of her mother's arms and throwing herself against Tony's legs.

Tony effortlessly scooped her up with his free hand, dangled her at his side. "Who's going to win the Super Bowl?" he challenged.

"Bengals!" Wyatt shouted.

"That's my boy."

"Bengals, Bengals!" Montana screamed even louder, not to be outdone.

Good God, the Super Bowl, Chris thought, self-consciously covering her mouth with her hand. She'd forgotten all about it. She had so much to do, and she hadn't even thought about what to serve for dinner.

"Chris," Tony was saying as he ushered Montana and Wyatt out of the room. "Look, if you wouldn't mind not saying anything to anyone about my losing my job . . ."

"Of course not."

"At least not today."

"Sure."

"No point spoiling the party."

"I understand." Chris smiled.

Now I have two secrets, she thought.

Two

The women were grouped around the circular pine table that occupied much of Chris's small kitchen. Several bottles of wine—one white, one red—stood open in the middle of the table, surrounded by at least a half dozen glasses in various stages of use. Between casual gossip and sips of chardonnay, Chris absently scraped the skin off a bunch of large carrots, Vicki played with the ends of a recent, ill-advised perm, and Susan and Barbara laughed over the contents of the most recent issue of *Cosmopolitan.* They were dressed casually in warm sweaters and jeans, except that Vicki's jeans were leather. Only Barbara wore a skirt. It was royal blue velvet and reached the floor. "This is a Super Bowl party," Vicki quipped when she saw her, "not a wedding."

"I know," came Barbara's easy response, accompanied by fluttering fingers. "I know. I know."

"She can't help herself," said Susan.

In the rec room immediately below, their husbands were drinking beer and alternately screaming their encouragement or bellowing their displeasure at an indifferent TV screen. In the living room, their assorted children—seven in all, five girls, two boys—were eating popcorn and giggling over their umpteenth screening of *Pete's Dragon,* under the watchful, if tired, eye of Vicki's weekend nanny.

"So what do you think her secret is?" Susan asked suddenly.

Chris's hands froze in mid-scrape, feeling all eyes directed her way. How could they know? she wondered, feeling her cheeks blush orange, like the shorn carrot in her hand. She'd said nothing, confided in no one. Were they so finely attuned to one another's needs? After a friendship of only four years, was their protective radar so intense? Could she keep nothing from them, no matter how personal, how shameful?

Slowly, Chris raised her head, the lies already forming on the tip of her tongue: *Secret? What secret? No, of course there's nothing wrong.* And if still they pressed her, if they stubbornly refused to accept her heartfelt protestations, dismissed the lie for the obvious fiction it was, what then? Could she really tell them the truth?

But when Chris looked up, she saw that no one was looking at her with sad, questioning eyes. She saw that no one was looking at her at all. Susan and Barbara were still engrossed in their magazine. Even Vicki had stopped playing with her wayward perm and joined them in ogling a photograph of Raquel Welch spilling out of a tiny white bikini and practicing yoga on a sun-soaked Malibu beach.

"Her secret?" Barbara repeated. "Are you kidding me?"

"Don't tell me plastic surgery," Susan said.

"Of course plastic surgery," Barbara pronounced.

"You say that about everyone."

"Only because it's true. Come on, guys, she's over forty."

"I heard she had a couple of ribs removed," Vicki offered.

"I believe it," Barbara said.

"Do you think she had her boobs done?"

"No."

"Yes."

"If she did," Barbara said, "I want her doctor. He did a great job."

"Yeah," Vicki agreed. "Usually when you have a boob job, you get these two big blobs in the middle of nowhere, with these nipples about three inches higher than they're supposed to be. They look ridiculous. Everyone knows they're not real."

"Men don't care," Barbara said, as a great roar emanated from downstairs. "They like 'em no matter how fake they look."

"Would you ever have plastic surgery?" Chris asked, letting go of the frightened air trapped in her lungs and joining the conversation.

"Never," Susan said, closing the magazine with a decisive hand.

"Never say never," Vicki told her, pouring herself another glass of red wine.

"I'm gonna have the works done." Barbara patted the ample bosom beneath the pale blue silk of her blouse. "The minute these babies sag, I'm getting a new pair. First sign of a wrinkle, I'm on the operating table. And none of this 'just make me look rested' nonsense. I want to look like I just emerged from a wind tunnel."

The women laughed. "You're nuts," Chris told her. "Why would you ever want to mess with that beautiful face?"

"Whatever happened to growing old gracefully?" Susan asked.

"Oh, please," Barbara said. "What's so graceful about growing old?"

"That's why you all should have married older men," Vicki told them. "That way you're always the young one."

"Yeah, but isn't it a trade-off?" Barbara asked, raising one carefully tweezed eyebrow.

"What do you mean?"

"I mean *you* may stay young"—Barbara winked—"but do *they* stay hard?"

A raucous squeal escaped Chris's throat as the blush in her cheeks turned from orange to red. She jumped from the table, quickly dropped the carrot scrapings into the garbage pail under the sink and the carrots into the large wooden salad bowl on the white tile countertop.

"Chris, get your ass back here," Vicki instructed. "This is very important stuff we're discussing."

"I don't think we should be talking about this sort of thing," Chris said, trying not to see Tony's erect penis dancing before her eyes, not to feel it slamming against the inside of her mouth.

"We always talk about this sort of thing," Vicki protested.

"I know, but . . ." Chris glanced toward the living room. "You know the saying about little pitchers having big ears?"

"Big pitchers are exactly what we're talking about," Vicki said with a laugh. "Besides, I've been challenged. You know I can't walk away from a challenge."

"So, there are no problems in that department?" Barbara asked, deliberately egging Vicki on. "I mean, Jeremy's what . . . sixty now?"

"He's fifty-seven," Vicki corrected.

"And?"

"And everything's working very nicely in that department, thank you very much." Vicki took a long swig of the wine in her glass. "Besides, Jeremy's pitcher isn't the only one in the ballpark."

"What!" the other women gasped as one.

"Oh, my God!" Barbara said. "What are you saying?"

"Hey, can you keep the noise down?" Tony called up from downstairs.

"You need some help up there, darlin'?" Jeremy's voice rang out.

"We're doin' just fine, darlin'," Vicki called back.

"What exactly *are* you doing?" Susan asked.

Vicki smiled. "Well, we all know that variety is the spice of life."

Chris quickly returned to her seat at the round pine table. "You're having an affair?"

"Don't look so shocked. It doesn't mean anything."

"How can it not mean anything?" Susan asked.

"It's just sex," Vicki told the other women, as if this fact were self-explanatory. "Are you saying you'd never have an affair?"

"Absolutely that's what I'm saying," Susan said.

"Never say never," Vicki admonished her again.

"What if Jeremy finds out?"

"He won't."

"How can you be so sure?"

"Because he never has before."

"Oh, my God!"

"I don't believe it!"

"What's going on up there?" Tony called out.

"You've been holding out on us," Barbara said, brown eyes narrowing accusingly.

"Timing is everything," Vicki told her.

"Mommy!" one of the children called from the living room.

"Yes," the four women answered in unison.

"Whitney's head is too big. It's in my way."

Susan sighed. "Her sister's head is too big," she announced to understanding nods. "Give it a kiss, Ariel," she called back. "It'll shrink."

"Speaking of getting head . . ." Vicki said.

"You are so bad," Barbara said, laughing as Chris lowered her gaze to her lap. "Look, you're embarrassing our hostess."

"Really? I love that. Chris, am I embarrassing you?"

"Maybe we should talk about something else," Chris suggested again.

"Like what?"

"I don't know. Politics, literature. Anybody read any good books lately?" Chris looked toward Susan. Susan was always reading something.

"I read the new John Irving over the Christmas holidays."

"Any good?"

"I liked it."

"Boring!" Vicki pronounced with an exaggerated yawn. "Come on, you guys. This isn't the time for intellectual discussions. Let's get to the good stuff." She pointed to one of the headlines on the cover of *Cosmopolitan.* "Multiply Your Orgasms," the words all but screamed. "So who here, besides me, of course, has multiple orgasms?"

"I don't believe this," Barbara said. "You don't give up."

"You have multiple orgasms?" Chris heard herself ask.

"Sometimes," Vicki said with a shrug. "You don't?"

Chris raised her glass of wine to her lips, took a long sip. What the hell? she thought. She was keeping enough secrets. "I've never had an orgasm."

"You mean you've never had a multiple orgasm," Vicki corrected.

"I mean I've never had an orgasm at all."

"You can't be serious."

"I haven't either," Barbara admitted after a slight pause, her voice a whisper.

"Get out of here," Vicki said. "I thought Ron was supposed to be so great in bed."

"He is," Barbara said, rushing to her husband's defense. "It's not his fault I don't have orgasms."

"Whose fault is it?" Vicki asked simply. Then, she shifted her penetrating gaze to Susan. "What about you?"

"Time to check on the kids," Susan said, quickly pushing herself off her chair and disappearing into the living room. "How's everyone doing in here?" Chris heard her ask the assorted throng.

"Whitney's head's still too big," Ariel protested loudly.

"Which brings us back to oral sex," Vicki said, returning her attention to Barbara and Chris.

"What? Whoa! How'd we get back there?"

"It's the surest way to have an orgasm. Trust me, a patient tongue is better than a stiff prick any day. Your husbands like to do it, don't they?"

Chris and Barbara exchanged furtive glances. "Mostly, Ron likes to be on the receiving end," Barbara admitted as Chris looked toward the floor. The truth was that Tony refused to perform oral sex at all.

"Who was it who said it's more blessed to give than to receive?" Vicki asked.

"Not Ron," Barbara told her.

"I think it was Jesus," Chris said.

"Are you guys still talking about sex?" Susan asked, coming back into the room.

"Apparently even Jesus talked about it," Vicki said.

"You're going to burn in hell. You know that, don't you?" Barbara laughed.

"We're all going to burn," Chris concurred, thinking this was probably true.

"Something burning?" Tony asked, bounding into the kitchen, kissing Chris on the forehead before heading for the fridge.

"Is the game over?" Chris watched her husband grab a handful of ice-cold beers from the freezer.

"Are you kidding? We've only just begun to fight."

"Who's winning?"

Tony winked. "The good guys."

"Isn't that an oxymoron?" Vicki asked.

"Watch who you're calling a moron," Tony warned playfully. "What are you girls talking about in here anyway?"

"Politics," Barbara answered with a straight face.

"Literature," Susan said.

"Well, that certainly explains all the hootin' and hollerin' going on," Tony said on his way out the kitchen door.

The women laughed, watching him leave.

"Are you going to tell me that sexy man doesn't like to give head?" Vicki asked. "I think that may be grounds for a divorce. Speaking of which, I have a joke," she continued almost in the same breath. "Why is divorce so expensive?"

"Why?" the women asked, waiting.

"Because it's worth it."

Chris could still hear the women laughing long after everyone had left. She closed her eyes, savored the sound.

"Chris," Tony called from upstairs. "Aren't you coming to bed?"

"I'm just finishing up with the dishes," Chris called back, removing the last of the beer glasses from the dishwasher, returning them to their shelves.

She moved slowly, enjoying the feel of the warm glass in her hands, captivated by the gentle curve of the tall, slender glasses. It had been a good party, she thought. Everyone had contributed something to the dinner—Barbara an eggplant dip, Susan her famous twice-baked potatoes, Vicki a spectacular chocolate mousse, although she'd admitted her housekeeper had made it. And everyone had raved about Chris's new recipe for prime rib. Just the right amount of garlic, served just rare enough. Not a slice left over, Chris realized, although she had enough salads to last till spring.

Even if Cincinnati had ultimately lost to San Francisco, 26–21, Tony was happy, having perversely bet on the 49ers and collected $60 from his fellow revelers. There'd only been a few tense moments. "What were you girls really talking about?" he'd asked several times during the evening. "I saw Vicki looking at me kind of funny," he remarked at one point. "You say anything to her?"

"Of course not," Chris told him. "Don't worry, Tony. It's okay."

Was it?

Chris closed the cupboard door, left the kitchen, and walked through the darkened living room, the smell of buttered popcorn bouncing off the sofa and chairs, following her into the front hall. She jiggled the front door to make sure it was securely locked, then opened it instead, stepped outside into the cold air. It was a clear night. A three-quarter moon illuminated an ink-blue sky heavy with stars. Snow covered the front lawns of the single-family, old-fashioned Georgian-style homes. Chris looked up and down the quiet street. Four houses down, the Albrights were replacing their old roof with cedar shingles, their decaying brick chimney with gleaming new copper. Tony said they were crazy, that the copper would eventually turn green, look ugly. Chris disagreed. She thought it would look nice.

Other changes were coming. The O'Connors, who lived halfway down the block on the other side of the street, were talking about adding another room to their red-brick house in the spring, an idea that was causing considerable muttering among several of the neighbors who thought the integrity of the neighborhood might be threatened. "Some people are just uncomfortable with change," Susan had remarked earlier, adding that she and Owen had been toying with the idea of extending their kitchen three feet into the backyard. Chris had suggested a glassed-in solarium. She'd always loved glassed-in solariums.

"Chris?" Tony called from inside the house.

She turned toward the sound of his voice, knew she should probably go back inside. It was late. Most of the houses were already dark, their inhabitants bedded down for the night. Was anyone watching her from behind the neat row of quaint mullioned windowpanes?

What if she were to start running right now? Just close the door behind her and take off down the street? Would anyone see her? How far would she get without a coat or winter boots, without money or identification? How long before Tony realized she was gone and came looking for her? How many miles could she put between herself and her children before she had to turn back? How could she leave them? And where in God's name would she go?

"Chris?" Tony called again.

She heard him moving around inside, felt his footsteps on the hardwood floor of the foyer. Her body swayed toward the street, as if she were standing on the high ledge of a building. One foot lifted into the air, poised for flight. Go, a voice inside her urged. Don't look back.

The door opened behind her.

"Chris?" Tony asked. "What are you doing out here?"

Wordlessly, Chris allowed herself to be drawn back inside the house.

"It's freezing outside, for God's sake." Tony began rubbing

her arms with his hands. Only then did she become aware of the cold. "What were you doing?"

"Nothing. Just looking. It's such a beautiful night."

"Are you feeling okay?"

Chris nodded.

"You sure? You've been acting kind of funny the last few days."

"I'm fine." Chris noted the worry in his eyes. Her hand reached out to caress his cheek. "The kids okay?"

"Sleeping. Like babies." He smiled, his arms wrapping around her waist. "Speaking of which . . ." He lowered his chin, raised one eyebrow.

Chris felt the air immediately constrict in her lungs. "Tony, this probably isn't the best time to be thinking of having another baby."

"I'll find another job, Chris. If that's what you're worried about."

"I'm not worried."

"Good. Then what's the problem?"

"No problem," Chris said quickly.

"Good." Tony tightened his grip on her waist. "Then let's get to bed."

Three

"Excuse me. Are you Barbara Azinger?"

Barbara looked up from the menu she'd been studying for the past half hour—she'd been reading it for so long, she should have it memorized by now, she thought—and nodded. "I am," she said, her voice even, soft, her large brown eyes peeking at the waiter from beneath heavily mascaraed lashes. Did the young man find her at all attractive? she wondered, turning her head just slightly to the left, affording him a glance of what she'd always considered her better side. Did he even suspect she'd once worn the crown of Miss Cincinnati, that she'd been second runner-up to the title of Miss Ohio? Her eyes darkened. It was entirely possible, she realized, that the young man hadn't even been born when she was proudly transporting her overflowing bouquet of red roses down the runway.

"There's a phone call for you." The waiter, despite his

youth, had already perfected the art of bemused superiority endemic to such establishments as The Foxfire Grille, located on Belvedere Street in the heart of the Mount Adams District. A reporter had once likened the admittedly charming old quarter of Cincinnati to San Francisco, and the district had never quite recovered, wearing its pride like a suit of heavy armor that occasionally threatened to overwhelm the tiny area altogether. "At the bar," the waiter said, pointing toward the front of the narrow terra-cotta-tiled restaurant with his chin.

Barbara removed the peach-colored linen napkin from the skirt of her powder blue suit, careful to smooth out the wrinkles that had gathered at her hips, an unpleasant confirmation that the scale she'd stepped on first thing this morning was probably right—she'd put on two pounds in as many weeks. Nonsense—it was just a little water retention, she told herself, listening to the sound of her high heels clicking against the tile floor as she made her way to the bar, reliving that fabulous walk down the runway in a bathing suit and heels very similar to these, feeling the eyes of the other patrons following her. Barbara lifted the receiver to her ear, careful not to disturb her imaginary tiara. Do they recognize me? she wondered. Or are they just feeling sorry for me? They've seen me sitting alone at my table for the better part of thirty minutes. They suspect I've been stood up. Barbara pushed her long, dark hair away from the phone, but her hair, secured by an invisible wall of high-powered spray, barely moved. Maybe it was Susan calling to say she could make it after all. "Hello?"

"Barbara, it's Vicki. I'm really sorry. There's no way I can make lunch."

"What?"

"I'm stuck in this stupid meeting. I didn't call earlier because I kept thinking it was about to end, but they've just ordered in sandwiches, and there's no way I'm going to be able to get away. And I was really looking forward to the butternut-squash ravioli, so you have to have it for me. It's to die for. And apologize to Chris and Susan. I'm really sorry. Oh, God, they're calling me back. Gotta go. Bye."

Vicki hung up before Barbara had the chance to tell her that Susan wouldn't be coming either. Apparently Susan had been up half the night with the girls, both of whom were suffering from nasty spring colds, and so she hadn't had time to finish an essay that was due on her professor's desk by the end of the day. "I'm really sorry," she'd said. "Give my apologies to Vicki and Chris."

What can you do? Barbara thought with a shrug, returning to her table. She couldn't very well expect Vicki to put important clients on hold in favor of a frivolous lunch with friends, nor could she expect Susan to be late handing in an important essay. Thank God for Chris, she thought, sitting down and immediately biting into another roll. Except where was Chris? It was very unlike her to be this late.

Ten minutes later, Barbara was still waiting, and debating her next move. She'd already finished all the rolls in the basket, drunk two glasses of mineral water, had the waiter remove two sets of cutlery. Where on earth was Chris? "Excuse me," she said, as she wound her way gracefully back toward the bar, "could I make another quick call?"

The bartender, a young woman wearing black trousers, a crisp white shirt, and a crooked red bow tie, nodded and smiled, one of those slightly scary smiles that revealed half her gum line as well as both rows of teeth. Shouldn't do that, Barbara thought, her fingers automatically locating the fine lines around her own mouth, lines that even heavy concealer could no longer altogether hide. She glanced at herself in the bottle-lined mirror behind the bar, startled for an instant by the middle-aged woman staring back. Don't be silly, she told herself, brown eyes wide with alarm. Thirty-six was hardly middle-aged. It was young, for God's sake. She was in her prime. Yes, it might be eighteen years since she'd proudly worn the crown of Miss Cincinnati, but, like a fine wine, she'd only improved with age. At least that's what her friends all said whenever she complained of waking up to find her eyes a little swollen, or her skin a little patchy, or her clothes a little tight. Inadvertently, Barbara reached down to tug at the wrinkles of her skirt. No way she looked thirty-six, she silently rebuked her reflection, running a delicate tongue across the pale rose gloss of her lips. *Twenty*-six was more like it, possibly even twenty-five. In fact, with a little more effort, she might even be able to pass for one of her husband's nubile young students.

"No way I'd want to be a teenager again," Susan had once proclaimed, Vicki and Chris nodding their agreement.

I'd give anything to be a teenager again, Barbara thought then, as now. To be the most beautiful girl in Cincinnati, with roses in my arms and the city at my feet. She felt tears sting her eyes and quickly dialed Chris's number, thinking it was very unlike Chris not to call if she was running late.

"Hello?" the male voice answered on the third ring.

"Tony?" What was he doing home in the middle of the day? Hadn't he started a new job just last month? "It's Barbara," she said, when she could think of nothing else to say. "I'm looking for Chris. We were supposed to meet for lunch."

"I'm afraid Chris can't make lunch. She's not feeling very well."

"She's not? She was fine when I spoke to her this morning."

"Yeah, well, what can I say? She's not feeling so great right now. She called me at work, asked me to come home."

"Have you called a doctor?"

"Just got off the phone two seconds ago. He says there's this crazy flu going around."

"Really? I hadn't heard."

"Listen, Barbara, I've got to get my ass moving. I'll have Chris call you as soon as she can get her head out of the toilet, okay?"

"Sure," Barbara said to the dial tone that followed. She hung on, pretended to be listening, in case anyone was watching her, trying to rid her mind of the unpleasant image of her best friend with her head in the toilet. "That was sudden," she said, thinking Chris had been quieter than usual the last few days. Maybe there had been something in her system. Was it possible she was pregnant? Chris had confided Tony was eager for more children, but she'd also confided she was still on the pill.

Barbara slapped the receiver against the inside of her palm, deciding she'd drop by Chris's later, find out exactly what was going on. The more immediate question was what to do right now. She couldn't very well just leave, not after occupying a prime table for four for almost an hour at one of the city's most popular eateries. Nor did she particularly feel like eating alone, notwithstanding the restaurant's to-die-for ravioli. Was there anyone else she could call? Her mother-in-law? She was always complaining that Barbara didn't spend enough time with her. No, the woman would only spend the entire lunch crowing about her other daughter-in-law, the supremely skilled and skinny Sheila, the baby-making machine. Four children and she still weighed what she had on her wedding day. Not only that, but she just kept popping those children out with no trouble at all. Like a chicken laying eggs, Barbara was always tempted to say, but had never worked up the nerve. Yes, sir, super Sheila not only managed a house and four children under the age of eight, she ran a successful party-planning service out of her home and was already working on baby number five, while Barbara hadn't managed to produce a single sister or brother for almost-seven-year-old Tracey, despite having nothing but time on her well-manicured hands. The least she could do was get a job, her mother-in-law occasionally hinted, but Barbara didn't want to take any job that meant she wouldn't be home for Tracey at the end of the school day. Besides, Ron had no objections to her being a stay-at-home mother, nor had he ever complained that Tracey was an only child. Not that they weren't trying to have more children. It just hadn't happened yet. But there was still time. She was still young. She was in good shape, despite the addition of a few extra pounds. Thirty-six certainly wasn't too old to have another child.

Again, Barbara checked the mirror, deciding she looked too pale. She immediately felt her forehead. Maybe she was coming down with whatever had felled Chris. Or more likely the shade of blush she'd recently purchased wasn't quite right. Perhaps she needed something with a little more depth. Maybe that's what she'd do now, she thought, returning the receiver to its carriage, smiling at the bartender without moving her lips, showing her the way it should be done, although the careless young woman failed to notice and was already busy chatting up another customer. Why was it that people were always hanging up on her before she was finished talking, or walking away from her while she was still standing there? She was still a strikingly beautiful woman; she presented herself well. What was it about her that failed to register?

Maybe it was her hair. People had trouble taking big hair seriously. Probably she should cut it. Barbara had once overheard her mother-in-law sniggering on the phone to a friend—"She looks like she was frozen in the sixties," she'd said, then pretended she'd been talking about an acquaintance from high school whom she'd run into that afternoon. "You see how stylish Sheila's short hair is," her mother-in-law had remarked just the other day. "There comes a time when a woman gets too old for long hair."

Maybe such a time would come, Barbara thought, returning to her seat, but that time was not now. She liked her long hair. Maybe she'd grow it as long as Crystal Gayle's, past her knees, right down to the floor. How would her mother-in-law like it then? Barbara signaled the waiter for the bill, feeling like a petulant child. "My friends won't be coming," she told him, bracing herself for his unpleasant scowl, but his back was already to her.

It was just as well the others hadn't shown up. She could do without lunch, even if she did get headaches whenever she missed a meal. Besides, she'd eaten all those rolls. It wasn't as if she would starve to death. And there were other things she needed to do. She'd promised Tracey she'd buy some fabric that matched a dress she'd recently purchased and have her dressmaker make the child one just like it. And there was that project Tracey's first-grade teacher had assigned on spring flowers. Tracey wanted hers to be the best project in the class, so Barbara, who had quickly realized she knew nothing about spring flowers other than that daffodils were yellow and tulips top-heavy, had promised to get her daughter all the necessary information. She could stop at the library, maybe buy a bunch of fresh flowers for Tracey to give to Miss Atherton. Maybe she'd take a bunch over to Chris later on.

"Eight dollars for two glasses of water!" Barbara sputtered when she saw the bill, unable to hide her shock and dismay. What would her mother-in-law say about that? Probably that her son worked much too hard for his wife to throw away his hard-earned money on something as frivolous as designer water. And she'd be right, Barbara thought, dropping a $10 bill on the table and fleeing the restaurant, pursued by her mother-in-law's silent but steady recriminations. Did she have no regard for how hard Ron worked to support his family? A university professor's salary wasn't exactly a king's ransom. Couldn't she show at least a little restraint? Look at Sheila . . .

By the time Barbara stepped out onto Belvedere Street, she was blinking back the renewed threat of tears. Dabbing at her bottom lashes with the side of her index finger, careful not to disturb what she prayed was water-proof mascara, she reached into her purse for her sunglasses, shoving them none too gently over the bridge of her nose, trying to obliterate the image of her mother-in-law's ferretlike face. Was it fair that her own mother, a woman as warm and caring as she was beautiful, had died of acute lymphatic leukemia shortly after Tracey's birth, while Ron's mother, who was as cold and mean-spirited as she was unattractive, would probably live forever? "Damn it," Barbara said into the palm of her hand, realizing just how much she'd been looking forward to lunch with her friends, especially to seeing Chris.

Of all the Grand Dames, Chris was Barbara's favorite. Susan was great—genuine and down-to-earth, if a little too practical for Barbara's taste, and Vicki was . . . well, Vicki was Vicki, dynamic and lots of fun, but she could be very indiscreet. Barbara had learned long ago not to tell Vicki anything she wouldn't feel comfortable seeing on the front page of the *Cincinnati Post.* It was with Chris that Barbara felt the closest bond. Perhaps because neither worked outside the home, Chris always had time for her. She never made Barbara's concerns seem shallow or unimportant; she never walked away from her in midconversation, never made her feel insignificant. Thank God Tony had finally found another job. Not that Chris had ever complained. Still, the situation couldn't have been pleasant, which might account for why she'd suddenly come down with the flu. Didn't the experts claim depression weakened the immune system? Although it had been weeks since Tony had started his new job, and still Chris seemed preoccupied. Something was wrong. She'd have to talk to Chris when she was feeling better, get her to open up.

Barbara stood for several seconds in the middle of the sidewalk in front of The Foxfire Grille, her stomach rumbling its confusion. She needed food and she needed reassurance that all was right with the world. She checked her watch. Closing in on 12:45. If she hurried, she could just make it to the university in time to take her handsome husband out to lunch.

Less than ten minutes later, Barbara pulled her black Sierra into a newly vacated spot on Clifton Avenue, more commonly referred to as Fraternity Row because of the plethora of fraternity and sorority houses that lined the right side of the street, and raced toward the campus of the University of Cincinnati, America's second-oldest and second-largest municipal university. Hurrying past the towering white concrete structure that was the Brodie Science and Engineering Center, she located the more modest two-story red-brick building that housed the Department of Social Studies, where her husband taught courses in basic psychology and human behavior. Nodding a vague hello to several denim-and-leather-clad students gathered near the front steps, Barbara pulled open the heavy oak front door and proceeded down the long hallway, her high heels in noisy contrast to the sneakers everyone else seemed to be wearing.

It was a beautiful old building, Barbara thought, picking up her pace just slightly as she turned right and continued on down the corridor, lined with old black-and-white photographs of long-ago alumnae. Lots of dark wood paneling, leaded windows, fine old archways. The way a university was supposed to look. Creaky and grand and just slightly intimidating. Not that she should feel intimidated, Barbara decided, climbing the wide staircase at the far end of the hall. Just because she hadn't gone on to college after winning her title didn't mean she was stupid, didn't mean she had anything to feel inferior about. She might not be able to quote Shakespeare, the way Susan could, or spout legal precedents, like Vicki, and truth to tell, she'd be hard-pressed to differentiate between psychology and sociology, but she could still hold her own in conversations with her husband and friends. Besides, it wasn't too late. If she was interested, she could always sign up for a few courses, work slowly toward her degree, the way Susan had been doing over the years, one course at a time, whenever home life and babies permitted. Of course she'd have to find something she was really interested in, and it couldn't be so demanding it would take away from her time with Tracey or Ron. Barbara shrugged, picturing herself as Scarlett O'Hara in *Gone With the Wind*: she'd think about these things later—tomorrow was another day. Quickly checking her image in the glass reflection of an old photograph outside her husband's classroom, seeing Vivien Leigh stare back, Barbara pulled open the door and went inside.

The classroom was large, its seats descending, as in a stadium, from top to bottom, where her husband, a tall and ruggedly handsome man of forty, stood behind his podium in front of a large chalkboard and delivered his lecture to approximately three hundred students hanging intently on his every word. Barbara slipped into an empty seat at the back, aware of numerous eyes turning toward her, including those of her husband, who acknowledged her presence with an almost imperceptible nod of his head while continuing to speak to the class. "One of the major difficulties in the field of attitude research has been the tendency to oversimplify problems in terms of a narrow theory of motivation," he was saying. "The gestalt school, to look at one such example, believes that people are always striving toward a more inclusive and stable organization of the psychological field, where the individual is constantly trying to reconcile conflicting impressions in order to make sense of the world around him, thereby maximizing his potential for fitting in."

Barbara heard the frantic scribbling of pens on paper as, all around her, students struggled to record each word. Do they actually have any clue what he's talking about? Barbara wondered, trying hard to concentrate so that she could discuss these theories with her husband over lunch. But already she was losing the thread of his lecture, her mind wandering back to Chris, wondering how she was feeling, if there was anything she could do to help her.

"Another motivational model follows the reward-punishment pattern," her husband was saying, brown eyes circling the room. "This model sees attitudes as part of an adaptive response to the social world where group norms are of primary importance and the individual seeks acceptance and support from his group."

Was he speaking English? Barbara wondered, feeling like a new immigrant, fresh off the boat. Where had he learned to talk like that? She surveyed the predominantly female gathering, the students hovered over their small desks, eager pens racing after each word. Not one of these girls knows a thing about makeup, Barbara thought, shaking her head with dismay. They may know plenty about motivational models, but they know zippo about contouring and blending.

"And finally, we have the personality theorist who emphasizes the internal dynamics underlying attitudes in which the individual's need to preserve his self-image and integrity becomes more important than external rewards and punishments." Ron stopped suddenly and smiled. "We'll continue with this tomorrow. Please read pages 121 through 139 in your text. Thank you."

The students immediately rose from their seats, gathering up their belongings and ascending the stairs, ignoring Barbara as she made her way down the steps toward her husband's podium. "What a pleasant surprise," Ron said, a smile spreading across his perpetually tanned face. "What brings you out here?"

"I thought I'd take my gorgeous husband out to lunch," Barbara said, invisible fingers crossed behind her back, her eyes all but shouting, Please say yes.

"I thought you were having lunch with the girls," Ron said, looking around the room as if for something in particular. "Amy," he called out suddenly. "Amy, I need to talk to you for half a minute about your essay."

Barbara watched the long-haired girl in the seemingly requisite tight blue jeans and black leather jacket stop near the top of the stairs, whisper a few words to her friends, then make her way down the steps. "It got canceled," Barbara explained, "so I thought I'd take a chance and see if you were free."

"Sounds wonderful," Ron said, and Barbara breathed a deep sigh of relief. "Give me two minutes to take care of this."

"No problem. Is there a washroom nearby I can use?"

"Top of the stairs. Turn right."

"I'll meet you in the hallway."

"I'll just be two minutes," Ron repeated as Amy

approached, nervous fingers pushing her long brown hair behind her ears.

A little mascara would give that girl all the confidence in the world, Barbara thought as she made her way back up the stairs. She turned back briefly, noticed that the girl was standing perhaps an inch too close to her husband, that the side of her breast was brushing against the side of his arm, that he made no effort to move away. Don't be silly, Barbara told herself, exiting the room. She was being paranoid again. The girl was standing only as close as was necessary to hear what Ron was saying. It only looked as if her breast were pressed against his arm because of where Barbara was standing.

Barbara quickly located the washroom, adjusted her hair and lipstick in the long rectangular mirror over the row of sinks, then tugged at the skin around her eyes until the small lines that surrounded them, like parentheses, disappeared. "You don't look any older than any of those girls," Barbara whispered to her reflection, wondering how Ron managed to maintain his youthful appearance without benefit of either diet or exercise. All those hours of lying out in the sun hadn't seemed to hurt him either. He was still as handsome as the day she'd first spotted him sitting at the bar at Arnold's, surrounded by women even then. Uh-oh, she remembered thinking as their eyes had connected. Trouble.

Of course she was aware of the rumors circulating about her husband. There'd been rumors throughout the ten years of their marriage. But Ron had assured her repeatedly that those rumors were base and unfounded, and she'd decided long ago to place no stock in them. She'd also decided that, even if the whispers were true, even if her husband did engage in the occasional outside dalliance, it meant nothing. Wasn't that what Vicki had said about her own extracurricular activities? That it was just sex?

Barbara unbuttoned her blue jacket, tucked her white silk blouse inside her skirt, and was deciding whether to use the toilet when the door to the washroom opened and the girl from her husband's class—"Amy, I need to talk to you for half a minute about your essay"—walked inside and approached the mirror. "Hi," Barbara said, as the girl dropped her books to the sink and immediately begin brushing her hair in a series of long, fluid strokes. She was a pretty girl, with a pale, thin face, and large, dark eyes that made her look more interesting than she probably was, Barbara decided, but still, she wasn't winning any beauty contests. Miss Congeniality maybe, Barbara thought with a smile, trying not to notice the round little bottom filling out the tight jeans, the small, high breasts that could only be described as perky. The young didn't have to be beautiful, Barbara realized. It was enough they were young.

"Hi," Amy said to Barbara's reflection.

"You're in my husband's class," Barbara said, straining to sound casual.

The girl shrugged. "Hmm."

"He's a good teacher," Barbara continued, although the girl was clearly not interested in pursuing a conversation.

Amy returned her brush to her floppy black leather bag. "The best," she said, her eyes connecting briefly with Barbara's in the mirror, lingering a beat too long, as if issuing a silent challenge. And then she was gone, out the door with her long brown hair flying after her, her bag slapping at her side.

Barbara remained in front of the row of sinks for several

more minutes, trying not to think of what her unexpected arrival might have interrupted, trying not to think at all. Sometimes it was better not to think. Thinking only got you in trouble. The dumber you were, the happier you were, she decided, applying blush to newly ashen cheeks. Once again, she adjusted her blouse and straightened her skirt. Then she waited until her breathing returned to normal, took one last look in the mirror, and stepped out into the hall to find her husband.

Four

Chris heard the doorbell ring, thought about answering it, decided it was better just to let it ring. Tony would answer it, tell her friends she was busy, that she'd call them later. Except that when later came around, she'd probably be busy with something else, and then it would be too late to call them back, and another day would pass, and then another. Lately a whole week could go by without her seeing or even speaking to her friends. She'd missed Susan's birthday lunch, begged off shopping with Barbara, turned down Vicki's latest invitation to dinner. Here it was halfway through September, and they'd gotten together what . . . three times since June? They used to speak every day. Nothing important. ("Hi, just checking in. I'm going to the store. You need anything?") Stuff like that. ("Wait till you hear what Ariel did yesterday." "You should have seen how cute Tracey looked in her new outfit." "Kirsten says day camp sucks.") The stuff of everyday life. ("Talk to you later." "Wait till you hear this." "Call me tomorrow.") The stuff that kept you sane.

("I love you.")

I love you too.

When had she stopped returning their calls? When had she become too busy to see her friends?

She heard Tony at the front door. "Well, hello, girls. This is a pleasant surprise."

And then three voices speaking at once. "Where is she?" "We won't take no for an answer." "Chris, get your ass down here."

"I'll be right there," Chris called down the stairs, her heart thumping as she hurried into her bedroom and checked her reflection in the bathroom mirror. "I look okay," she assured herself, pulling a comb through her shoulder-length hair, securing it into a ponytail with a purple scrunchy. She exchanged the stained gray sweats she'd been wearing the last two days for a pair of white cotton slacks, replaced the faded yellow T-shirt she had on with a pale lavender clone. Why the fuss? she wondered. Where was she going? Just downstairs to say hello.

"Chris, what the hell are you doing up there?" Vicki yelled up the stairs.

"Be right down." Chris didn't move. Maybe if enough time elapsed, they'd get tired of waiting and go away.

"I'm counting to ten, then I'm coming upstairs," Barbara warned.

Chris took one last glance in the mirror, then rushed into the hall. She appeared at the top of the steps just as Barbara was starting her climb.

"There she is!" Barbara announced with delight. "She's real. She exists. We didn't just make her up."

In the next instant Chris was in Barbara's arms, the warmth

of the other woman's embrace like cashmere against her skin, the subtle musk of Barbara's perfume dancing around her head like fairy dust. Chris closed her eyes, buried her head against Barbara's neck, inhaled the wondrous scent.

"Is everything okay?" Barbara whispered, squeezing Chris tightly.

An involuntary cry, half-squeal, half-sigh, escaped Chris's lips, and she pulled back, away from Barbara's arms.

"What's the matter?"

"Apparently you don't know your own strength, Barbie doll," Tony said, laughing, joining the two women on the stairs, putting his arm around his wife, leading her gingerly down the stairs and into the front hall where Susan and Vicki were waiting. "Chris is a little bruised up. She told you about falling down the stairs last week, didn't she?"

"What?" Susan.

"You fell down the stairs?" Vicki.

"My God, are you okay?" Barbara.

"It was just the last two steps," Chris assured them. "And, yes, I'm fine. Can't say the same for Wyatt's train, I'm afraid, which I pretty much destroyed when I landed." She tried to laugh, but the painful throbbing at her ribs cut the laugh short.

"Let's see." Barbara was instantly at Chris's side, lifting up the bottom of her T-shirt, her fingers gently grazing the large, round, mustard-colored stain on Chris's left side.

"Whoa, girl," Tony said. "Anything going on with you two I should know about?"

"That's a pretty nasty-looking bruise," Vicki said.

"Maybe Owen should have a look at it," Susan offered.

"I'm fine," Chris protested. "Really. It's nothing."

"Mommy fell down the stairs and squished Wyatt's train," Montana announced, entering the hall from the kitchen.

"So we hear," said Vicki. "That wasn't very smart of her, was it?"

"She's always falling down," Montana said matter-of-factly.

"Maybe if you and your brother would pick up your toys occasionally . . . " Tony said.

Montana frowned, grabbed her mother's fingers, started tugging on her arm. "Come on, Mommy. You said we'd make cookies."

"Why don't you get your daddy to help you make cookies?" Susan suggested.

"Yeah, we're gonna take your mommy out with us for a little while," Vicki said.

"No!" Montana protested.

"Don't frown," Barbara warned. "You'll get wrinkles."

"I can't go," Chris said, as Montana continued pulling on her fingers. "Wyatt'll be up any minute, and I promised Montana . . ."

"I can look after the kids," Tony offered. "Go on, hon. You haven't been out of the house in weeks."

"No!" Montana said again, her delicate features crowding together in the middle of her tiny face as her long blond hair whipped from cheek to cheek with each stubborn shake of her head. "She said we'd make cookies."

Tony immediately scooped his daughter into his arms. "What's the matter, kiddo? You don't think your daddy knows how to make chocolate chip cookies? I'll have you know I'm an expert on chocolate chip cookies. In fact, I make much better cookies than your mommy. Didn't you know that the best chefs in the world are men?"

Montana wiggled out of her father's arms, glared at her mother. "I don't like you anymore. You're not a good mommy."

"Montana . . ."

"It's okay, Chris," Tony said, as Montana ran back into the kitchen. "She'll get over it. You go with your friends."

"You'll be a good mommy later." Vicki quickly guided Chris toward the front door.

"Really, I shouldn't . . ."

"We'll have her back in time for dinner." Susan opened the door, pushed Chris outside.

"Where are we going?" Chris asked, taking a deep breath, sucking in the warm September air. She raised her face to the sun, closed her eyes, felt the sun sear into her cheek like a hot iron. Had it left a mark? she wondered, lowering her head, looking back to the house, catching Tony's shadow watching her from behind the sheer curtains of her living room.

"We're kidnapping you," Vicki announced, leading the women toward the pearlized-beige-colored Jaguar parked halfway down the street.

"Really," Chris said, coming to an abrupt halt. "I can't do this. I have to get back."

Vicki unlocked the car doors as the women surrounded Chris, blocked her escape. "Get in the car," someone said.

Chris peered out the rear window of the large luxury car, watching one winding road disappear into another. They'd only been driving for ten minutes, and already it seemed as if they were in another world, a magical world untouched by the mundane concerns of harsh reality. A world where large estates sat well back from the road, and traffic signs announced horse trails and crossings. A world where peaceful, rolling green hills created the calming illusion of country life, although it was situated less than half an hour from downtown Cincinnati. Lots of money, both new and old, Chris thought, in the twenty square miles that comprised the tony suburb of Indian Hill. Had these people been affected by the recession at all? Did they even know about it? "What are we doing here?" she asked.

"Just looking," Vicki said. "See anything you like?"

"Only everything," Barbara said from the seat beside Chris.

Chris felt Barbara's hand resting on top of hers, wondered if Barbara was keeping it there to prevent her from bolting from the car. She's so beautiful, Chris thought absently, fighting the urge to run her free hand across Barbara's soft cheek. She doesn't need all that makeup and hairspray. She doesn't need anything at all.

"Did I tell you what Whitney said the other day?" Susan asked from the front passenger seat, her voice resonating quiet maternal pride. "We were getting ready to take a walk when it started raining, so I told her we'd have to go later, and she said, 'That's okay, Mommy. We take *open* umbrella.'" Susan laughed. "I thought that was pretty good for two years old, that kind of deductive reasoning."

"Amazing," Barbara said.

"Puts Einstein to shame." Vicki laughed.

"Well, I thought it was pretty smart for two years old."

"I remember when Tracey was two," Barbara said, "and I'd been playing with her all afternoon, and I was just exhausted, so I told her I had to go lie down for a while, and of course, she wasn't tired, because she was one of those kids who never slept, so I went into my room and lay down on the bed, and a few minutes later, I heard these little feet come padding into the room, and I opened one eye and saw her struggling with this big blanket, which she finally managed to throw over me, and then she climbed into the chair on the other side of the room and just sat there, watching me. Next thing I knew I'm sound asleep. I woke up an hour later and she's still sitting there, she hasn't moved, she's just sitting there staring at me."

"Josh is a bit like that," Vicki said of her four-year-old son. "Kind of creepy."

"I didn't mean to imply Tracey was creepy," Barbara protested.

"Josh is definitely creepy," Vicki said matter-of-factly. "I mean, I love him and everything, it's just that he's a little weird. You know what he asked me for the other day? Tampax!"

"Tampax! Why, for heaven's sake?"

"He said he heard you swim better with it."

The women hooted with laughter. Even Chris found herself laughing out loud. Immediately she felt the tug at her ribs.

"And Kirsten," Vicki continued. "She's a hard one to figure out. I never know what she's thinking."

"It's better that way," Susan said. "Ariel tells me every thought in her head. Most of them have to do with hating her sister. I don't think she's ever going to forgive me."

The women chuckled, fell silent, stared out the windows at the magnificent expanse of rolling hills.

"So, when are you going to tell us what's going on?" Barbara asked Chris, managing to make the question sound casual, although the stiffening of her fingers on Chris's hand gave her away.

Chris felt her breath catch in her lungs. Even though she'd been expecting the question ever since climbing into the backseat of Vicki's car, still its directness startled her. She'd been lulled into a false sense of security by the women's laughter, by the easy familiarity of their shared confidences. "I don't understand what you mean," she said, the words sounding unconvincing even to herself. Barbara sat back, raised one eyebrow; Susan twisted around from the front passenger seat; Vicki's eyes narrowed in the rearview mirror. All looked skeptical, concerned, even vaguely frightened. "What are you looking at?" Chris asked. "What's the matter with everyone? There's nothing going on. Honestly."

"We hardly see you anymore, you never return phone calls, you're always busy—"

"You know how it is," Chris protested.

"We don't know."

"Tell us."

"There's just a lot going on," Chris said.

"You just said there was nothing going on," Vicki reminded her.

"What?"

"Which is it, Chris? You can't have it both ways."

"Careful. You're starting to sound like a lawyer."

"I'm your friend," Vicki said simply.

"Sorry," Chris apologized. "It's just that you're all making a big deal over nothing."

"Are we?" Susan asked.

"Are you angry at us?" Barbara asked. "Did we say anything, do anything to offend you?"

"Of course not."

"Then why don't we see you anymore?"

"It's just that things have been a little hectic lately, that's all," Chris insisted. "Wyatt's sick all the time, he seems to pick up every bug out there. Well, you know how kids are—they're these little incubators for disease. So first he gets sick, and then I get sick. Except it takes me longer to recover. And then I have all this catching up to do around the house."

"So why'd you fire the cleaning lady?" Barbara asked.

"You fired Marsha?" Susan asked, referring to the woman whose services they all shared.

"Tony wasn't happy with the job she was doing," Chris tried to explain, "and I'm home all day. There's no reason I can't do it."

"Do you *like* doing it?" Vicki asked, as if this thought were beyond her comprehension.

"I don't mind," Chris said. "Really. I don't."

"You're not getting agoraphobic, are you?" Susan's voice was low, her eyes wide.

"What's *agoraphobic?*" Barbara asked.

"Technically, it's a fear of the marketplace," Susan explained.

"I hate the marketplace," Vicki interjected.

"It means being afraid to leave your house."

"I'm not afraid to leave the house."

"You seemed afraid this afternoon."

"Is everything all right with Tony?"

"What do you mean?"

"Are you two getting along okay?" Barbara asked.

"Of course. We're fine. I mean, it's been a little tense lately because Tony's not very happy with his job, and I think he lost a lot of money in the stock market."

"You think?" Susan asked. "You don't know?"

Chris shook her head. "You know how hopeless I am about money."

"Since when?"

"You have your own bank account, don't you?" Vicki asked.

"We have a joint account. Why would I have my own account?"

"Every woman should have her own account. Just in case. And at the first sign of trouble, she should start socking money away."

"But that's so dishonest," Chris protested.

"No," Vicki told her. "It's self-preservation. Besides, you don't want to have to go to Tony for every little thing. You don't, do you? Go to Tony for every little thing?"

"Of course not." Chris felt her cheeks flush angry red. What business was it of Vicki's how she and Tony handled their finances? Vicki was married to a wealthy man. She had no understanding of what it meant for a man to work at a job he hated in order to keep food on the table. Money was tight right now. Tony was right to have her on a strict allowance, to make her account for every dime.

"First thing Monday morning," Vicki was saying, "I want

you to go to the bank and open your own account. You hear me, Chris?"

"I hear you," Chris said, deciding it was easier to agree than argue.

"I'll go with you," Barbara volunteered, patting Chris's hand. "I'm embarrassed to say I don't have my own account either."

"God, I don't believe you two," Vicki said. "What century are you living in anyway?"

"Why don't we pull over," Susan suggested as they turned right onto Sunshine Lane. "Walk for a bit."

Immediately, Vicki pulled her car to the side of the road. Four doors opened. The women stepped into the warmth of the September afternoon.

"It's so peaceful here," Barbara said, grabbing on to Chris's hand, swinging it back and forth, as if they were schoolgirls. Vicki walked several paces ahead, Susan several paces behind.

"Can we slow down just a little," Susan asked.

Even twenty pounds overweight, Susan was lovely, Chris thought, with her fine brown hair curving toward her strong jaw, the roundness of her cheeks erasing any telltale signs of age, making her look even younger than she had at their first encounter.

"Come on, ladies, I can't walk this slow," Vicki groaned. Typical, Chris thought. Vicki's patience was limited. Hadn't she gotten tired of waiting for her perm to grow out and impatiently hacked her hair off to within an inch of its life? Luckily, the pixie do suited her. Chris smiled. Vicki had a way of spinning even the dirtiest straw into gold.

They walked along the side of the road till they reached Cayuga Drive.

"That's it for me, ladies," Chris said, stopping abruptly, feeling suddenly sick to her stomach. "The heat's getting to me." She felt her knees buckle, give way, watched the ground rushing up to meet her as she fell to the pavement.

Comforting arms immediately surrounded her.

"My God, Chris, what happened?"

"Did you hurt yourself?"

"Take deep breaths."

Chris tried to push away their concern with a wave of her hand, bursting into tears instead.

"What is it, Chris? What's wrong?"

"I think you need to see a doctor."

"I don't need a doctor," Chris said.

"How long have you been falling down like this?"

"It's nothing."

"Chris, you fell down the stairs. Montana said you fall down all the time. Now you collapse in the middle of the street."

"It's hot."

"Not that hot."

Chris took a deep breath, pushed the seemingly unstoppable flow of tears roughly toward her ears, burying her hands beneath the ponytail at the back of her neck. "Oh God," she wailed.

"What is it?"

"Please, Chris. You can tell us."

Chris searched the worried eyes of her friends. Could she tell them the truth? Could she? Dear God, what would they think of her? "I think I'm pregnant," she whispered.

"You're pregnant?" Barbara repeated. "That's wonderful." She paused. "Isn't it?"

Chris lowered her head to her chest, her shoulders shaking as she cried.

"Is it wonderful?" Susan asked quietly.

"I don't know," Chris heard herself wail, hating the sound. It sounded weak and desperate and ungrateful. "It's not that I don't love my children."

"Of course not."

"I love my children more than anything in the world."

"We know that."

"And it's not that I don't ever want more kids. Maybe in another year or two, when things have settled down a bit. It's just that the timing seems so wrong." Chris raised her arms in defeat, then dropped them to her sides. "We had to take out a second mortgage on the house last month, and Tony hates his new job, he's already talking about quitting, going off on his own, starting up his own agency, working from home. And it all just seems like too much sometimes, you know. Like I'll never have a minute to myself. And I know how bad that sounds, because I know how much Tony loves me, I appreciate all the things he does for me, what good care he takes of me and the kids, I really do, but sometimes it feels like I can't breathe. And another baby right now . . ."

"You don't have to have this baby," Vicki said simply.

There was silence.

"I can't have an abortion." Chris began shaking her head as Montana had earlier, her ponytail whipping back and forth across her cheeks. "I can't. I can't."

"You should talk this over with Tony," Barbara suggested gently.

"I can't talk to him about this. He'd never understand. He'd never forgive me for even considering . . ."

There was another moment's silence, then, "He wouldn't have to know."

Chris stared at Vicki in disbelief. She broke free of her friends' comforting arms and pushed herself to her feet, pacing back and forth along the side of the road. "No. I can't. You don't understand. Tony would know. He'd know."

"How would he know?" Barbara asked.

"He'd know," Chris said, her head bobbing violently up and down. "He keeps track."

"What do you mean, he keeps track?" Susan asked. "Are you saying he keeps track of your periods?"

"He's been wanting another baby ever since Wyatt was born."

"What about what *you* want?"

"I don't know what I want." That's why she was so lucky to have Tony, Chris almost screamed. He knew what was best for her.

"He keeps track of your periods," Susan repeated wondrously, as if trying to make sense of the words.

"It's not as bad as it sounds. Look, I've blown this whole thing way out of proportion. I do that all the time."

"No, you don't."

"Yes, I do."

"Who says you do?" Barbara asked. "Tony?"

"You don't blow things out of proportion, Chris," Susan said. "Chris, are you listening to me?"

"I have to go home," Chris said, spinning on her heels, walking back toward the car. "If you won't drive me, I'll hitch a ride." She looked up and down the road, saw no one.

"Of course we'll drive you," Vicki said, chasing after her.

"Chris, wait up!" Chris heard them call from somewhere behind her.

"Chris, please, we're on your side."

Were they?

"We didn't mean to upset you," Barbara said as they climbed back inside the car.

Chris kept her head down on the drive back to Mariemont, her eyes in her lap. "I really want this baby."

"Of course you do."

"We want whatever you want."

"Don't worry about me," Chris said as Vicki pulled her car onto Grand Avenue. Chris saw Tony's shadow watching from behind the living room window as she pushed open the rear door and climbed out of the car. Had he been standing there all this time?

"We love you," Barbara called after her. "You know that, don't you?"

"I know that." Chris wrapped the words around her like a shawl. "I love you too."

Her front door opened. "Hey, baby," Tony said. "You're home early."

"I missed you," Chris told him, stepping across the threshold, closing the door behind her without looking back.

Five

"Mommy! Mommy!"

Susan flipped over onto her right side, strained to look through the darkness toward the clock radio by her husband's side of the bed. Not even 4 A.M. "Oh, God," she moaned, knowing less than two hours had passed since she'd finally drifted off to sleep, a sleep plagued by worried thoughts and restless dreams. Guess I'm not the only one, she thought, listening to Ariel's repeated cries, about to toss off her blankets and see what was bothering the child when her husband's hand on her arm stopped her.

"I'll go," Owen said, sounding as tired as she felt.

"You're sure?"

"Get some sleep." His lips brushed against Susan's forehead as he climbed out of bed.

Susan heard her husband wrestling with his bathrobe at the foot of the four-poster bed, felt the vibrations of his bare feet on the carpet as he walked briskly from the room. "What's the matter, sweetheart?" she heard him ask as he pushed open the door to Ariel's room.

"I had a nightmare," she heard Ariel sob.

Susan knew all about nightmares. One nightmare in particular, she thought, closing her eyes, immediately seeing herself hunched over her desk in her Medieval Drama class, frantically trying to tame an unwieldy assortment of papers, to pummel them into some sort of coherent order, failing miserably, and then hearing her name shouted out loud, as if over a PA system: "Susan. Susan Norman. We'll hear your presentation now," as Professor Currier's bald head bobbed up and down and Susan gathered her errant papers together and squeezed herself out of her seat, making her way to the front of the classroom.

It was always at this moment in the dream that Susan realized she was naked. Alarmed, she'd try to preserve some modesty by hiding behind her papers, scrunching her shoulders forward, her pendulous breasts crushing against the small but bothersome roll of flesh at her stomach. But this new posture only emphasized the abundance of her exposed backside, and she'd hear the laughter of the other students, see their mocking fingers pointing toward her. Quickly she'd bring one hand around behind her, the sudden action sending her papers scattering, as she was forced to her hands and knees in a vain effort to retrieve them, the cruel laughter around her building to an almost deafening crescendo.

That was usually the moment when she woke up, Susan thought gratefully, watching Owen tiptoe back across the carpet toward the bed. He threw his bathrobe across the nearby chair and climbed under the covers, snuggling against her. "What was the problem?" she asked.

"She wet the bed," her husband said matter-of-factly.

Susan's entire body tensed. She had a class first thing in the morning, and she couldn't just hand her mother a load of soiled linen as soon as the poor woman walked in the door. Could she? *Hi there. Ariel wet the bed again. I know you baby-sit every day and this wasn't exactly part of our deal, but could you maybe do a few loads of wash and change the sheets since I have an important class and you're just sitting around doing nothing but taking care of my children?*

"It's okay," Owen said, as if she'd been speaking out loud. "I changed the sheets and put the wet ones in the washing machine."

Susan sat up in bed, stared down at her husband of eleven years. "You did all that?"

"Piece of cake," he mumbled, eyes closed.

"How'd I get so lucky?"

"Get some sleep." A satisfied smile settled into the lines around Owen's eyes and mouth.

"I love you," Susan whispered, curling into the crook of his arm. Owen Norman might not be considered especially good-looking—he was of medium height and build and his features were too ordinary to be considered either distinguished or interesting—but he was a kind and decent man, not to mention a wonderful doctor, and everyone who knew him, patients and friends alike, trusted and admired him.

Susan turned onto her left side, felt Owen turn with her, his hand falling across her generous expanse of hip. She was restless. The incident with Chris this afternoon had unsettled and upset her. Clearly, something was very wrong, something more than Chris was letting on, something more than the prospect of another baby, however ill-timed its conception. The women had discussed it over coffee at Vicki's house, tried to devise strategies for drawing Chris out, ultimately decided they had no choice but to wait until Chris was ready to come to them. Whatever problems she was having, whatever Chris wasn't telling them, was her business. They had to be patient, understanding, and above all quiet. Or they risked losing her altogether.

Susan flipped onto her back, tried to determine the precise moment Chris had begun her withdrawal. Had there been one defining moment, or had the changes in Chris's relationship with the others changed gradually over time? Had their friendship soured as slowly and imperceptibly as a long-standing marriage in the final stages of decay?

Was that the problem? Susan wondered, rolling onto her other side. Were there cracks in Chris and Tony's marriage? Chris had denied it, but if Tony was seriously considering starting his own agency, that would be very expensive, and money was obviously tight. A third baby . . .

He keeps track of her periods! Susan thought, kicking the blanket from around her feet.

"Susan," Owen was saying, "what's wrong?"

"Wrong?" Susan returned to her back, saw Owen's concerned face looming above hers.

"You haven't stopped twitching since I got back into bed."

"I'm sorry." Susan recalled the fear in Chris's eyes when she confided she might be pregnant. What exactly was she so afraid of? *He keeps track of her periods!* Susan thought again. "I just can't seem to get comfortable," she said.

"Still worrying about Chris?"

"No." After a pause, Susan admitted, "Well, trying not to." What was the point in pretending otherwise? She'd never been able to fool Owen. Never really wanted to, she realized, thinking again how lucky she was.

"Luck is only part of the equation," her mother had once said. "You've worked very hard for what you have. And you had the good sense to choose well."

In the end, her mother had told her, we are the choices we make.

"I love you," Susan told her husband again, wondering if she said it often enough. She lifted her head toward his, kissed him on the lips.

"I love you too," he said, responding with surprising eagerness to her kiss, their sudden desire catching them both off guard, but building quickly, so that what began as an innocent expression of gratitude soon became something quite different. Susan felt her body stir in response to her husband's gentle touch, her senses, only moments ago on the verge of total collapse, suddenly heightened and wide-awake, anticipating each new caress.

"Are you ready?" he asked some moments later, and Susan nodded, wrapping her legs around his waist as he entered her. Their bodies rocked together quietly, harmoniously, until Owen asked again, "Are you ready?" and again, Susan nodded, and Owen raised himself onto his knees, thrusting deeper inside her until her head was buzzing, her body tingling, her entire being vibrating. They never tell you about this part in health class, she thought, everything inside her poised to explode. They use cold, clinical words like *climax,* which works better as a literary device, or *orgasm,* which sounds as if it's something that should be confined to a laboratory, but they never get close to what actually happens when two people make love: the pure and utter joy of total surrender.

"Who has multiple orgasms?" Susan remembered Vicki demanding on that Super Bowl Sunday some eight months ago.

"I've never had an orgasm," Chris had admitted, and Barbara had confessed to always faking hers. Even Vicki had confided she didn't experience orgasm through intercourse. When pressed, Susan had declined comment and left the room. Better to appear shy than smug, she'd decided, choosing not to tell the others she experienced orgasm on an alarmingly regular basis. Sometimes all Owen had to do was touch her in a certain spot on the side of her neck . . .

Maybe I'm just easier to please, Susan thought now, although she'd never considered herself particularly sexual. Certainly, she didn't see herself as sexy. Attractive enough, yes, especially if she were to lose a few pounds, but nowhere near as pretty as Barbara, Chris, or Vicki. And certainly no one looking at Owen would fight to get into his bed. They'd choose Barbara's husband, Ron, because he was tall and good-looking, or Vicki's husband, Jeremy, because he was rich and powerful, or Chris's husband, Tony, because he was cocky and full of bravado. And they'd all choose wrong.

In the end, we are the choices we make.

"How are you?" her husband was asking now.

"Good," Susan said, a purr in her voice. "I'm good."

Seconds later, securely nestled inside her husband's arms, Susan closed her eyes and drifted off to sleep.

"In our survey of the liturgical beginnings of drama," Professor Ian Currier was explaining to the class of approximately forty-five less than enthusiastic students, "we've talked about the handful of twelfth-century plays that had real artistic merit, most notably those from the Fleury playbook."

Susan fidgeted in her hard seat of polished wood, struggled to keep her eyes from closing. I have to get more sleep, she decided, although how she was going to accomplish this feat was open to question. Between going to classes, writing essays, studying for tests and exams, looking after two young daughters—although mercifully, Whitney was easier in every respect than Ariel, which only made Ariel all the more difficult—and making sure her husband didn't feel neglected, Susan understood there simply weren't enough hours in the day or, more precisely, in the night, when she needed them most. She pushed herself up straighter in her chair, arched her back, stifled a yawn, returned her attention to the soft drone of Professor Currier's voice, a voice that all but shouted his been-there, done-that, hate-doing-it attitude. What was she doing here? Where exactly did she think a degree in English literature was going to take her?

"Yet even the Fleury plays were tied closely to very specific liturgical occasions and were sung during intervals in regular church services," Professor Currier continued. "As we'll see in *The Conversion of St. Paul,* this play, which was probably staged on the Feast of the Conversion of St. Paul on January twenty-fifth, adheres pretty closely to the biblical account of his conversion as related in the Acts of the Apostles."

Around her, Susan heard the movement of pens scurrying across paper like a bunch of tiny wild mice and realized she hadn't copied down a thing since the lecture had begun. She opened her notebook, reached toward the large canvas bag at her feet for a pen. Immediately, she felt something glom on to her finger, like a leech from a freshwater lake, she thought, recalling the unpleasant incident from her childhood when her parents had taken Susan, along with her older brother and younger sister, to the cottage one summer, and Susan had insisted on going in the water that very first afternoon, even though her mother had cautioned there might be leeches. But Susan was too busy showing off for her little sister to fully appreciate her mother's warning, and she'd emerged from the water with several hideous black blobs fastened to her arms and legs, only to see her little sister run from her in terror. Susan had tried pulling at them in a vain effort to dislodge them, but that only made things worse, and blood soon trickled down her limbs in thin, squiggly red lines. Her mother had explained that the horrid things couldn't be pulled off without damaging the skin below, and that they could only be removed by a liberal sprinkling of salt. "And then you have to eat them," her older brother had teased gleefully, sending Susan scrambling across the sand, screaming and shrieking her dismay, until her mother caught up to her and calmed her down by assuring her that if anyone was going to have to eat the nasty things, it would be her brother.

Susan extricated her hand from her bag, relieved, yet simultaneously dismayed, by the sight of Ariel's half-eaten orange lollipop sticking to the inside of her index finger. "Great," she said, much louder than she'd intended.

"I'm sorry, Mrs. Norman," Professor Currier said immediately, "did you have something to share with the class?"

Damn those big ears, Susan thought, shaking her head. They don't miss a thing.

"Sorry," she muttered, pulling the offending lollipop off her finger with more force than necessary, so that it came apart, and several stray pieces fell to the floor, shattering like chips of glass.

"A little snack, Mrs. Norman?" Professor Currier asked, chin lowering as his eyes peered over the top of his round, wire-rimmed glasses.

Did he possess X-ray vision as well? Susan wondered, as several nearby students laughed nervously, perhaps grateful at not being the object of his considerable and much feared derision.

"I would think you'd be well acquainted with the perils of eating between meals," the professor remarked, his gaze returning to the podium in front of him before the full import of his remarks had time to register. "In *The Conversion of St. Paul,*" he said, as if one thought followed naturally upon the other, "we have the familiar elements of twelfth-century church drama, including the conversion of a sinner to grace and a narrow escape from dangerous enemies, as well as the continuing conflict between worldly power and the power of God's salvation."

Susan felt her skin on fire beneath her white sweater, her neck flushing pink, her cheeks burning bright red. How dare he speak to her that way! How dare he make fun of her weight!

Was that what he was doing? she backtracked immediately. Or was she being overly sensitive? Maybe his comments weren't intended as anything more than a slight rebuke for her having disrupted the class. He probably knows he's as boring as hell, she thought, and he takes advantage of certain situations to inject a little much-needed levity into the proceedings. In the future, she'd be careful not to present him with any more such opportunities at her expense. Let the other students bear the brunt of his mean-spirited barbs. They could take it. They were tougher and stronger and at least a decade younger than she was.

Whom was she kidding? Susan thought, casting a furtive glance around the overheated old room. They were babies, for God's sake, most still in their teens, their faces unfinished canvases, awaiting the brushstrokes of experience to complete them. What was she doing here among them when she so clearly didn't belong? What distorted ego had persuaded her to keep pursuing a university degree that would gain her nothing in the long run? Except an education, she reminded herself. Except the satisfaction of a job well done.

And who was to say her degree in English literature might not prove practical after all? Vicki was constantly encouraging her to speak to her husband about a job at one of his magazines. Maybe when she had her diploma safely in hand and her children were both ensconced in school all day, well, then, she might just visit Jeremy Latimer's ever-expanding empire after all.

"The chief aim of church drama of the twelfth century was not to educate the masses, but rather to create beautiful works of piety and wisdom, and the use of many different poetic forms and literary genres, as well as classical references, suggest a level of considerable literary sophistication." Professor Currier looked up from his notes, surveyed the classroom. "Fine, then. All right. For next Friday, I want to see a five-thousand-word essay comparing the Digby and the Fleury versions of *The Conversion of St. Paul*. There will be no extensions, and this paper will be worth twenty-five percent of your term mark. But," he continued with a wink, "women with big breasts get an automatic pass." With that, he placed his notes in his worn leather briefcase and snapped the case shut. "That's it." The boldness of his smile accentuated the baldness of his head. "Class dismissed."

There was some laughter along with some embarrassed tittering as the students gathered their belongings together and exited the room. Only Susan remained in her seat, unable to move, scarcely able to breathe.

"Problems, Mrs. Norman?" Professor Currier asked.

Susan shook her head, her gaze rooted to the floor. Tears stung the corners of her eyes, as if she'd been slapped. What was the matter with her? Why didn't she just get up and leave?

"Is something the matter?" Ian Currier pressed.

Slowly Susan lifted her eyes from her feet, floating them toward the professor's general vicinity, although she was careful not to look at him directly. If she looked at him, she might say something she'd regret. And he was her professor after all, the man who decided whether or not she passed her course, achieved her much coveted degree.

"Susan?"

So now her name was a question in itself, Susan thought, wanting to run away and hide, as she had that afternoon on the beach when confronted by her brother's cruel taunts. Avoidance—her first reaction to any kind of unpleasantry. Followed by the conciliatory gesture. Anger was a tremendous waste of energy. Most problems could be solved with a few soft, well-chosen words. Besides, what exactly was she so upset about anyway? An innocent remark, obviously intended as a joke, that no one took seriously, that no one else in the class seemed the least offended by. She was making a mountain out of the proverbial molehill, probably because she was still smarting from Professor Currier's earlier comment about her weight, although she'd undoubtedly misinterpreted that one as well. She was being much too sensitive. Probably because she was so tired. She really needed to catch up on her sleep.

Susan heard movement, looked toward the podium only to find it abandoned, and Professor Currier walking toward the door. Leave well enough alone, she thought. "Professor Currier," she said.

Ian Currier stopped at the sound of his name and swiveled toward Susan, so that by the time she reached his side, he was facing her head-on. "I thought there might be something on your mind," he said, waiting.

He's not that much older than I am, Susan realized, pushing her hair behind her ears, trying to decide what she wanted to say. "I thought that was a rather inappropriate comment," she began, thinking, *Damn, too general, way too vague.*

"Which one was that?" he asked, as she'd known he would. He was smiling, his dark eyes challenging hers.

"What you said about women."

"Women?"

"Women with large breasts."

"Ah, yes, women with large breasts," he repeated, his lips twitching in obvious amusement at her discomfort.

"I didn't think it was appropriate."

"You don't think women with large breasts are appropriate?"

He's playing with me, Susan thought, growing bolder, refusing to back down. "I didn't think your comment about automatically giving passing grades to women with large breasts was appropriate."

He nodded, his gaze lowering to the front of her white turtleneck sweater. "I don't see where you have anything to worry about, Mrs. Norman. Your chest appears more than ample to secure a passing grade." His smile tugged at his cheeks, widening, showing teeth.

Like a snarling dog, Susan thought. Instinctively, she took a step back.

"Now if you'll excuse me," he said.

"I won't excuse you." The words were out of Susan's mouth before she had time to consider them.

"What?"

"I won't excuse you. I think your comments are out of line. I think you owe the class—and me—an apology."

"I think you're the one who's out of line here, Mrs. Norman," he said quickly, biting off her name and spitting it into the space between them. "Now I know it's the eighties, and women's lib has seized control of common sense, but really, Susan, have you no sense of humor?"

"I have no sense of *your* humor," she retorted.

Professor Currier shook his head sadly, as if he were the one offended. "I look forward to your essay," he said, then walked briskly from the room.

Six

So, how are you feeling?"

"Okay, I guess."

"Nervous?"

"A little."

Chris reached over to take Barbara's trembling hand, her arm brushing up against her hugely pregnant belly. Chris felt the baby inside her immediately lean forward, press its ears against the inner layers of her flesh, as if on instant alert. Who is this woman? the baby inside Chris demanded silently, a sharp kick reminding her not to get too close. This woman is an interloper, not a friend, the kick warned, someone who makes unreasonable demands on your time, who takes your focus away from your family, where it belongs. You shouldn't even be here. Didn't Daddy tell you not to come? Another kick, harder, sharper than the first. What would Daddy say if he knew?

A wave of nausea washed over Chris as she swallowed the bile pushing its way up her throat. Oh, please, no, she thought, eyes frantically scanning the long hallway for an exit sign. You can't be sick. Not here. Not in a hospital corridor, for God's sake. Although what better place? she thought, and almost laughed, except she was too afraid to laugh. She was always afraid, she thought, fighting off the impulse to gag and hiding her fear behind a smile. She smiled a lot these days. "It'll be okay," Chris said, as much to herself as to her closest friend. "I understand they do these procedures all the time now." She wondered if this was true or something she'd made up. Tony said she was always making things up, substituting gibberish for fact, trying to disguise her lack of education. But nobody was fooled, he said.

"I know." A slight widening of Barbara's eyes signaled a smile of her own. "It's no big deal. I shouldn't have asked you to come."

"Don't be silly. I want to be here."

"Ron said he'd try to get here as soon as his classes were over."

"I'm really glad I could make it."

"Thanks." Barbara stared into her lap. "I know it probably wasn't easy for you to get away."

"Easier than you think." Chris stole another look down the busy hospital corridor, searching for familiar eyes peeking out from atop sterile hospital masks. "Tony had to go out of town on business."

"Business? Did he get a new client?"

"I'm not sure," Chris said vaguely, embarrassed less by the fact she wasn't able to elaborate than by the fact she'd been so relieved when Tony had said he had to leave town for a few days that she hadn't asked him either where he was going or what he was going to do when he got there. Such was her joy at his unexpected announcement that she'd had to hang on to the kitchen table to keep from jumping up and down.

"What's the matter, sweetheart?" Tony asked, folding her into his embrace. "I won't be gone long. You don't have to worry."

What was the matter with her? Chris asked herself now. Tony was her husband, for God's sake, the father of her children. He worked so hard to provide her with all the creature comforts she took for granted. How could she be so ungrateful, so hard-hearted, so selfish, as to wish him anywhere but at her side, the only place on earth he wanted to be? Why was she always giving him such a hard time? Was it so hard to just keep quiet and do the things he asked: keep the house in order, the children in check, her friends at bay? Tony was right—if only she would worry half as much about him as she did her precious friends . . .

Maybe if she just had some time to herself, Chris thought. But ever since Tony had started working out of the house, he'd seemed more preoccupied with how Chris spent her days than he did his own. In the seven months since he'd converted the den into his office, he'd reorganized Chris's schedule entirely, and while she grudgingly had to admit that the house ran much more efficiently now, still, a few days to herself had sounded awfully nice. She could relax, call her friends without worrying about Tony's bruised ego, maybe even meet Susan or Vicki for lunch, definitely accompany Barbara to the hospital for her scheduled laparoscopy, an idea Tony had initially vetoed. "Sure, that's great thinking, Chris," he'd scoffed when she'd told him of Barbara's initial request several weeks earlier. "You, with your baby practically bursting out of your stomach going to the hospital with a woman having a procedure to find out why she can't have another kid! Real sensitive of you."

Absently, Chris patted her stomach, feeling the baby inside her kick at the palm of her hand, as if kicking her away, warning her to keep her distance, as if aware of her ambivalence toward him, as if he'd judged her in advance and found her wanting. The ultrasound had revealed the baby was a boy. Tony had already picked out a name. Rowdy, he told her, after some cowboy Clint Eastwood had once played on TV. What kind of name was Rowdy? she wondered, but hadn't bothered to ask. What was the point? "You're sure this doesn't upset you?" she asked Barbara, her voice a whisper. Both women looked toward Chris's stomach.

"Are you kidding? It gives me hope. Reminds me why I'm doing this." Barbara reached over and caressed Chris's pregnant belly, eager palms obviously hoping to feel signs of life. The baby inside Chris fell instantly quiet, refusing to move so much as a finger until Barbara eventually gave up in defeat and withdrew her hand.

As if he knows, Chris thought. As if he's not moving on purpose.

Barbara patted her own stomach. "Think I could talk them into a tummy tuck while I'm here?"

Chris laughed. "You look great."

"I don't know. I can't seem to get rid of this pot. At least you have an excuse."

"You look great," Chris repeated, amazed at how put-together her friend was even less than an hour away from surgery, sitting primly beside her in high heels and Chanel-style suit, shoulder-length black hair framing her perfectly made-up face, brown eyes highlighted by pale mauve shadow, lush pink lips outlined in red, her cheekbones blushing pale peach.

Chris brought her hand to her own cheek, still echoing with the sting of Tony's palm. Of course, it had been an accident. He hadn't meant to hit her. Yes, he was angry, but he'd merely raised his hand in frustration; he hadn't expected her to turn her head. Why had she chosen precisely that moment to turn her head?

"God, baby, I'm so sorry," she heard him cry, his voice echoing down the hospital corridor, bouncing off the walls. "Are you all right? You know I didn't mean to hurt you. Please forgive me. You know it was an accident, don't you? You know how much I love you. Please say you forgive me, baby. I promise you it'll never happen again."

"Something wrong?" Barbara asked.

"Wrong?"

"You're rubbing a hole in your cheek."

Chris felt her neck grow hot and her cheeks flush red. "Feels like I'm getting a pimple," she lied. She was getting good at lying to her friends.

"You'd think we'd be past that crap by now." Barbara moved closer, examined Chris's cheek with a practiced eye. "I don't see anything."

"It's one of those under-the-skin things."

"They're the worst." Barbara looked around, sighed. "It's times like this I wish I smoked."

"You're nervous?"

"A little. Heard any good jokes lately?"

"What did one wall say to the other?" Chris asked timidly.

"Meet you at the corner?"

"Pretty lame," Chris acknowledged, and both women laughed. "That's what happens when you get your jokes from a four-year-old."

Barbara released a deep breath from her lungs, the sigh rippling audibly into the air. "What if they discover I can't have any more kids?"

Chris took her friend's hands in her own. "That's not going to happen."

"What if it does?"

"I'll give you one of mine," Chris said softly, as Barbara lay her head against Chris's shoulder. Immediately, Chris felt the baby inside her kick, as if he'd heard her, as if by laying siege to her body all these months, he was privy to everything she said and felt and thought. And he hated her for those thoughts, hated her already. Rowdy, she repeated silently, trying to get used to the sound, as the baby inside her unleashed a barrage of well-aimed kicks at her bladder. I didn't mean it, Chris tried to explain. It was just a joke. I could never give you up. You're my flesh and blood. I'd never desert you. It's not that I won't love you, that I don't love you already. It's just . . .

Just what? Just that the timing isn't right? Isn't that what you told your friends? That a third child is the last thing you need right now? Because you have so many other things to do, so many better things to do. Because you'd rather be with your friends than your family, she heard the baby inside her accuse in Tony's voice.

"No!" Chris jumped to her feet.

Barbara was instantly on her feet beside her. "What's the matter? Did your water break?"

Both women looked toward the floor. Mercifully, it was dry, as were Chris's thighs and legs. What was the matter with her? Had she lost all self-control? "I need to use the washroom."

"Do you want me to come with you?" Worry clouded Barbara's mauve-framed brown eyes.

That's just great, Chris thought. She's worrying about me when I'm the one who's supposed to be taking care of her. She's the one going in for surgery. She's the one who's going to be sedated and cut and prodded and poked, and all I was supposed to do was sit here and keep her company until she goes in, that's my whole job, and I can't even do that. I'm a complete incompetent. My best friend is putting herself through this ordeal because she wants to have another baby more than anything else in the world, and here I am practically giving birth—to baby number three, no less—right in front of her. Talk about insensitive! Tony was right. I should never have come.

"Chris? Are you all right? You don't look so hot."

"I'm okay," Chris lied.

"Maybe you should go home." Barbara checked her watch. "They'll be coming for me any minute now, and Ron'll be here before I'm out of recovery. There's no reason for you to stay. Here, let me give you some money for a cab." She reached inside her purse, grabbed two $20 bills, pushed them into Chris's hand.

Chris flushed with shame. How could Tony have forgotten

to leave her any money? "I'm not going anywhere," she insisted, stuffing the money back inside Barbara's purse. "Except to the bathroom. I'll be right back."

Chris walked on unsteady feet along a corridor that seemed to grow longer with each successive step. "Where is the damn bathroom?" she muttered. "There's got to be a bathroom, for God's sake."

"Can I help you?" a man asked from somewhere beside her.

Chris lifted her eyes toward the familiar voice, her heartbeat quickening, sweat breaking out across her forehead. He'd found her, she acknowledged, closing her eyes, bracing herself for her husband's anger. She'd gone against his wishes, leapt at the first opportunity to deceive him, put her family at risk by exposing her baby to potentially lethal germs. Hadn't Tony told her not to go? He had every right to be angry.

"Are you looking for anything in particular?" the man asked, as Chris forced her eyes open.

The man Chris saw, the man staring at her with kind blue eyes from a height of at least six and a half feet, looked absolutely nothing like Tony. Nor did he sound anything like him, Chris realized, as he directed her to the washroom located around the corner to her right. "Thank you," she said, allowing him to take her elbow and escort her part of the way. "Thank you," she said again as she reached the bathroom door, although the young man was already gone. "Thank you," she repeated a third time, standing in front of the mirror, throwing water on her cheeks and watching as it dribbled down her neck toward the white collar of her navy blue sweater.

Several minutes later, her bladder emptied and her nerves calmed, Chris retraced her steps, only to find Barbara gone.

She stood for several seconds in the middle of the hall, not sure what to do next, whether to sit down and wait for Barbara to come back from surgery or whether to go home, as Barbara had suggested. Except she had no money, only $10 to give Mrs. McGuinty for looking after Wyatt. So she had no choice but to wait for Ron to show up. That was okay. Montana was in school. Wyatt was being well looked after. It was peaceful here. Quiet. No one was telling her what to do or how to do it, no one was telling her she was lazy or stupid or selfish.

It was then that she felt a hand on her back, familiar fingers pressing into the flesh beneath her blouse. Oh, God, she thought, stifling a cry in her lungs, her shoulders stiffening. He'd found her. She'd been a fool to think he wouldn't find out, a fool to think he wouldn't know where to look.

"Are you Chris Malarek?" a woman's voice asked.

Chris spun around so quickly she almost knocked down the middle-aged woman in the white nurse's uniform standing before her. Chris nodded vehemently.

"Mrs. Azinger was taken into surgery," the nurse explained. "She asked me to give you this and said she'll call you later." The nurse dropped five new $20 bills into Chris's hand.

"Thank you," Chris whispered. "Thank you very much." In the next minute, she was sobbing wildly on the other woman's shoulder.

She had to leave him.

Pregnant or not, she couldn't live this way any longer, always looking over her shoulder, afraid of her own shadow. "I can't live this way," Chris was saying, her hands trembling as she fought with her key to open the front door. "I can't live this way anymore. Afraid to leave the house. No money of my own. Lying to my friends. Collapsing in front of total strangers. I can't do it."

She looked down the street, at the taxi that was disappearing around the corner. She loved this street, Chris thought, pushing open the front door. Especially now, in early April, when the cool, damp air was so full of promise. How could she leave it? How could she leave her friends, the wonderful women of Grand Avenue, whom she loved with all her heart? Her best friends in the world. Chris smiled as each beautiful face flashed before her eyes. Still, her friends would understand why she had to leave. They'd known for months that something was wrong. Only her great shame had prevented her from telling them the truth.

She'd pack a small suitcase, pick up Wyatt from Mrs. McGuinty's and Montana from school, spend the night at a hotel, decide then what to do next. She still had a credit card, didn't she? Maybe not. No. Tony had taken away her credit cards, said they were in enough debt as it was, and she was so careless with money. He was right. Money had always slipped through her fingers with alarming ease. That's why he'd found it necessary to take away her credit cards, to stop her weekly allowance, to give her only a few dollars a day, to make her account for every cent.

It wasn't so awful. This way she didn't have to worry about spending too much or planning too far ahead, because she'd never been good at planning too far ahead, her mind was always racing from one thing to another, which was why they'd decided she really shouldn't be driving, because she was so easily distracted, and they both knew she'd never forgive herself if she were to get in an accident, especially if the kids were involved. Besides, what did she need with a car anyway, especially now that Tony was home all day and he could drive her anywhere she needed to go? No, the second car had been an unnecessary extravagance, one they simply couldn't afford to indulge anymore. If necessary, if he wasn't available, then she could always hop in a cab. "Hop in a cab," Chris repeated, stepping into the foyer. "Hop in a cab. Hop in a cab."

Just hop in a cab and go. Go where? Chris thought, dropping her coat and purse to the floor, stepping over the small heap as if it were a puddle. She was eight months pregnant, for God's sake. Where was she going to go? Home to mother? That was a laugh. Mother was in California with husband-to-be number three. Daddy was in Florida with wife number four. And were either of them any happier than they'd been when they were together? She doubted it. No, they'd destroyed the family, uprooted the children, taken off for parts and partners unknown, turned everyone's life inside out, and for what exactly? So that they could be just as miserable somewhere else. Was Chris seriously thinking of doing the same thing to her own children? To Tony? To herself?

Could she really abandon her husband on a whim, uproot her family because she was feeling a little down in the dumps? And that was all it was. She was being moody, the way she always got when she was pregnant. That's all it was. Her hormones were making her so anxious about every little thing, causing her to talk back to Tony, to question his every utterance, to resent him for being concerned about her, for being so attentive. Didn't he have her best interests at heart? Wasn't he always trying to help her, to protect her, even when that meant protecting her from herself, if need be? "You're your own worst enemy," he told her, and he was right.

Maybe she should see a therapist, she decided, inching her way up the stairs to her bedroom, feeling her feet sink into the worn carpet, as if into quicksand, her shaking hand heavy on the wooden banister. It needs dusting, she thought idly, pulling one leg after the other, the muscles of her inner thighs twisting and cramping with the strain. I don't need a therapist, she decided. I need a cleaning lady.

Or a lawyer, Chris thought, reaching the top of the stairs, gasping out loud. "A lawyer," she repeated out loud, rolling the word around her tongue as she waddled into her bedroom and plopped down on the side of her bed, feeling as unwieldy, as stranded, as a beached whale. The baby inside her registered his displeasure with her thoughts by a sharp kick. "It's okay, baby," she tried to reassure him. "It's okay."

But it wasn't okay, Chris knew, catching sight of her reflection in the bedroom window, barely recognizing the lost soul looking back. Her eyes squinted toward the image, but the harder she looked, the faster she faded, until one quick turn of her head, and she'd disappeared altogether, lost in an errant streak of sunlight. What had happened to her? Chris wondered. Where had she gone?

In the next second, her hand was on the telephone, and she was punching in a series of numbers, refusing to think about what she was doing, to question it, to stop it. "Vicki Latimer, please," she said into the phone, surprised by the strength she heard in her voice.

"I'm sorry. Mrs. Latimer is in a meeting."

"This is Chris Malarek, a friend of hers. It's very important I speak to her as soon as possible." Was it? Chris wondered. What exactly was she planning to say to Vicki? Was she planning on asking for her advice? For a loan? For the name of a good divorce lawyer? "I just need to know my options," she said, not realizing she was speaking out loud.

"I'll let Mrs. Latimer know you called," Vicki's secretary said.

Chris sat with the receiver pressed to her ear long after the secretary had hung up, the dial tone resonating against her brain, like the sound a heart monitor makes after the patient has died. She wasn't sure how long she sat like that, shoulders slumped forward, swollen breasts balanced on her belly, the phone buried into her ear, her eyes staring blankly toward the window, the baby inside her surprisingly still. Nor was she sure at what precise moment she became aware that she wasn't alone. Perhaps she caught a glimpse of Tony's reflection in the glass of the window or heard the sound of his breathing from somewhere behind her back. Maybe there was a ripple, a stirring in the air that disrupted the room's normal flow of oxygen. Maybe she'd smelled him, the way a doomed gazelle catches a fleeting whiff of the hungry tiger in the instant before he strikes. Or maybe she'd known all along he was there, Chris realized, a dull certainty settling into the pit of her stomach, the baby inside her shifting to accommodate the intruder.

"Hang up the phone, Chris," she heard Tony say, his voice the serrated edge of a blade.

"Tony . . ." The word froze on Chris's tongue.

"Hang up the phone and turn around."

Chris felt the phone drop from her shoulder, bounce toward the floor. It dangled from its cord, like a man dropped from the gallows. She made no move to pick it up, to return it to the security of its carriage. Instead she watched it sway back and forth above the steel-blue broadloom, like the pendulum of an old grandfather clock, ticking off the moments of her sad, stupid existence.

"Turn around," Tony said again.

Chris took a deep breath, lay a protective hand across her stomach, then slowly, reluctantly, did as she was told.

"Looks like I decided not to go away after all." Tony smiled. "What's the matter, Chris? Aren't you happy to see your husband?"

Chris watched Tony's smile twist into a sneer as his right hand swooped into the air, his fist flying toward her with mesmerizing speed. And then, suddenly, the world split apart in a flash of blinding light, and she saw nothing.

Seven

"When did you say she called?"

"Not more than two minutes ago. Right before you walked in."

"And she said it was important?"

"Said she wanted to speak to you right away."

Vicki brought the arched slivers of her eyebrows together at the bridge of her nose, wondering if something had gone wrong during Barbara's surgery. "Was she calling from the hospital?"

"She didn't say."

"What exactly *did* she say?"

"Just that she was a friend of yours and that it was very important she speak to you as soon as possible."

"She didn't give any hint what it was about?"

"Said something about reviewing her options," the secretary said.

What options? Vicki wondered, reaching across her cluttered desk for her phone and punching in Chris's number, listening impatiently to the subsequent busy signal. What options could Chris have been talking about? She immediately redialed the number, received the same annoying signal, slammed down the receiver. Vicki took busy signals personally. They offended her in ways she recognized were completely irrational, having little to do with either logic or common sense. Still, she couldn't help but feel that some intentional malice was directed at her by the person tying up the other end of the line. Busy signals slowed her down, got in her way, proclaimed she was just one of the crowd. Grab a number, get in line, wait your turn. Vicki sighed, glared at the phone. "Well, I guess she's going over her options with someone else." Vicki dismissed her irritation with a wave of her long fingers, her large diamond flashing through the air as she walked around her desk and sank into the high-backed, black leather chair. "Any other calls?"

"Your husband, reminding you that dinner is at seven o'clock sharp in the restaurant of the Cincinnatian Hotel, and you should prepare yourself for at least an hour of speeches."

Vicki groaned. Another boring dinner honoring her husband. Not that he wasn't deserving of the myriad hosannas that continually came his way, just that she was getting awfully tired of attending parties where she was the only person in the room not collecting social security.

"And your daughter phoned twice. Apparently, she wasn't feeling very well, and the school sent her home." Vicki's secretary nodded toward a huge stack of memos resting by the phone. "And those, of course. I told everyone you were in meetings on and off all day and it was unlikely you'd be able to return any calls until tomorrow."

"Thanks."

The young woman turned to go. "Oh, and some man called at least three times. He wouldn't leave his name, but he didn't sound happy."

Vicki frowned. She had a pretty good inkling who the unhappy caller might be. "If he calls again, tell him I'm out of the office for most of the week. And Michelle . . ."

Michelle looked at Vicki expectantly, watery blue eyes lost beneath a limp fringe of thin brown hair.

("Just give me five minutes with that unfortunate girl," Barbara once proclaimed.)

"Keep trying this number for me." Vicki quickly scribbled Chris's phone number on a piece of paper and held it toward her secretary. "Let me know as soon as it's free. Oh, and get me the number of University Hospital in Clifton."

"Will do."

Vicki watched her secretary slump out of the room. ("Walk proud," she heard Barbara call after her. "Head high, shoulders back, stomach in.") Again she wondered whether Chris's call had anything to do with Barbara's surgery. True, a laparoscopy was a relatively simple procedure, but a general anesthetic still carried all sorts of risks, and the courts were full of medical malpractice suits, several of which she'd instigated herself. But Chris hadn't mentioned anything about Barbara, only something about reviewing her options, whatever that meant.

"Okay, what to do first?" Vicki muttered, eyes flitting nervously around her desk, coral-colored lips twisting from side to side, as she rifled through the stack of pink memos. "Should call your daughter," she said out loud, deciding to call her husband first, punching in his private number on her private line. "Talking to yourself again," she said with a resigned laugh. Vicki regularly talked to herself. It helped her focus, added weight to her thoughts, significance to sometimes insignificant musings. Besides, she'd always liked the sound of her own voice.

"Hey, darlin'," her husband was saying seconds later. Jeremy Latimer had been born and raised in Ohio, but had spent almost a decade in Atlanta before resettling in Cincinnati, and a casual Southern attitude still clung to certain words and turns of phrase. Of course, he could turn the honey-dipped drawl on and off at will, Vicki recognized, just as he could that quasi-Southern charm he was becoming increasingly famous for.

"Hey, darlin', yourself. How you doin'?" Vicki effortlessly slid into the same lazy territory, a mythical land in which pesky nouns and verbs disappeared at will, and apostrophes often replaced the letter *g*.

"Kickin' along," he told her.

Vicki pictured him running a lazy hand through luxuriously thick gray hair. Thank God he hadn't gone bald, like so many other men in their fifties. Or allowed his waistline to thicken with the excesses and inevitabilities of midlife. No, Jeremy Latimer had been blessed with a full head of hair and worked hard to maintain his naturally slim physique, eating wisely and exercising regularly. Vicki liked to take credit for that. Maybe having a wife almost a quarter of a century his junior had provided her husband with the motivation to maintain a healthy, youthful appearance. Or maybe the rich really were different.

"Rosie called," Jeremy said, referring to the nanny of their two young children. "Apparently, they sent Kirsten home from school with a bit of a fever."

"Yeah, Kirsten phoned here a couple of times. Poor baby. I'll call her, see how she's doing."

"Think you'll have to stay home with her tonight?"

"I'm sure it's nothing Rosie can't handle. Don't you worry," Vicki assured her husband. "I'll be at that dinner tonight with bells on."

"Darlin'," Jeremy said with a laugh before hanging up, "I love it when you wear those bells."

Vicki called home and was relieved to hear her daughter was sleeping comfortably. Now she wouldn't have to waste precious time trying to make intelligent conversation with a seven-year-old. She glanced at the silver-framed photograph of her two children, Kirsten's freckled arm draped protectively around the shoulder of her younger brother, both children smiling for the camera, although Josh's smile was tight and tentative, while Kirsten's grin stretched wildly from one ear to the other, her mouth open in a giant "Ahh" that threatened to swallow the photographer whole. Her two front teeth were missing. "Yeah? Want to make something of it?" the child's eyes challenged merrily.

What had she done with those teeth? Vicki wondered absently, remembering Barbara had given her a little silver tooth holder in which to keep them. She'd always meant to keep a scrapbook of her children's development, but she'd never quite gotten around to it. Now it was too late. Baby teeth were gone forever, red-gold locks swept away, first words long forgotten. It wasn't that she wasn't a good mother, she assured herself. Just that she'd be a better mother when her children were older and more interesting. Vicki buzzed her secretary. "What's happening with that number I gave you?"

"Still busy. But I have the number for University Hospital you asked for."

"Thanks." Vicki scribbled it down. "Keep trying Mrs. Malarek for me."

Vicki placed a quick call to the hospital, found out that Barbara was out of surgery and in the recovery room, ready to be released as soon as her husband, who was apparently running late, arrived. "She's fine," Vicki informed the empty office, returning the phone to its carriage, picking it up again, trying Chris's number herself, getting that same annoying busy signal. Who the hell was Chris talking to for so long? She never talked to anyone for more than a couple of seconds. Tony always seemed to be standing over her, interrupting her, calling her away. She didn't have time for normal conversation. She didn't have time for her friends. She didn't have time for anything anymore. But then, who needs time when you don't have a life? And Chris had no life, for God's sake. Was that why she'd been calling? Were those the kind of options she was talking about? Options for getting her life back?

The phone rang. Vicki picked it up before her secretary could answer it. "Chris?" she asked, holding her breath.

"Mrs. Latimer?" the male voice asked in return.

Immediately, Vicki regrouped, refocused. "Who's this?"

"It's Bill Pickering."

Vicki looked warily toward the closed door of her office, lowered her voice to a whisper. "Have you found anything?"

"We might have something in Menorca."

"Menorca?"

"It's a small island off the coast of Spain."

"I know where Menorca is, Mr. Pickering," Vicki said impatiently. "It's my mother I'm trying to find. Is she there?" Again Vicki glanced toward the door. Could anyone be listening?

"A woman matching all her particulars has been living there for the last six months under the name Estella Greenaway."

"Alone?"

"No. She's living with a man named Eduardo Valasquez, a local artist."

"Have you spoken to her?"

"Not yet. We—"

A sudden commotion outside her office propelled Vicki to her feet. In the next instant, her office door flew open and a tall, muscular man with wild, angry eyes shot toward her desk. His right arm was extended and he was waving a crumpled piece of paper in his hand as if it were a gun. "What the fuck is this?" he screamed.

"I'll have to get back to you," Vicki told Bill Pickering, calmly returning the phone to its receiver, tucking short red hair behind her ears.

"I'm sorry, Vicki," her clearly flustered secretary said from the doorway. "I couldn't stop him. Should I call security?"

Vicki stared at the imposingly handsome man shaking with rage in front of her, his fist in the air, remnants of the college football hero he once was clinging to the square set of his jaw, the firm cast of his shoulders. "I don't think that will be necessary. Do you, Paul?" she asked him.

"What's going on here, Vicki?" the man demanded.

"Why don't you sit down." Vicki indicated the chair in front of her desk, as she sank back into her own, watching her short black wool skirt slide up her thigh, making a conscious decision not to pull it down. "Michelle, maybe you'd be good enough to get us some coffee."

"I don't want any goddamn coffee." The man slammed the letter in his hand onto Vicki's desk, sending the other papers scattering, several of them wafting gently toward the floor. "I want to know what the hell you think you're doing."

"Sit down, Paul," Vicki instructed, her secretary lingering in the open doorway. "It's okay," she told the young woman, whose eyes seemed to be looking for a safe place to hide. "Mr. Moore is finished yelling. Aren't you, Paul?"

Paul Moore said nothing. Instead he kicked at the chair in front of Vicki's desk until it spun around, then plopped down noisily into it, the leather cushion exhaling a loud whoosh upon contact. In that instant, he looked exactly like the young boy Vicki had sat beside in grades two through six at Western Elementary School, the same unruly blond hair hovering above restless green eyes, the same forbidding scowl distorting the otherwise pleasing lines of his full lips.

"Two coffees," Vicki told her secretary. "One black. One double cream, no sugar. I think that's how Mr. Moore takes it. Am I right?"

"Are you ever wrong?" Paul Moore asked in return.

Vicki smiled, waited until her secretary was out of the room before continuing. "I take it you're my mystery caller," she stated, not at all surprised by his visit. She'd been expecting him for several days.

"You want to tell me what the hell is going on?" Paul Moore

demanded yet again, clearly as flustered by his own behavior as he was with the reason for his visit.

"Obviously, your sister has informed you."

"Obviously my sister has informed me," Paul Moore mimicked, squishing the handwritten letter in his hand into a round ball before hurling it across the room, where it bounced against the window, then dropped silently to the floor. "Obviously my sister has informed me; obviously my sister has informed me," he repeated, like a record stuck in a groove, the phrase growing more ominous with each repetition. "How could you do this?"

"Your sister has hired me to represent her."

"You're suing my mother, for God's sake!" He banged his fist on Vicki's desk.

"Paul, this kind of behavior isn't going to do either of us any good. By all rights, you shouldn't even be here. I'm sure your lawyer would advise you—"

"Fuck my lawyer!"

Vicki suppressed an untimely smile. I have, she thought, picturing the lanky, sandy-haired attorney who was representing Paul Moore's family. A weeklong interlude several years ago, a pleasant way to while away the time while her husband was in California on business. She bit down on her lower lip, pushed the lanky lawyer into the back recesses of her mind. "You can't take this personally, Paul."

"Not take it personally?" Paul Moore was incredulous. "How else am I supposed to take it? You're tearing my family apart, for God's sake."

"It's not my intention to hurt your family."

"What else do you think this lawsuit is going to accomplish?"

"Your sister has hired me to represent her in challenging your father's will. She feels she was deliberately and unfairly overlooked—"

"I know what she feels!" Once again, Paul Moore was on his feet, his hands flailing angrily at the air. "The whole world knows how she feels! Why? Because she's always telling everyone! Because my sister is a crackpot! Because she always has been! And you know that. Christ, Vicki, you've known her since you were four years old."

"Which is why, when she came to see me last month, I couldn't just turn my back on her."

"You could have told her you had a conflict of interest. For God's sake, Vicki. We were next-door neighbors, classmates, for how long? My mother was always there for you, especially after your mother left."

Now Vicki was on her feet as well, pulling her skirt toward her knees. "None of this is relevant," she said impatiently, picturing her mother, still as young and beautiful as she'd been the day she walked out on her family almost three decades ago, on a beach in Spain cavorting with someone named Eduardo Valasquez.

"This isn't right," Paul Moore was muttering. "It isn't fair. How can you hurt my mother this way?"

"I'm not trying to hurt anyone. I'm merely trying to do my job." Vicki was amazed at the coldness in her tone. She and Paul had been buddies since childhood. She was friends with his wife. Still, did that give him the right to dredge up the past, to use it against her, as if it were some sort of bargaining chip? What right did he have to make this personal, to talk of fairness? It was the law, for God's sake. It had nothing to do with fairness.

There was a slight tapping on the door before it opened and Vicki's secretary proceeded timidly into the room, round shoulders caving toward her flat chest, head down, thin brown hair falling across her face as she deposited the two mugs of hot coffee on the desk and quickly exited the room.

"Look, let's take five minutes and catch our breath," Vicki said, her eyes following her secretary out of the office. "Neither one of us can be enjoying this." She hoped her voice didn't belie her words. The truth was that she was enjoying herself immensely. This scene was exactly why she'd chosen the law as a career in the first place. Doors bursting open, voices raised in fury, raw nerves jangling, high drama unfolding. The glorious, unmitigated, unscripted chaos of it all.

Why do you want to be a lawyer? her husband had asked when she was still dating his son. *It's so much work, and most of it is so dry and boring.*

Only as dry and boring as the lawyer involved, Vicki had shot back.

That was the moment he'd fallen in love with her, Jeremy had confided later.

"Adrienne is a nutcase, and you know it," Paul Moore was saying, still pleading his case.

"Adrienne is a very unhappy woman. She doesn't want to go to court any more than you do."

"And that's why she's suing?"

"She's suing for her fair share of her father's estate. I'm sure she'd be willing to settle out of court."

"I'm sure she would."

"Then perhaps you could talk to your mother and your brother and have your attorney get back to us with a reasonable offer."

"No chance," Paul Moore said angrily.

"Then you leave us with no options." Options, Vicki repeated silently, thinking of Chris, glancing toward the phone.

"You're really going to do this?" Paul Moore began pacing back and forth in front of Vicki's desk, disrupting the steady flow of steam rising from the two untouched mugs of coffee, causing it to ripple, like smoke rings, in the air. "You're really going to drag my family through the mud? You're going to let my sister get on the stand and lie her goddamn head off?"

"I would never allow your sister to lie on the stand."

Paul Moore stopped dead in his tracks. "What are you saying? That you believe the things she's been telling you?"

"You know I can't discuss our conversations."

"You don't have to. I know exactly what she's been saying. I've been hearing the same crap out of her mouth all my life: my father never loved her; nothing she did was ever good enough for him; he called her 'dummy' because she wasn't as smart as me or my brother; he didn't take her seriously, wouldn't let her into the family business. Forget about the fact she refused to go to college and never showed the slightest interest in the family business. That's beside the point. That's irrelevant, as you would say. And let's not forget that he didn't approve of her wardrobe, her boyfriends, or her husbands. Doesn't matter that he was right, that she dressed like a whore, that her boyfriends were a bunch of pathetic losers, and that my father footed the bill for both her divorces. She probably forgot to mention that. Just like I'm sure she's conveniently forgotten about the hell she put my parents through all those years she was living at home, the horrible lies she told that finally got her kicked out of the house."

"What kind of lies?"

"Oh, let's see. Where to begin, where to begin?" Paul Moore sank back down into the waiting chair, lifted the coffee to his lips. "There was the time just after Adrienne turned sixteen that my father caught her out with some lowlife he'd expressly forbidden her to see, caught her in the elevator of a hotel as she and this guy were going up to his room." Paul shook his head, cool green eyes burning with disbelief. "And is she at all apologetic? Is she at all contrite? No. What's little Adrienne's response to being caught red-handed in the elevator of some out-of-the-way hotel with some scruffy drug dealer? She accuses my father of being at the hotel with a paramour of his own, says this right in front of my mother, mind you, doesn't give a damn who she hurts. Doesn't care that my father was at the hotel on business, that the woman was a client in town overnight. None of that matters. And when he punishes her by grounding her for a month, what does she do? She sneaks out of the house in the middle of the night, steals the car, smashes it into a neighbor's fence. Spends time in Juvenile Hall. Comes home, drops out of school, sits around drinking, doing drugs, telling more lies."

"Such as?"

"Such as the reason her father hates her isn't because she's wasting her life, or that she's a druggie or an ingrate, but because she's got his number, because she knows all about his secret life. His women. She's heard him talking on the phone, arranging secret rendezvous. She knows about the mistress in Dayton, his affair with her old baby-sitter, the pass he made at one of her friends. Lies, lies, and more lies. The real surprise here isn't that he cut her out of his will, it's that he didn't cut her out of his life much sooner than he did."

Vicki chose her next words carefully. "I think you should think long and hard about settling this case out of court."

Paul Moore lowered his coffee to the desk without having taken a sip. "And why is that?"

"It's expensive to go to court, Paul. You know that. Expensive and messy. I think we have a good case. I also think it could get very ugly. I don't want to see your mother hurt any more than you do."

"Bullshit!"

"Make your sister an offer, Paul. Don't let this thing go to trial."

"What are you trying to tell me? That you found the mystery mistress in Dayton? That you unearthed the phantom baby-sitter?" He laughed, but the laugh was forced, hollow, scared.

"Talk things over with your wife, Paul," Vicki answered cryptically. "Then get back to me." She lowered her eyes to her lap, as if signaling the meeting was over.

"What do you mean, talk things over with my wife? She doesn't have anything to do with this."

"Joanne has a lot to do with this," Vicki said evenly, looking Paul Moore straight in the eye. "If this goes to trial, I'll have to call her as a witness."

"What are you talking about? What lies has Adrienne been feeding you about my wife? Don't tell me she's accused my father of making a play for Joanne!"

"No," Vicki admitted. "I don't think Adrienne has any idea about what happened between your father and Joanne."

For a moment, the air was so still and heavy it felt as if Vicki were standing underwater. There was no motion, no sound, no breath. And then suddenly, Paul was on his feet, and the room was spinning and swirling around her, as if someone had pulled the plug and she were being sucked into a giant vortex. Vicki grabbed hold of her desk, hung on tight, lest she be swept away by the angry current radiating from his eyes.

"My father and Joanne! What kind of sick joke are you playing?"

"It happened a long time ago, just after the two of you were married. Apparently your father had sent you out of town on business."

"Something happened while I was away?"

"Your father showed up at your apartment. He tried to force himself on your wife. She was able to fend him off, but just barely. Needless to say, she was pretty shaken up by the incident."

"You're lying."

"I'm not lying."

"And you know all this because . . . ?"

"Because Joanne told me about it."

The color drained from Paul Moore's face in a sudden rush, as if a major artery had been severed and he was rapidly leaking blood. His arms fell limply to his sides, as if the muscles had been cut. His knees buckled visibly beneath crisp navy trousers, and he had to grab the back of his chair to keep from sliding to the floor. For a minute, Vicki was afraid he might faint. "My wife told you?" he repeated, his tongue having trouble with the words, as if they were stuck to an unruly wad of bubble gum.

"Yes," Vicki said, afraid to say more.

"When?"

"Soon after it happened. She needed someone to talk to; I

happened to be there. She swore me to secrecy. Said she didn't want to create any problems for the family. She especially didn't want to hurt your mother."

Paul Moore shook his head. "I don't believe you," he said, although the sudden appearance of tears indicated otherwise.

"Settle this out of court, Paul."

"You'd really use this? Something my wife told you in confidence nearly eight years ago? Something no other lawyer would be in a position to know? That can't be ethical."

"It's perfectly ethical. How I obtain my information is not relevant." That word again.

"Neither is what my father might or might not be guilty of. He had every right to cut my sister out of his will."

"A judge might disagree," Vicki told Paul plainly. "It's a crapshoot, of course. A judgment could go either way. But do you really want all this to come out? Do you want it aired in open court? Settle, Paul. Settle this before it goes any further, before anyone else gets hurt."

Paul Moore's head slumped against his barrel chest, almost as if he'd been shot. He stood this way for several minutes, Vicki monitoring the ragged rise and fall of his shoulders for signs he was still breathing. Then, without saying another word or even looking in her direction, he spun around on his heels and walked out of the room.

"Are you all right?" Michelle asked timidly from the doorway after he was gone.

"Get Adrienne Sellers on the phone for me," Vicki instructed her secretary by way of a reply. "Oh, and did you have any luck with Chris's number?"

"Still busy."

Vicki shook her head as Michelle left the room. Who the hell could Chris be talking to all this time?

"I have Adrienne Sellers on line one," her secretary informed her minutes later.

"Adrienne," Vicki said, a sudden rush of adrenaline pushing her shoulders back, her head high. "I think I might have some good news for you. Looks like we might be talking settlement." Then she took a deep breath, closed her eyes, and laughed out loud.

Eight

Someone was laughing.

Or maybe it was shouting. Shouting her name. Chris tried turning her head, but a sharp pain at the base of her neck warned against further movement. She opened her mouth, tried to speak, but the only sound she heard was a low, ragged wail. Someone's in terrible trouble, she thought, wondering why she couldn't make out who it was. "Chris!" she heard from a distance, someone pulling on her arms, as if she were a rag doll. "Chris, open your eyes. I know you can hear me. Please, baby. I'm so sorry. You know I didn't mean it. Please, Chris, open your eyes. Stop playing around."

Playing around? she repeated, strange arms tugging her this way and that, adjusting her shoulders, slapping gently at her cheeks. What was she doing? What kind of game was she playing? Why did her head ache? Why couldn't she see anything?

"Please, Chrissy, open your eyes," the voice pleaded.

The voice was growing increasingly desperate, and Chris struggled to obey. But her eyes refused to cooperate. All Chris saw was darkness. It must be her brother. He'd locked her in that old chest again, and even now he was sitting on its lid triumphantly, refusing to let her out. *Let me out of here!* Chris hollered, though no sounds emerged from between her swollen lips.

What happened here? Chris wondered, bringing a hand to her mouth, feeling something sticky against her fingers.

Gerry, you let me out of here right now! Chris yelled, swatting at the air. *When I get out of here, you're going to be sorry. You're going to be very sorry.*

"I'm sorry, Chris," someone was saying. "I'm so sorry."

What was happening? Why couldn't she open her eyes? Why did her shoulders ache and her jaw throb? Had she been in some kind of accident? Had she fallen? Hit her head? Been hit by a car? Think! she told herself, trying to gather together the thoughts that were bouncing wildly around in her brain. Try to piece together what's happening. Try to get it together, she repeated, her head lolling off to one side, eyes blinking open, seeing nothing, before rolling back in her head.

"Don't pass out on me again, Chris," the voice begged, panic underlining every word.

She felt a strong kick to her stomach, and then another. From the inside, she realized with growing horror. Somehow, someone had reached inside her body, was pummeling her from the inside out. Chris tried to scramble to her feet, to run, to get away, but her ankles only twitched and her legs went nowhere. She couldn't get away. She was going nowhere.

Help me! she called toward a group of women watching from

the shadows. *Please do something. Get me out of here. Tell me what's happening.*

The largest of the silhouettes stepped forward. *He keeps track of your periods?* Susan asked, round face pushing through the darkness.

Barbara was immediately at her side. *Maybe you should go home. They'll be coming for me any minute now. There's no reason for you to stay.*

You were calling me? Vicki asked, pushing her way in front of the other two.

Yes, I was calling you, Chris answered in her mind, fighting to remember why. She'd been at the hospital. With Barbara. Without Tony. Oh, God. Barbara having some surgical procedure. Me there to lend moral support. Tony out of town on business. Oh, God. The baby kicking. Feeling queasy. Coming home. Tony away on business. Oh, God. No car in the driveway. Montana at school. Wyatt with Mrs. McGuinty. The house empty. The phone call to Vicki. Need to know my options. Tony's reflection in the window. Oh, God. *Hang up the phone, Chris.* Oh, God. *What's the matter, Chris? Aren't you happy to see your husband?*

Oh, God. Oh, God. Oh, God.

"Wake up, Chris. Please, honey, open your eyes. Goddamnit, Chris!"

Chris saw Tony's fist flying toward her, braced herself for the wallop of his knuckles as they smashed against her jaw, was surprised by a splash of cold water instead, filling her nostrils and seeping into her mouth. Her eyes shot open as she sputtered into full consciousness. "What's happening?" she cried, feeling the baby inside her trying to push her to her feet.

"It's okay, babe," Tony was saying, an empty glass in his

hand. "You're gonna be fine now. Everything's gonna be okay. You just had a little accident."

"An accident?"

"You know I didn't mean it, sweetheart. You know I'd never do anything to hurt you or the baby." His hands were all over her. On her face. In her hair. On her stomach.

Chris tried pushing his hands away from her, but they kept coming back, as if she'd stumbled blindly into a spider's web. "Don't touch me."

"Oh, please, baby. Don't be like that. I'm just trying to help you, sweetheart. You know I didn't mean to hurt you."

"You hit me, Tony." Chris struggled to stand up, teetering on knees that threatened to give way. "You knocked me unconscious."

"It was an accident. You know that."

Chris stumbled into the bathroom, stared at her battered face in the mirror over the sink, Tony right behind her, his reflection hovering over hers in the glass. Who are you? Chris asked the frightened woman staring back at her. Who is this pathetic lost soul?

I vaguely remember you, one set of eyes cried out to the other from atop a jaw that was scratched and discolored, cut and swollen lips dripping blood onto the white collar of her navy sweater, her hair dripping with the water Tony had flung in her face to revive her. What's happened to you? What happened to the feisty little girl who used to chase her older brother around the house, who regularly caught him and wrestled him to the ground? Where had she disappeared? "Oh, God. How could you do this? You promised me it would never happen again."

"How many times do I have to tell you it was an accident?"

Anger suddenly replaced the concern in Tony's voice. "It never would have happened if you hadn't lied to me."

"Lied to you?" Chris was incredulous. What was Tony talking about? "When did I lie to you?"

"You lied to me about going to the hospital."

"I never lied to you."

"You said you wouldn't go."

"You said you were going out of town."

"What difference should that make?"

"You weren't here," Chris argued, trying to turn around, to escape the confines of the small bathroom. "I didn't see the harm."

"You didn't see the harm?" He spun her back toward the mirror, forcing her face toward her bruised reflection. "You didn't see the harm? Do you see it now? Do you?"

"Tony, please," Chris whimpered. "You promised after the last time you wouldn't hit me anymore."

Immediately Tony dropped his hands to his sides, walked from the room, began pacing back and forth in front of the bathroom door. "Why do you make me do these things? You know I don't want to hurt you. Why can't you just leave well enough alone?"

Chris said nothing, running some cold water from the tap, applying a wet compress to her lips, trying to make the thin red lines of blood that were etched into her skin disappear.

"Didn't you agree not to go to the hospital with Barbara?" Tony asked, refusing to let the matter drop. "Isn't that what you decided?"

"*You* decided."

"You agreed. Didn't you?"

"Yes." What was the point in saying anything else?

"But you lied."

"I didn't . . ." Chris stopped. "I didn't mean to."

"You never mean to do anything," Tony said with a shake of his head.

"You lied too," Chris heard herself say, the words out of her mouth before she could stop them.

"What?"

"You said you were going away on business. Why did you do that?" Chris realized she was genuinely curious.

Tony leaned against the doorframe, his body filling the doorway that separated the bedroom from the bathroom. "I had my suspicions. Thought I should check them out."

"Suspicions about what?"

"What do you think?"

"About me? Why? What have I ever done to make you suspicious?"

"Oh, I don't know. How about ignoring your children to go off gallivanting with your friends?"

"I'm not ignoring my children. Montana's at school," Chris said, trying to inject some logic into the proceedings, "and I only left Wyatt with Mrs. McGuinty for a few hours so that I could be with Barbara at the hospital. That's hardly gallivanting. Wait." Chris stopped, trying to retrace the path of the conversation. "How did you know I went to the hospital?"

"What?"

"You said I lied to you about going to the hospital. How did you know that's where I was?"

A smile slid across Tony's face, settling into his eyes and mouth. He said nothing.

"You followed me?" Chris asked, although she already knew the answer.

"Saw you and the Barbie doll get in a taxi, watched you smile sweetly at the driver. Black guy, wasn't he? I hear they're very well endowed. . . ."

"Tony, for God's sake." Chris could feel Tony's anger building in the pit of her stomach. This was Tony's pattern, the way such scenes always played themselves out. Anger. Violence. Contrition. Kind words becoming false accusations until suddenly it was all her fault. Always her fault. Her fault she walked into his fist, her fault she tripped over his feet, her fault she was covered with bruises.

"It's the same old story," Tony was saying. "Your friends are more important to you than your family. Susan and Vicki mean more to you than your own kids. And Barbara. She's the worst. She calls; you jump. What is it with the two of you anyway? You got something going on you want to tell me about?"

"She was scared, Tony. Scared about the operation. Scared she won't be able to have more children."

"So you volunteered to give her one of ours."

Chris gasped, fell back against the sink, the full impact of his words hitting her as strongly as his fist had earlier. So, her instincts had been correct after all. He'd been right there in the corridor with them, right beside them, for God's sake, right under her nose. She tried to conjure up the busy hospital corridor, saw people marching purposefully back and forth, patients trailing IVs, doctors conferring, nurses scurrying, an orderly hunched over a set of charts, a man down the hall mopping the floor, another man buried behind an old magazine, visitors disappearing in and out of patients' rooms.

Which one had he been? How long had he been watching her?

"That's right, Chrissy," Tony said, as if he'd heard her. "I was right there. I heard every word you said. I heard you offer to give our baby away."

"I was joking," Chris whispered, her hands trembling at her sides.

"Yeah, you were having a high old time, weren't you, babe? Laughing and joking with the Barbie doll. And how about that handsome young doctor I saw you cuddling with?"

"What?"

"You didn't think I'd miss that one, did you? No, I saw the two of you making a spectacle of yourselves in the hall."

Chris fought to remember what man her husband was talking about. What doctor had she been cuddling with? "I don't know—"

"Come on, Chris. Nice-looking guy. Real tall, just the way you like 'em."

The image of the young doctor leapt before her eyes. "Tony, he was just giving me directions to the bathroom."

"Escorted you there personally," Tony corrected. "Took hold of your arm."

"He was just being nice."

"A little overly familiar, wouldn't you say?"

"Absolutely nothing happened. You saw that."

"I saw a man with his arm around my wife."

"He touched my elbow." Chris stopped. This was crazy. Tony had been right there. He knew exactly what had happened. Why was she defending herself?

"What'd he say to you, Chris? What plans did the two of you make?"

"We didn't make any plans. This is ridiculous."

"Did you slip him your number? Tell him your husband was out of town?"

Chris shook her head, said nothing. Tony wasn't interested in answers. He was interested only in terrorizing her.

"Should have told the poor guy he didn't stand a chance," Tony continued. "Not with the Barbie doll around."

"I don't know what you're talking about." Chris tried to twist past Tony into the bedroom, but his arms reached out, blocked her escape.

"Where you going, Chris? Got a heavy date?"

Chris shook her head, felt it throb. "I promised Mrs. McGuinty I'd pick Wyatt up by two o'clock."

A look of panic flooded Tony's face. "Don't you want to get cleaned up first? I mean, you don't want to have anybody see you looking like you just got run over by a truck." Dark eyes narrowed accusingly. "Or do you? Is that part of the plan?"

"There is no plan," Chris said, feeling one of her teeth loose against her tongue.

"You sure about that? No instructions from one of your gal pals? From little Vicki Rich Bitch? I heard you calling her, Chris. I heard you say you needed to talk to her as soon as possible. What was that all about?"

"I just wanted to tell her about Barbara," Chris told him, her bruised cheek burning red.

"I didn't hear you say anything about the Barbie doll. I heard you say something about options."

"No."

"What options would you be talking about, sweetheart?"

"I don't know," Chris replied truthfully. What options

could she have been talking about? What possible options did she have?

"You wouldn't be thinking about leaving me, would you?"

Tears formed in Chris's eyes, fell the length of her cheeks, mingled with the blood at her lips.

"Because I don't think I could stand it if you left me, Chris. I'd go crazy without you. I wouldn't want to live."

Chris tasted the salt of her tears in the dried blood around her mouth.

Tony inched his way toward her. "I love you, Chrissy. Please tell me you know that."

"I know that," Chris whispered.

"You know I never meant to hurt you."

Chris nodded without speaking.

"It's just all this pressure I've been under, trying to get clients, trying to keep our heads above water. The bank turned down our loan application."

"What?"

"I didn't tell you about it because I didn't want you to worry."

"They turned down our loan?"

"I don't want you to worry about it, Chris. It's gonna be all right. Everything's gonna be all right as long as we're together, as long as I know you're with me, that I can count on you. It's just that you make me so crazy sometimes. I want to trust you, but I can't. You won't let me. And it makes me crazy because I love you so much." He reached for her, wrapped her in his suffocating embrace, buried his face in her hair. "Tell me you love me, Chris. Tell me you love me as much as I love you."

"Tony, please . . ."

"I need to hear the words, Chris. I need to hear you say them."

"I . . ." Chris tried pushing the words from her mouth, but they clung stubbornly to a small clump of dried blood, refusing to fall.

"Don't make me beg, Chris. Please don't make me beg." His hands were groping her from behind, his tongue grazing the bottom of her ear.

"Oh, God," Chris muttered. "I'm going to be sick." She pushed her way out of Tony's arms, fell to her knees in front of the toilet, threw up into the bowl. "Oh, God," she moaned as she felt something inside her snap, a torrent of water bursting out from between her legs. Not now. Dear God, not now.

"What's happening? What the hell are you doing?"

"My water broke." Chris pressed her face against the toilet bowl, her body racked by a series of painful spasms. This couldn't be happening.

"The baby's not due for another month," Tony said, as if correcting her, as if warning her to stop playing games.

"He's coming now," Chris wailed, wishing she were dead. Women used to die in childbirth all the time, she thought, as her husband struggled to get her to her feet.

"Hang on, Chris. Don't panic. We're gonna get you to the hospital in plenty of time."

"I can't move."

"It's just a contraction, babe. You're an old pro at this." He guided her through their bedroom to the stairs. "One step at a time, sweetheart. Take it real slow."

"I can't do this," she screamed. "I can't. I can't."

" 'Course you can. 'Course you can. Just take it slow and easy. I'm with you every step of the way."

"Oh, God."

Somehow Tony managed to get her down the stairs and out onto the street. "Car's parked just around the corner," he told her, as if suggesting somehow it had ended up there on its own, as if he hadn't parked it there deliberately to hide it, to fool her into thinking he'd gone away.

Chris glanced at the front of her blood-and-vomit-stained sweater, her damp hair plastered against a forehead dripping with perspiration, her slacks clinging to her wet thighs. I want to die, she thought. "I can't make it," she said.

"I'm not going to leave you, babe."

By the time they made it to the car, Chris was doubled over with dry heaves. Please just let me die, she thought, as Tony carefully guided her into the front seat.

"What are you going to tell them at the hospital?" he was asking, jumping in beside her and starting the engine. "When they ask about the cuts and bruises." He pulled the car away from the curb. "I think you can tell them you slipped while giving Wyatt a bath, slammed your jaw against the bathtub, split your lip, you feel real foolish, stuff like that. You're in labor, they're not gonna argue."

"Tony . . ."

"What?"

She turned her face toward him, watched him drift in and out of focus. "This can never happen again. You have to give me your word it will never happen again."

"It won't," he agreed, reaching over to grab her hand.

"You have to promise." Chris wondered why she was being so insistent. How many times had Tony broken this promise already? What made her think it would be any different this time?

"I promise," he said easily. "You'll see, Chris. As long as I know you love me, everything's going to be okay."

As long as I know you love me. The words slammed against her brain, like a series of hammer blows, harder than her husband's fists. Chris cried out, feigning the tug of an approaching contraction. Dear God, she thought, closing her eyes as the real thing took over, trying to adjust to the fresh onslaught of pain, to go with it, lose herself in its almost hypnotic power. In a short time, she'd be the mother of three young children. What had she possibly have been thinking of earlier? Where exactly had she been planning to go?

It's going to be all right, she tried assuring herself as Tony sped through the streets of Mariemont. It had to be. She was all out of options.

Nine

"Your house is absolutely gorgeous."

"Thank you. Come on in. I forgot you haven't been here before."

Chris stepped across the marble threshold of Vicki's palatial new home in the suburb of Indian Hill, Tony right on her heels, like a shadow. "Of course I'll never forgive you for leaving Grand Avenue."

"We brought you a house-warming present," Tony said, two-year-old Rowdy fidgeting in his arms as he handed Vicki a box of expensive gourmet jams. "Apparently it's a tradition to bring something sweet into a new home."

"Thank you," Vicki said, but Chris could see what she was thinking. She was thinking, "Well, not exactly new. We've been here over a year. Nice of you to finally get around to paying us a visit." That's what she was thinking.

"You cut your hair!" Vicki squealed. "I can't believe it."

Chris immediately brought her hand to the back of her head, her fingers fluttering around her bare neck. She fought the impulse to burst into tears.

"I can't believe no more ponytail. Turn around. Let me have a look."

Chris lowered her head, swiveled in a self-conscious arc. She noticed a stain on the front of her pink T-shirt, maybe food, maybe old spit-up, most likely the ghost of dried blood. Tears filled her eyes. Don't cry, she admonished herself. If you start crying, Tony will make you go home. He'll say you're doing it on purpose, that you only came to this party to create a scene. Don't cry. Don't you dare cry.

"What's the matter? Don't you like your hair short?" Vicki asked, as if sensing the tears lurking behind Chris's blue eyes. "I think it's real cute. A little uneven maybe, but that can be fixed. Who did it?"

Chris tugged on the ragged ends of her hair, kept her eyes on the white marble tile of the foyer floor. "Some guy in Terrace Park. I was walking by his salon, and next thing I knew, the ponytail was gone." Please don't ask me any more questions, Chris prayed. I'll be all right if we can just start talking about something else.

"You know how impulsive Chris can be," Tony said.

"Well, no, actually," Vicki demurred.

"I wasn't too happy about it at first," Tony said. "But I'm getting used to it." He ran a playful hand through Chris's amputated locks.

Chris twisted her neck to one side, squirmed out of her husband's reach, and looked toward the driveway where Montana and Wyatt were conducting an impromptu game of tag in the summer sun, scurrying between Vicki's new red Jaguar and Jeremy's classic silver Porsche. Parked directly behind the two luxury cars were two more: Susan and Owen's dark green Seville and Ron and Barbara's chocolate brown Mercedes.

"Kids, get in here," Chris called, grateful when they responded quickly, pushing each other out of the way in order to be first at the front door. "No pushing," Chris cautioned.

In response, six-year-old Wyatt punched his older sister in the shoulder.

"No hitting," Chris said.

"It's okay, Chris, they're only kids," Tony said. "Kids fight. Leave 'em alone."

Montana's response was to poke her brother in the ribs.

"Stop that," Chris warned, as Montana rolled her eyes toward her father. "You remember Mommy's good friend Vicki, don't you, Montana? Wyatt, do you remember Mrs. Latimer?"

"The last time I think I saw you," Vicki said, pointing at Montana while ushering everyone inside the large marble foyer and closing the front door, "was about a year ago. Right before we moved. And look how much you've grown," she said to Rowdy, who promptly buried his face in his father's shoulder. "Everyone's out back. They can't wait to see you guys. Come on, I'll take you." She offered Montana her hand.

Montana looked at her father, as if asking his permission. Tony smiled. Montana followed Vicki through the large front hall, her hands clasped tightly behind her back.

"Did your mother ever tell you the story of how we met?" Vicki asked brightly.

"You make it sound like some sort of love story," Tony said, hoisting Wyatt into his arms beside Rowdy, entering the cavernous living room.

"Well, I guess it is in a way." Vicki grabbed Chris's hand, squeezed it inside her own. "It's so good to see you."

"It's good to see you too. We brought a birthday gift for Josh." Chris extricated a brightly wrapped present from the large canvas bag she was carrying.

"Thank you. That's really sweet. Can you believe how fast they grow up?" Vicki took the small box from Chris's hand, depositing it on a gilt-edged antique table along with the gourmet jams, as she led Chris and her family toward the rear of the house. "I remember so clearly the day he was born."

Chris couldn't help but be amazed. Vicki was anything but sentimental. The only dates she normally kept track of were those she had to be in court.

"God, what a mess that was!" Vicki exclaimed. "I was right in the middle of this big case, and I'd taken all my stuff with me to the hospital, and there I am on the phone, I'm in labor, I'm in transition, for God's sake, I don't have to tell you what that's like, and here I am trying to hammer out this settlement while the nurses are telling me I'm fully dilated, we have to get to the delivery room. 'Mrs. Latimer, you have to get off the phone,' they're telling me. I say I'm not ready yet, I need two more minutes. They're screaming they can see the baby's head. God, what a scene. They finally took the phone right out of my hands, but not before I got a verbal commitment from the other side. Yes, sir, that was some afternoon. Never forget it."

Chris laughed. She remembered calling Vicki at the hospital the day after Josh was born only to be told that Mrs. Latimer and son had already checked out. Vicki was back at the office a scant three days after Josh's birth.

"I love what you've done with the house," Chris marveled, peeking into each enormous room as they walked past. "Everything is so beautiful."

"Well, the decorator did it all," Vicki admitted. "I just told him that I liked antiques and Jeremy preferred modern, so he went with a combination of old furniture and modern art, and I don't know, somehow the whole thing works."

"Looks great," Tony said, aping Vicki's confident stride behind her back, causing the two children in his arms to laugh out loud.

"Something funny?" Vicki asked.

Rowdy immediately returned his face to Tony's shoulder, but Wyatt laughed even louder. The abrasive sound hacked at the air, like an annoying cough. Rowdy promptly covered his ears and started screaming.

"What's the matter, Rowdy?" Chris asked.

"Leave him alone, Chris. He's fine," Tony said.

"I can give you a tour later, if you'd like," Vicki said, seemingly oblivious to the little scene being played out behind her back, although Chris knew Vicki was oblivious to nothing, that those small hazel eyes didn't miss a thing. "Everything all right?" Vicki asked Chris as they passed through the kitchen, where stainless steel appliances mixed easily with antique walnut furniture.

"Fine."

"You look a little pale."

"Just tired."

"Have you lost weight?"

"Maybe a few pounds."

"Maybe more than that."

"Daddy says it's rude to whisper," Wyatt said.

"Your daddy's absolutely right," Vicki agreed. "So, everybody, look who's here," she announced to the small gathering milling about the stone patio in front of the large, gated pool. Everyone turned to greet them.

Her friends, Chris thought gratefully, wanting to pull them to her and never let them go. Her wonderful, dear friends: Susan and Owen, tanned and smiling, arms around each other's waist; Barbara and Ron, glamorous and tall, Barbara's red lipstick an exact match with Ron's golf shirt; Jeremy Latimer, casually distinguished and very proud, beaming at the whirling dervish that was his wife.

"Hi there, stranger." Susan extended her arms toward Chris. "I can't believe we live on the same street and we had to come all the way out here to see you."

"It's been way too long," Owen agreed, shaking Tony's hand.

"Everything all right?" Susan asked.

"She cut her hair!" Barbara squealed, wiggling toward Chris on three-inch heels and gripping her friend in a tight bear hug. "When did you do this?"

Chris winced as Barbara's arms pressed against a recently acquired bruise on her lower back.

"I see congratulations are in order." Tony turned to Chris. "Why didn't you tell me Barbara was expecting?"

There was a collective intake of breath.

"What?" Barbara said.

"What are you talking about?" her husband asked.

"I'm not pregnant."

"Oh. I'm sorry," Tony said quickly. "I just assumed . . ." His hands made vague circles in the direction of Barbara's round stomach.

"It's the blouse." Barbara's large brown eyes glistened with the threat of tears as she pulled on the front of her lilac-and-white-striped top. "Guess I should have tucked it inside the pants." She brushed an imaginary fleck of dirt off the thigh of her white slacks, stared toward the large gray stones of the patio.

"I'm really sorry," Tony repeated, but Chris saw the glint in his eyes and wasn't so sure.

"How're things going?" Ron asked.

"Never better," Tony said

"I take it this little guy is Rory."

"Rowdy," Tony corrected.

"Rowdy. Yes, that's right. Montana, Wyatt, and Rowdy. Such interesting names."

"The names were Tony's idea. He's the one with the imagination," Chris said, her lips struggling with a smile. "I'd have called them Anne, William, and Robert."

"You hear that, Montana?" Tony asked. "Mommy would rather you had a boring name like Anne." The child's pinched expression duplicated her father's.

"Well, I certainly hope you kids brought your bathing suits," Jeremy Latimer said, glancing toward the large free-form pool that occupied only a small portion of the sprawling backyard. The other children—Kirsten, Josh, Ariel, Whitney, and Tracey—were having a great time splashing around and jumping off the diving board, under the watchful supervision of the Latimers' nanny and housekeeper.

"Oh, no, I forgot about their bathing suits." Panic laced through Chris's words.

"You what!" Montana demanded.

"You big dummy!" Wyatt gave his mother a push.

"Stop that," Chris said, eyes appealing to Tony for help.

Wyatt barked his loud, abrasive laugh. "Dummy Mommy," he said, then again, "Dummy Mommy."

"Okay, Wyatt, that's enough of that," Tony instructed. Instantly Wyatt fell silent.

"I think we have some bathing suits that will fit you guys," Jeremy Latimer offered quickly. "Maya," he called toward one of the staff milling by a long table of food that had been set up on one side of the patio. "Could you take the children inside and find them some swimsuits?"

The young woman flipped her long blond hair over the shoulder of her formfitting white uniform and approached Chris's three children. Chris noted the furtive smile that floated between the girl and Barbara's husband as she took Rowdy by the hand and led the children back inside the house. "Dummy Mommy," Rowdy was chanting happily to himself. "Dummy Mommy."

Chris stood in the middle of the stone patio, a plastic smile fastened to her mouth, like a pair of wax lips. This is your own damn fault, she was telling herself. Vicki told you to bring their bathing suits. If you weren't so stupid, this wouldn't have happened. Wyatt's right. You are a dummy. Dummy Mommy. Dummy Mommy. Don't you cry, Dummy Mommy. Don't you dare cry. "So, how are you enjoying living in the country?" she asked in a voice she barely recognized.

"Love it," came Jeremy Latimer's quick response.

"And it's only twenty-five minutes from my office," Vicki said.

"How many acres you got here?" Tony lifted a tall bottle of beer from a nearby cooler, downing almost half of it in one prolonged gulp.

"Five point something," Jeremy said. "Don't ask me about the square footage. I can never remember."

"The house is just under ten thousand square feet," Vicki offered, taking over from her husband. "Fourteen rooms, six bedrooms, five and a half bathrooms, first-floor master wing. Come on, Chris, I'll give you a tour." She grabbed Chris's hand, pulled her toward the patio doors.

"I'm coming too," said Barbara.

"Wait for me," Susan said.

Tony downed the rest of his beer. "Think I'll come too."

"Sorry," Vicki said quickly. "This tour is for girls only. Jeremy'll show you around later."

"Relax," Owen said to Tony, depositing a second beer in his hand and leading him toward a row of deck chairs. "Tell us about what you've been up to lately. I understand you're thinking of leaving the advertising business."

Chris felt Tony's eyes searing a large hole in the back of her pink T-shirt as she allowed Vicki and the others to drag her back inside the house. "Kitchen," Vicki said, perfunctorily waving her hands in the air as she strode purposefully from one room to the next. "Dining room. Living room. Hunt room, whatever the hell that is." She pulled Chris toward the so-called master wing, brought the finely carved double doors closed behind them. "So, what's going on?" she asked Chris, as Susan and Barbara gathered around her protectively.

Chris looked nervously past the billowy muslin curtains hanging from the canopy of the antique four-poster bed toward the long wall of floor-to-ceiling windows that looked onto the outside patio. Even from this distance, she could see Tony pacing nervously back and forth in front of the deck chairs, refusing to sit down despite Owen's repeated entreaties. "What do you mean? There's nothing going on."

"You're a nervous wreck," Susan said. "Look at you. You're shaking."

"I'm just tired. You know—three kids, only two hands."

"You don't look so great," Barbara said.

"She's lost weight," Vicki said to the others.

"It's my hair," Chris insisted, eyes flitting between the women and the window. "I never should have cut it."

"Well, I have to admit it's not the most flattering do." Barbara examined the uneven ends of Chris's hair. "Who'd you go to anyway?"

Chris held her breath, said nothing.

"Chris?"

Tears sprang to Chris's eyes. Immediately she lowered her gaze to the thick mint-green carpet, refusing to look up.

"Chris, talk to us," Susan said. "You can't keep insisting nothing's the matter. Let us help you."

Chris said nothing. No one can help me, she thought. "I really should be getting back."

"Talk to us, Chris," Susan said again.

"I can't."

"Listen," Susan prompted. "It's been obvious to all of us for a very long time that you and Tony are having serious problems. Maybe if you could persuade him to see a marriage counselor . . ."

Chris felt her hands begin to tremble, her knees begin to wobble, and her head begin to bob up and down involuntarily, until her entire body was shaking so hard, she could barely maintain her balance. Her shame was about to spill out, to erupt from deep within her, like lava from a volcano. There was nothing she could do to stop it. "Oh, God."

"Chris, what is it?"

"You don't understand."

"Understand what? Tell us, Chris. What don't we understand?"

"He did it." Dear God, she'd said it.

"What? Who did what?"

"Tony." Her secret was out. Her secret had a name.

"Tony did what?" Vicki demanded.

"My hair." A low wail escaped Chris's throat. Could she tell them? Could she tell them everything?

For an instant there was total silence.

Then, "Tony cut your hair?" Barbara asked in disbelief.

"What do you mean, he cut your hair?" Susan said, her voice low. Then again, even lower: "What do you mean, he cut your hair?"

"We took the kids over to Kenwood Towne Centre last Saturday. We were walking past this hairdressing salon, and I stopped to look at this girl who was getting her hair cut real short, and I said something like, 'I wish I were brave enough to do something like that.'" Chris stopped the lifeless recitation of facts, swallowed, struggled to continue. "Everything was fine. We kept walking. We got the kids ice cream. I thought we were having a good time." Again she stopped. What was the matter with her, for God's sake? What made her think she was entitled to a good time?

"What happened, Chris?" Susan asked.

"We got home. I made dinner. I got the kids settled down for the night. I climbed into bed to watch TV." A frightened cry ferreted its way into her voice, as Chris searched for words to describe the horrible nightmare that followed. "Tony came into the room. I could see he was upset about something, but I didn't know what. He started pacing back and forth in front of the TV. I asked him what was the matter, and he said I knew what was the matter. I said no, I had no idea. And he said, 'You think I like it when my wife flirts with other guys when I'm standing right beside her?' Honest to God, I didn't know what he was talking about. I said, 'I don't know what you're talking about,' and he said, 'You think I didn't catch the looks between you and that hairdresser in the mall?' and I said, 'What are you talking about? I was just watching him cut that girl's hair.' But he wouldn't believe me. He kept saying over and over how I made a fool of him, how everyone around us saw how I was looking at this guy, how he was looking at me, and I said no, I wasn't, that the guy didn't even know I was there, that he was probably gay anyway, I was just looking at the haircut.

"And suddenly, Tony had me by my ponytail and he was pulling me out of bed toward the bathroom, and I was pleading with him to stop, and he was telling me to be quiet, I'd wake up the kids, so I tried to be quiet, I thought, don't give him a hard time, just let him work all this crazy stuff out of his system, he'll calm down, he'll realize he's being ridiculous. I never even looked at this guy."

"Of course you didn't," Susan said.

"You don't have to explain yourself to us," Barbara told Chris.

"Should have kicked the fucker in the balls," Vicki said.

"And that's when he did it?" Susan asked. "That's when he cut your hair off?"

"He got me in the bathroom, and he started opening the drawers, rifling through them like he's looking for something, and he's getting madder and madder because at first he can't find it. Meanwhile he's still got me by my ponytail, he's pushing my head down, I'm all hunched over, I can't see what he's doing. And then I hear this sound, I don't know what it is at first, and then I realize it's scissors, and he's making snipping noises in the air with them, and I said, 'What are you doing?' and he was saying, 'You like short hair? You want a new haircut? I can cut your hair for you.' And I'm screaming, 'No!' and he's yelling at me to shut up, I'll wake up the kids, and then I feel this horrible tug on my head, and I hear that awful snipping sound, and I see my hair falling past my eyes, I see my ponytail hit the floor."

Barbara took Chris in her arms. "My God, he's a lunatic."

"What else has he done to you?" Susan asked.

Chris shook her head, her eyes racing toward the window, searching the outside patio. Where was Tony? She couldn't see Tony.

"How long has this sort of thing been going on?" Barbara asked.

"Does he hit you?" Susan asked.

"It's my fault as much as his," Chris insisted, locating Jeremy and Ron, unable to find either Owen or Tony. Maybe they were engrossed in conversation just out of her sight line. "I egg him on. I mean, he has a temper. Of course he has a temper. And you know how easily he takes offense at things. He's very sensitive."

"He's an asshole," Vicki said. "I say, shoot the bastard! How dare he lay a hand on you!"

"It's not that cut-and-dried," Chris argued. "It takes two to make a fight, remember. It's not all his fault. I'm not blameless. I know exactly what buttons to push, how to provoke him."

Susan looked confused. "You're saying it's your fault he hits you?"

"I didn't say he hit me. You're putting words in my mouth. I never said that."

"He cut your hair off, for God's sake."

"I shouldn't have argued with him. I should have just apologized. Maybe I did look at that guy."

"For God's sake, listen to yourself," Susan said, grabbing Chris's arms, forcing Chris's eyes to hers. "You are not responsible for your husband's bad behavior."

"What's going on here, Chris?" Vicki asked. "In my book, any woman who stays with a man who beats her must like to be beaten."

"I don't think that's true," Susan said, her round face a mask of confusion.

"He doesn't beat me," Chris insisted. "We have arguments, just like everybody else."

"Not like everyone else," Barbara said.

"Let me talk to someone at my office. I'm sure we can find a good divorce lawyer."

"I can't get a divorce. That's out of the question."

And then they were all talking at once, their voices blending, emerging as one. You don't have to be afraid. He doesn't have a hope in hell of getting custody of the children. What other choice has he left you? You can't stay in that house. He's a monster. You have to get away from that man. You have to get away before it's too late.

And then the double doors burst open and Tony exploded into the room. "What's going on in here?" he demanded.

"Hen party," Vicki said, jumping directly between Tony and Chris. "No men allowed."

"Looks like my wife's been crying. What have you been saying to her?"

Vicki shook her head in disbelief, her fists clenching and unclenching at her sides. "Look, we'll be out in a few minutes."

"Now. I'm taking my wife home now. Kids!" Tony called toward the three youngsters coming down the stairs newly outfitted in bathing suits. "Go get your clothes back on. We're going home."

"What!" Wyatt yelled in angry disbelief.

"Your mommy isn't feeling too well. She wants to go home."

"Oh, jeez!" Wyatt protested, spinning around on his heels.

"She never feels well," Montana muttered.

"Dummy Mommy! Dummy Mommy!" Rowdy said.

"Dummy Mommy! Dummy Mommy!" the other children chimed in, picking up the chant, carrying it with them back up the stairs.

Chris stood in the center of the commotion, too numb to speak or offer any resistance. Around her she was aware of bodies jostling for position, of Owen in the doorway, of Jeremy and Ron lingering just behind.

Tony lifted his hands into the air. "I don't know what stories my wife's been feeding you."

"How could you?" Barbara asked.

"Barbara," Ron said, coming forward, touching his wife's arm as if advising her to back off. "We shouldn't be getting involved here. This is obviously a private matter, something between a husband and wife."

"You don't know," Barbara said, refusing to be silenced. "You don't know what he's capable of."

"What I'm capable of?" Tony asked. "Well, let's see. Am I capable of cheating on my wife every chance I get with every little coed who crosses my path?"

"That's enough," Ron cautioned.

"Your husband fucks anything that moves and you don't do a damn thing about it," Tony told Barbara. "I hardly think you're in any position to be advising my wife."

"I think you've said quite enough," Jeremy Latimer interrupted as Barbara's face went white behind her heavy layer of blush. "Party's over."

Tony smiled. "I couldn't agree more. Chris . . ." He held out his hand, beckoned her forward.

"She's not going anywhere with you," Barbara told him. "How dare you lay a hand on her. You're nothing but a weak, despicable little man."

"And you're nothing but a washed-up second runner-up to Miss Ohio. Not even first runner-up, for Christ's sake. You can't do anything right, can you? Can't satisfy your husband, can't have another kid—"

"Shut up, Tony," Owen said.

"Another quarter heard from. The good doctor, no less.

Tell me, doctor, what's it like being married to Moby Dick?"

Susan shook her head. "Just ignore him," she cautioned her husband.

Tony laughed. "So, the little woman calls the shots, does she? The not-so-little woman, I guess I should say. Don't blame you, Doc. She's pretty formidable."

"A rather big word for you, isn't it, Tony?" Vicki asked bitterly.

"I guess it is," Tony said, obviously in his element. "But maybe we should check with the professor here. Make sure I got it right. Poor guy, can't be easy being married to a dyke. No wonder he can't keep it in his pants."

"You bastard!"

"What's a dyke?" a small voice asked as all eyes turned toward the sound.

"Tracey, honey!" Barbara said, racing toward her ten-year-old daughter, who stood in the doorway of the massive master suite, dark, wet curls clinging to her doll-like face, her bathing suit dripping chlorine onto the carpet at her bare feet.

"I heard yelling."

"It's okay, sweetie." Ron scooped his daughter into his arms and carried her quickly from the room.

"What's a dyke?" the child was asking as they disappeared from view.

"You're a class act," Vicki told Tony.

"You know what you need, don't you?" Tony whispered, just out of her husband's earshot. "Now, if you'll excuse me, my wife and I will be leaving."

Tony broke through the women forming a protective cocoon around his wife and grabbed Chris's hand, pulling her to his side. Chris offered no resistance. What was the point?

"Oh, God, somebody do something!" Chris heard Barbara cry as Tony opened the front door and pushed her outside.

"What can we do? It's her choice to go with him."

"But he's liable to kill her one of these days."

It's okay, Chris wanted to tell her, as Tony pushed her down the front path toward their car. You don't have to worry. Tony promised it would never happen again.

Part Two

1988-1990

Barbara

Ten

Barbara woke with a start from a dream in which she was being chased around her bed by a knife-wielding toddler in diapers. "Dear God," she whispered, reaching over and shutting off the alarm before it could go off. "What was that all about?"

Beside her, her husband snored peacefully. Ron was lying on his side, his back to her, his dark hair starting to thin a bit on top. Still he was handsome, she thought, watching the green-striped comforter rise and fall with each breath, fighting the urge to kiss his bare shoulder. It might disturb him, and she had a lot of work to do in the half hour before he got up. Barbara reset the alarm for six-thirty and slipped out of bed.

"Oh, God," she said as she confronted the mirror in her bathroom, the same thing she said every morning, although in truth she didn't look half-bad. Her skin was way too pale, of course, but her eyes, courtesy of the lift Dr. Steeves had given her two years earlier—a fortieth birthday present to herself—were unlined and alert. Maybe a little too alert for six o'clock in the morning.

"You're crazy," Susan had told her at the time. "What's so horrible about a few tiny lines?"

"Why mess with perfection?" Vicki had asked. "Wait a few more years."

Chris, of course . . .

Dear God, poor Chris.

Barbara closed her eyes, banishing thoughts of Chris from her mind. There was nothing she could do. Hadn't the police told her as much?

Barbara replaced the silk scarf she always wrapped around her hair before going to sleep with a plastic shower cap and stepped out of her white nylon nightgown and into the shower, careful to keep the water tepid and away from her head. She soaped her newly sculpted breasts, kneading them the way Dr. Steeves had shown her to keep them from getting hard, then moved on to the problem area of her stomach. Probably she should see the good doctor about a tummy tuck, although she'd heard they were very painful and carried a high risk of infection. Still, exercise wasn't doing anything. Three hundred crunches a day, and still the stubborn little pot refused to disappear.

Barbara finished her shower, dried herself off, brushed her teeth, stuck a handful of hot rollers in her hair, and sat down at the mirror to begin her daily ritual. First the eye cream, then the moisturizer. Almost $200 for a little false-bottom jar. Was she crazy? Her mother-in-law would have a heart attack if she knew. "Maybe I should tell her," Barbara whispered, applying a stroke of concealer under each eye. Next she covered her skin with a light makeup base, blending it into her temples and neck in a series of long, careful strokes before brushing powder blush across the apples of her cheeks. "And a little on the nose and forehead," she said. To give the illusion of a natural tan. Not that Barbara would ever allow the harmful rays of the summer sun anywhere near her skin. Even in the heart of the grayest Cincinnati winter, Barbara always wore number 30 sun block.

She outlined her eyes with plum and her lips with cherry red, then applied rich black mascara and deep coral lipstick. She pulled out the hot rollers and brushed out her dark hair, teasing it where necessary, smoothing it around her shoulders, securing it behind her ears with several hidden bobby pins, wondering if her roots could use a touch-up. Barbara Bush might favor the more natural look, but the sight of even one gray hair was enough to have this Barbara reaching for the Prozac. She stepped back into her nightgown and returned to bed just before the alarm clock went off at six-thirty.

"Ron, honey," Barbara whispered, her voice hinting at the remnants of sleep as she leaned across him, her breast grazing the side of his arm. "It's time to get up."

He made some sort of sound, more than a sigh, less than a grunt, but didn't move.

"Ron, sweetheart. It's six-thirty."

He flipped onto his back, opened his eyes, stared at the ceiling fan whirring softly above their heads.

Barbara leaned over, planted a series of soft kisses across her husband's throat. He barely stirred. "Are you all right?" she asked, returning to her previous position.

He said nothing, continued staring at the ceiling.

"Ron, are you feeling okay?"

"I'm fine," he said, sitting up, avoiding her gaze. "Just tired."

"You've been tired a lot lately. Think you should see a doctor?"

"I don't need a doctor."

"What *do* you need?" Barbara asked provocatively, forcing herself into his line of vision, dropping the straps of her nightgown, pushing her newly inflated bosom against his chest. He may not have noticed when she'd had her eyes done, but he'd sure noticed when she'd come home with these. So what if they got a little cold in the winter? So what if her nipples weren't as sensitive, as responsive, as before? At least they got his attention.

In the next minute, he was on top of her and inside her. Moments later, he was pounding his way to a climax while she faked her orgasm and wondered what she was doing wrong. Ron kissed her forehead perfunctorily as he slipped out of her, then left the bed without looking back.

Was he this way with his other women?

Barbara leaned back against the shiny ebony headboard, listening to the shower running in the bathroom. She had to stop torturing herself by constantly thinking about Ron's other women, the possibility of infection, the horrifying prospect of AIDS. How could she expect satisfaction if she didn't relax? Surely Ron used a condom when he felt the need to stray, she prayed, too afraid to bring the subject up, to ask him to don protection when they made love. Asking her husband to wear a condom when they were in bed together was tantamount to admitting she believed all the whispers, the innuendos, the outright lies, that had shadowed her marriage from its inception.

And things had been so much better between them since Tony's horrible outburst that afternoon at Vicki's some three years ago, the terrible things he'd implied—no, not implied, stated outright, called her a dyke, for God's sake, accused her of not being woman enough to keep Ron in line, throwing her husband's affairs in her face in front of all her friends, and her friends looking as if they wanted to melt into the carpet at their feet, because they knew, they knew all about Ron's escapades, everyone knew. On the drive home, she'd actually apologized to Ron for Tony's outburst, as if it had somehow been her fault. "That horrible little man," she remembered saying. "How could he say such awful things?"

"Don't worry about it," Ron had said. "Nobody pays any attention to that moron anyway."

For a while after that, it seemed as if Ron were working overtime to prove Tony wrong. He was loving, charming, and attentive. And Barbara was determined to be the best wife she could possibly be, the best companion, the best cook, the best lover. She pored over sex manuals and exotic cookbooks—the only books she had the patience to actually finish—and spent hours concocting special recipes, so that her husband would want to be home in time for dinner, and indeed, he was always inviting guests over, fellow members of the faculty, and then small student groups, groups that boasted an ever-increasing number of young girls who openly worshiped their handsome professor.

"You're being paranoid," Barbara whispered impatiently. Just because Ron had been a little distant these last few months didn't mean he was having an affair. He was preoccupied, that's all. He had a lot on his plate, what with the extra summer courses he'd taken on. A few late nights didn't mean anything. She had nothing to worry about. Hadn't they just made love, for heaven's sake?

"Busy day?" she asked him when he emerged from the bathroom, freshly shaved, slender hips wrapped in a large white towel.

"The usual." He opened the closet, rifled through his shirts. "I thought maybe we could go out to dinner tonight. Just the two of us."

Barbara almost had to sit on her hands to keep from clapping. When was the last time her husband had asked her out for a romantic dinner? "Sounds wonderful."

"I'll make reservations at Fathom. Seven o'clock all right?"

"Perfect." Fathom was Cincinnati's restaurant du jour, the place to be and to be seen. It was always mobbed. "You think we'll be able to get a table?"

"I'll see what I can do." He got dressed quickly in a blue pinstriped shirt and black pants. "What's the weather like out there?" He motioned toward the bedroom window.

Barbara immediately pushed herself off the bed and pulled up the green-and-beige flowered Russian blinds, peering into the sun-soaked backyard. "Looks like it's going to be a beautiful day."

Fathom was located on Sixth Street in the heart of the Fountain Square District, in the very center of Cincinnati. Nearby, gourmet restaurants were bracketed by old-time chili parlors, exclusive boutiques framed expansive department stores, impressive new skyscrapers highlighted historic landmarks. The taxi let Barbara off in front of the graceful, century-old Tyler Davidson fountain that stood in the middle of one of the busiest public squares in America. People were everywhere, strolling, laughing, even dancing to the live music that wafted through the warm July night. Horse-drawn carriages lined the streets. Maybe she could persuade Ron to go for a romantic ride after dinner.

The restaurant was decorated to look like the bottom of the ocean. Brightly colored exotic fish swam in large aquariums that lined sea-green walls; lamps made out of coral and swathed in seaweed sprang from the blue-tiled floor. The bars at either end of the room were carved out of rock. The chandeliers hanging from the high ceilings resembled free-floating octopi.

"Is Ron Azinger here yet?" Barbara asked the pretty young woman at the front desk. The girl looked like all young girls her age—tall, curvy, blond, minimal makeup. She barely acknowledged Barbara as she led her inside the large room toward the glass-topped table where Ron sat waiting.

"Your waiter will be right with you." The girl smiled at Ron, lingering perhaps a beat longer than necessary as she deposited the large blue fiberglass menus on the table. "Enjoy your evening."

"Have you been here long?" Barbara asked.

"Just got here two minutes ago."

"Good. I was worried."

He seemed surprised. "What were you worried about?"

He was right, Barbara thought. Why was she so worried all

the time? "Susan invited Tracey over for dinner," she explained anyway, "so I had to drop her off, and then I ran into Laura Zackheim, and boy, can that woman talk."

"Who's Laura Zackheim?"

Tears immediately sprang to Barbara's eyes. Her voice fell to the floor. "You know, the woman who bought Chris's house."

Ron reached across the table, patted Barbara's hand. His touch was electrifying even now, after all these years. "That was more than two years ago," he said gently.

"I know." Would she ever be able to say Chris's name without crying?

"I think we could both use a drink. What'll it be?"

"Some white wine?" Barbara asked, as if she weren't sure.

Ron signaled the waiter, conferred with him over the wine list as Barbara dabbed at her eyes, tried not to think about Chris. Laura Zackheim was a perfectly nice woman who was always inviting Barbara over to see what she'd done to the house, but Barbara hadn't been able to bring herself to go. Maybe it was time to put the past behind her, to bury old ghosts, banish old fears.

"I ordered the Pouilly-Fuissé," Ron was saying, and Barbara smiled, thinking he looked especially handsome tonight, even though he'd come directly from work and a troubled look was in his eyes.

"Perfect. So, what happened to you today that you could use a drink?"

"I had a run-in with that asshole Simpson."

Barbara suppressed a sigh of relief. Whatever was bothering Ron had nothing to do with her. It was that asshole Simpson, bless his little heart. "What kind of run-in?"

"To tell you the truth, I'm not sure what he was on his high horse about this time. There's always something bothering him. Anyway, there's no point in getting into it now. I'll just get upset all over again. What about you? How was your day?"

Barbara shrugged. "I drove Tracey to camp, went to exercise class, met Vicki for a quick lunch, had my nails done." She waved her long, red extensions in the air. "Then I picked Tracey up, took her shopping for some new T-shirts." She paused. Was there anything she could say that would make her day seem more exciting? It sounded boring, even to her. "I was thinking of taking some classes," she heard herself say. Was she?

"Really?" Immediately Ron's face registered interest. "What kind of classes?"

"Current affairs," she lied, saying the first thing that popped into her head. Where had that come from? She'd never had any interest in current affairs. She barely managed to get through the Lifestyle section of the newspaper.

"I think that's a great idea." Ron smiled.

"Yes, well, there's more to me than just a pretty face, you know," Barbara said with a laugh. *Was* there more to her than just a pretty face? Her face had brought her everything—attention, accolades, adoration. Would there be anything left when that was gone?

The wine arrived and Barbara watched as the waiter filled their glasses, then deposited the bottle in an ice bucket that looked like a pail you take to the beach. "Would you like to hear our specials?" the waiter asked, and Barbara listened as he rattled off the chef's suggestions for the day.

"I'll have the sea bass," Ron said. "And the house salad with raspberry vinaigrette."

"Sounds good," Barbara agreed. "But could you put my salad dressing on the side?" After the waiter left, she told Ron, "I'm trying to lose five pounds." She was hoping he'd look at her with that funny little expression he sometimes got whenever she said something particularly stupid and ask why on earth she'd want to lose any weight when she was perfect just the way she was, but he only smiled and raised his glass.

"Cheers. Health and wealth."

"To good times," Barbara added, clicking her glass against his.

"Good times," he seconded, then took a long sip, swirling the wine around in his mouth. "And good wine." He lowered his glass to the table. "You're looking very beautiful tonight."

"Thank you. So do you."

He laughed. Barbara sipped her wine, felt it warm inside her chest. She loved the sound of her husband's laughter. It made her feel secure.

"I was thinking of calling your mother," she offered, his laughter making her feel surprisingly expansive, "inviting her to dinner one night next week."

"You don't have to do that."

"No, I'd like to. We haven't seen her in a while."

"I saw her yesterday."

"You did?"

"I stopped by her apartment on my way home from work."

"Any particular reason? I mean, she's okay, isn't she?"

"She's fine. There were just some things I wanted to run by her."

"Such as?"

"Just things," Ron repeated, taking another drink, looking around the noisy room, which was quickly filling up.

Barbara followed his gaze. "Amazing you were able to get a table at such short notice."

"Actually, I reserved the table a week ago."

"You did?" What was he saying? That a previous engagement had fallen through, that she was a last-minute substitution? "I don't understand."

"I need to talk to you about a few things. I thought this would be a good place to do it."

Barbara took another look around the crowded room. Why would he pick the middle of a busy restaurant to talk to her? Surely if it were anything important, he would have chosen the privacy of their home. She held her breath, almost afraid to ask what he wanted to talk to her about.

"I'm leaving," he said without further prompting, smiling as a couple brushed by their table on the way to their own.

"You're leaving? You mean right now? Are you sick?"

"I'm not sick. That's not what I mean."

"What do you mean? Where are you going?"

"I'm moving out."

"You're moving out?"

"Yes."

"I don't understand."

"Our marriage isn't working," he told her simply.

"What do you mean, our marriage isn't working?"

"It's not working," he said again, as if this would clear everything up.

The waiter approached with their salads. "And here's your dressing," he told Barbara.

"You invited me out to dinner to tell me our marriage is over?" Barbara asked incredulously.

The waiter dropped the small cup of salad dressing to the table and hurried away.

"This can't come as a total shock," Ron said. "You must have had some idea."

Barbara fought to make sense of his words. Had she missed something? "When you left this morning, everything seemed just fine, thank you very much. How could I have had any idea? Why wouldn't I be shocked? What are you talking about?"

"Could you keep your voice down?"

"We made love, for God's sake. What, should that have been my first clue something was wrong?"

"That was an accident. I never meant for that to happen. You caught me by surprise."

"I forced you?"

"Of course not."

"It just wasn't part of the plan."

"No," he said, grabbing his fork, waving it over his salad.

If he takes even one bite, Barbara thought, I'll stab him through the heart with my butter knife. "This isn't happening." After all these years, after she'd turned a blind eye to all his infidelities . . . "Is there someone else?" she heard a voice ask, barely recognizing it as her own.

"No." His eyes told her there was.

"Who is it?"

"There's no one."

"Who is it?" she asked again, her voice louder, more insistent.

He dropped his fork to the table. "Pam Muir," he said softly, as if she should recognize the name.

"Pam Muir?" An image was slowly taking shape in Barbara's

mind of a young woman in her early twenties with a round face and pale, almond-shaped eyes. "Pam Muir," she repeated, as the image came into sharper focus. Strawberry blond hair cascading down her skinny back, small, hopelessly perky breasts, and big, sultry lips. Men took one look at those lips and thought of only one thing, she remembered thinking the first time Ron had introduced them.

Stupid, pie-faced little girl, Barbara thought now. With pimples on her chin, no less. One big one, two smaller ones hovering just below the surface of her ash-white skin. A nose smeared with freckles, like peanut butter on white bread. How dare her husband leave her for a pimply, freckle-nosed, pie-faced coed he'd brought into their home, right into their living room, into their dining room. She'd fed her, for God's sake!

"It was so nice of you to invite the study group over for dinner, Mrs. Azinger," pimply, freckle-nosed, pie-faced Pammy had said, helping Barbara stack the dirty dishes in the dishwasher.

"My pleasure," had come Barbara's immediate response.

Dear God. "Pam Muir."

To think she'd felt almost sorry for the girl. She might have a brilliant mind, as her husband had espoused on more than one occasion—the smartest student he'd taught in almost twenty years of teaching, he'd said—but she didn't have a clue how to make a good impression, how to make the most of her appearance. As if long blond hair, small, perky breasts, and blow-job-sculpted lips weren't enough, Barbara thought wryly.

All right, so he'd been having an affair. She'd suspected as much. So what? He'd been having affairs throughout their marriage. It didn't mean he had to leave. It didn't mean they couldn't work things out.

"It just happened," Ron was saying, although she hadn't asked him to explain.

The waiter warily approached with their sea bass.

"Are you hungry?" Ron asked, and Barbara shook her head, although strangely enough, she was famished. Ron waved the waiter away.

"What can I do?" Barbara asked. Tears filled her eyes and she lifted her chin to prevent them from falling. Ten years off her face, the doctor had promised when she'd had her eyes done. Ron hadn't even noticed. Should have asked for twenty, Barbara thought.

"There's nothing you can do," he told her. "It's not your fault."

But of course it was her fault, Barbara understood. Simply put, she wasn't the girl he'd married; she'd grown up, grown old. Despite the makeup and the plastic surgery, new wrinkles kept a constant vigil just below her skin's surface, waiting to ambush her at the first sign of complacence. Gravity continued its relentless assault on all sides, even while she slept. Perfect plastic breasts only emphasized the imperfections everywhere else.

"There's nothing you can do," he said again.

"There must be something I can do to change your mind," she begged, hating the neediness in her voice, hating herself even more. "I'll do anything." She would have gotten down on her knees if they hadn't been in the middle of the most popular restaurant in town. She lifted her hands in the air, as if to implore him, thought better of it, and returned them to the table in defeat, her skittish fingers inadvertently sending the cutlery flying toward the floor.

"Was that necessary?" Ron asked, as if she'd done it on purpose.

"*Was this?* I guess I should be grateful you didn't surprise me on the Phil Donahue show."

Ron clearly had no idea who Phil Donahue was. "I just thought that being in a public place would help keep things on an even keel."

"Crowd control," Barbara muttered.

"Something like that." He smiled.

Barbara slumped back in her seat. "Coward."

"I was hoping we could avoid the name-calling."

"Asshole." What the hell? She'd lost him anyway.

"Okay, I understand you're upset."

"You don't understand a damn thing." Did *she*? What exactly was she so upset about? That her husband was leaving her for another woman? That that woman was half her age? Half her size? That he'd had the temerity to bring her into their home, introduce her to his wife and daughter? That he'd chosen this most public of venues to break the news? That he'd made love to her this morning knowing he was going to dump her tonight? That he'd been planning his escape for at least a week? "That's why you went to see your mother last night," Barbara said, realizing this was true only as she spoke the words. "You told her you were leaving me."

"For what it's worth, she said I was making a mistake."

"Well, she's certainly right about that," Barbara said, speaking over her surprise, deciding to call Vicki as soon as she got home, to take the bastard for everything she could get her hands on—the house, his pension, his precious Mercedes.

Except she didn't want any of those things. What she wanted was her husband back.

Why?

Because she was used to having him around? Because she didn't like the idea of being a single mother, a lonely statistic, of sleeping alone night after night? Because she was afraid of growing old alone? Any or all of the above?

Or did she want him back so that she could do it right this time, so that she could be the one to walk out, the way she should have done years ago, when she was still relatively young, when she was still heart-stoppingly beautiful, when she still had some pride? When was the last time she'd felt proud about anything? Except for Tracey, of course. The only thing in her life she'd managed to get right. Perhaps if she'd been able to have more children, if she'd been able to give him a son . . .

"What will we tell Tracey?" she asked, her voice a monotone.

"That we love her," Ron said, sounding much too mature for a man who was leaving her for a girl half his age. "That my leaving won't change that. That just because her parents can't make it work—"

"Because her father can't keep his dick in his pants!"

Ron's face glowed an angry red as he glanced toward the nearby tables. Somewhere beside them, a woman tittered nervously. Ron lifted his napkin from his lap, threw it across his salad, rose to his feet. "Maybe this wasn't such a good idea."

"No. Please. Allow me." Barbara jumped up from her seat

and raced toward the washrooms in the far corner of the restaurant. She pushed open the heavy blue door, feeling it whoosh shut behind her. She leaned against it, took a series of long, deep breaths, gulping for air, as if she were drowning. A good description, she thought with a crazed chuckle as she surveyed the walls of deep blue mosaic tiles, heard the trickling of water from the long waterfall that doubled as a sink. "He can't be doing this," she cried, hearing an embarrassed cough from inside one of the stalls.

Except that he was doing it. As always, Ron Azinger was doing exactly as he pleased. Yes, sir. It was business as usual, and she had no choice but to carry on with her life. She had to be strong, if not for herself, then for Tracey. Besides, she was hardly unattractive. There were plenty of other fish in the sea. "Fish in the sea," she said out loud, as a burst of hysterical giggles escaped her throat. "Nothing like keeping with the theme." She laughed again.

A toilet flushed, although no one emerged from any of the stalls. Probably afraid to, Barbara decided, straightening her shoulders, sucking in her stomach, pushing out her impressively augmented bosom. She opened the bathroom door and stepped back into the main part of the restaurant, not surprised to discover that Ron had already left.

"The gentleman took care of the bill," the waiter informed her.

Barbara smiled, wondering at what precise moment her life had slipped out of her grasp. She'd just turned around for half a second, she thought, and it was gone.

Eleven

Susan awakened slowly from a dream in which she was delivering an important speech to the President's Council on Physical Fitness, her eyes opening at the precise moment she realized she was standing completely naked in front of the large crowd that included the president and virtually his entire cabinet. "Why do I always have to be naked?" she moaned, looking at the clock beside her bed. Seven twenty-nine. Seven twenty-nine! Hadn't she set the alarm for seven o'clock? Susan reached across her sleeping husband and grabbed at the clock accusingly, forgetting it was plugged into the wall, so that the electrical cord slithered roughly across Owen's nose and mouth. He immediately bolted up in bed, swatting at his face, frantic fingers trying to pluck the offending object away from his lips. "I'm sorry," Susan said quickly, trying to calm him. "I was just trying to check what time I set the alarm for."

Owen exhaled a deep breath of air, scratched at his balding head. "I was having a dream about being on safari. Suddenly I felt this thing moving across my face. I thought it was a snake."

"I'm so sorry." Susan fought the urge to laugh. Her husband always looked so vulnerable first thing in the morning, especially when he'd spent the night trekking through the jungle. "Are you all right?"

Owen leaned over to kiss her just as the alarm went off in Susan's hands. They both jumped, Susan dropping the clock to the bed, then having to ferret through the billowing white comforter to retrieve it and turn the damn thing off. "God, that's loud," she said.

Owen returned the clock to its position on the nightstand. "Seven-thirty on the dot. Same as always."

"Damn. I meant to change it."

"What's the problem?"

"I'm speaking to Ariel's class this morning about my job. It's career week or something, and I promised I'd take part. Anyway, I was really hoping to finish up some work before I went into the office."

"What time did you come to bed last night?"

Susan rubbed the sleep out of her eyes, hearing Barbara tell her to stop that at once. The skin around the eyes is delicate, Barbara would say. Especially as women get older. Didn't she actually read any of the stories she edited? "I guess it was sometime after midnight. I was working on that article about what makes investment banking sexy." She laughed, although the work had been slow and tedious. So much of being an assistant editor involved correcting the writer's grammar, rearranging ill-conceived concepts, trying to organize a series of jumbled parts into a well-constructed whole. Is that what she'd say to Ariel's class?

"I'll bite. What makes investment banking sexy?" Owen asked.

"I think it has something to do with money." Susan smiled, throwing a white terry-cloth robe over her shoulders and sliding into a pair of fuzzy pink slippers. She shuffled out of the room and down the hall toward her daughters' bedrooms. The shower in the bathroom between the girls' rooms was already running.

The door to Whitney's room was open and her bed was empty, the nine-year-old's clothes arranged neatly on the bed, awaiting her return. Susan smiled. Whitney was always the first one out of bed in the morning, the first one dressed, the first one finished with breakfast, the first one out the door. In school, hers was the first hand to shoot up in answer to a teacher's question, to volunteer for a special assignment, to offer to read her composition out loud. She didn't have to be reminded to wash her hands after she went to the bathroom or to brush her teeth after every meal or to go to bed at the appropriate hour. She was unfailingly polite and sweet-tempered. In every respect, a living doll.

Which was precisely why Ariel hated her.

"She's an alien," Ariel regularly scoffed. "Haven't you noticed how she never spills anything, how her hands are always clean, how she's always got this stupid smile on her face? She's not normal." Ariel would tell her sister to her face, "You're an alien."

"You're just jealous," Whitney would calmly reply.

"Oh, yeah, right. Like I'd be jealous of an alien."

Whitney never rose to the bait. She'd shrug and walk away, which, of course, only enraged Ariel all the more.

"A fat and ugly alien," Ariel would call after her, but Whitney never looked back.

"Ariel, honey," Susan called from the doorway to her older daughter's room, "time to wake up." A large hand-printed sign taped to the door with a Band-Aid proclaimed: KEEP OUT! PRIVATE! ABSOLUTELY NO ALIENS ALLOWED! Susan knocked gently, then again, louder the second time so that her daughter, who was buried under an avalanche of pink blankets and whose radio was loudly blasting rock music into her ear, might hear. "Who am I kidding?" Susan asked herself, stepping over the threshold and negotiating her way through the clothes littering the floor. "I know there's a carpet under here somewhere." Susan tried to find it with her bare toes, thinking, Two children raised by the same two parents in the same house with the same set of values, and they couldn't be less alike. She reached the bed, lifted the blankets from Ariel's shoulders while removing the pillow from her head, then leaned down and kissed her daughter's sleep-warmed cheek. "Wake up, sweetie pie."

Without opening her eyes, Ariel reached up and grabbed the pillow from her mother's hands, returning it to her face.

"Come on, sweetheart. Help me out here. I'm already running late, and we have to leave here by a quarter to nine at the latest."

"Big deal if we're ten minutes late. Who cares?" came the muffled reply.

"I care. If I'm late for your class, that makes me late for work and . . . " She stopped. Why was she explaining herself to a thirteen-year-old girl who obviously couldn't care less? "Just get up," Susan said, and walked from the room.

"Hi, Mommy," Whitney greeted her cheerfully, emerging from the bathroom wrapped in a soft yellow towel.

Susan loved to be called Mommy. Just the sound of the word infused her with pride and joy. In another year or so, Whitney would undoubtedly abandon the word for the less childish Mom or the dreaded Mother, as Ariel had taken to calling her lately. She felt a twinge of sadness, already mourning its loss. "Hi, beautiful girl," she said.

"She's not beautiful. She's an alien," came the cry from the other room.

Amazing what Ariel could hear and what she couldn't, Susan thought, folding Whitney into a warm embrace, the child's skin damp against her cheek.

"Close my door!" Ariel barked. "Something out there smells bad."

"Get up and close it yourself," Susan called back as Whitney disappeared into her room to start getting dressed. "Two girls raised in the same household," Susan muttered, entering her en suite bathroom and starting the shower, "with the same two parents and the same set of values." She was still muttering as she undressed and stepped under the hot rush of water. "Just let her be out of bed by the time I'm ready to go."

Of course Ariel wasn't out of bed, and when Susan finally succeeded in getting her up, she couldn't decide what to wear, then she couldn't decide what to have for breakfast, so of course they were late getting to the school, which meant Mrs. Keillor got to give her speech first, and Susan was forced to sit through an incredibly boring recitation of exactly what was involved in being a dental hygienist, followed by a question-and-answer period that Susan prayed would be brief—surely the woman had covered everything in her speech—but the question-and-answer session proved to be fairly lengthy as well, due in large part to Ariel's sudden and inexplicable interest in the subject. Question after question on territory already covered, but Mrs. Keillor seemed flattered by the attention, and went over everything with Ariel patiently again.

She's doing it on purpose, Susan realized, trying not to show any signs of impatience or discomfort. *She knows how much I hate being late for anything, and she knows all these questions are going to make me really late getting to work. She hates that I have a job, just like she hated when I went to school. Wasn't she always sick the night before a big exam? Wasn't she always the most demanding when I had a big paper due?* Had anything changed in the two years since Susan had finally earned her diploma and went to work at Jeremy Latimer's latest project—a glossy women's magazine named after his wife?

When it was Susan's turn, she delivered her speech as concisely and quickly as possible, and none of the students had any questions to ask, least of all Ariel, who'd been talking to the girl beside her or staring out the window the entire time. Susan politely excused herself before Danny Perrelli had a chance to expound on the joys and sorrows of running a successful dry-cleaning business.

An accident on I-75 held up traffic a good twenty minutes, so by the time Susan arrived at the stately brown-brick building on McFarland Street that served as home base to the ever-expanding Latimer publishing empire, it was after eleven o'clock and Susan had missed the morning meeting in its entirety. "Peter was looking for you," a coworker announced from the next cubicle. "He seemed upset you weren't at the meeting."

"Great." Susan glanced toward the wall of glassed-in offices at the far end of the square-shaped room, hoping for a glimpse of Peter Bassett, a handsome string bean of a man in his late forties who'd joined the staff less than a month ago and who was her immediate supervisor. But he wasn't in his office. Nor could she see him parading up and down the ersatz halls between the cubicles, strutting his skinny stuff and generally making like a cock of the walk, wearing his arrogance like an expensive cologne. What was it about him she found so damned attractive? Susan wasn't even sure she even liked the man.

The editorial division of *Victoria,* where Susan worked, was comprised of thirty small cubicles, arranged in six rows of five, that were divided one from the other by attractive Japanese-style screens. Floor-to-ceiling windows lined three of the office's four walls and normally guaranteed plenty of light, but the October sky had turned threatening, and a gray pall was slowly leaking into the room, casting long shadows across the field of computer screens. Susan rifled through her messages, noted that they included one from each of the three writers whose articles she was working on, one from Carole in the art department, another from Leah, the magazine's chief fact-checker, one from Barbara, and two from her mother. That was unusual. Her mother never called her at work.

She was reaching for the phone to call her mother when it rang.

"Susan," the male voice said in a voice that announced it had no time for pleasantries. "It's Peter Bassett. I was wondering if I could see you in my office in, say, ten minutes?"

"Of course." Susan replaced the receiver, wondering if she was about to be fired. The magazine was struggling, and one associate editor had already lost her job since Peter Bassett has been brought on board to help turn things around. Rumors had been circulating for weeks that more heads were going to fly in the coming months. Jeremy Latimer might have been instrumental in getting her hired, but that didn't make her invulnerable. She might have worked her tail off to advance through the ranks to her current position, but that didn't mean she couldn't get her ass fired.

Susan loved her job. Despite the daily frustrations and occasional late nights, she felt blessed to be working at something that brought her so much pleasure. Not everyone was so fortunate. Hadn't she told Ariel's class as much this morning?

Susan rested her head in the palm of her hand, stared at her blank computer screen. Missing this morning's meeting couldn't have helped her cause. She was still staring at the blank screen five minutes later when the phone rang again.

"The slut is pregnant," Barbara announced by way of hello. "Can you believe it? They're married less than six months and she's pregnant already."

"Are you all right?" Susan asked.

"I don't know what I am. I need to vent. Are you free for lunch?"

Susan rubbed her forehead, looked toward Peter Bassett's

office, although her view was blocked by the tall beige partition. "I'm not. I'm sorry. Look, why don't you come for dinner tonight? We can talk then. Bring Tracey. I'm sure Ariel would love to see her." Why had she said that? Ariel was never happy to see anyone.

After Barbara hung up, Susan placed a quick call to her mother. She knew something was wrong the minute she heard her mother's shaky hello. "What's the matter?"

"Dr. King's office called," came her mother's tentative reply, as if she were speaking a foreign language she hadn't quite mastered. "Apparently something suspicious showed up on my mammogram. They want me to come in for a biopsy."

Susan tried to speak, but no sound emerged.

"It's probably nothing," her mother continued, saying all the things Susan would have said had she been able to find her voice. "It's very small, and they said these things are usually benign, so I should try not to worry."

"When do they want you to come in?" Susan pushed the reluctant words out of her mouth.

"Tomorrow morning at ten."

"I'll come with you." Susan's calendar indicated another staff meeting for tomorrow at ten, but Peter Bassett would just have to understand. Or he wouldn't, Susan thought.

"Thank you, dear." The relief in her mother's voice was palpable. "I really appreciate that."

"I'll pick you up at nine-thirty. Does that give us enough time to get there?"

Her mother agreed it was more than enough time, and Susan said she'd see her in the morning. She hung up the phone and closed her eyes. Please let my mother be all right, she said in silent prayer. "My job doesn't matter," she whispered into the cowl neck of her lime green sweater. Take my job, she continued without words. Just let my mother be okay. She felt a trickle of tears sting her cheeks.

It took Susan a few minutes to regain her composure, and another minute until she felt sure enough of her feet to stand up. Exactly fifteen minutes after Peter Bassett's phone call, Susan stood outside the glass wall of his office.

He was on the phone, but he motioned her inside with a wave of his free hand. "Close the door," he whispered, hand over the receiver. "Have a seat. I'll just be a minute."

Susan closed the door, pulled out the blue, straight-backed chair across from his desk, lowered herself slowly into it, tried not to eavesdrop on his conversation.

"On the contrary," he was saying. "This is the school's responsibility. If I take this on, if I tell Kelly she can't go out on the weekend if she continues to skip classes, then I'm only giving myself more problems at home, and I'm doing nothing to solve the problem at school. It's up to you to impose a consequence. Consequences mean nothing if they're arbitrarily imposed from outside. You know that as well as I do." He rolled his eyes impatiently, turned a brass-framed photograph of three attractive adolescents toward Susan.

Susan examined the picture: two smiling teenage boys on either side of a scowling teenage girl. So what else is new? she thought, liking Peter Bassett more already because he was obviously going through the same kind of problems she was, even if he was about to fire her.

"What am I suggesting?" Peter Bassett asked. "I'm suggesting you do your job. Next time my daughter skips a class, give her a detention. If she skips the detention, then suspend her. That's the way things work in the real world."

Susan closed her eyes. She'd skipped the morning meeting. She was about to be suspended. Permanently.

"Sorry about that," Peter Bassett apologized, hanging up the phone. He pointed at the photograph. "Kelly's fifteen and a major pain in the butt. Her brothers are also pains in the butt, but at least they're not skipping school. So, how are you?"

"Fine, thank you."

"We missed you at the meeting this morning."

"Yes, I'm very sorry about that. I was giving a talk to my daughter's class about my job. It's career day, or whatever they call it. Anyway, Sarah knew about it. She'd given it the go-ahead," Susan said, referring to the woman Peter Bassett had replaced.

"Hope you got in a few plugs for the magazine." Peter Bassett's piercing gray eyes had an engaging twinkle that Susan found almost unbearably appealing.

"Every chance I got," Susan said.

"Good. We need all the help we can get."

"Yes, sir," she said when she could think of nothing else to say.

"Oh, God, please don't call me sir. *Peter* will do just fine." He rose from his chair, walked around to her side of the desk, perched on the edge, long, skinny legs dangling toward the floor. "What do you think is wrong with the magazine?" he asked, catching Susan completely off guard.

"What do I think is wrong?"

"I'm interested in your opinion."

"Why?" Susan couldn't help but ask.

"Because I asked everyone else at this morning's meeting, and I didn't get any satisfactory answers. And I was especially looking forward to hearing what you had to say because I think you're smart, and the articles you work on are consistently the best articles we print."

"Thank you," Susan said, straightening up in her seat, realizing she wasn't going to be fired after all.

"So, what's *Victoria*'s problem? Why do you think sales are down?"

Susan took a deep breath. Could she really tell him what she thought was wrong with the magazine? "I think our focus is wrong," she heard herself say. "It's like we're trying to be *Cosmopolitan,* but why should women want to read us when they can buy the real thing? Also," she continued, growing bolder as his smile widened, "there are already too many women's magazines out there going after the same market, and we're at a disadvantage to begin with because we're operating out of Cincinnati and not New York or Los Angeles."

"And the solution?"

Was he playing with her? Susan wondered, distracted by the intensity of his gaze. "I think we should stop trying to compete with the big guys on their turf and start carving out our own niche," she began, gradually warming to her subject. "This is a local magazine. We should concentrate on what interests the women of Cincinnati. Forget about profiling visiting B-list celebrities and start creating some celebrities of our own. Stop doing fashion spreads with skinny New York models wearing clothes no one in this city would be caught dead in, and start doing stories about real women with real problems, and let those stories be more than one thousand words in length. Why are we so afraid of a little depth?

"I think we should start publishing fiction," she continued, not pausing long enough to let him interrupt. "If we're going to copy anyone, let it be *The New Yorker.* We could publish one original short story a month, maybe even run a short-story contest.

"It's almost the nineties. Today's women are interested in more than just fashion and horoscopes. We want to know about issues and politics and how the decisions being made in Washington today are going to impact on our lives in Cincinnati tomorrow. We have to stop appealing to the lowest common denominator and start setting our sights higher. We have to stop following the leader and start leading our own parade. Toot our own horn. Let the others copy us." Susan stopped abruptly. "I'm sorry. You must think I'm a complete lunatic."

Peter Bassett laughed out loud. "On the contrary, I admire your passion. I'm not sure I agree with everything you said, some of it's not very practical, but I'd like to give it some thought. Perhaps we could toss over some of these ideas with the others at tomorrow's meeting."

"That would be great. . . . Oh, no. No, I can't. I'm sorry."

"Is there a problem?"

"My mother has to go to the hospital for a biopsy tomorrow morning. I said I'd take her." Susan braced herself for an onslaught of recriminations: We're running a business here, Susan. How are we going to implement some of these big ideas if you continue to place your personal life ahead of your job? The reason sales are down, the *only* reason sales are down and this magazine is in trouble, is because of people like you, people who talk a good game, but are too damn busy visiting their daughters' schools and taking their mothers to the doctor to attend important meetings. This is the real world, Susan. Which is it going to be? Your family or your career?

"Of course," Peter Bassett said instead.

What? "What?"

He shrugged. "No big deal. We can discuss your ideas another time. The magazine isn't about to change its focus overnight, and the important thing right now is your mother. She needs your support."

"Thank you," Susan whispered. She wondered if she looked as shocked as she felt.

"Don't mention it." Peter pushed himself away from his desk, his athletic body swaying into the space between them. He approached her chair, lay a soft hand on Susan's shoulder, his fingers warm through her thin sweater. "It'll be all right. Think positively."

"I will," Susan said, and held her breath.

"Please give your mother my regards." Peter Bassett removed his hand from her shoulder, gave her a sad but reassuring smile, then returned to his seat behind his desk.

Susan stood up, swiveled toward the door, stopped, turned back, about to thank him again. For being so understanding, so patient, so wise. When was the last time anyone had listened to her with such active interest? But Peter Bassett was already busy typing something into his computer. Susan's eyes floated to the picture on his desk of his three children, noticing for the first time another photograph, this one of an attractive woman slightly younger than herself, short, dark hair framing an engaging smile. Mrs. Bassett, no doubt, Susan surmised, thinking she looked very much like her two sons and not at all like her difficult daughter.

You're a lucky woman, Mrs. Bassett, Susan told the picture with her eyes. I hope you appreciate what you have. Then she opened the door and left the office.

Twelve

"Tracey, look at this, sweetie. This outfit would look great on you. What do you think?"

Tracey closed the book she was reading, crossed the floor of the doctor's spacious waiting room, and sat down beside her mother, glancing at the latest issue of *Victoria* in Barbara's hand. "I don't think it would suit me," she said of the striped-blue-and-white jersey and skinny navy pants the young blonde was modeling for the camera.

"Why not?"

"Well, look at her, Mom." Tracey nodded toward the young model cavorting on the page. "She has no thighs. In case you hadn't noticed, I do."

"That's just baby fat," Barbara assured her, although she wasn't entirely convinced. In the last year, Tracey's body had undergone radical change. With the advent of her period, Tracey had morphed from a skinny adolescent into what might kindly be described as a young woman of substance. Not that Tracey was fat, or even overweight. Just that she'd filled out in all the wrong spots, wide where she should be narrow, flat where she should be full, something she'd undoubtedly inherited from Ron's side of the family, Barbara decided bitterly. "You'll lose that soon enough. All you have to do is cut out the junk food. Start eating right. Come with me to the gym one afternoon. You know what we could do?" she continued almost in the same breath, although Tracey had already returned her attention to her book. "I could make an appointment with a nutritionist, and we could go together. Because I think I could stand to lose a few pounds myself, and I think that would be a great idea. What do you think?"

Tracey looked at her mother with blank eyes. "Sure."

"Good. Because I think that's a great idea. I don't know why I didn't think of it before." Barbara looked guiltily into her lap. She'd been thinking of little else for weeks now, wondering just how she could approach the subject without hurting her daughter's feelings. And she'd done it. Accomplished her objective without ruffling Tracey's feathers. She stared at her daughter's profile. She's such a pretty girl, Barbara thought. It would be a shame to have her miss out on things just because she'd gotten a little careless, because she didn't pay enough attention to her appearance. And appearances were important, no matter what people tried to tell you these days. If you looked like you didn't give a damn about yourself, well, then, nobody else would give a damn either.

Barbara reached over, stroked her daughter's cheek. Tracey smiled without looking up from her book. What was she reading anyway? "What are you reading?"

Tracey flipped the book over, showed her mother the cover.

Barbara took the book from Tracey's hand, turned to the opening chapter, read the first few lines. "Sounds pretty good," she said, about to hand the book back when she saw the signature scrawled along the inside of the cover. *Pam Azinger* looped across the top of the page in bold red ink. Like blood, Barbara thought, dropping the book back into Tracey's lap. *My* blood.

"She thought I'd like it," Tracey muttered, laying the book down on the chair beside her. "But it's pretty silly. I won't read it." Her voice drifted to a halt.

"Nonsense. If you like it . . ."

Tracey shook her head. "No. I don't. It's not very good."

Barbara took a deep breath. "How is Pam making out with the new baby?" She cleared her throat, practically scraped the words out of her mouth.

"Not so great. He cries all the time."

"That's too bad." Barbara smiled. Thank you, God, she thought. "What's his name again? I keep forgetting."

"Brandon. Brandon Tyrone."

Stupid name. No wonder she could never remember it.

"He's a cute baby. He just cries all the time." Tracey looked straight ahead, eyes focused on nothing in particular.

Had she always had that little bump on her nose? Barbara wondered. Maybe while they were here, she'd have the doctor take a look at it. "Excuse me," Barbara said from her chair, banishing thoughts of baby Brandon Tyrone Azinger from her mind. "How much longer do you think we'll have to wait?"

"Just a few more minutes," the receptionist said from behind a glassed-in partition, staring in Barbara's general direction, as if she were looking through a dense fog.

Sure. Why not? What were a few more minutes? She had nothing better to do with her time anyway. She didn't have to rush home to tend to a colicky newborn. She didn't have to prepare formulas or change diapers. She didn't have to get dinner on the table for her hardworking husband. No, she had nothing pressing, nothing urgent that required her attention. So what better way to while away a humid summer afternoon than by sitting in the plushly appointed waiting room of Cincinnati's most respected cosmetic surgeon? Time wasn't important. Wasn't that why she was here? To do away with time.

The doctor could get more comfortable chairs at least, Barbara thought, flicking an errant thread from the deep purple velvet of her seat. They'd been re-covered in the two years since her last visit. Barbara glanced at the peach-colored walls, trying to remember what color they'd been at the time of her last consultation. Obviously nothing in Dr. Steeves's life was allowed to show any signs of age.

The office door opened and a woman with a large blue chiffon scarf obscuring most of her face stepped into the waiting area. She conferred quietly with the receptionist, then walked from the room without so much as a glance in Barbara's direction. Nobody sees me anymore, Barbara thought, feeling strangely slighted. It's like I don't exist.

"Mrs. Azinger," the receptionist said, looking just past her, "you can go in now."

"I shouldn't be too long," Barbara told Tracey, who was staring at a lithograph of flowers on the opposite wall. The girl nodded without looking at her mother. As if I don't exist, Barbara thought again.

"Barbara," Dr. Steeves greeted her, extending his hand. "Good to see you again."

"Nice to see you," she agreed, although she couldn't help but notice that Norman Steeves was looking a little tired underneath his clear blue eyes. And he'd put on a few pounds since her last visit, a slight jowl pushing against the salt-and-pepper of his beard.

"You're looking well. How's life treating you these days?"

"Pretty good." My husband's concubine recently delivered a seven-pound baby boy named Brandon Tyrone and my daughter is sprouting hips the size of Ohio, but I'm just fine and dandy, thank you very much.

"Tell me what you think I can do for you." Dr. Steeves motioned toward the purple armchair in front of his large mahogany desk. Barbara sat down, waited to speak until the doctor was seated and she was sure she had his complete attention.

"It's my stomach," she told him. It's my life, she thought. "I mean, I've always had this little pot, but lately it's not so little."

Dr. Steeves peeked at his charts. "How old are you now?"

"Forty-four," Barbara said, coughing into her hands to mitigate the harsh sound.

"How many children?"

"One." Barbara looked into her lap, trying not to think of baby Brandon Tyrone. "I was thinking of a tummy tuck."

"Well, why don't you get undressed and let me have a look. Not everyone is a candidate for this kind of surgery." He handed her a blue cotton robe and walked to the door. "You can keep your panties on. Just tell the nurse when you're ready."

Less than five minutes later, she was lying stretched out on the examining table, the blue cotton robe pushed aside to reveal a pair of black lace panties pulled low on her hips, and Dr. Steeves's well-practiced hands were running along the raised scar of her cesarean section. "Muscle tone's not bad at all, considering," he was saying, neglecting to specify. "We could cut into the existing incision."

Barbara winced, remembering her earlier surgery, the months it had taken her to recover. Did she really want to go through that kind of pain and discomfort again?

"So what do you think about Iraq invading Kuwait?" Dr. Steeves asked suddenly. "Think Hussein will invade Saudi Arabia?"

Barbara thought she must have fallen asleep, that she was having another of the peculiar dreams she'd been having lately. Could she really be lying here naked save for an expensive pair of black lace panties pulled down almost to her pubis, while a man caressed her stomach and talked of Saddam Hussein? Had she disappeared altogether?

Surely she was still capable of commanding a man's attention, of turning a man's head. Surely all she had to do was put herself out there, make herself available, send out the appropriate signals. Surely to God someone would notice.

I need someone to notice me, she thought.

"Why don't you take a few days and study the literature," Dr. Steeves said when he'd concluded his examination, and Barbara nodded, wondering why doctors always referred to the pamphlets they gave out as "literature." "Talk it over with your husband, and let me know what you decide."

Barbara grimaced, but the doctor was already walking to the door. "How soon could you do it?"

"You'd have to check with my receptionist. She has my schedule."

"How much . . . ?"

"It's in the literature."

I need someone to show me I'm still desirable, she thought.

"What's all this stuff?" Tracey asked moments later, indicating the pamphlets in Barbara's hands as they waited for the elevator.

"Literature," Barbara said with a laugh, noticing Tracey was empty-handed. "You forgot your book . . ."

"I left it there." Tracey smiled. "It's a stupid book." She shrugged. "I'll just tell Pam I lost it."

"You're a good girl."

I need a man, Barbara thought.

The man, it turned out, was scarcely more than a boy, which was exactly the point when you thought about it, Barbara decided, admiring the hard, naked body looming above hers. About the same age as putrid Pammy. Hell, if Rotten Ron could find happiness with a bovine-faced bimbo, so could she.

His name was Kevin. At least she thought it was Kevin. Weren't they all named Kevin these days? And he was tall and buff and good-looking in that bland Calvin Klein–billboard way, all pouty arrogance and rippling abs. That's what he called them, Barbara thought with a smile. *Abs.* As if it involved too much time and effort to say *abdominals*. Or maybe that's what he thought stomach muscles were actually called. *Abs.*

"I've got some great exercises for upper and lower abs," he'd said when she'd first approached the muscular young trainer at the gym the day after her consultation with Dr. Steeves. "You don't need surgery," he'd told her with a sly smile. "Spend a month with me. I'll whip you into shape." That was all the encouragement Barbara needed to decide that Kevin Young Hardbody was just what the doctor ordered.

Kevin had been working at the health club in Vicki's office building for the last six weeks. Personal trainers were the coming rage, Vicki had proclaimed. Worth every penny. Barbara had promptly signed on with Kevin for eight private sessions, two times a week, despite the fact her credit cards were already maxed to the limit, and Ron was making grumbling noises about all the money she was spending. Yes, he'd agreed to pay her credit cards bills for five years as part of the divorce settlement, but within reason.

Screw you, Rotten Ron, Barbara thought. Then, with a laugh, no, screw me! Which Kevin was doing nicely, thank you very much. Barbara adjusted her rear end to accommodate the continued thrusting of Kevin's narrow hips. Talk about the stamina of the young, she thought, stealing a glance at the clock beside Kevin's too hard double bed. Did everything about him have to be so damn hard? she wondered, and almost giggled, except her laughter might be misinterpreted.

Who was she kidding? He wouldn't hear her. He probably didn't even know she was still there, he'd been pounding away for so long. Almost forty minutes if that clock could be believed. It was two o'clock in the morning. Didn't he ever get tired? She'd lost interest in the proceedings at least twenty minutes ago, when it became obvious she wasn't going to experience orgasm. Promising tingles had become painful irritations. Instead of excitement, she was feeling sore. If she didn't get some sleep soon, the bags under her eyes would be down to her chin. It was time to speed things up a bit. Time to take matters into her own hands. As it were.

She grabbed his buttocks, groaned, the beginning of her well-practiced routine. A series of short moans followed, accompanied by a slight thrashing of her head. Nothing too violent, just enough to let the boy know she was ready, that he didn't have to work so hard. Kevin continued pounding away, oblivious. Groans turned to squeals, squeals became gasps. Still, the boy kept pounding.

Like a runaway train, Barbara thought, collapsing back against the pillows, trying to get comfortable. Obviously she wasn't going anywhere. She thought of pushing herself off the bed, pictured the young man attached to her torso, like a dog humping a reluctant leg. I could be anyone, she realized, flattery turning to dismay. She didn't exist for Kevin any more than she existed for Ron, or for Dr. Steeves, or for Saddam Hussein, for that matter. She'd vanished into that nether world of the discarded, a foggy arena filled with women over forty who functioned much like extras in a movie, there to fill out a scene, to occupy space without diverting attention from the key players. A blur in the background. An attractive blur perhaps, but a blur nonetheless.

Above her, Kevin kept pounding away, his eyes tightly closed.

He doesn't see me, Barbara thought, closing her eyes as well, reviewing the various things she had to do the next day. Tracey would be coming home from spending the weekend with Ron at about three o'clock. Probably she should get groceries, straighten up the house a bit, maybe make Tracey her favorite macaroni-and-cheese dinner before they had to drive out to Indian Hill to catch Kirsten Latimer's performance in the high school production of *Oliver!* No, Barbara decided, wrapping her legs around Kevin's tight little buttocks, she'd take Tracey out for dinner. Charge it to dear old Dad. Take that, Rotten Ron, she thought, thrusting up violently with her hips. And that, you bastard. And that. And that.

In the next instant Kevin, perhaps caught off guard by the unexpected ferocity of her thrusts, let out a loud cry, stiffened, as if he were poised to take flight, and then suddenly collapsed on top of her, like a puppet whose strings had been severed without warning. "Wow," he said, his body glowing with satisfied sweat. "That was amazing. You're something else, you know that?"

Barbara smiled. An apt description, she thought, as an increasingly familiar sense of dislocation surrounded her head, like a fine mist. She'd become something foreign, even to herself.

Something other.

Something else.

Barbara left Kevin's small apartment at three in the morning and drove home, having made some excuse about having to be up first thing in the morning for Tracey. "I could wake you up," he told her with a wet kiss on her neck, and Barbara refrained from saying that was exactly what she was afraid of.

The last thing her poor body needed was another marathon session with the boy wonder. Talk about feeling your age.

Besides, all her makeup and creams were at home, and there was no way she was going to let Kevin see her bare-faced, any more than she'd allowed him to see her naked. "It's sexier this way," she'd insisted when he'd tried to remove her pink satin teddy. "Leave it on."

There was no way she was going to sleep, she realized as she pushed open her front door. She was too restless, too frustrated, too damn sore. I'll probably get a bladder infection, she thought, heading for the kitchen at the back of the darkened house. Or a yeast infection. Or worse, she thought with a start. What was the matter with her? Why hadn't they used a condom? Weren't the papers full of warnings about the need for safe sex? Did she think she was invulnerable, that middle age was the antidote to AIDS?

"This calls for a cup of coffee," she said out loud, her words echoing through the empty house as she plugged in the kettle, spooning a heaping teaspoon of instant coffee into a mug. Barbara hated when Tracey wasn't here, as if Tracey's absence diminished her even further. She found herself talking out loud whenever Tracey was away, the sound of her voice lending assurance that she was really there. Lately Tracey had taken to sleeping in her mother's bed. Probably she should put a stop to that, Barbara thought, pouring the water into the mug before it fully boiled. But what was the harm? It felt good to wake up with her daughter's arms around her. Her daughter's arms carried her through the day.

The coffee tasted bitter even with two teaspoons of sugar, so Barbara added a third, which made it too sweet, but so what?

she decided, looking through the fridge for the remainder of the strawberry tart left over from the other day. But it was gone, which meant Tracey had eaten it, which was no good. She'd better get moving, make that appointment with the nutritionist, get Tracey on a diet before things got out of hand. "You can pay for that too," Barbara said, thinking of Ron, glancing at the white phone on the wall.

In the next instant, she was at the phone, punching in a series of numbers, listening as the phone rang once, then again, before being picked up. "Hello?" said a sleepy female voice, halfway between a woman's and a child's. Poor Pammy had probably just fallen back to sleep after baby Brandon's 2 A.M. feeding. What a shame someone had to call and wake her up.

"Hello?" Pam said again, the word a question.

"Who is this?" Ron's voice assaulted Barbara's ears, reaching through the phone and filling the small kitchen.

Immediately, Barbara dropped the phone back in its carriage, her heart pounding. She began pacing back and forth between the phone and the kitchen table. "That was pretty stupid," she said out loud, then laughed. "Hello?" she repeated in Pammy's little-girl voice. "Hello?"

She sat down, finished her coffee, feeling strangely exhilarated. Calling Ron's house might have been stupid, but it sure was fun. More fun than she'd had in a long time, and that included tonight's workout. For one brief and shining moment, she'd been the one calling the shots, the one in control, determining who slept and who didn't. Not that Ron would suffer unduly. He'd simply take a few seconds to reassure his frightened child bride, then turn over and fall back to sleep. But poor little Pammy was a different story. She'd drift back slowly into a restless sleep, perhaps dreaming of faceless men with knives outside her door, only to be awakened by baby Brandon Tyrone's untimely cries.

A few more weeks of this kind of thing and who knew? Pam might soon be paying a visit to Dr. Norman Steeves herself.

A jolt of fear brought Barbara to her feet. What if Ron and Pam suspected she was the one who'd placed the call? But, no, she decided, resuming her earlier pacing, there was no way to trace the call, and there was no reason for them to be suspicious of her. She'd done nothing to alert them. People got nuisance calls all the time. She was in the clear. Nobody had any idea. She could try it again a week from now, and still nobody would suspect her. Or tomorrow night. Or even right now . . .

Barbara returned to the phone, waited a full five minutes, long enough for hearts to stop pounding, for tired imaginations to be easing toward oblivion. Then she punched in Ron's number, listened eagerly while it rang.

"Hello," Ron's angry voice bellowed into the phone. "Hello? Hello?"

Barbara dropped the phone back into its carriage with a satisfied grin. No reason she should be the only one up all night. Then she climbed the stairs to her bedroom, stepped out of her clothes, and crawled into bed. She was asleep before her head hit the pillow.

Thirteen

Vicki woke from a dream in which she was trying desperately to claw her way out of a deep, dark pit. Her fingers flailed at the wall of her prison, small clumps of earth breaking off in her hands and clinging to the undersides of her nails.

"Ow!"

She opened her eyes to see her husband sitting up in bed beside her, nursing a nasty scratch on his arm.

" 'Fraid you're gonna have to cut those nails, darlin'," Jeremy Latimer said with a smile.

"Oh, God, I'm so sorry. I can't believe I did that to you. Poor baby." Vicki lifted her husband's arm to her mouth, ran her tongue along the narrow line of blood just below the skin's surface.

"I think you might have scratched me a little lower down." An impish grin stretched the width of Jeremy's pale cheeks.

Vicki laughed and pushed herself out of bed, pretending not

to see the invitation in her husband's eyes. Did the man never get tired? He was sixty-five, for heaven's sake. Wasn't he supposed to be slowing down? She marched naked into the bathroom, stepped into the shower, disappeared under a torrent of hot water. She had too much on her mind to enjoy the luxury of a morning quickie. She had to be in Louisville by one o'clock, and she needed to do something before that, something she'd been putting off for weeks that she needed to deal with.

Vicki heard the bathroom door open, saw the shadow moving toward her, felt a whoosh of cold air as the shower door opened and her husband stepped inside.

"Thought you could use a little help." Jeremy took the soap from her hand and turned her around. "You know, for those difficult-to-reach areas."

His strong hands gently massaged the nape of her neck, before sliding down her spine to cup her bony backside. Don't they ever grow up? Vicki wondered. It didn't seem to matter whether they were sixteen or sixty—they were all the same. Well, maybe not quite the same, she thought, remembering the sixteen-year-old boy who'd been her first lover, feeling his lean, hard body pound against hers as her husband's fingers reached between her legs. But hard bodies weren't everything. Look at her own body, Vicki thought, deciding not to. It was changing every day, and not for the better, despite the personal trainer who came to the house twice a week. Kevin kept telling her she looked great, but that was part of his job. He was supposed to make her feel good about herself. And in truth, she did. Being forty wasn't so terrible. She still turned plenty of heads. Certainly her husband found her sexy and desirable, she knew, deciding not to fight the pleasurable tingling that was spreading across her body, to enjoy the impromptu interlude, even though it would throw her off schedule.

"Busy day?" Jeremy asked later at breakfast.

"Some things I have to get done." Vicki was already on her feet, dropping the morning paper to the table, kissing her husband good-bye.

"Where are you going?" Kirsten asked, entering the kitchen, her brother hanging on to the rear pocket of her jeans.

"Work." Vicki blew kisses at her children as she walked briskly to the front door.

"It's Sunday," Kirsten reminded her.

"I'll be back later."

"The play starts at eight."

"I'll be back in plenty of time. Don't worry. Break a leg."

Vicki was in her car and halfway to Cincinnati before she allowed herself time to think. She checked her watch. Only ten o'clock. She had plenty of time. Don't worry, she assured herself. You're doing the right thing.

I'm so glad you could make it, Mrs. Latimer," the nurse was saying. "He was asking about you just the other day."

Vicki followed the portly black nurse down the long, peach-colored hall of the nursing home, holding her breath, trying not to inhale the heavy, stale air. Like everything else in the four-story, yellow-brick building, the air carried the scent of decay and despair. No matter how brightly you painted the walls, how vigorously you scrubbed the floors, how often you disinfected the rooms, there was always this stench—the sad smell of the discarded, of those who were taking too long to die.

"He asked about me? What did he say?"

"He asked why his daughter hadn't been around to visit him for so long."

Vicki ignored the well-intentioned rebuke, deciding not to respond. What was the point? Besides, what could she say? The nurse was right. It had been months since her last visit, months since she'd last stared into her father's blank eyes hoping for some sign of recognition, months since she'd stood beside his bed hoping to hear him utter her name. "How's he doing?"

"Seems a bit better today. He ate all his breakfast. Went for a little walk down the hall."

"Did he really ask about me?" Vicki stopped in front of the door to her father's room.

"Well, not in so many words," the nurse admitted. "But he looked at me in that way—you know, that cute little look he gives sometimes—and I knew he was thinking about you."

"Thank you," Vicki said, thinking that *cute* was not a word she would have used to describe her father.

"I'll be right down the hall if you need me."

Vicki looked down at the well-scrubbed floor, exhaled a deep breath of air, then pushed open the door to her father's room.

The man in the single bed in the middle of the small room was the color of pale yellow chalk. "You almost match the walls, Daddy," Vicki said, inching toward the bed, staring at the frail figure of the man who was only five years older than her husband.

He stared at her through watery hazel eyes a shade lighter than her own and smiled the same tight grin Vicki remembered from her childhood, but she could tell instantly he had no clue who she was. It had been at least a year since he'd had any memory of her at all.

"So, how are they treating you, Daddy?"

"Good," came the immediate response. "Very good."

"I'm sorry I haven't been around to see you in a while."

"You've been busy," he said, as if he understood.

"Yes, I have. Do you remember what I do, Daddy?"

"You've been very busy," her father said again, staring at the painting of a snowy landscape that hung on the wall across from his bed.

"I'm a lawyer, Daddy. Just like you. With Peterson, Manning, Carlysle, over on Mercer Street. You remember them, don't you?"

"Of course," he said, his head nodding up and down atop his skinny neck, his Adam's apple jutting out at such a pronounced angle it looked as if a child's building block were wedged in his windpipe.

Vicki leaned forward, smoothed down the few white hairs jutting from the top of her father's balding head, adjusted the collar of his blue flannel pajamas. "I was made a full partner last year. I'm not sure if I told you that."

"You've been busy."

"Well, I don't have to tell you how crazy things get at a major law firm. But it's been good. I won a huge judgment in the McCarthy case. You may have read about it in the papers. It made the front page." She stopped. What was she babbling on about? Her father wouldn't have a clue what she was referring to. She doubted he'd glanced at the front page of a newspaper in years.

"That's very good," her father said. "Good for you."

Yes, good for me, Vicki thought, pulling up the chair that was resting against one wall and plopping down into it, savoring the irony. "Good for you"—probably the nicest thing her father had ever said to her, and he had no idea what he was saying. She almost laughed, looking past her father at the tree brushing against the window on the far wall, its bright October leaves slapping against the leaded panes. "It's pretty warm for this time of year," she said.

"Yes," her father agreed.

"You should get them to take you outside for a walk."

"Outside for a walk. Yes, it's pretty warm for this time of year."

Vicki pulled the red cardigan she was wearing more tightly around her. Despite the unseasonably warm temperatures and the overheated room, she was feeling cold. "So, I should fill you in on everything that's been going on." Her voice resonated fake cheer.

Her father smiled his tight little grin, the same grin he'd used when mocking her for losing the fifth-grade spelling bee competition, for placing second on the debating team in high school, for getting only an eighty-seven on her final English exam at college. Nothing she did was ever good enough. Was it, Daddy? Vicki thought now, wishing she could wipe that awful grin off his face. Nothing anybody ever did was good enough.

Is that why her mother left?

"Your grandchildren are doing very well," Vicki said loudly, trying to block out the rumble of unpleasant thoughts. "Kirsten is growing like a weed. She's thirteen now, and almost a full head taller than I am. Wait, I have a picture." She fished inside her large black Bottega bag for her wallet, extricated a slightly crumpled snapshot of Kirsten, stretched it toward her father. "Well, actually, this one's a few years old. Damn, I thought I had a more recent one." She was pretty sure Kirsten had given her the latest school picture for her wallet. What had she done with it? "Anyway, you can see how pretty she is. Her face has thinned out quite a bit since this was taken, and her hair's much longer. She's letting it grow to her waist. And she's doing very well in school. First in her class last year. You'd be very proud."

Would he? Vicki doubted it. *Eighty-seven?* she could hear him sneer. *Hardly a figure to be proud of.*

"She doesn't have a boyfriend or anything yet. Well, she's still so young." Vicki sank back into her chair, fought back the surprise threat of tears. She'd been barely fourteen when she'd lost her virginity. Was it possible Kirsten was similarly active? That she was having sex?

No way, Vicki decided, although how would she know? She wouldn't have known that Kirsten had started menstruating if the housekeeper hadn't complained of Kotex plugging up the toilet. Kirsten was relatively guarded about such matters, and she rarely confided in her mother, preferring to keep personal matters private, which was fine with Vicki. If she wants to know about anything, she knows where to reach me, Vicki reasoned. At least she knows where her mother is, which is more than I could ever say about *my* mother.

"She got the lead in the school play," Vicki said out loud, tiring of her inner monologue. "Nancy in *Oliver!* You remember the musical *Oliver!*? 'Oliver, Oliver,' " she sang softly, as her father bobbed his head to the gentle beat. "Well, luckily, she has a better voice than I do, although I have to tell you, the thought of a thirteen-year-old girl singing 'As Long As He Needs Me' is kind of horrifying. Anyway, I'm going to see her tonight. It's the last performance. I couldn't make it for opening night. It was on Wednesday and I had to work late, so . . ." Vicki stopped when she saw her father's eyes drift to a close. "Daddy? Daddy, are you asleep?"

"You're very busy," he said, almost as if he'd been listening.

"Anyway," Vicki persisted, "we're all going. Jeremy and Josh, who isn't much of a student yet, but that could change, you never know, stranger things have happened. And my friends Susan and her husband, and Barbara, plus their kids, they're all going to be there. Not Chris," Vicki said, hearing her voice drop. "Nobody's seen or heard from Chris since they left Grand Avenue. It's like she disappeared off the face of the earth."

Like someone else we know, Vicki thought.

"I'm going to see her," she said suddenly.

"What? Speak up," her father demanded, as the tears that had been lurking behind Vicki's eyes gathered force, threatened to break free. *Did you hear me? I said speak up. You think I'm going to let you go to the dance with marks like these?*

Vicki waited until the threat subsided before she spoke. "I said I'm going to see her."

"Oh," her father said, not asking for further elaboration. Not interested in explanations.

"Mother," Vicki said, the word feeling heavy on her tongue.

"You're very busy."

"In Louisville." Vicki was speaking for her own edification now. "At least I think it's her. I won't be sure until I actually see her, talk to her. I've had detectives looking for her for some time now. Off and on. They thought they found her a few years back living off the coast of Spain. But it wasn't her. I mean, she was American and she fit the general description and everything, but once I saw the pictures, I knew it wasn't her. This woman in Spain was much too tall to be her. But this woman living in Louisville sounds like she could be the one. She's the right height and age, and she calls herself Rita Piper, which, of course, was Mother's maiden name. She's not married. Apparently she lives alone. So, it sounds like it could be her. And the pictures the investigator sent me look like she might look now. Of course, it's hard for me to remember because I was so young when she left, but—" Vicki's voice came to an abrupt halt. "You don't really care, do you?" she asked her father bitterly. "You don't care at all. That's why she left, isn't it?"

Except why did she have to leave me too? Vicki asked silently. Why couldn't she have taken me with her?

"Beats the shit out of me why I'm doing this," Vicki said, throwing her hands into the air, feeling them slap her thighs when they landed. "I mean, it's not exactly like she's been knocking herself out trying to keep in touch. It's not like she doesn't know where to find me."

And she hasn't tried. Not once. In all these years.

"So, I'm not sure what the point of this little exercise is, but, hey, it's a nice fall afternoon, and I feel like a drive."

"It's a nice afternoon," her father agreed.

Vicki checked her watch. "Anyway, it's getting late. I really should get going. I have to be back in time for Kirsten's final performance. Can't miss that. I told you she got the lead in *Oliver!*, didn't I?" Vicki jumped to her feet. Now she was the one who couldn't remember things. She had to get out of here before the nurses mistook her for one of the residents. She leaned forward, her lips hovering around her father's dry forehead. She kissed at the air, patted his shoulder, felt him shake off her touch. Even now, she thought. "I'll drop by again soon. Let you know how I make out."

"Yes," her father said, as if answering a question.

Vicki stood in the doorway for several seconds, watching her father watching the wall, feeling years of indifference pushing her into the hall. "Good-bye, Daddy," she said, and closed the door behind her.

It took a little over an hour to reach the small, white clapboard house in Louisville. Vicki drove by the house three times, circling the block repeatedly, trying to decide how best to approach the woman who could be her mother. Probably she should have phoned ahead of time, given her time to prepare for their meeting. Given her time to pack up her bags and flee, Vicki thought, which was why she'd decided not to call. Her mother was very good at packing her things and leaving town. She wasn't going to give her another opportunity.

No, it was better to surprise her, to confront her directly, although what exactly she was planning to say to her, Vicki couldn't be sure. She'd been trying out various speeches for days, ever since Bill Pickering had called her office with the news he'd located a woman named Rita Piper matching her mother's description, and she wasn't living off the coast of Spain, she wasn't holed up in a rustic log cabin in Wyoming, she hadn't fled to Canada. She was living right next door in Louisville, Kentucky, not more than a stone's throw away from the daughter she'd abandoned thirty-six years ago. Close enough to keep an eye on her, to follow her accomplishments in the paper, to keep tabs on her. Close enough for her daughter to find her, should she choose to go looking.

"Hi, Mom. Remember me?" Vicki said out loud, pulling the car to a stop halfway down the block. She couldn't very well park right in front of the house. Shiny new red Jaguars weren't the least inconspicuous of cars. She didn't want to alert her mother that someone was watching the house, give her the opportunity to escape through the back door. Vicki put the car in park, breathed deeply, and watched a small square of the front window fog with her breath. "You probably don't remember me," she started again, then stopped. "Excuse me, are you my mother?" she asked with a roll of her eyes. Sure. Great. That'll do it.

"What do I say?" Vicki asked the neat white house, not much different from any of the other homes on this decidedly working-class street. Why haven't you tried to contact me? You have to know who I am, whom I married, what I've achieved. There's no reason for you to be living in such modest surroundings when you could be living in the lap of luxury. Jeremy is a generous man. He'd do anything to make me happy. "And you don't have to worry about *him* anymore," Vicki said, knowing, as she had always known, that her father was to blame for her mother's abrupt departure. Not that he'd been physically abusive, like Chris's husband. Vicki doubted her father had ever had to raise his hand in anger to make his displeasure felt. All he had to do was look at you with those cold hazel eyes, and you knew you'd been judged and found wanting, that try as hard as you could, you would always be a disappointment to him.

No wonder her mother had left.

Vicki checked her watch. Almost one o'clock. Bill Pickering had told her that the woman calling herself Rita Piper volunteered every Sunday morning at a local hospital and was usually home by one. Of course, she might have gone shopping or stopped off for something to eat. Vicki felt her stomach rumble. Probably she should have stopped at McDonald's for a Big Mac and a strawberry milk shake. Maybe an order of fries. The very real odor of imaginary food immediately filled the car. "Maybe there's time for me to get something," Vicki said, about to put her car into drive when she saw the old-model, green-and-tan Plymouth round the corner and pull into the driveway of the small white house. "Oh, God," Vicki said, holding her breath, watching as the car came to a stop and the driver got out.

"Mother . . . ," Vicki whispered, peering through the Jaguar's front window at the small, auburn-haired woman who emerged from the front seat, laughing as she closed her car door. Why was she laughing?

And then the door on the passenger side of the car opened and another woman got out. She was taller, broader, bigger in every way than Rita Piper, her hair permed into a big blond ball on top of her head, and she too was laughing. Obviously someone had said something funny. Maybe told a joke. What kind of sense of humor did her mother have? Vicki didn't know. Her father had refused to speak about her mother after her desertion. He'd destroyed all photos of her, except one that sat on the dresser in Vicki's room, a picture of mother and daughter he'd probably forgotten about, and which Vicki later secured under her mattress, sensing it was in danger.

Vicki reached into her purse, extricated the small picture hidden behind her driver's license, stared at the photograph of a beautiful young woman, only twenty at the time of her daughter's birth, shoulder-length red hair pressed against her baby's smooth cheek, joy and sadness present in equal measures behind luminous green eyes. "I got my father's eyes," Vicki noted, tucking the red hair she'd inherited from her mother behind her ears. "Lucky me," she said, watching as the two women entered the white clapboard house and closed the door behind them.

Now what?

She couldn't just go knocking on the door to claim her birthright when her mother had company. She'd have to wait until the visitor left. Vicki leaned back against the black leather seat, wondering how long that would be. She turned off the car's engine, closed her eyes, trying to ignore the hunger gnawing at her stomach, and quickly drifted off to sleep.

The sound of something smacking against the side of the car woke her up.

"Sorry, lady," a small voice called out as Vicki bolted upright in her seat. A young boy darted in front of the car to retrieve a blue rubber ball from the road, then threw it to the other young boy waiting across the street.

What was happening? Where was she? What time was it?

The answers came as quickly as the questions. She was sitting in her car in Louisville, Kentucky, waiting to confront her mother, and it was almost four o'clock in the afternoon. "Four o'clock!" It couldn't be four o'clock. She couldn't have been asleep for three hours! It was impossible. She never took naps in the middle of the day. Something must be wrong with the clock. Damn Jaguar. Something was always wrong with the stupid thing.

She checked her watch. "No, this can't be. It can't be." Her head shot toward the white clapboard house. "No, I don't believe this. Please just let this be another crazy dream." But even as she was saying the words, Vicki understood it wasn't a dream, that the green-and-tan Plymouth was no longer sitting in the driveway of the white clapboard house, that her mother was gone. "Where did you go? Where did you go?" she screamed, banging her hands against the steering wheel so that the horn blasted into the surrounding air, drawing the unwanted attention of the two boys playing ball across the street. She quickly waved away their puzzled looks, and they returned to their game, although they kept stealing guarded glances in her direction. "Idiot! How could you fall asleep?"

Can't you do anything right? she heard her father say.

"Now what?" she asked again, out loud this time. What do you do now? "Okay, okay," she said, speaking into her hands in case the boys were watching her. "Where could she have gone?" Maybe she was just driving her friend home, which meant she'd be back soon. Except Vicki didn't know what time she'd left. "Maybe they went to a movie," Vicki moaned. "Oh, God, I can't stand it. How could you be so stupid? You had her. She was right here."

She checked her watch one more time. After four. She had to be back in Cincinnati by eight. Eight at the very latest. She'd promised Kirsten. How long could she afford to wait? "I'll give it one more hour," she said. Surely Rita Piper would be back by then.

It was ten minutes to five when the green-and-tan Plymouth pulled into the driveway and Rita Piper climbed out of the front seat, her arms full of groceries.

"Thank God." Vicki closed her eyes with relief, then opened them immediately, lest the woman disappear again. Okay, so she was home. Time to get this show on the road. "What am I supposed to do? Run out and help her carry her groceries inside the house?" Wouldn't that be cozy? Mother and daughter getting reacquainted while restocking the refrigerator. No, better to let the woman get inside the house, give her time to get everything put away, time to catch her breath. "And mine," Vicki said, opening her door and gulping at the outside air.

Five minutes later, Vicki was knocking on the woman's front door. *Hi, I'm Vicki Latimer. Your daughter. Remember me?*

"Just a minute," came the response from inside the house. A nice voice, Vicki thought, searching for echoes of her own voice in the sound, hearing none. "Who is it?" the woman asked without opening the door.

"Rita Piper?" Vicki asked, her heart pounding.

The door opened a fraction. Curious dark green eyes peeked across the threshold. "Yes?"

"My name is Vicki Latimer. I was wondering if I could talk to you for a few minutes."

"You're not selling anything, are you?"

Vicki shook her head. "No," she said, and almost laughed.

"Is there something I can help you with?"

Even before the door was fully open, Vicki understood that the attractive, sixty-year-old woman with dark red hair and questioning green eyes standing in front of her was not her mother. "I'm sorry. I've made a big mistake." Then she burst into a flood of bitter, angry tears.

Without another word, the woman who was not her mother wrapped her arms around Vicki's shaking shoulders and led her inside the house.

Fourteen

Barbara's arms were shaking.

And I haven't even started exercising yet, Barbara thought, lowering the heavy bags she was carrying to the green marble floor and struggling with the imposing glass door at the entrance to Bodies by Design Fitness Center, located on the sixteenth floor of the Sylvan Tower Complex on Mercer Street in downtown Cincinnati.

"Somebody's been doing some serious Christmas shopping," the blond and bronzed receptionist chirped from behind her similarly colored desk as Barbara passed by on her way to the machine room at the very back of the center.

"Damn right," Barbara called back, then laughed. Wait till Ron got this month's Visa bill. Yes, sir, Santa Claus was being especially good to his former family this year. An Armani suit for Barbara, a Gucci jacket for Tracey, matching watches from Cartier. Leather bands, Barbara sniffed, passing a crowded mirror-lined room filled with sweating, middle-aged white women trying to keep up with their tireless, young black aerobics instructor. She hadn't had the nerve to buy the gold bands she preferred. Maybe next year.

1990 was almost over. They were inching toward the new millenium.

God only knew what surprises the decade had in store. "Can hardly wait," Barbara muttered into the black fox collar of her green tweed coat, last year's Christmas present from her outraged former spouse. Didn't know you were such a generous man, did you? Barbara thought, and smiled, although the surface of her face remained still.

"Four more!" the aerobics instructor was shouting into the microphone around her neck, as she extended first her well-toned right arm, then her left, into the air. "Three more."

"No more," Barbara sang out, readjusting the packages in her arms, wobbling on high-heeled winter boots toward the rear of the facility, wondering if Susan and Vicki were here yet. Probably. She was at least half an hour late. Susan was always so punctual. And Vicki's office was only two floors down. Even though it was Saturday, she'd undoubtedly spent the morning working. Just as she'd most likely return to her office when she was finished here. Vicki was always working.

She hadn't even bothered showing up to her daughter's school play last month. Working, she claimed. Some lame excuse about getting stuck with a client, not realizing the time, etc., etc. Was she having another affair? Barbara wondered, thinking that while it wouldn't be the first time Vicki had cheated on her husband, it would be the first time she'd decided to keep that information from her friends.

Not that Barbara had confided in either Vicki or Susan about her brief interlude with Kevin. Why hadn't she? she wondered. Was she embarrassed? Ashamed? Afraid of being judged? Afraid of being pitied?

Things had changed, Barbara realized sadly, although the women tried gamely to pretend they hadn't. The Grand Dames had somehow survived Vicki's move from Mariemont to Indian Hill intact, but Chris's untimely departure had dealt a fatal blow to the women of Grand Avenue. Slowly, subtly, inexorably, the group dynamic had shifted. This wasn't altogether unexpected. There were, after all, three women now instead of four, but more often than not, Barbara felt like the odd woman out. Especially since her divorce.

Barbara recognized that neither Vicki nor Susan meant to exclude her. They were simply an easier fit, both well-educated women with husbands who adored them, with healthy incomes and successful, satisfying careers. They couldn't understand what it was like to be in her position, to be uneducated, unloved, uncertain. Although Vicki and Susan never said it out loud, Barbara knew they were thinking it was high time she pulled herself together and started doing something constructive with her life. Ron was never coming back; it was time for her to move forward.

Except she couldn't move.

She was stuck.

And she didn't know how to get out of the mess that was her life.

If only she had Chris to talk to. Chris would understand. But Chris was gone, spirited off in the middle of the night by a monster who'd sold her Grand Avenue house out from under her and imprisoned her in a small rented house in the nearby suburb of Batavia. An investigator Vicki hired had quickly uncovered their whereabouts, and the women had driven to out to Elm Street and confronted Tony at the front door, then called the police when he refused to let them see Chris. But the police had informed them that nothing could be done in light of Chris's refusal to file a complaint, and they lectured the women sternly about minding their own business.

Barbara had ignored their warnings and, for the next few weeks, continued driving to Batavia almost daily, parking in front of the tiny brown wood bungalow, hoping for a glimpse of Chris. But the curtains were always drawn. There were no signs of life. A month later, Barbara pulled up in front of the house to find the front door open and the house deserted. Chris was gone.

There were no further attempts to locate her. "There's nothing we can do," the women took turns saying over the ensuing years, although Barbara didn't believe it, and she was pretty sure the others didn't either. Over time, their unspoken guilt thickened, then hardened, like a coat of protective varnish. They no longer kissed each other's cheeks in greeting, choosing instead to peck at the air. When they hugged, their guilt kept them an arm's length apart.

The Grand Dames weren't so grand without Chris.

Barbara reached the exercise room at the end of the long hall, spotted Susan slogging along on one of six treadmills, Vicki pounding away on the closest of three StairMasters. That can't be good for you, Barbara thought, pushing open the glass door with the weight of her shoulder, feeling an immediate wave of heat wash across her face.

"There she is!" Vicki called out, as five sweaty heads snapped in her direction. "We wondered what happened to you."

"We were starting to worry," Susan admonished.

"Sorry. I lost track of the time." Barbara dropped her parcels to the floor and slipped her coat from her shoulders, revealing a newly purchased blue-and-black-striped leotard underneath. She realized she'd forgotten her sneakers.

"That's a pretty outfit," Susan said. She was wearing a pair of loose gray jogging pants and a shapeless white T-shirt. Her chin-length brown hair was damp with exertion. "When did you get that?"

"This morning."

Susan shook her head, dislodging several large beads of perspiration that quickly dribbled from her forehead to the tip of her nose. "Something tells me a certain college professor isn't going to be very happy." A bead of sweat fell toward her mouth, teetered precariously on the bow of her upper lip.

"Next time he gets a divorce, he should read the fine print," Vicki said, jumping off the StairMaster, giving Barbara's arm a squeeze as she headed for the free weights in the center of the room. She wore black shorts and a matching T-shirt with a Bodies by Design logo over her left breast.

"She's pregnant again," Barbara announced, the words echoing against her ears, making her dizzy.

"What?"

"Who?"

"Rotten Ron and Putrid Pammy," Barbara told them, steadying herself against a nearby bench. "They're expecting another baby in June. Can you believe it? She's still nursing barf-faced Brandon, for God's sake."

"When did you find out?"

"Tracey called from Ron's first thing this morning."

"How's she taking it?"

"She's fine," Barbara marveled. "You know Tracey. Nothing fazes her."

"How about you?" Susan slowed the speed of her treadmill, looked at Barbara with concerned eyes.

"I'm okay." Barbara shrugged, although in truth she was anything but okay. She hadn't slept well in weeks, and the weekends Tracey spent with Ron were especially difficult. She'd gotten used to having Tracey sleep beside her in bed. The news of Pam's pregnancy had hit her with the force of a ten-pound barbell dropped squarely on her head. Spending her ex-husband's money had provided only temporary relief. Even the knowledge that it was her former mother-in-law who was most likely footing the bills brought with it only momentary satisfaction.

I've made such a mess, Barbara thought now, knowing how angry Ron would be at her continuing extravagance. Hadn't he already threatened to take her back to court if she didn't start controlling her spending? What was she trying to do? Didn't she know that by forcing his hand she could get slapped in the face?

Barbara spun around, trying to avoid her reflection in the walls of mirrors that surrounded her. What was there to see, after all, but a pathetic, middle-aged woman in a stupid blue-and-black leotard whose horizontal stripes only emphasized the thickening of her waistline. What was she doing here anyway? Exercise wouldn't help her. Nothing would help her.

"So, did you hear the news about Kevin?" Vicki was asking.

"Kevin?" Susan repeated, as Barbara's heart stopped.

Good God, she thought. He has AIDS. I'm dead.

"My trainer," Vicki said. "*Our* trainer." She extended a barbell in Barbara's direction. "*Ex*-trainer, I guess I should say."

"He's dead?" Barbara gasped.

"Dead! No, he just got fired, that's all. Why would you think he was dead, for God's sake?"

"Why did he get fired?" Barbara asked, ignoring the question, trying to regain her composure.

"Apparently he was sleeping with half his clients. Management got wind of it and fired his cute little ass."

"Did you?" Barbara asked, horrified by the thought she and her friend might have been sharing the same cute little ass.

"Did I what? Sleep with Kevin? Are you kidding? I make it a practice never to sleep with anyone prettier than I am. Did you?"

"What? Of course not."

"Too bad," Vicki said, returning the ten-pound weight to its stand, picking up two fives, lifting them behind her neck and above her head. "I guess I don't have to ask you," she said, glancing at Susan, whose only reply was an exaggerated roll of her eyes. "Didn't think so. Anyway, I'm going to have to cut this short, I'm afraid. I have a client coming in at two o'clock."

"It's Saturday," Susan reminded her.

"It's business," Vicki replied. "How's lunch on Friday? I checked my calendar, and I actually have an hour free."

"Can't," Susan said. "I'm having lunch with my supervisor on Friday."

"Ooh, that sounds interesting. What's he like anyway?"

"Very nice. Very smart."

"Very cute I understand."

"I hadn't noticed."

Now it was Vicki's turn to roll her eyes. "God, Susan, you're no fun. Is she, Barbara?"

Barbara shrugged, waited for Vicki to extend the luncheon invitation to her. But Vicki continued lifting the weights above her head in silence, and nothing more was said about lunch on Friday.

"Okay, got to go. Talk to you guys later," Vicki announced minutes later, dropping the weights, gathering up her belongings, throwing kisses at the air, and exiting the room in a series of abrupt moves that made her look like a blurred photograph.

It's only a matter of time till she's out of my life entirely, Barbara thought, watching the door close behind her. First Chris had left her, then Ron. Now Vicki and Susan were drawing closer together, sharing time and confidences, increasingly leaving her out in the cold. Hell, even Kevin's cute little ass was gone. How long before Tracey decided she'd rather live with her father? How long before she had no one?

"Barbara?"

Barbara saw Susan dismount the treadmill, take several steps toward her.

"Barbara, what's going on?"

"Going on? What do you mean?"

"I've been talking to you for the last two minutes, and you haven't heard a thing I've said, have you?"

"I'm sorry."

"Are you all right?"

"Sure. Why? Is there a problem?"

"You tell me. You're just standing there in the middle of the room. You haven't moved since you took off your coat."

Barbara swallowed the surprising threat of tears. What was

the matter with her? "I guess I just don't feel much like exercising today."

"What *do* you feel like?"

"Graeter's ice cream," Barbara responded softly, waiting for Susan's gentle rebuke.

Instead Susan laughed. "Sounds wonderful."

"You game?"

"Can't," Susan apologized. "Owen's picking me up in half an hour. We're going to visit my mother."

Barbara felt instantly guilty she hadn't inquired about Susan's mother, who was in the hospital recovering from her most recent surgery. Poor woman—a mastectomy last year, and now another operation to remove a cancerous lymph node from her neck. "How is she?"

Susan tried to smile, but her lips only wobbled weakly before disappearing one inside the other.

"She'll be all right."

"I know." Susan climbed onto one of the stationary bicycles, then immediately climbed back off. "To hell with exercise. Life's too damn short, and I've got half an hour till Owen shows up. What are we waiting for? Let's go to Graeter's." Her arm slipped across Barbara's shoulder. "Have I told you lately that I love you?" she asked with a sad smile.

"Tell me again," Barbara said.

She was coming out of Saks when she saw him.

No, Barbara told herself immediately, wiping the late-afternoon sun out of her eyes, feeling the dampness of lingering tears. What was the matter with her? Why was she crying, for God's sake? The salesgirl hadn't meant to upset her. She was a child, for heaven's sake. What did she know of diplomacy, of tact, of life? "Lalique has just put out this wonderful new line of products for mature skin," she'd said when Barbara had asked about a new face cream. And suddenly Barbara was crying. Right there in the middle of the makeup department at Saks. Right there in front of the horrified salesgirl and curious passersby.

It seemed as if she were crying all the time these days, as if all anybody had to do was look at her the wrong way or say the wrong thing or even think it, and right away, she was bawling her eyes out, which Dr. Steeves would undoubtedly tell her was the worst thing she could do.

She was so tired. Tired of her days. More tired of her nights. Tired of coping. Tired of hurting. Tired of shopping, for God's sake. Tired of pretending that everything would be all right, that Ron would come to his senses and come home. He was never coming home. She knew that. He had Pammy and Brandon and another baby on the way. A whole new life. And what did she have? The scars from the old one.

Sometimes she thought it would be nice just to fall asleep one night and never wake up. Maybe the anesthetist will put me to sleep, she remembered thinking during her last cosmetic procedure, and something will go wrong and I'll never come to. It happens. She'd read about it often enough. And then Vicki could sue and make Tracey a wealthy young woman. Her friends would look after Tracey, and Barbara wouldn't have to worry anymore about staying young and pretending to move forward with her life. What life?

Barbara pictured the bottle of painkillers in her medicine cabinet at home. Surely if she swallowed them all, that would be the end of her misery. She'd literally feel no pain. Her pitiful excuse for a life would be over and done with, no more waiting around for her body to catch up to her soul. Except then Tracey would find her, and Tracey would no doubt blame herself, assume she'd failed her mother, and she couldn't do that to her daughter, she couldn't inflict that kind of horror on the one person who mattered more to her than anything else in the world. Barbara recalled how devastated she'd been at her own mother's death, how alone she'd felt, how black the world had seemed, how pointless her existence.

But Tracey had saved her. Barbara hadn't allowed herself the luxury of falling apart because she'd had an infant daughter to take care of, and the same was true now. Tracey might be a teenager, but she was still her baby. And she needed her mother. As much as ever. Maybe more. Together, they would get through this. Together they could get through anything.

What was the matter with her? Why couldn't she be more like Susan, who took difficult situations in her stride, or Vicki, who bulldozed her way right through them? Or Chris, who just seemed to accept whatever hardship and indignity life tossed her way. Oh, God, poor Chris. Poor, sweet, wonderful Chris. Why was she thinking about her so much lately? Was it because Christmas was only a month away, and Chris had always taken such a child's delight in the holidays? Losing Chris had been like an amputation. The limb had been severed, but even now, years later, the phantom pain remained.

Which would explain why she was seeing ghosts, apparitions that weren't there. Walking out of Saks, Christmas music ringing in her ears, seeing a stranger cross the street, his face buried against the collar of his heavy jacket, her mind playing tricks, thoughts of Chris swirling around in her brain like the errant flakes of snow the wind was pushing in her eyes, the glare of the sun slapping Tony's features onto the stranger's face, the man disappearing into the crowd, the apparition vanishing.

Of course it wasn't Tony.

Except suddenly there he was again, Barbara realized, as she was pulling her car out of the parking lot behind the post office at Fifth and Main. And this time there was no mistaking him for anything other than what he was—a vile, evil, little man. "My God," Barbara whispered, her heartbeat quickening, her breath creating small pockets of steam on the car's front window. "What do I do now?" she whispered out loud, slowing her car to a crawl, lowering her chin and her eyes in case Tony looked over and saw her.

He walked quickly, his strides long and confident as he turned left onto Sixth Street. Barbara steered her car around the corner, careful to keep a comfortable distance between them, pulling into an available space at the side of the road when Tony stopped for a second to tie his shoelace. Of course he wasn't wearing boots, Barbara thought derisively. Too damn macho for that.

Where were they going? How long was she planning to follow him?

At Race Street, Tony turned left. Now they were right in the heart of the hotel district, the Cincinnatian, the Clarion, the Terrace Hilton. Was it possible he was staying in town at one of these hotels? Probably she should get out of her car and follow him on foot, Barbara thought, deciding that was a stupid idea. She'd never be able to keep up with him, especially in these heels, and besides, what if he suddenly got into his car and took off, then where would she be?

They were back at Saks, she realized. Why? Where was he going? Was he walking around in circles? Did he know she was following him? Barbara ducked down in her seat, slammed on the brake. The man in the car behind her blared his displeasure with a loud blast of his horn. Barbara felt her breath escape in short, painful spasms. She was afraid to sit up, afraid to raise her eyes. What if Tony was standing beside her car window? What if he was standing there right now, looking down at her with that awful satisfied smirk across his face?

Behind her, impatient drivers honked their horns. Barbara slowly lifted her head, like a turtle emerging from its protective shell. Tony was gone. "Shit!" Barbara exclaimed, slamming her hand against the wheel, listening with horror to the sound of her own horn slicing through the outside air.

And then, there he was again, pulling an old blue Nissan into the traffic, turning right onto Elm Street. Barbara cut in front of a black VW, whose owner promptly gave her the finger, then passed another car on the inside lane. Tony turned right at Sixth Street, turned right again on Central Avenue and again at Seventh Street. And suddenly they were out of the Fountain Square District and on Gilbert Avenue. They passed the Greyhound Bus Terminal, bypassed the Mount Adams District, and headed into the 184 beautiful acres that made up the historic district of Eden Park.

What was Tony doing out here? Barbara wondered, rounding the bend of the city reservoir and driving by the Murray Seasongood Pavilion, built in 1959 to honor a former mayor. A few more twists and turns and they were in front of the Cincinnati Art Museum, then the Eden Park Water Tower, an Ohio Valley landmark that hadn't operated since 1908. They drove past the Irwin M. Krohn Conservatory, continued on past the stone eagles gracing the old Melan Arch Bridge, before arriving at the entrance to the Twin Lakes section of Eden Park. Twin Lakes was once a stone quarry, and various overlooks provided a wondrous view of the Ohio River, especially during the spring and summer months. Now, the trees were bare and the sidewalks dirty. There were no children playing at the water's edge, and only the occasional jogger. What was Tony doing here?

They drove past Edgecliff College on Victory Parkway, passed the magnificent old churches along Madison Road, and continued past the Summit Country Day School and the Cincinnati Country Club until they reached the Grandin Road Viaduct in Mt. Lookout. Was Tony planning to stop, enjoy the view? What would she do if he did?

He didn't. Tony continued along Grandin Road into a lovely residential area filled with spacious homes, wooded grounds, and river views. Was it possible this was where he and Chris were living? Barbara held her breath. Was it possible he was taking her to Chris?

But they drove right past the beautiful homes and landscaped grounds into the recreation area of Alms Park, at the brow of a high hill, before doubling back. Several blocks short of the entrance to the Columbia Parkway, Tony pulled his car to the side of the road and turned off the engine. In the next instant, he was out of the car and walking toward her.

Barbara froze. For one insane second she considered running right over him, then thought of jumping out of the car, fleeing on foot, but she did neither of those things. Instead, she threw her car into park and rolled down her window, watching the smirk plastered across Tony's face grow larger as he drew nearer. To think she'd ever considered him at all attractive. A diamond in the rough, the women had agreed.

"Hi, there, Barbie doll," he was saying, his words riding toward her on a white puff of air. "Enjoy the tour? I normally charge for that, you know."

"You knew I was following you," Barbara said, as much to herself as to Tony.

"Hard to miss that hair, sweetheart." Tony laughed. "Thought I might have lost you a few times along the way, but I got to hand it to you, you stuck right with me. I like that in a woman."

"Where's Chris?" Barbara asked, ignoring the sneer in his voice, the leer in his eyes.

"Chris is home where she belongs, looking after her children, cooking supper for her man. Is that why you were following me? Hoping to catch a glimpse of my bride? And here I thought it was my animal magnetism that had you all hot and bothered." His smile widened as he leaned closer. "Wouldn't mind seeing you all hot and bothered," he said.

"Go to hell."

Tony stiffened. "Go home. Mind your own business. Bad things happen to people who don't mind their own business."

"Are you threatening me?" Barbara asked in disbelief.

But Tony was already walking back to his car. She heard him call something over his shoulder. Half a beat later the message reached her ears: "Drive safely."

Fifteen

Chris walked gingerly down the stairs toward the small laundry room off the garage. She took her time, pausing at each completed step, taking shallow breaths because they caused her less discomfort, cradling Tony's shirts against her still sore ribs, looking neither left nor right, only down at her slippered feet. She didn't want to lose her footing. She couldn't risk another fall. Wasn't that what she'd told the doctors during her last visit to the emergency room—that she'd slipped on some ice, taken a tumble down the outside steps?

"You're sure?" the young intern had asked her, his voice low, the first doctor to question her well-rehearsed routine. "You're sure someone didn't do this to you?" He'd glanced beyond the curtain to where Tony paced impatiently back and forth, the dull thud of his footsteps echoing down the hall. She knew Tony was listening. Listening and waiting.

Waiting for her to make a mistake, to say the wrong thing.

She always did.

The one way in which she'd never disappointed him.

"I slipped on some ice," she'd insisted, as a knowing frown slid across the doctor's boyish face, like a shadow. "No one did this to me."

"What the hell was that all about?" Tony demanded on the drive home. "You were with that guy for almost half an hour. What the hell was going on in there?"

Chris stared out the car's side window, said nothing.

"What? You're not talking to me now? I drive your clumsy ass to the hospital and you don't talk to me? What's the matter, Chris? All talked out? Your new boyfriend has you too tired to talk to your husband? What is it with you anyway? You have to go after every guy you see? You have to embarrass me that way? What the hell is the matter with you?"

"I'm sorry." Tears fell toward her bruised chin, her mind already in their bedroom, trying to prepare herself for the brutality she knew would follow. The thought of her with another man seemed to excite him. He used his unfounded accusations as a stimulant. Such tirades were merely foreplay. The sex that resulted was always violent and nasty, his fist flattened against her mouth to block her screams. It didn't matter. No one ever heard.

They'd moved around a lot since leaving Mariemont, renting first a house in Batavia, then one in Anderson Township, one in Amelia, and now this, a furnished clapboard, two-story cottage in New Richmond. The farther they moved from her friends, the worse the abuse got, as if now that Tony no longer had her friends to worry about, he had the freedom to unleash the full range of his brutality. And why not? There was no one around to stop him.

Chris reached the bottom of the stairs, readjusted the floppy, pink slippers clinging to her otherwise bare feet, smiled at her children grouped around their father in the sparsely furnished living room. Montana was doing her homework; Wyatt was on the floor playing with his Game Boy; Rowdy was curled up in Tony's lap watching *Roseanne*.

"Where are you going?" Wyatt asked in his father's voice, staring at Chris accusingly.

"Laundry." Chris offered up the three shirts in her arms, almost as proof.

"You can do that later, sweetheart," Tony said, extending one arm toward her. "Why don't you sit down and relax for a while?" He patted the empty seat beside him on the worn navy corduroy sofa. "Come on, Chrissy. The laundry's not going anywhere."

He sounded so thoughtful, so reasonable, so loving, Chris thought. If only she could learn not to provoke him, everything would be fine. They could be happy again, like they were at the start of their marriage. Chris closed her eyes, tried to remember the last time she'd felt anything even vaguely approaching happiness.

"What's the matter, Chrissy? Don't you want to keep your husband company?"

Chris heard the threat implicit in her husband's soft voice. Don't be silly, she admonished herself. There was no threat. She was hearing things, just like Tony always said. Putting words in his mouth. Making false assumptions. Jumping to conclusions. Making trouble for herself.

Chris stood in the hallway, unable to move. She shifted from one foot to the other, her body swaying unsteadily as she watched her family huddled together in the other room. Where did she fit in? she wondered. Was there no place for her anywhere?

"Suit yourself," Tony said, withdrawing his invitation, returning his attention to the TV.

Chris remained frozen to the spot, trying to decide which move would cause her the least amount of repercussions later on.

"What are you waiting for?" Tony demanded flatly, his eyes never leaving the television. "Christmas?"

Rowdy exploded into a fit of childish giggles. "Christmas!" he repeated gleefully. "What are you waiting for? Christmas?"

Christmas, Chris repeated silently. She'd barely given a thought to Christmas, and here it was, less than three weeks away. Tony had said something about taking them all out this week to select a tree. Maybe she could talk him into giving her a little extra money so she could buy some cards to send to her friends. She hadn't seen them in so long. They had no idea where she was, that she was still in the greater Cincinnati area. That she was still alive.

"And while you're washing those shirts," Tony said now as she was turning to leave, "you might think about washing that nightgown you're wearing. You look like crap."

"Crap!" Rowdy repeated loudly. "Crap, crap, crap."

"Shut up, dummy," Wyatt ordered, and for an instant Chris thought he might be coming to her defense. She turned back, eyes tearing in gratitude, but all she saw was Wyatt angrily waving the Game Boy in the face of his younger brother. "I messed up because of you! You ruin everything!"

"Mommy!" Rowdy protested, climbing off his father's lap and running toward her, slamming against her knees, so that Tony's shirts flew from her hands, fell to the floor.

Tony was instantly beside them, forcefully removing Rowdy's hands from around Chris's hips. "What are you, some kind of momma's boy—running to your mommy instead of standing up for yourself? Go back in there and give your brother a punch in the nose."

"Tony!"

"Don't you have laundry to do?" Tony asked, as Rowdy ran back into the living room to confront his brother. Chris watched anxiously as a shoving match ensued between the two boys. She reached down, retrieved the shirts from the floor.

Tony smiled, gave her rear end a playful tap as she walked away. He's probably plotting something special for later, she thought, opening the door to the laundry room, closing it behind her, blocking out the sounds of her two sons fighting. Any minute now, Montana would slam down her books and run from the room in frustration, screaming toward her mother, "What's the matter with you? Can't you do anything?" And what could she say in response? Nothing. She was as useless as everybody claimed.

Chris ran the warm water, carefully lowered her husband's shirts into the large basin beside the automatic washer and dryer. Tony had long ago decided that dry cleaners were an unnecessary expense, that he preferred his shirts hand-washed and ironed. Chris had lots of free time. There was no reason she couldn't incorporate washing his shirts into her daily routine. *Hand*-washed, he'd insisted, even after she'd showed him the washing instructions that stated the shirts could be safely machine-washed and dried. The discussion ended with one resounding slap across the face, a slap that sent shock waves clear up to her eye, a slap that left an angry welt on her cheek that took three days to disappear.

At first, Tony used to watch her doing the laundry, criticize her every move. The water was either too hot or too cold, she used too much detergent or not enough, she was either too rough or too gentle on stains, what was the matter with her, couldn't she get anything right?

But after a while he'd grown bored and left her to her own devices, and Chris had discovered she actually enjoyed the ritual of washing Tony's shirts. The feel of her hands in the warm water, the steady motion of her fingers as they worked to get the sweat out of his collars, the subtle rhythm of the wet cotton as it slapped against the side of the white enamel basin. The peace and the quiet. The thrill of being alone. The laundry room became the only place she felt secure, the only room she could call her own.

A room of one's own, she thought, recalling the novel by Virginia Woolf. Susan had lent it to her, and she'd devoured it eagerly. How many years ago was that? A lifetime ago, Chris thought now. Another life where she was neither stupid nor useless. A life that included books and movies and good times. A life where she had a sense of humor, where she was capable of making people laugh, capable of laughing in return. I had such a life once, she remembered, wringing the soap out of Tony's shirts. I had joy. I had love. I had friends.

The Grand Dames, Chris thought with a smile, picturing the four young women perched precariously on the edge of the sandbox in the small park at the end of Grand Avenue. What happened to us?

She still kept track of them. Important details of their lives filtered toward her from a distance, in fits and starts, bits and pieces, like a dream. Occasionally she read about Vicki's exploits in the newspapers, heard about Jeremy's latest acquisition on the evening news. Once, when she was in a hospital waiting room, she'd seen Susan's name listed among the editorial staff in a discarded *Victoria* magazine. Tony had reported to her gleefully about Barbara's divorce. Chris had cried, knowing what Barbara must be going through, wishing she could help her friend, knowing she couldn't. How could she, when she couldn't even help herself?

Chris laid Tony's wet shirts on top of the washing machine and emptied the soapy water from the basin, watching the last of the soap bubbles dance around the drain before being sucked out of sight. Her life had slipped through her fingers just as effortlessly, she thought. It had disappeared before her eyes.

"What are you doing in there, Chris?" she heard Tony call. "How long does it take to wash a couple of shirts?"

"I'm almost done." Chris quickly ran the cold water to rinse out the shirts.

"I'm feeling a little hungry. Think you might like to fix your husband a sandwich?"

"In a minute."

"Make sure you don't wrinkle the collars like you did last time."

Chris's hands worked furiously to press the wrinkles out of the wet collars of Tony's pale blue shirts. But they were old shirts and they wrinkled easily. No matter how carefully she washed them, how meticulously she ironed them, still the collars wrinkled. "Damn these shirts," she whispered, panic building as her fingers unsuccessfully kneaded the stubborn fabric. "Damn these stupid shirts."

Tony's knuckles wrapped against the door. "Chris, what are you doing in there, honey?" The door opened. His head popped through. He was smiling. Chris held her breath. "I got you a little present," he said, his smile growing mischievous.

"A present?"

"For later."

Chris felt her heartbeat quicken, her mouth go dry.

"I'll leave it on the bed."

Chris nodded.

"Hurry up with those shirts," he said.

Just after the eleven-o'clock news, Tony announced it was time for bed. Montana groaned but otherwise offered no resistance. The boys were already in their rooms, although Chris doubted Wyatt was asleep. She pictured him under his covers furiously manipulating the controls of his Game Boy in the dark, and smiled. Any room for me under there? she wondered, wishing she could disappear as easily. But there was no room for her anywhere. She knew that. Especially in her children's lives. Tony had made sure of that. To them she was little more than a glorified housekeeper, someone they barked orders at or ignored, in equal measures.

Chris wasn't surprised at the boys—she'd pretty much expected they would follow their father's example. Rowdy was seven years old and growing up fast, and while she was still the one he ran to whenever anything went wrong, that would soon stop. Already she could feel she was losing him. Another six months, maybe a year—he'd be gone. Wyatt, she understood sadly, had never been hers. His father's son since the day he'd pushed himself roughly out of her womb.

It was Montana who surprised Chris the most. She'd always clung to the notion that Montana would see through her father's manipulations, his not-so-subtle bullying, his outright abuse. Maybe not when she was Rowdy's age, or even Wyatt's. But surely Montana was old enough now to grasp what was really going on. And yet, she blithely swallowed each sorry tale of her mother's supposed clumsiness, accepting as fact that her mother was simply "accident-prone." She ignored the evidence of her own eyes as steadfastly as she ignored the fear in Chris's. She had little patience, even less sympathy, for her mother's plight. Indeed, if Montana sympathized with anyone, it was her father. How could that be?

Chris recalled an article she'd read in the paper about how women jurors were often less sympathetic than their male counterparts to victims of rape. It was the women's way of distancing themselves from the victim, the article claimed. If the women jurors could find some way to hold the victim at least partly accountable for what had happened, then it made them feel safer, assured them that such a horrible fate could never be theirs. Sympathize with the victim—feel vulnerable. Identify with the abuser—feel powerful. Feel helpless or feel in control. That was the choice she was offering her daughter.

No wonder Montana chose to side with her father. What other option did she have?

"Well, what are you waiting for?" Tony was saying now, sitting on the end of the double bed, watching Chris as she turned over the small parcel in her hand. "Open it."

Chris quickly tore at the lurid purple tissue paper across which *Hot Times* was stamped at regular intervals in large hot-pink letters. She closed her eyes. Please, just let it be a scarf, she prayed, and almost laughed. Who said she had no sense of humor?

"Do you like it?"

Chris forced her eyes open, although she didn't have to see it to know what it was. Her drawers were full of cheap black teddies, frilly garter belts and stockings, uncomfortable red bustiers. Tony regularly bought them for her, insisted she wear them while parading around in front of him, striking *Penthouse*-style poses, all as a prelude to increasingly kinky sex. Dear God, what did he have in store for her tonight? Chris stared down at the sheer, lavender push-up bra and bikini panties, both trimmed with fake fur, a flowing chiffon cape attached to the bra's straps. He can't be serious, Chris thought, and might have laughed had she not been so horrified. "I can't wear this," she said, the words out of her mouth before she could stop them.

Tony was instantly on his feet, advancing toward her. "Why not? Don't you like it?"

Chris began backing up. "It's too small, Tony. I can tell just by looking at it."

"Too small's half the fun." He pressed himself against her, rubbed his hand between her legs. "Come on, Chris. Put it on."

Chris waited until he removed his hand, then shuffled shakily toward the bathroom. What was the matter with her? Why was she giving him a hard time? She was only prolonging the inevitable. Hadn't she learned anything by now?

Tony's voice stopped her at the bathroom door. "I've been thinking about your friend Barbara."

Chris turned around slowly, afraid to respond. Where was this coming from?

"I ran into her a few weeks back. Did I tell you?"

"You saw Barbara?"

"Did I forget to mention it?"

Chris nodded, knowing Tony never forgot a thing. "How is she?"

"Looks great."

Chris smiled, pictured her friend in her mind's eye, wondering how the years had changed her. "What did she say? Did she ask about me?"

"What did she say? Did she ask about me?" Tony mimicked cruelly. "Listen to yourself. You'd think you were lovers the way you're carrying on."

"I just meant . . ."

"Why don't you give the Barbie doll a call," Tony suggested suddenly.

"What?" Surely she'd heard him incorrectly.

"Call her up, seeing as you're so interested in how she's doing."

"I don't understand."

"She must be pretty lonely living in that ugly old house, no one to talk to but a teenage girl. She's probably getting a little desperate for some male companionship. How long you think it's been since she got laid?"

Chris said nothing, her mind racing ahead, trying to figure out where this conversation was going.

"How long?" Tony repeated.

"I don't know."

"Long enough, I bet. Which is a shame. She's looking pretty damn good, I tell you."

Chris twisted the flimsy undergarments she was holding until they disappeared into a tight little ball. "You wouldn't mind if I called her?"

"Why would I mind? Hell, call the Barbie doll. Invite her over."

"Invite her over? When?"

"When? When do you think? Tonight. Right now."

"Now?" What was he getting at? "It's late, Tony. She won't come over now."

"Sure she will. First sound of your voice, she'll be halfway out the door. She'll be here before you've had a chance to hang up the phone."

And then what? Chris wondered. "And then what?"

"And then we let nature take its course." Tony paused, ran a suggestive tongue along his bottom lip. "The three of us."

Chris shook her head. He had to be joking. Was he really hinting at a threesome involving her and her closest friend? That he thought there was even the remotest of possibilities Barbara might agree?

"What's the problem, Chrissy? You want to keep your little friend all to yourself?"

"You can't be serious," Chris whispered, aching to run for the phone, to call her friend, if only to hear her voice again.

"Didn't your mother ever teach you to share? Didn't she teach you it's not polite to keep your toys to yourself?"

"This is crazy talk, Tony."

"Excuse me? What did you say?" His head cocked to one side. "What's going on here, Chrissy? Am I going to have to teach you a lesson? Is that what you're going to make me do?"

Chris looked frantically from one dull mustard-colored wall to another, sweat breaking out across her forehead and upper lip. "Look, let me change into this nice outfit you bought me." She began unraveling it, smoothing it out across her thighs. "We don't need anyone else to have a good time."

"I see how you look at other women, Chris. I know you'd like to have a taste of some of that for yourself. I'm just trying to do something nice for you."

"You're the only one I want, Tony."

"Is that so?"

"You know it is."

"Because sometimes I don't feel appreciated," he was saying, as if talking to himself. "Sometimes I go to all the time and trouble to buy you something nice"—he indicated the still-crumpled lingerie in Chris's hands—"and you don't seem real happy about it. That's why I got to thinking that maybe you'd be happier if we were to bring another person into our lovemaking."

Oh, God, Chris thought. How long had this idea been brewing?

"It doesn't have to be the Barbie doll, if that would make you too uncomfortable. We could find somebody else."

"Really, Tony. I don't want anybody else. You're all I need."

"Is that so?"

She nodded vigorously. "Let me prove it to you. Please Tony, let me prove it to you."

"Get changed."

Chris ran into the bathroom, closed the door behind her, tears falling down her cheeks as her fingers scrambled with the top buttons of her nightgown. "Please, God, help me." What was she going to do? She knew Tony well enough to know that this latest idea hadn't just popped into his head, that he'd been mulling it over for some time, waiting for the right time to spring it on her. And it wouldn't go away. Just because he'd temporarily put aside such thoughts didn't mean he'd forget about them. No, Chris thought, pulling her nightgown over her head and stepping into the sheer, lavender panties with their ridiculous fake-fur trim, pulling them awkwardly over her hips. There was no way Tony was going to let go of this latest obscenity until he got her to agree. "I can't do it," she whispered, snapping on the ill-fitting bra with its ludicrous flowing chiffon cape. "I won't do it."

Except that he would make her do it, she knew. He would berate her and bully her and beat her until she not only gave in, she volunteered. Just as she'd done tonight. Hadn't she begged him? "You're all I need," she'd repeated more than once. "Please, Tony, let me prove it to you."

"You disgust me." She spat at the image in the mirror, watched a trickle of spit run down the glass. "Wonder Woman," she sneered, flicking at the fur-trimmed, lavender chiffon cape hanging limply down her back, thinking of her three children in their rooms down the hall, what they would think if they saw their mother dressed up like some sort of obscene cartoon. What the hell, she thought, opening the bathroom door, leaping into the bedroom, as if leaping off a tall cliff. "It's Supermom!" she announced, knowing she'd taken leave of her senses, that Tony would find nothing funny about her impromptu display, that she was courting disaster, sealing her fate, signing her own death certificate. Had she done so deliberately?

She prepared herself for Tony's fury, braced herself for his fists. Let's just get this over with, she thought. Finish me off. You can do it. One good kick to the head and it would all be mercifully over. Lavender Woman bites the dust!

Except that Tony kept his hands at his side, his feet on the thin brown broadloom. He stared at her calmly, his lips a flat line, his dark eyes hollow. Chris looked at him and understood that she was staring at her worst nightmare, that everything that had come before this moment was nothing compared to what was about to follow. "You think this is a joke?" he asked, his voice low, steady, controlled.

"I was just trying . . ."

"I'm just a big joke to you. Is that it?"

"No. Of course you're not."

"Call the Barbie doll."

"What?"

"Prove I'm not a big joke to you." Tony reached for the phone. "Enough of your stupid games. Call the Barbie doll right now. Invite her over. Now."

"I can't," Chris heard herself mutter. Then more strongly: "I won't."

"Can't?" Tony repeated wondrously, as if hearing the word for the first time. "Won't?" He made a face, as if he'd bitten into something sour.

Chris shook her head. There was no way she was going to call Barbara. No matter what Tony threatened, no matter what he did, no matter how desperately she wanted to see her, hear her voice. "I'll leave," she whispered, the words crashing against her skull with the ferocity of an unbridled scream. Immediately she tried to swallow the unexpected words, push them back down her throat, but it was too late. Already Tony was advancing toward her, one arm outstretched, angry fingers clawing at the air, a staccato burst of words, like machine-gun fire, shooting from his mouth.

"What did you say? You're going to leave? Is that what you said?"

"Tony, please . . ."

"You want to leave? Right now? Dressed like that? By all means." He grabbed Chris by the elbow, pushed her toward the hall.

"What are you doing? Tony, stop! Let go of me."

"Stop yelling, Chris. You want to wake the children?" He pushed her toward the stairs. "You want them to see you like this? Do you want their last image of their mother to be this?" He flipped the chiffon cape up over her head. It fell across her eyes like a veil.

Chris grabbed the banister, fought to stay upright as Tony pulled her fingers from the railing, kicked her feet out from under her, forced her down the top two stairs. "Last image? What are you talking about?"

"You think you'll ever see your kids again?" Tony grabbed

the flowing lavender cape and yanked Chris to her feet. "Get up! You want to leave? Go! Get the hell out of my house!"

"What are you doing? You can't throw me out dressed like this!"

Tony said nothing as he continued pushing Chris down the stairs. Every time she stumbled, he yanked her back up, pushed her farther down. She lost her footing, slipped down the last few steps, landed on her knees at the bottom of the stairs.

"Please, Tony. Let me put something on."

But he was already behind her, grabbing her arms, dragging her toward the front door. Dear God, was he really going to throw her outside in the freezing December cold in nothing but her underwear? With bare feet and no money? With nothing on her back but a goddamn chiffon cape?

"You can't do this!"

"Watch me." Tony opened the front door with one hand, pulled Chris toward it with the other.

Snow-filled wind swirled toward her, snapping at her exposed flesh. "No, Tony!" she screamed. "Don't do this! At least let me get dressed!"

He stopped. "Maybe some fresh air will clear your head," he announced calmly. Then he grabbed Chris beneath both arms and hurled her out the front door.

"Tony!"

The door slammed shut in her face.

"Tony!" Chris banged furiously on the door, the terrible cold of the landing burning into her bare feet, as if she were standing on hot coals. "Tony!"

She took several steps back, glanced frantically around

the empty, snow-dusted street, wondering what to do next. Shivering, she looked up at the house to see Montana watching from her bedroom window. “Montana,” she cried out, but the word was carried away by a gust of icy wind. Chris watched helplessly as her daughter turned away from the window and, one by one, all the lights in the house went dark.

Sixteen

Barbara was in bed, trying to get past the first chapter of a book everyone said was wonderful, but she was having a hard time concentrating. She'd read the last paragraph at least four times, and still she had no idea what it said. She flipped the book closed, dropped it to her knees. Beside her, Tracey lay sleeping, her pillow flattened across her eyes to block out the bedside light. "Sweet girl," Barbara whispered. "What would I do without you?" She returned the book to the night table and switched off the lamp, then carefully removed the pillow from Tracey's face and smoothed the matted hair away from her forehead, absorbing her daughter with her eyes, the way a sponge absorbs water. Tracey stirred, flipped onto her back. Her eyes fluttered, as if they were about to open.

"Tracey?" Barbara asked hopefully. Sometimes Tracey's subconscious seemed to sense when Barbara couldn't sleep, and she'd wake up, prop herself up in bed, and they'd talk. About movies, fashion, cosmetics, celebrities. Barbara realized that she was the one who did most of the talking, Tracey the bulk of the listening. Sometimes Barbara would go further—confide her fears, her disappointments, her insecurities, and Tracey would calmly reassure her. Occasionally Barbara thought she might be piling too much on Tracey's adolescent shoulders. But Tracey never complained. She seemed comfortable in her role as the designated adult. When had their roles reversed? Barbara wondered now. When had the thirteen-year-old girl in the blue-and-white polka-dot flannel pajamas become the parent and she the child? Wasn't she the one who was supposed to know everything, the one who was supposed to be wise and capable and patient and strong? Instead, she was foolish, inept, weak. A fraud. She knew nothing. Did Tracey sense that? Was that why she shared so little of herself with her mother?

Not that Tracey was secretive or rude or even difficult. No, her daughter was unfailingly polite, supportive, sweet. She answered all her mother's questions—about school, her friends, boys—with candor and ease. In a nutshell, school was fine, her friends were great, there were a few boys hovering on the horizon. When Barbara occasionally pressed her for more details, Tracey provided them immediately, relaying the mundane facts of her days with precision and care, as if she were reciting a poem in front of her class. She seemed to have no real ambition, no burning desire to be this or that, and as a consequence, was rarely, if ever, disappointed or depressed. She'd taken her parents' divorce in her stride, adapted well to her growing new family, went on about the business of getting on with her life in a way her mother could only stand back and admire because she was so incapable of doing it herself.

"Tracey?" Barbara asked again, but Tracey's eyes remained stubbornly closed.

Barbara stroked her daughter's cheeks, understanding she didn't know her only child very well at all.

You're doing a wonderful job, her friends assured her. Tracey's a great kid, they agreed.

Which couldn't be said of all the daughters of Grand Avenue.

While Vicki's daughter, Kirsten, had turned out remarkably well—remarkable in light of the fact she'd been raised by a succession of nannies and rarely saw her mother at all, a direct reflection of how Vicki herself had been raised, Barbara realized—Susan's first-born, Ariel, was a sullen child at best, and downright surly at her worst. Which was most of the time, according to her mother. Ariel was rebellious and combative, quick to anger and slow to forgive, in almost every way the exact opposite of Susan.

As for Chris's daughter, Montana . . .

Barbara said a silent prayer, then closed her eyes. Chris had rarely left her thoughts since her run-in with Tony several weeks earlier. But she couldn't afford to think about Chris now. If she allowed Chris entry into her thoughts, she'd be there all night, and it was late, she was tired, it was time to get some sleep. Barbara flopped onto her back, thoughts of Chris circling behind her eyes, like a lost plane searching for a runway in the dark.

She told herself to relax. Start with your toes, she remembered reading in a recent issue of *Victoria*. Toes, relax, she instructed silently, feeling them twitch beneath the covers. Now move up your body slowly. First your feet. Feet, relax. Now the ankles. Ankles, relax. Probably if she were to start wearing more practical shoes, her feet wouldn't take so long to get comfortable, Barbara thought. Calves, relax. Now the knees. Next the thighs. My big fat thighs, Barbara thought impatiently. She used to have such great legs, won the bathing suit competition hands down. Now look at them! No, don't look at them. All you'd see was cellulite and varicose veins and unsightly ingrown hairs. "Legs, relax," Barbara ordered out loud, bouncing restlessly on the bed. Now your ass, she thought. Oh, that's a good one. My big, fat, ever-expanding rear end. If she relaxed it any further, it would take over the whole bed. "Relax, damn you," Barbara hissed, her thoughts wrapping around her stomach. My big, fat, bloated stomach, Barbara thought with disgust. Stupid goddamn thing. First thing in the morning, she was calling Dr. Steeves, making an appointment, to hell with the pain, to hell with what it cost, to hell with everything.

Barbara lurched up in bed and threw off her covers. Well, that little exercise was a roaring success, she thought, her adrenaline pumping. She might as well have mainlined a dose of caffeine. Now she'd be up all night. "Goddamnit!" She searched out Tracey in the dark. "Tracey? Tracey, are you awake?"

Tracey's response was to sigh, roll over onto her side, face the opposite wall.

"Damn." Barbara's head turned restlessly from side to side. She debated getting out of bed, going to the bathroom, decided she couldn't be bothered. She reached for her book, grabbed the phone instead. "Almost midnight," she noted with satisfaction, punching in the numbers her fingers knew by heart. "You should be all comfy by now."

The phone rang once . . . twice . . .

"Hello?" The young woman's voice was heavy with sleep.

Barbara smiled. Oh, you poor thing, did I wake you?

"Hello?" the voice asked again.

Stupid girl, Barbara thought. You'd think she'd learn.

"Barbara, is that you?" Pam asked suddenly.

Barbara dropped the phone into its carriage, her fingers burning as if they'd been sprayed with acid. Her heart was pounding so wildly it threatened to burst out of her chest. Dear God, what had she done?

Calm down. Relax. "Heart, relax," she said, and laughed out loud, a high-pitched shriek that chipped at the darkness like a pick through ice.

"Mom?" Tracey murmured, turning her head toward her mother.

"It's okay, sweetie." Barbara patted her daughter's shoulder. "I just had a bad dream. Go back to sleep."

It's okay, she repeated silently. Everything was all right. Pam was just guessing, throwing out the first name that popped into her head. There was no way she could prove anything. It's okay. Lie down. Try to get some sleep.

It took a few minutes, but gradually Barbara's heartbeat returned to normal. Exhausted, frightened, spent, she finally drifted into a restless sleep in which she was being chased down Grand Avenue by a rabid Doberman. The dog was nipping at her heels, about to take a bite of her flesh, when it suddenly stopped, turned its head, listened. To what? Barbara found herself wondering.

Then she heard the noise.

Barbara bolted up in bed, glanced at the clock. Ten minutes

after midnight. She waited, deciding the noise had been part of her dream, praying the phone call to Pam had been part of that same dream. She was about to lie back down when she heard the noise again.

What was it?

Her first thought was that it must be Tracey, that she'd gotten up, gone to the kitchen to make herself a snack. But Tracey was sleeping soundly beside her, Barbara understood without looking, which meant it was something else, some*one* else, and that someone was moving around downstairs. A burglar?

Why would a burglar choose her house when there were so many nicer homes on the street, homes that didn't speak of abandonment and neglect? Why would anyone choose this house?

Unless they knew who lived here. Unless there was a personal reason for the visit.

Tony.

It had to be, Barbara realized, holding her breath. He'd threatened her. *Bad things happen to people who don't mind their own business,* he'd said. Those were his exact words. And now he was here to make good on his threat.

Dear God, what could she do? If he so much as touched Tracey . . .

Barbara was reaching for the phone to call 911 when she felt the dull thud of footsteps on the stairs, heard the familiar voice.

"Barbara," the voice said, then again, with greater insistence, "Barbara."

She closed her eyes, not sure whether to laugh or cry. She

didn't have to ask who it was. She knew that voice as well as her own. Wordlessly, Barbara climbed out of bed and gathered a dark blue housecoat over her powder blue nightgown. She glanced back at Tracey, still sleeping soundly, then pushed her feet toward the hall.

He was waiting for her at the top of the stairs, angry shoulders rigid beneath his heavy winter coat.

"What are you doing here?" she asked.

"What the hell are *you* doing?" he asked in return.

Barbara brought her fingers to her lips. "Tracey's asleep," she whispered. "We should go downstairs."

"What the hell do you think you're doing?" he asked again before they reached the living room.

"I might ask you the same thing," Barbara said, feeling surprisingly calm as she confronted her ex-husband face-to-face. Didn't Vicki always claim the best defense was a good offense? "How did you get in?"

"I have a key," Ron reminded her.

"I'd like it back."

"This is my house."

"Not anymore. You have no right to come barging in here in the middle of the night."

"*I* have no right?"

"Could you lower your voice please? I don't think you want Tracey to hear you."

"Maybe I do. Maybe I think it's time Tracey found out what her mother does with her spare time."

Oh, God. "Ron, this is unnecessary."

"Unnecessary? *Unnecessary?"*

"Please, let's just calm down."

Ron paced back and forth in front of her, waving his hands in all directions at once, so that flakes of snow flew off his black coat, as if he'd brought the weather inside. Even in his fury, he was handsome, Barbara couldn't stop herself from thinking. Even now, she had to fight the urge to throw herself into those angry arms, beg him to come back to her. What was the matter with her? Had she no self-respect?

"What the hell do you think you're doing, calling my house at all hours of the night, upsetting my wife?"

"I don't know what you're talking about." Did she really expect him to believe that?

"Don't bullshit me, Barbara. I know it's you making those calls. What I don't know is why. You get some sort of perverse thrill from upsetting my family? Is that what it is? Because I've had it. We've all had it. And I'm here to warn you that if it doesn't stop, and stop right now, I'm going to the police."

"The police?"

"And the courts."

"The courts? What are you talking about?" What was happening? When had she lost control of the conversation, the situation? What had happened to her best defense?

The separation agreement appeared miraculously in Ron's hands. He waved it in front of her face. "This isn't written in stone, you know. If I have to, I'll go back to court."

Barbara heard Tracey's footsteps overhead, understood her daughter was listening at the top of the stairs. "I think you need to calm down."

"I've had it, Barbara. I'm warning you. One more call, I make a few calls of my own."

"There won't be any more calls," Barbara said quietly, watching Ron's hands fall to his sides.

"Place is a mess," he said, almost to himself.

Barbara looked at the fashion magazines scattered across the floor, at the water marks on the coffee table in front of the crumpled green floral sofa. He was right—even softened by the moonlight, the place was a mess. "I had to cut back on the cleaning lady. There isn't enough money."

"I give you plenty of money."

"It's not enough."

"It's more than enough."

"This house is expensive to maintain."

"So, sell it."

"And give you half?"

"That's the deal you signed."

"The deal says I get to stay here until Tracey finishes high school."

"In a house you can't afford to maintain properly?"

"In a house I love."

"You could find something smaller."

"I don't want anything smaller."

"You could rent, for God's sake. Or buy a condo. There's all sorts of great deals on the market right now."

"I don't want a condo. I don't want to rent," Barbara told him, trying to keep up with the conversation. "I don't want to uproot Tracey."

"Tracey is fine. She'd have no problem with moving."

"*I'd* have a problem with moving."

"Why? Half your friends have moved away. What's keeping you here except spite?"

"I don't have to justify myself to you."

"I'm a professor, Barbara," he said, trying to sound reasonable. "I don't make a lot of money. I can't afford to maintain two families."

"Maybe you should have thought of that before you left," Barbara said bitterly, "before you decided to have more children."

"Is that what this is about?" The look in Ron's eyes hovered between pity and contempt. "That I have a son? That Pam and I are expecting another baby?"

"Tracey is your child too."

"I know that. And I fully intend to provide for Tracey. Be reasonable, Barbara. It's not like I'm asking you to live on the streets."

"I won't leave Grand Avenue."

"You're just doing this out of spite."

"Doing what? Surviving?"

"Surviving very nicely I'd say, judging by my Visa bills."

"That was your idea."

"The idea was that it be used only in the event of an emergency."

"Really? That's not how I interpreted it."

"It doesn't matter," Ron said, shaking his head resolutely. "As of this minute, consider your credit canceled."

"What?"

"Your credit's no good, lady."

"You can't do that."

"Just watch me."

"I'll call my lawyer."

"And I'll call mine. I'm sure a judge will be very understanding of the three-thousand-dollar Armani emergency you had last month, especially in light of the late-night phone calls you've been making to my house."

Barbara glanced toward the stairs. "Would you please lower your voice!"

"Do me a favor, would you, Barbara? Next time you go to the doctor for a face-lift, have your head examined."

The force of Ron's venom slammed Barbara back against the wall. "Get out of here," she said quietly, too numb to move. "I want you out of my house right now."

Ron gathered his coat around him, strode toward the front door. "You need help, Barbara. You've turned into a bitter, bloodsucking, dried-up old prune, and all the plastic surgery in the world isn't going to do a damn thing to change that."

The front door slammed shut behind him. Immediately Barbara's knees gave way, collapsing under her. She slithered down the wall to the floor, lay in a crumpled heap, like laundry someone had piled up, then forgotten.

She was still sitting there when Tracey ventured meekly down the stairs a few minutes later. "Mom? Mom, are you all right?"

Barbara nodded, said nothing, not trusting her voice.

"He's just angry," Tracey said, kneeling beside her mother on the tired green broadloom. "You know he didn't mean any of the things he said. Mom?"

The word trailed a host of unspoken sentences behind it. Mom, what was Dad doing here? Mom, why was he so upset? What phone calls was he talking about? Mom, please talk to me. Tell me what tonight was really all about. Was it my fault?

"Mom?"

Barbara smiled at Tracey through eyes heavy with tears, amazed, as she always was, by the miracle she'd produced. Tracey stared back at her mother with round, dark eyes that revealed nothing. What does she really think of me? Barbara wondered, reaching up, gently stroking her daughter's hair, her fingers becoming enmeshed in the twisted maze of sleep-tossed curls. Does she see what Ron sees—a pathetic, middle-aged divorcée, abandoned by her husband, left sitting alone in the dark, clinging to fading dreams of past glories? A bitter, bloodsucking, dried-up old prune? "You should be asleep," Barbara said to her daughter.

"So should you."

Maybe she should take Ron's advice, however acrimoniously it had been hurled at her head, and see a therapist, someone who could help her deal with her problems, someone who could help her get on with her life. Except that therapists cost money, and Ron had informed her in no uncertain terms that the bank was closed. "You should go to bed," Barbara told Tracey.

"So should you."

"You go, sweetie. I'll be up in a few minutes."

"I'll wait."

"No, you go," Barbara insisted. "Please, sweetie. I'll be fine. I just need a few minutes."

Tracey looked at her mother through eyes too tired to argue, then pushed herself to her bare feet. "You promise you won't be long?"

"Two minutes."

Tracey leaned down, kissed her mother on the forehead, then slowly backed out of the room.

"Thank you," Barbara said.

"For what?"

"For taking such good care of me."

"Try not to think about what Daddy said," Tracey advised, as if she could read her mother's thoughts, as if they were emblazoned on her forehead, as if they were glowing in the dark.

"It's already forgotten," Barbara lied, closing her eyes to the soothing blackness that surrounded her as Tracey reluctantly left her side.

"Mom?" Tracey called down from upstairs almost immediately. "It's two minutes. Are you coming up?"

With a weary smile, Barbara pushed herself off the floor, walking, as if in a trance, toward the stairs. She was on the first step, her hand on the railing, when she heard a car in the driveway, footsteps on the front path. Ron? she wondered. Returning to spew more hatred at her, to share some choice words he'd forgotten during the first go-round? Would he knock this time or just use his key? She'd have to go to the hardware store tomorrow, arrange for all the locks to be changed. Send Rotten Ron the bill. Show him the dried-up old prune had a few more wrinkles up her sleeve.

But the knock on the door was gentle, even timid, although as she hesitated, it was growing in insistency. Barbara approached the door slowly, stared through the peephole into the bitterly cold night. "Oh, my God."

"Mom," Tracey called from upstairs. "Who is it?"

Barbara opened the door and extended her arms. In the next instant, Chris collapsed inside them.

Seventeen

My God, what happened to you?" Barbara's hands fluttered all around Chris, not sure where to land. She touched her trembling shoulders, her snow-dampened hair, her tearstained face. "Tracey, bring me some blankets. Hurry!"

Chris looked back toward the driveway, at the cabdriver who was leaning against the car door, watching nervously. "It's his jacket," she whispered hoarsely, slipping the ratty black leather jacket off her shoulders. Barbara caught it before it reached the floor. "I don't have any money."

"We'll take care of it." Barbara wondered what the hell was going on tonight. Had everyone gone crazy? There wasn't even a full moon, she thought distractedly as Tracey raced down the stairs with an armload of blue and green blankets that Barbara immediately wrapped around Chris. Dear God, what was she wearing? "Give this jacket back to the cabbie and get some money out of my purse," Barbara instructed Tracey while leading Chris toward the living room. "And I need some heavy socks," she called out as Tracey ran upstairs to get her mother's purse. "I can't believe you were out in that freezing cold with bare feet. Your poor toes," she said, massaging them.

"I'll make some hot tea," Tracey volunteered minutes later, having returned from paying the cabdriver, assuring him that everything was fine. "Are you all right, Mrs. Malarek?" She watched her mother slip the heavy gray-and-white gym socks over Chris's blue-tinged feet.

Chris's body was shaking so hard, it was impossible to know whether the nod she offered was intended or not.

"Are the socks okay?"

"They're fine, sweetheart," Barbara told Tracey. "And tea would be great."

Barbara quickly enveloped her shaking friend in her arms, rocked her gently back and forth, like a baby. She couldn't believe Chris was actually here, that she was holding her in her arms. How she'd longed to see her. And how beautiful Chris was, despite the passage of time, the horrors she'd undoubtedly endured. Barbara kissed Chris's icy forehead, her bitterly cold cheek, and watched the years, the pain, melt away. Suddenly, they were back in the sandbox at the far end of Grand Avenue. They were laughing and happy and carefree, like the children playing at their feet. Nothing bad could ever happen to them. Not as long as they had each other. "Can you tell me what happened?"

Chris stared at Barbara with confused, terrified eyes. "Tony and I had a terrible fight." She trembled, but Barbara couldn't tell whether it was from the cold or from the memory. "He bought me this." Chris opened the front of the blankets, stared blankly at the costume she was wearing. "He insisted I put it on. Can you believe it?" she asked in growing disbelief. "I mean, I felt like such an idiot in it, with this stupid fur trim and flowing cape. I couldn't believe he was really serious."

Barbara glanced toward the kitchen, heard Tracey at the sink, pouring water into the kettle. "What happened?"

"I tried to make a joke. 'It's Supermom,' I said. I thought maybe he'd laugh, but he got so mad. I've never seen him so angry."

"Did he hit you?"

Chris regarded her curiously, the question taking a long time to sink in, as if it had to penetrate layers of frozen skin to reach her. "No," she said after a long pause. "Isn't that strange? He didn't hit me."

"Why is that strange?"

"Because he always hits me."

Barbara felt her cheeks flush with shame. "What happened, Chris? What made you run out of the house without any money, without even getting dressed? Because we can call the police . . ."

"Please don't call the police."

"Why not? If he threatened you—"

"He didn't threaten me."

"What *did* he do?"

"He threw me out." Chris laughed, a brittle sound that snapped upon contact with the air, like an icicle from an eaves trough.

"He threw you out of the house practically naked?"

"Please don't call the police."

"Why not? The man's a lunatic. You could have frozen to death."

"He told me I'd never see my children again."

"Well, he's full of shit," Barbara said adamantly. "If anyone won't see his kids again, it'll be him."

Chris tried to smile. "He can't stop me from seeing my kids, can he, Barbara?"

"Of course not. We'll call Vicki first thing in the morning. She'll know who you should talk to."

"If we call the police, it'll only make things worse."

"How could it make things any worse? They'll arrest the bastard, Chris. Take him to jail."

"He'll get out, come back. It's my word against his. And the children's," Chris added softly. "He can't stop me from seeing my kids, can he?"

Barbara heard the kettle whistling in the kitchen. "No, he can't stop you from seeing your kids."

In the next minute, Tracey appeared with two mugs of steaming tea. "It's herbal." She pushed several magazines out of the way as she deposited the mugs on the coffee table in front of the sofa. "Strawberry-kiwi. It's new."

"Thank you." Chris leaned forward, warmed her hands over the rising steam.

The comforting smell of exotic fruit filled the air. "Thank you, sweetheart," Barbara said, feeling a tremendous sense of pride in her only child. Let Ron produce baby after baby with his young bride. She'd already gotten the best of his seed. "Why don't you go back to bed now, darling? You have school in the morning."

"Can I get you anything else, Mrs. Malarek? Some cookies, maybe?"

"No, thank you, Tracey. You're very sweet."

Tracey lingered, shifting from one bare foot to the other, as if trying to imagine what it would be like to have snow between her toes, ice clinging to her heels. "Good night, Mrs. Malarek. Good night, Mom. I'll be in my room, if you need anything." She kissed her mother's cheek, disappeared upstairs.

Barbara lifted one of the mugs from the table, held it close to Chris's lips, watched Chris slowly suck at the air, coaxing the hot liquid inside her mouth.

"It's good," Chris said, taking the mug from Barbara's hand, surrounding it with her own.

"So, he just threw you out into the street," Barbara prodded, needing to put the facts into context, to hear the details that would make the story make sense. Had Chris run to her neighbors? Had they refused to take her in? How had she found a cab to take her to Mariemont at almost one o'clock in the morning, looking like some mad escapee from a horror movie?

"I didn't know what to do." Chris's eyes darted back and forth, as if looking for answers. "I couldn't believe what was happening, that Tony had thrown me out of the house practically naked, that I was really standing outside in the freezing cold with no coat and no shoes and no money, and he wouldn't let me back inside. I banged on the door. I ran around to the back. I even thought of breaking one of the windows. But I was afraid if I did that, he'd get even angrier. And then I thought . . . oh God, this is terrible because my kids are still there . . . I thought, no, I don't want to go back inside that house. I'm out. I'm actually out. He's not standing over me.

He's not breathing down my neck. He's not forcing his way inside me."

"Oh, God."

"I'm free." Chris looked around Barbara's living room in grateful disbelief. "I'm out."

Tears filled Barbara's eyes. "Yes, you are. You never have to go back there."

"But my kids . . ."

"We'll get your kids out of there. No court in the land would give that monster custody."

Chris nodded, took another long sip of her tea. "I thought of going to the neighbors," she continued, picking up the thread of her narrative. "But it was almost midnight. Everyone's house was dark. I knew they'd all be asleep. I couldn't wake people up, people I barely know, let them see me this way. So I just started running."

"You ran? Where? How?"

"I don't know. In circles. I slipped, fell a few times, finally found myself on a main street. Some cars went by and honked, but nobody stopped. I think I probably scared them. And then suddenly, there was this cab. And it pulled over, and the driver didn't speak much English, but he knew I was in trouble, and he said he'd take me to the hospital or to the police, but I said, no, take me to Mariemont, to my friend Barbara, that you'd pay him when we got here. And then he took off his jacket and wrapped it around me." Her voice trailed off. She looked toward the front door.

"It's been taken care of," Barbara reminded her.

"Yes. Thank you." Chris finished the rest of her tea, returned the mug to the table.

Immediately Barbara put the second of the hot mugs into Chris's hands. "Did the kids hear anything of what went on?" Barbara was thinking of Tracey listening at the top of the stairs during her earlier confrontation with Ron. Say what you will about the SOB, Barbara thought now, at least he wasn't Tony.

"The boys were asleep."

"And Montana?"

Chris shook her head, as if she didn't know. Tears began falling the length of her cheeks.

"You'll be all right. You're safe now. He can't hurt you anymore."

"He has my kids."

"Not for long. We'll call Vicki first thing in the morning. She'll know what to do. In the meantime, you're going to stay here with me. And as soon as we get your kids, they'll stay here too, at least until everything gets sorted out. Which it will, I promise. Now, let's go upstairs. You're going to get out of those ridiculous clothes and I'm going to pour you a nice hot bath, and you're going to get a good night's sleep. How does that sound?"

Chris smiled. "Too good to be true."

Barbara sat on the side of the tub, watching the water gush from the tap, occasionally stretching her hand toward the flow, checking and adjusting the temperature. Hot, but not too hot. Not so hot Chris wouldn't be able to sit down comfortably. No way she wanted to add to her injuries. Dear God, what had the woman been through? Clearly, the things she'd told Barbara tonight were just the tip of the iceberg. Although why should that surprise her? Hadn't Tony been abusing Chris for years? Hadn't he hacked off her hair, for God's sake? And hadn't she sat back—hadn't they all sat back—and done absolutely nothing?

The Grand Dames. Friends for life.

Some friends.

Barbara closed her eyes in shame and regret. It was too easy to conclude there was nothing anyone could have done. Too easy to put the responsibility squarely on Chris's shaking shoulders and Tony's brutal fists. They were all responsible.

And yet, what could she have done?

"It's not your fault," Chris said suddenly, coming into the bathroom, sitting down beside Barbara on the edge of the tub. She was wrapped in Barbara's voluminous white terry-cloth bathrobe, and her hair, grown back to shoulder length, was pushed behind her ears.

The ponytail was gone forever, Barbara thought, realizing how much she missed it. "I should have been there for you," she whispered. "At the very least, I should have been there for you."

"You were." Chris reached over, took Barbara's hand inside her own.

"No. I stopped trying to find you."

"What choice did you have?"

"I thought about you all the time."

"I know."

"We all did. Grand Avenue was never the same without you."

"How are the others?" Chris asked, her eyes suddenly hungry for information. "Vicki and Susan? Owen and Jeremy? The kids?"

"Everyone's fine."

"Still together? Still well?"

"Still together. Still well."

"I'm so glad. And you, how are you?"

Barbara smiled. "Better now that you're here." She stroked Chris's beautiful face, as if to convince herself she was really there and not just a figment of her lonely imagination. "Please tell me you'll never go back to him," she said, almost afraid to say the words out loud for fear of what Chris might say in return.

"I'll never go back to him." Chris's voice was surprisingly strong.

"No matter what he says or does."

"I'll never go back," Chris said again, even more forcefully the second time.

"You promise?"

Chris nodded. "I promise."

Barbara pushed herself off the side of the tub. "Take your bath."

Chris undid the belt at her waist, shedding the oversize terry-cloth robe, like a butterfly emerging from a cocoon, Barbara thought, averting her eyes, about to leave the room when Chris's voice stopped her. "Don't go."

Barbara said nothing. Instead she lowered the lid of the toilet seat, sitting down and watching as Chris slipped naked into the tub, her body quickly submerging beneath the hot water. Had she always been so thin, so terribly fragile? Barbara wondered, wincing at the sight of the myriad bruises that stained Chris's body, dusty yellow blotches along the insides of her arms, neon purple circles on her thighs, flat blue shadows everywhere. There were other marks as well, Barbara realized, unable to turn away. Scratches on Chris's neck and around her ribs, what appeared to be several bite marks on her left shoulder and breast, just above the small, earth-brown nipple. "How's the water? Too hot? Too cold?" Barbara realized she was talking strictly for the sake of hearing her own voice, that she was afraid if she didn't talk, she might start crying and never stop.

"It's perfect."

"You must be exhausted."

"I was thinking the same thing about you."

"Don't worry about me," Barbara said.

"Don't worry about *me.*"

The two women nodded silent understanding. "Would you like me to wash your back?" Barbara asked after a pause of several minutes.

Chris smiled, grabbed the bar of soap from its container, handed it to Barbara. Then she raised her knees and leaned forward over them, hugging her thighs to her chest, as Barbara soaked a washcloth in the water and began rubbing it across her back. Chris moaned, twisted her head from one side to the other, closed her eyes.

"Too hard?"

"Feels great. Feels perfect."

Barbara rubbed soap into the washcloth, letting the cloth glide across Chris's back and neck, the gentle ablutions hypnotizing both of them. "Promise me you'll never go back to him," Barbara said, as she had said earlier.

And again Chris promised, "I'll never go back."

Only later, with Chris safely back inside Barbara's white terry-cloth bathrobe, her wet hair securely tucked inside a thick, white towel, both women sitting on the side of Barbara's bed, did Barbara notice Chris looking at her with newly inquisitive eyes, as if seeing her for the first time. "What is it?"

"Your face." Chris lifted her hand to Barbara's cheek. "Something's different."

Barbara patted her hairline with self-conscious fingers. "I had a little surgery a while back."

"Surgery?"

"Just a few little nips and tucks. A girl's got to stay beautiful."

"You always look beautiful."

Barbara felt her eyes sting with tears.

"You *are* beautiful." Chris gently wiped the tears from Barbara's face.

"Thank you." Barbara folded one lip inside the other to prevent a sob from escaping.

"I've missed you so much."

"I've missed *you,*" Barbara hugged the other woman to her, both women crying freely.

At the same moment, each pulled back, began drying the other's tears. "I love you," Chris said.

"I love you too."

And suddenly Chris leaned forward, pressed her lips against Barbara's, so tenderly Barbara wasn't sure they were really there at all.

My God, what's going on? Barbara asked herself, trying to pretend what was happening was a dream, that this whole crazy night was a dream, except she knew it wasn't. What she didn't know was how to respond. What she didn't know was what to do next. She loved Chris. Loved her with her entire being, her heart and her soul. But she'd never thought of Chris in any sexual sense, never so much as fantasized anything like this happening between them. And Chris was frightened and vulnerable and confused. She'd just escaped from a crazy man. She was grateful and relieved and desperate for warmth. For affection. For love.

That's all it was.

One lost soul reaching out to another.

And then they heard the noise, and the women quickly pulled apart. "What was that?" Chris asked, fear instantly returning to her eyes as they shot from the bedroom window to the hall, then back to the window.

Barbara ran to the window, peeked under the heavy curtains toward the backyard. She peered into the darkness, trying to catch sight of anything, anyone. But all she saw was a silent wintry tableau—a postage-sized yard liberally sprinkled with snow, the ice-encrusted branches of the small trees swaying precariously in the cold wind. Had one of the branches snapped off, fallen to the ground? Had someone thrown a pebble at the window? Barbara checked the ground for debris, the window for scratches, saw nothing out of the ordinary. Had Tony figured out where Chris had gone? Was he out there now, waiting in the dark, watching the house?

"Stay here," Barbara instructed, heading for the hall. Or was it possible that Ron had returned, was even now ransacking the house for items he'd forgotten the first time around?

"Where are you going?"

"I'll be right back."

Barbara crossed the hall, opened the door to Tracey's room, looked toward the bed. Tracey might have gotten up to use the bathroom. Maybe that was the noise they'd heard. Except that Tracey was sound asleep in her bed, her breathing steady and rhythmic. "Sleep well, my sweet girl," Barbara said, kissing Tracey's warm forehead, securing the blankets around her shoulders, tiptoeing from the room.

She approached the stairs, her fingers trailing across the wall as she inched her way down the steps in the dark, bracing herself for the sudden touch of unfriendly hands on her shoulders. But there was nothing. No unwelcome guests lurked inside. No sinister ghosts lingered. Both the front and side doors were securely locked. Again, Barbara peeked outside, saw no one. "Go away, whoever you are," Barbara said to the ominous silence. "Stay away."

"Barbara?" Chris's voice wobbled toward Barbara from the top of the stairs.

"It's okay. There's nobody here."

"It was probably just the house," Chris said once Barbara was safely back upstairs. "You know how houses sometimes make noises when it gets really cold."

Barbara looked around warily. "That's probably what it was."

The two women stood awkwardly in the middle of the room. The first time they'd ever felt awkward with one another, Barbara thought sadly.

"Barbara," Chris began, then stopped, undoubtedly feeling the same way.

"You should get some sleep," Barbara said, trying not to think about what had passed between them only moments before. "You must be absolutely exhausted."

"Yes," Chris agreed readily. "I am."

Barbara nodded gratefully. "Me too."

"About what happened before . . ."

"I understand," Barbara said quickly.

"Do you? Because I'm not sure I do."

Barbara tried to give Chris one of her patented beauty-pageant smiles, but the smile refused to stick to her lips. "Can we talk about it in the morning?"

"Sure."

Without another word, the two women crawled into Barbara's bed, Chris's back curved into Barbara's front, like two spoons, Barbara thought, allowing her arm to fall gently across Chris's side. "Good night," Chris murmured, sleep already softening the consonants, so that the word emerged more as a sigh.

"Sleep well," Barbara whispered, as Chris's body relaxed beneath her arm. In the next minute, Chris was asleep. Barbara clung stubbornly to consciousness, refusing to give in to sleep. She lay awake for the balance of the night, watching the darkness bleed from the sky until it was light, keeping watch over her beloved friend until morning.

Part Three

1991–1992

Susan

Eighteen

"Ariel, have you seen my purple cashmere sweater?" Susan stood in the middle of her walk-in closet, a pile of discarded sweaters scattered around her bare feet. She could hear the radio blasting from Ariel's room, so she knew her daughter was in her room, probably still in bed. Susan checked her watch. Eight thirty-five. Which meant Ariel would be late for school. Yet again. Which was something Susan wasn't prepared to get into at this particular moment. She had a nine-o'clock editorial meeting, and right now her missing purple sweater took priority over her chronically tardy teenager. "Ariel?"

Owen's head poked around the closet door. "Something wrong?"

"My purple sweater is missing. I'm sure Ariel has it."

"You're not going to accomplish anything standing in the closet screaming."

Susan smiled, but what she really felt like doing was hurling a shoe at her husband's head. Did he always have to be so damned logical? Besides, she wasn't screaming. "Ariel, honey," she called, louder this time, "have you seen my purple sweater?"

This time the response was fast and furious, blasting through the wall between them like a stick of dynamite. "How would I know where your stupid sweater is!"

"Don't say anything," Susan warned her husband, who promptly backed off, then disappeared from view. She took a deep breath and returned her attention to the shelves she'd been searching through. "You can't fight if you don't bite," she intoned solemnly, the mantra Dr. Slotnick had suggested she repeat whenever the urge to throttle her difficult older daughter—or her easy-going husband—threatened to overwhelm her. According to the esteemed family therapist Susan had briefly consulted, Ariel was merely testing the waters, rebelling because rebelling was what teenagers were supposed to do. It was the child's way of separating from her parents, the good doctor had explained, her way of becoming her own person, asserting her unique, independent self. Susan should try not to take it personally. Which she might be able to do were it not for the fact that Ariel's unique independent self was so singularly unpleasant.

Owen, on the other hand, seemed to have no difficulty following Dr. Slotnick's advice. He dealt with their ill-tempered daughter with the same good grace he dealt with his patients. He was gentle, understanding, and unfailingly respectful, no matter how rude or disrespectful Ariel might be in return. He was a role model for proper parental behavior, Susan thought, and he was really starting to get on her nerves.

Susan pulled open the top drawer of her built-in dresser,

her hand rifling through the neat stacks of bras and panties, not surprised to discover the sweater wasn't there. Why would she have put her sweater anywhere but with her other sweaters? She slammed the drawer shut, forgetting her finger was still inside. "Damn it! Damn it, damn it, damn it!" She began hopping around the small space, waving her fingers in the air, as if she could shake out the terrible sting.

"What's the matter now?" Owen asked from the bedroom.

Not what's the matter, but what's the matter *now?* Where was all that famous patience where she was concerned? Susan padded sheepishly into the bedroom. "I closed the drawer on my fingers." She held her hand out toward her husband.

"You'll be fine." He cast a cursory glance in the direction of her wiggling fingers. "Stop waving them around like that."

"They hurt." Can't you at least kiss them and make them better? she almost said, but didn't. She was tired of the perfunctory little kisses that dotted her days. A kiss good morning at the breakfast table, a kiss good-bye as each left for work, a kiss hello on their return, a kiss good-night as, exhausted, they climbed into bed. Kisses as punctuation marks, Susan thought, wondering when pleasantry had replaced passion in her marriage, when their lovemaking had become so routine, something they did because it was expected, almost *polite.* While they still had the ability to satisfy one another, they'd lost the ability to surprise. When was the last time they'd tried a new position or technique? When was the last time they'd made love in the morning? Why not right now? Susan found herself thinking, taking a step toward her husband. Maybe I could ambush him, unbutton his freshly laundered white shirt, unbuckle his shiny black leather belt.

"Don't you think you should get dressed?" Owen asked.

Susan stopped cold, glanced down at the flesh-colored bra and panties she was wearing, and felt as if she'd been doused with a bucketful of cold water.

"Are you all right?" her husband asked.

"Fine."

"Running a bit late, aren't you?"

"Damn it," Susan said, realizing the time, returning to the closet, struggling with a pair of panty hose, pulling a beige silk dress off its cedar hanger and dragging it down over her head, pushing her arms through its long sleeves, then tugging it roughly across her hips. She marched into the bathroom, ran a brush cursorily through wayward chin-length hair, scowled at her reflection in the mirror. She was putting on weight again. No wonder Owen was losing interest. Not that he was in such great shape himself. Not like Peter Bassett, who worked hard to keep his body trim with thrice-weekly visits to the gym.

"You should join me there one night," he'd suggested just last week, and she'd laughed, although she wasn't sure why she was laughing and said she'd think about it.

What was there to think about? No way she was going to let Peter Bassett see her in unflattering sweatpants, or worse—a leotard. She was so out of shape, she probably wouldn't last ten minutes on the treadmill. She hadn't worked out in ages. Which was stupid. Not only would regular exercise help her shed those extra pounds, but it would give her fresh focus. She spent altogether too much time worrying about her mother, fighting with her daughter, and eating everything that crossed her path. "I look awful," she said out loud.

"You look okay," Owen said, coming up behind her, kissing her cheek.

"Thanks," Susan said dully. *Okay* was not exactly a ringing endorsement.

"Have a good day," he told her as he left the room.

A minute later, Susan heard the rumble of the garage door as it opened and closed. "You too," she muttered.

"Talking to yourself again?" Ariel asked dryly, popping into view, her newly spiked blue-black hair sitting like a nest of dyed porcupine quills on top of her head.

Susan jumped, as she always did these days when she saw her older daughter, this delicate little angel she'd nursed at her breast, her soft golden hair so full of wonderful baby smells and future promise. The promise of what? Susan wondered now, trying to take Dr. Slotnick's advice and think positively.

Well, let's see: Ariel had beautiful eyes, even if she insisted on surrounding them with what appeared to be layers of black soot; she had lovely skin, although it was sometimes hard to see it under all that white powder; she had a beautiful figure, although the oversize rags she wore were far from flattering; she had a sharp mind.

And a sharper tongue.

Think positively. Think positively.

She had a mind of her own.

Was that a positive?

"Where'd you get that dress?" Ariel's question had the sting of an accusation.

Same store I got my purple sweater, Susan thought but didn't say. "Shouldn't you be in school?" she said instead, then silently cursed herself. Definitely the wrong thing to bring up when you were trying to avoid a confrontation. Hadn't Dr. Slotnick advised her to let the school deal with Ariel's chronic lateness? It's their issue, the balding therapist had stated, not yours.

Susan suddenly recalled the first time Peter Bassett had summoned her to his office. He'd been on the phone with his daughter's school, discussing this same problem. No wonder he seemed to understand her so well. They had a lot in common, Susan thought with a smile.

Surprisingly, Ariel also smiled, pronounced dimples breaking through the coat of white powder that covered her face but stopped at her neck, so that she looked as if she might be the victim of some creeping skin disease. "Yeah," she admitted, cracking the knuckles of her left hand with the fingers of her right as Susan tried not to cringe visibly. "I'm late, and there's a big math test first period."

"Then you'd better get going." Susan checked, then rechecked her watch. Closing in on nine o'clock. Even if Ariel left right this minute, the odds were she wouldn't make it to school on time. And she wasn't even dressed yet. Or was she? Susan tried not to stare at the dirt-stained sweatshirt and baggy, ripped jeans her daughter was wearing.

"Something wrong?" Ariel's tone was a dare in itself.

Susan shook her head no, gazed at her toes. *You can't fight if you don't bite.*

"I was hoping you'd give me a lift."

"A lift?"

"To school. So I won't miss my test."

Susan held her breath, silently counted to ten, opened her mouth to speak, then closed it, counted to ten again. They'd been through this how many times? "We've been through this."

"Come on, Mom. One time . . ."

She's never going to learn if you keep rescuing her, Dr. Slotnick had warned. You have to let her face the consequences of her actions. "I can't," Susan heard herself say.

"What do you mean, you can't?"

"Ariel, I have an important meeting at nine o'clock. I don't have time to drive you."

"It'll only take a minute."

"I can't."

"You can't or you won't?"

"I have to get dressed."

"You *are* dressed."

"I look awful."

"So?"

The question was stunning in its simplicity. Who cares if you look awful? the word asked. Who looks at you anyway? Who sees you? You're a middle-aged woman, for God's sake. Don't you know you're invisible?

"So, I'm afraid you'll just have to get to school on your own."

"And be late for my test?"

"Maybe you should have thought of that half an hour ago."

"Maybe you should go to hell," came Ariel's blistering response.

"Now just one minute, young lady," Susan began, but Ariel had already vanished in a puff of self-righteous fury, her feet bullying their way down the steps. The front door opened and slammed shut, the unpleasant reverberation thundering through the house as Susan raced into Ariel's bedroom and propelled herself toward the window overlooking the street. "Didn't take an umbrella," Susan muttered in frustration, watching her daughter pull a pack of cigarettes out of her back pocket and light up, seemingly oblivious to the late-April rain beating down on her head as she sauntered lazily toward the corner. "It's pouring rain and she doesn't even notice."

She should have driven Ariel to school. One more time. One less cigarette. It was raining, for God's sake. Now her daughter would be late for class and she'd fail her test and probably get pneumonia to boot. Susan stood in the middle of Ariel's room, this room that looked as if a tropical storm had just ripped through it, and almost cried. What an unsightly mess! The bed, the desk, the floor, every available surface was littered with clothes, makeup, tape cassettes. Abandoned pennies lay scattered across the carpet like a trail of bread crumbs. A used plastic tampon tube stood upright on the floor at the foot of the bed. Susan closed her eyes, praying she didn't find its discarded other half as she bent down to scoop it up, then dropped it in the empty wastepaper basket, probably the only item in the room that wasn't filled with something. "God, how can she live this way?" Automatically, Susan began retrieving items of clothing from the floor, shaking them out, folding them neatly. She opened the closet door, pushed soiled and neglected items aside, made room for more of the same.

It was then that she saw it—scrunched into a tight little ball and pushed to the far end of the second shelf. Her purple cashmere sweater. The sweater she'd spent half the morning searching for, the sweater that Ariel had disavowed any knowledge of, the sweater she'd wanted to wear to the meeting this morning, the one Peter said brought out the violet in her eyes. "I'll shoot her," Susan whispered, seeing another of her sweaters, a white angora turtleneck she hadn't seen in months, peeking out from underneath a stack of crumpled T-shirts. She grabbed the sweaters and returned with them to her room, although she knew they were too dirty, too riddled with smoke fumes, to be worn anywhere anytime soon. Think positively, she thought. Maybe it meant Ariel's taste was improving. "She lied to me," Susan said, stopping in her tracks, hearing her daughter's voice echo in her ears.

How would I know where your stupid sweater is?

"Try not to take it personally," she heard Dr. Slotnick advise.

"Fuck off," Susan told the good doctor, returning to her closet and slipping into a pair of new brown heels. They were a little higher than she normally wore, higher than she was comfortable wearing, but she was in need of a little lift, she decided.

God knows I need something, she thought.

"Susan, could I talk to you for a minute?" Peter Bassett asked as she was leaving the boardroom at the conclusion of the morning meeting.

"Of course." Susan flexed her toes inside the shoes that had been pinching her feet all morning and watched the other editors and their assistants file from the room.

"Why don't you close the door."

She immediately closed the door to the large room, one of

only two rooms on the floor that wasn't surrounded by glass. Peter preferred this room for meetings because it provided few distractions. There were no windows, either interior or exterior, nothing to entice a wandering eye. Four beige walls surrounded a long wooden table and sixteen uninteresting beige chairs. The only color in the room came courtesy of three rows of framed *Victoria* covers that lined one wall. The other walls were blank. A coffeemaker sat on a counter at one end of the room. A plate of untouched muffins sat beside it.

Susan had been fighting the urge to grab one of those muffins since she'd first walked into the room, but she'd been ten minutes late and the meeting was already well under way. Besides, she noted no one else at the table was eating anything. They'd all obviously had time for breakfast, those of them who actually ate anything. Damn all those skinny thighs anyway, Susan cursed, thinking she was starting to sound like Barbara. When had she started worrying about such things? "I'm sorry I was late," she said before her boss had a chance to upbraid her.

"Everything all right?"

Susan shrugged. The shrug said, Same old stuff.

"Daughter still giving you problems?"

Susan smiled. "I shouldn't let her get to me."

"It's hard sometimes. Trust me, I know."

"Anyway, it's no excuse for being late." Shouldn't he be the one saying this? Susan wondered.

"Forget it," he said instead. "It's not the end of the world. How's your mother doing?"

"Not great."

"Sorry to hear that."

"Thank you." She returned to her chair, not sure why she

was here. She'd assumed Peter was going to chide her for being late, remind her that, much as he sympathized with her plight, they had a magazine to produce, that she couldn't let her personal problems get in the way of her doing her job. Hadn't Judi Butler been given her walking papers for exactly that reason several months ago? Instead, here was her boss telling her not to worry, it wasn't the end of the world. And he was smiling, not scowling, his legs stretched out in front of him, his hands curved behind his head, his head resting inside his entwined fingers. "Was there something you wanted to talk to me about?" she broached cautiously.

"I wanted to give you a progress report."

"Progress report?" What was he talking about?

"You didn't think I'd forgotten about your suggestions for improving the quality of the magazine, did you?"

It took Susan a minute to figure out what Peter Bassett was referring to. It had been so long since they'd had that initial conversation, she couldn't even remember what her suggestions had been.

"Things move very slowly in the magazine business. The people in charge don't like to tamper with a successful formula, even when that formula is getting pretty stale. I'm having a hard time convincing the powers that be to change the basic mandate, especially in light of increasing sales figures. Management argues that *Victoria*'s readership will continue to expand only if it remains glossy and pretty and, above all, shallow." He shook his head. We're in this together, the motion said. "But I want you to know that I haven't given up, that I intend to keep pressing for improvement. And I am more determined than ever to sneak in a few articles of substance."

"How can you do that?"

"Very carefully," he said with a wink. "Sneak in a page here and a page there. Provide more background, more context, greater depth. Eventually—who knows?—we might even be able to insert a more serious-minded article into the mix."

"That would be great. Actually, I have a whole bunch of ideas."

"Such as?"

"Well, I've been hoping we could do something on this new hormone replacement therapy that the medical establishment is all excited about. Actually, it's been around a long time, but suddenly it's all the rage. I know it's not something that will necessarily appeal to our younger readers but—"

"Can you make it sound sexy?" Peter interrupted.

"What?"

"Sexy. Like your shoes." He winked again.

Susan felt her cheeks burn bright red. Good thing she hadn't worn her purple sweater, she thought. She'd clash terribly. "I guess we could give it a sexy kind of title," she stammered, trying to concentrate on her idea. "Something like 'HRT—the New Fountain of Youth?'"

Peter tilted his head, as if trying to picture the headline in his mind. "I think you might be onto something."

"You do?"

"Absolutely." Peter Bassett pushed himself to his feet, walked around the table to where Susan was sitting, and sat down in the chair beside her. His knees brushed lazily against hers, though he didn't seem to notice.

Susan felt a shock similar to the one she'd experienced earlier that morning when she'd slammed her fingers in the drawer, except this time it was the insides of her thighs that were tingling.

"Why don't you try writing it yourself?" he said.

"What?"

"It's your idea. Why don't you run with it?"

"Really?"

"I'm not promising anything, of course."

"Of course." She tried standing up, but he was sitting so close to her, she had nowhere to go. "I'll get right on it."

"What's your hurry?"

She laughed, a silly schoolgirl laugh, she thought, hating the sound.

"Did I say something funny?" he asked.

Susan shook her head as he leaned in closer. My God, was he going to kiss her?

"You have something under your eye," he told her, wetting his finger with his tongue. "Hold still." He leaned forward until their lips were only inches apart. His left hand reached up to steady her chin, while the middle finger of his right left a moist trace of saliva beneath her left eye. She felt as if her skin were melting under his touch, as if the rest of her were about to dissolve into a puddle of hot lava. How long had it been since Owen's touch had so electrified her? "There," he said. "That's better."

Was he going to kiss her?

What would she do if he did?

He leaned back in his seat, smiled. My God, what was the matter with her? Of course he wasn't going to kiss her. He was her boss, and he could have any woman he wanted. And the rumor was that he'd already had several. Not overweight, middle-aged mothers of two, who wore beige dresses that made them look as if they were part of the furniture, Susan castigated herself, but attractive younger women like Rosa Leoni and Judi Butler, both of whom no longer worked for the magazine. Not that Susan believed any of the office gossip. She understood that Judi's frequent lunches and private meetings with her boss had been strictly work-related. Still, she hadn't been unhappy to see either Rosa Leoni or Judi Butler leave. Not that she was jealous, for heaven's sake. She was a married woman. A *happily* married woman, Susan reminded herself emphatically, clasping her hands together primly in her lap. Good God, what was the matter with her? Where were these strange thoughts coming from?

"Tell me something personal about yourself," Peter Bassett was saying.

Susan paused, not sure what he was getting at. "I'm not sure I understand. What would you like to know?"

"Whatever information you can spare. You're a woman of mystery, Susan Norman."

Susan might have laughed out loud had she not been so absurdly flattered. "Hardly."

"I can't get a handle on you."

"You can't?"

"We've been working together, how long? Almost two years now? And still you intrigue me."

"I intrigue you?" Susan repeated, hypnotized by his choice of words. She was forty-three years old. She'd never intrigued anyone in her whole life.

"You're a fascinating woman."

Mysterious, intriguing, and now fascinating, Susan thought.

There was no question about it—Peter Bassett was flirting with her and she knew it, and he knew she knew it, and it was all so obvious and so silly that Susan would have rolled her eyes and laughed in his face had she not needed all her energy to keep from jumping into his lap and wrapping her thighs around his waist. Dear God, what was the matter with her?

"I'd really like to kiss you right now," Peter whispered.

Susan said nothing. A sound, like someone having trouble breathing, reached her ears, and she knew it was her own body giving her away. Peter leaned closer until she could almost taste his breath on the tip of her tongue. His eyelashes fluttered against hers. His lips grazed her own. She felt a spark, like the flick of a match, ignite her skin. What was she doing? she wondered, as his lips pressed deeply against hers, and his tongue played gently in her mouth.

I'm too smart for this, she thought, watching from somewhere outside herself as his arms drew her closer still. Who is this woman? Surely not principled, practical, overweight Susan Norman, the good doctor's wife? Hadn't she once told Vicki there was no way she'd ever consider cheating on her husband?

Never say never, Vicki had warned.

A knock on the door split them suddenly apart.

"Yes?" Peter asked, on his feet and at the door, fully in control.

"Jason Elliott is waiting in your office," Susan heard his secretary say.

"Be right there." He turned back to Susan, who was still sitting in her seat, unable to move. "Later," he said.

Nineteen

The sound of the phone ringing woke Vicki from a dream in which she was chasing a faceless woman down an unfamiliar street. Just as the woman stopped and turned around, Vicki ran smack into the proverbial brick wall. She saw stars, heard bells, realized it was the phone, dragged herself reluctantly into consciousness. "Hello," she whispered into the receiver, trying to rub a budding headache away from her forehead. Too much red wine, she thought, trying to remember how many bottles they'd gone through.

"Good morning. This is your six-thirty wake-up call."

Vicki automatically checked the clock beside the king-size bed. Six-thirty on the dot. Exactly as requested. Who said Holiday Inns didn't offer four-star service? "Thank you." She replaced the receiver, sat up in bed, brought her knees to her chest, the crumpled white sheet falling from her small, bare breasts. How could it be six-thirty already? Hadn't they just gotten into bed? "Hey, you, sleepyhead," she said to the naked man beside her. "Wake up, darlin'. Time to start the day."

"Says who?" The man's voice was a low purr, full of the sands of sleep, as if he'd been gargling gravel.

"Says me." Vicki jumped out of bed, headed for the bathroom. Okay, so it wasn't exactly the Ritz, she thought, running the shower, stepping into the tub and under the sputtering spray, feeling her body coming gradually awake under the uneven outpouring of hot water. She groaned, soaping herself with the expensive bar of Chanel soap she'd brought from home, and slowly rolled her neck back over the top of her spine, the water licking at her exposed throat like a lover's tongue.

She heard a noise, felt a cold whoosh of air as the bathroom door opened, saw the shadow moving toward her, pulling back the curtain, shadow becoming flesh as the naked man stepped into the tub behind her and lifted the soap from her hand. "Let me do that," he said.

Jeremy always liked making love in the shower, Vicki thought with a smile. Said it reminded him of their honeymoon in Hawaii, where they'd managed to find a private waterfall not far from their hotel and make love under the stars every night.

Except this wasn't Hawaii.

And it wasn't Jeremy.

Vicki sighed as the man's soapy hands curled around her, cupped her breasts. Jeremy was in Florida negotiating with some local TV station about becoming a partner, while she was here at the Holiday Inn Cincinnati-Airport, which was actually located in Erlanger, Kentucky, with assistant state's attorney Michael Rose, with whom she'd been having a fairly torrid affair for the past three months. It was probably time to end it, Vicki thought, as he entered her quickly from behind, his fingers digging into the tiny daisy tattoo she'd recently had etched into her inner thigh as he pounded her with such early-morning vigor she almost slipped and fell, her hands shooting out to balance herself against the white tile of the walls.

That's all I'd need, she thought, adjusting to the tempo of his thrusts. A broken arm or leg. How to explain that one? Although she doubted Jeremy would ask for an explanation. Ask me no questions, I'll tell you no lies. Wasn't that their silent agreement? She doubted her husband spent his many nights away from her all by himself, although he'd been slowing down of late, so maybe sex wasn't such a big deal to him anymore.

"God, that feels good," she heard herself say, glad he was taking her from behind. This way she didn't have to look at him, pretend he was more than he was. It was enough he was young, at least five years younger than she was, and didn't have to be coaxed into action. Vicki loved her husband, but God, sometimes he was hard work. She'd be on her knees for twenty minutes, and for what? A thirty-second payoff. Men like Michael Rose were her way of evening out the equation.

"You're something else," he whispered in her ear.

Why did men find it necessary to talk? Especially when they weren't really saying anything. *You're something else*. What the hell did that mean? Vicki grunted appreciatively, but in truth, she didn't feel particularly appreciative. What was she doing that was so praiseworthy? Just standing there, hanging on for dear life. It wasn't exactly rocket science, as her son, Josh, might say. God, what would the boy say if he could see his mother now?

And what of Kirsten?

"I don't understand. Why won't you be home tonight?" her daughter had demanded indignantly when Vicki had informed her of her plans to be away overnight.

"I told you. A client is flying in from New York and we're meeting at the airport. The meeting's liable to go on half the night. It'll be easier if I just stay over."

"I don't understand," Kirsten said again, although maybe she did, Vicki thought now. Maybe she understood all too well. She was almost fifteen, after all. Vicki pictured her daughter, an exact replica of herself at that age, all skinny limbs and knobby knees, small, pert breasts, concave stomach. Only the hair was different. Kirsten's red hair was a shade or two darker than her mother's, and it hung lazily down her back and over her forehead, hiding a face that was more interesting than beautiful, a face still growing into its potential. She probably wishes her eyes were bigger and her nose smaller, Vicki thought, just as she had wished at that age.

Had her mother wished the same thing?

Vicki shook her head free of her mother's unexpected intrusion into her reveries. She hadn't thought about her mother in months, had finally, after all this time, dismissed the private detective she'd hired to find her, informed him his services were no longer required. Enough was enough. She had neither the time nor the patience anymore for this prolonged game of cat and mouse. If her mother had any interest in seeing her again, well, then, it was her turn to do something about it. Vicki was calling in the troops, waving the white flag of surrender. You win, she was saying. I give up.

So what was her mother doing here now, uninvited and unannounced? Vicki thought impatiently, shaking her head again, this time so strongly her whole body shook. Michael Rose mistook her sudden moves as an indication she was approaching orgasm and immediately picked up the pace, ferociously slamming his body against hers until she was pressed so tightly against the wet wall of the shower, she could barely breathe. She heard Michael shudder to a climax, felt his lips brush against the top of her shoulder as he slipped effortlessly out of her.

"You're something else," he said again.

Was that all he could think of to say? Vicki wondered, grabbing the soap and washing what remained of him from between her legs. No wonder his summations to the jury left something to be desired. No wonder she never had any trouble beating him in court. *You're something else,* she repeated silently, rolling her eyes directly into the water's spray.

I'm something else all right, she thought, picturing Jeremy asleep in his bed at the Brazilian Court in Palm Beach. She should have gone with him. A few days in Florida might have done her some good. She needed a rest, and surely her office could have managed without her. Although then she would have missed Susan's phone call, and whatever it was Susan wanted to discuss sounded like it couldn't wait. She was coming over first thing this morning. Eight o'clock, before she went to work. Vicki shut off the water, stepped around assistant state's attorney Michael Rose, and out of the tub. What was so damned important Susan couldn't wait?

Vicki was almost dressed by the time Michael emerged from the bathroom, dark hair falling across his broad forehead, a towel wrapped around his slim hips. Tall, dark, and traditionally handsome, Vicki thought, not quite looking at him, preferring the generic to the specific, careful, as always, not to become too engrossed in particulars. It was easier that way to keep your distance. To say good-bye.

"I should get going," Vicki said.

"Now? I thought we'd order room service."

"No time." Vicki adjusted her gray A-line skirt so that the seams fell correctly on her hips and grabbed her matching jacket from the blue velvet chair beside the bed.

"It's early." Michael Rose checked his bare wrist where his watch normally sat.

Vicki tried not to notice the question in his eyes, the budding hurt in his voice. "I have a client coming in at eight o'clock." She ran a quick comb through her short, wet hair.

"How about tonight? Dinner at Dee Felice Cafe?"

"Can't." She pushed her hands through the sleeves of her jacket, did up the fake-pearl buttons.

"I thought your husband was away till the end of the week." An unflattering pout was working its way between the syllables of his words.

"He is. But I have two children, remember?"

"So you tell them you're working late."

"Can't."

"Vicki . . ."

"Michael . . ."

He laughed, but the laugh crackled with the static of defeat. "How about tomorrow?"

"Michael . . ."

"Vicki . . ."

Her turn to laugh, but the laugh crackled with the threat of bad news. "I think maybe it's time we give this a rest."

"Give what a rest?" Surprise, concern, then disbelief traveled back and forth between his eyes and mouth. "Us?"

"There is no us, Michael." Vicki stopped adjusting her clothing, looked directly at him for the first time since they'd woken up. "I have a husband. You have a wife."

"So?"

"So . . ." Vicki lifted her hands into the air, as if asking, Isn't that explanation enough?

"That's never stopped you before." Disbelief was morphing rapidly into anger.

Vicki felt the air constrict in her chest, as if she were being squeezed. "I'm sorry. I didn't mean to hurt you."

"I don't think you give two shits how I feel."

"Michael, please. Is this necessary?"

Michael looked helplessly around the room. "I thought we had something going here."

"We did." Going, going, gone, she thought. "It's nothing you did, Michael."

"You're not going to insult my intelligence be giving me that old 'It's not you, it's me' speech, are you?"

"No, of course not," Vicki lied. "Look, I'm really sorry."

"I just don't understand how the roles got reversed," he said after a pause, stroking his hair in disbelief as Vicki headed for the door. "I mean, I'm the one who's supposed to be hurrying off to work. You're supposed to be the one standing naked under a towel begging me to stay."

So that's what this little scene was really about, Vicki marveled. Not love or even lust. Not disappointment or distress. It was about wounded egos, about wanting to be the first to leave. "Sorry, Michael," Vicki said again, although she was feeling less so, and then, because she couldn't resist: "I guess I'll see you in court."

Okay, so what's the problem?" Vicki settled in behind her desk, a cup of hot black coffee in her hand, and raised her freshly penciled-in eyebrows at her friend. She'd had just enough time to finish putting on her makeup before Susan arrived, ten minutes early, for her scheduled appointment. Susan smiled, but looked distinctly uncomfortable, which was unusual for Susan, who'd always seemed very comfortable in her skin. Now she was shifting restlessly in her chair, looking from the window to her lap, then back again, ignoring the coffee on the desk in front of her, obviously dreading what she'd come here to say. She was wearing a stylish olive green pantsuit, and her hair fell about her round face in soft waves. That was one of the pluses of being overweight, Vicki thought. Your face was fuller; there were fewer age-revealing lines cluttering the skin around your eyes and mouth. Vicki noted the pale peach lipstick that added fresh lushness to Susan's already full lips, the hint of blush that gave definition to her round cheeks. There was an unfamiliar sparkle to her eyes. Vicki was astounded to realize that Susan was actually glowing. "You're not pregnant, are you?" she gasped.

"Are you crazy?" Susan gasped in return.

Vicki laughed with relief. "So what's going on? What's the problem?"

"No problem really."

"Which is why you had to see me first thing in the morning, in my office."

"I thought we'd have a little more privacy this way."

"And we need more privacy because . . . ?"

"I'm not sure where to begin."

It wasn't like Susan to equivocate. Normally she came right to the point. It was one of the things Vicki liked best about her. Unlike Chris, who'd always been too shy to push her point on others, or Barbara, whose great charm was that she never seemed quite sure what the point was, Susan was one of those rare people who refreshingly said what she meant and meant what she said. "How are the girls?" Vicki asked, giving Susan an opportunity to collect her thoughts.

"Fine."

Okay, not the girls. "Owen?"

"Fine."

Another one fine, Vicki thought. "Your mother?"

"The same."

"I'm sorry to hear that." Not her mother. "Still liking your job?"

"I love my job."

Vicki shrugged, a shrug that said, I'm running out of options here. "Any more threatening calls from Tony?"

"Not lately. You?"

"No. He seems to have calmed down since the court awarded him temporary custody."

Both women shook their heads in disbelief.

"How did that happen? Can you tell me?"

"Beats the shit out of me," Vicki said honestly, still bristling at the judge's decision. "I guess the fact the kids all said they wanted to stay with their father more or less sealed the deal."

"Asshole," Susan muttered.

"Motherfucking, cocksucking asshole," Vicki elaborated. "But that's not why you're here," she said pleasantly to Susan.

"No."

"Are you going to tell me, or do I have to keep guessing?"

Susan took a deep breath, looked toward the window. "There's a man."

Vicki followed the path of Susan's eyes to the window. How could Susan see anyone from here? "A man? Where?"

Susan lowered her head, laughed softly. "No. I don't mean . . ."

"Oh," Vicki said, surprised to have been caught so off guard. Could Susan really be saying what she thought she was saying? "You mean . . . a *man?*"

A natural blush flooded Susan's face, turning it bright pink.

"A man who isn't Owen?" Vicki asked, careful not to make wrong assumptions.

"A man who isn't Owen," Susan repeated, covering her mouth with her hand, as if to push the words back inside.

"You're having an affair?" Vicki tried—and failed—to keep the astonishment out of her voice.

"No. Of course not," Susan said quickly.

"Of course not," Vicki repeated, trying to navigate the dizzying loops of the conversation. Susan had been in her office ten minutes, and Vicki still had no idea why she was here or what she was talking about. "I don't understand."

"I need some advice."

"I need some information."

"Sorry. This is very hard for me."

"Take your time." Vicki stole a surreptitious glance at her watch. She had a client coming at eight forty-five, but, hell, this was too good. If necessary, her client would have to wait.

"There's this man . . ."

"At work?"

"No!"

"Good," Vicki said, not entirely convinced. Susan's denial had been a little too quick, a tad too emphatic. "It's never a good idea to shit where you eat."

"I beg your pardon?"

"Jeremy always says, 'You should never shit where you eat.'" Vicki pushed thoughts of a naked Michael Rose from her mind. "It means—"

"Business and pleasure don't mix."

"Exactly. So, where did you meet this man?"

Susan hesitated. "Is that important?"

"I don't know. Is it?"

"I don't think so."

"Okay. What is?"

"I don't understand."

Vicki threw up her hands in exasperation. "Susan, at some point, you have to tell me *something.*"

"There's this man I find myself very attracted to."

"Okay."

"And I'm not sure what to do about it."

"What do you want to do about it?"

"I don't know."

"I think you do."

Susan brought her hands together, twisted her fingers in her lap. "I love my husband."

"This has nothing to do with your husband."

"It doesn't?"

"Unless you're in love with this other man. Are you?"

"Good God, no! I'm not even sure I like him."

Vicki almost laughed. Sometimes Susan could be so naive. "Okay, you've met some guy. You're attracted to him. You want to sleep with him. Is that it?"

"I don't know if I want to sleep with him. I don't know what I want. It's just that . . ."

"You've been married a long time," Vicki said, finishing Susan's sentence.

"Yes."

"Things aren't as exciting as they used to be."

"It's not that Owen doesn't try."

"But this guy makes you feel special. He hangs on your every word. When he looks at you, you go weak in the knees."

"Nobody's ever looked at me that way before."

"Don't do it," Vicki said, surprising herself even more than Susan. She'd been preparing to tell her friend to go for it, cut loose, have a little fun. Join the club. Instead she'd said just the opposite.

"What?"

"Don't do it." God, she'd said it again. What was the matter with her?

"Why? I thought you'd tell me . . ."

"That it's okay? It is. For some people."

"But not me?"

"Not you."

Susan looked as if she didn't know whether to laugh or cry. So she did both.

"Look at you. You're crying already, and you haven't even done anything. Have you?" Vicki asked, just to make sure.

"We kissed."

"That's all? You're positive?"

Susan nodded.

"Okay, so you kissed some guy who isn't Owen, and it made you feel tingly all over, and you were thinking maybe you'd like to do more, so you came to the expert in the field of adulterous relationships. . . ."

"I didn't mean to insult you."

"Insult me? Who said anything about being insulted? Hell, I'm flattered."

"I just need some advice."

"I think you want more."

"What?"

"I think you want permission."

"Permission?"

"And I won't give it to you," Vicki said, her voice adamant. "You can't have an affair. Okay? Go home to Owen. Be a good girl."

Susan jumped to her feet. "Damn it. I'm tired of being a good girl. I've been a good girl my whole life!"

"Which is why it's too late to change now. Trust me, you don't want to do this."

"I don't?"

"No. What you're looking for is a little romance, like in high school. You want to hold hands and go for long walks and maybe make out a little in a parked car before you say goodnight. I know you, Susan. You want soft kisses, not hard penises. You'd be miserable. You'd hate yourself in the morning. And you'd be so racked with guilt that you'd probably confess everything to your husband, and that could spell the end of your marriage, and your marriage is one of the good ones, and I won't let you do anything to screw it up."

Susan smiled, shook her head. What more was there to say? Vicki was right. They both knew it. "Sometimes you amaze me."

"Sometimes I amaze myself. Now get out of here so I can amaze the people who pay me to amaze them. And don't do anything stupid," Vicki added as Susan reached for her office door. "You're my hero. You remember that."

Susan stopped, looked back, her eyes brimming with grateful tears. "And you're mine."

Twenty

"Susan, I need to see you in my office when you get a minute," Peter Bassett said in passing as he strolled by her cubicle.

Susan nodded without speaking, although he was already gone. He expects you to follow him, Susan thought, unable to move. She'd been avoiding him all week, making sure they were never alone, that she was in the office by nine and out by five, that she was busy, busy, busy. No time for lunch, no time for coffee breaks, no time for stolen kisses in locked boardrooms. Oh, God, what was the matter with her? She had to banish such thoughts from her mind.

Susan squirmed in her seat and stared at the pile of work on her cluttered desk. When was the last time she'd seen its scratched oak surface? It was starting to resemble the floor of Ariel's room. There was simply too much stuff, and nowhere to put it all, exactly as Ariel regularly—and loudly—proclaimed. Maybe she'd been too hard on her older daughter. Maybe it was time to pay closer attention to what she was saying. *Shouting,* Susan immediately amended, knowing Peter was waiting for her, possibly even watching her from his office across the hall.

Maybe Ariel shouts so much because she thinks I don't hear her, Susan realized.

Maybe she's right.

Susan rolled her eyes back in her head, found herself staring at a spider creeping slowly across the top of the Japanese screen that separated her cubicle from the one next to it. The spider was one of those deceptively flimsy-looking things, its legs delicate silver threads that protruded at awkward angles from the tiny black button of its body. Why is it those legs don't just collapse? Susan wondered, following the insect's leisurely stroll across the top of the beige partition, imagining a series of minuscule muscles propelling the spider along, wondering if spiders had brains, minds, feelings.

"You're starting to think like an undergraduate again," she muttered, watching the spider disappear over the top of the screen, aware she was stalling for time. What was she doing sitting here musing about the secret life of spiders when she should be on her way to Peter Bassett's office? "Come into my office, said the spider to the fly," she said out loud.

"Sorry," came the voice from the next cubicle. "Did you say something?"

Susan shook her head, realized Carrie couldn't see her. "No. Sorry."

Carrie's head poked around the partition. Her face was thin, pale, angular, surrounded by a sloppy mass of strawberry blond curls that looked as if they'd been impatiently grafted onto her scalp. She was twenty-five, already twice-divorced, with a slight astigmatism in her left eye that made her look vaguely cross-eyed. "You all right?"

"Fine."

"The Great Man on the warpath?"

"Nothing I can't handle," Susan said, wondering if this was true. "Watch out for the spider," she warned as Carrie leaned her head against the partition.

Without so much as shifting her position, Carrie reached up and slammed her fist against the side of the screen. It wobbled back and forth as Carrie proudly displayed her open palm, the remains of the spider splayed across the inside of her hand like an abstract tattoo. "You too," Carrie said, and then was gone.

Susan took a deep breath, unable to ignore the irrational feeling of outrage building inside her. Why did she have to kill the damn thing? It wasn't doing anything. It was simply walking along minding its own business, and then Wham! One minute it was alive; the next minute it wasn't. Squished beyond all recognition, Susan thought melodramatically, marveling at the carelessness of the young. Have they no idea how precious life is? Had she, at Carrie's age?

Besides, it was bad luck to kill a spider. If you killed a spider, her mother always said, it meant it was going to rain.

Susan glanced toward the surrounding walls of windows, noting the heavy, dark clouds gathered at one end of the sky, felt them already moving toward her. Nature imitating the thoughts of man, Susan thought, recalling the expression from one of her English classes. Pathetic fallacy. At least that's what she thought the proper term was. Her years at university were starting to blur, leak one into the other. Already she'd forgotten so many things. Already she was starting to wonder, What was the point? So she had her degree. Big deal. Could her degree slow the merciless progression of her mother's cancer? Could it make her older daughter love her? Could it save her from making the biggest mistake of her life? Too bad they didn't teach common sense in university, she thought as the phone rang.

"Hi, sweetheart," she heard Owen say. "Am I catching you at a bad time?"

"Is everything all right?"

"Everything's fine." Susan could see his gentle smile through the phone wires. "I just had a call from Ed Frysinger asking if we're free for dinner on Friday night. I said I'd check with you and get back to him."

"Friday sounds good."

"Great. I'll tell him."

"Okay. See you later."

"I love you."

"I love you too." Susan hung up the phone, buried her head in her hands.

The phone rang again.

"I need to see you," Peter Bassett growled in her ear. "Now," he added, just before the line went dead.

Susan reluctantly pushed herself to her feet, smiling thinly at Carrie as she passed by her cubicle. Before she reached the end of the narrow corridor, she reached up and closed the top button of her pink cotton shirt. Then she took another deep breath—she'd taken so many she was starting to feel dizzy—pushed her shoulders back, and walked toward Peter Bassett's office.

The door was already open. Peter was sitting behind his desk, seemingly absorbed in something he was reading. "Close the door," he instructed, not bothering to look up, as if unconcerned with preliminaries.

Susan cleared her throat, then closed the door behind her, her heartbeat quickening. Don't be silly, she told herself, forcing herself to look directly at her superior, although he continued to ignore her. There's nothing to be concerned about. Nothing is going to happen. Not now. Not in the middle of the afternoon in a glass-walled office surrounded by curious workers.

"You're driving me crazy, you know that?" he asked, still not looking her way.

Susan felt her breath catch in her lungs. Oh, God, she thought, feeling the now familiar tingle between her legs.

"I've been sitting here trying to work all day, and I can't get anything done because I can't stop thinking about you." He raised his head, looked directly at her.

He's not even that handsome, Susan tried telling herself. He's too thin and hawklike. Owen is a much pleasanter looking man. Except when was the last time Owen had looked at her with such unadulterated lust? Adultery, Susan repeated silently, damning her overactive brain. Did it never take a rest?

Peter Bassett suddenly jumped to his feet, thrusting a stack of papers in her hands. "Follow me," he directed, out the door before she had time to ask why.

She knew where they were headed even before he turned toward the boardroom. Please let it be occupied, she prayed, waiting while Peter knocked first, then pushed open the door.

"Coast is clear," he whispered with a laugh, then said louder, so that those nearby could hear, "Just spread all that stuff across the table."

Susan was laying the papers across the table as directed when she heard the door close, then lock, behind her.

"What are you doing?"

"I thought you wanted . . ."

"You know what I want." And suddenly he was standing right behind her, his breathing loud and heavy. Susan could feel it slowly wrapping itself around her, invisible velvet ropes pinning her arms to her sides. "You're so tense," he was whispering, expert thumbs finding the tender muscles between her shoulder blades. "Try to relax." His hands slipped around to cup her breasts. Before she could protest, they'd already dropped to her thighs, were pulling at her skirt. Good God, was he really going to make love to her right here in the middle of the office? Was she really going to let him?

Don't do it, she heard Vicki say.

"Don't," she heard herself whisper, unconvincing even to herself.

"I want to kiss you," he said, spinning her around, his hands groping their way under her skirt, tugging at her pantyhose. His lips found hers, his tongue pushing her lips apart. "I want to kiss you all over."

Oh, shit, Susan thought.

Be a good girl, Vicki told her.

"Relax," Peter said hoarsely, fumbling with the zipper of his fly.

Go home to Owen.

Owen, Susan thought, hearing his voice on the phone, innocently making plans for Friday night. Owen, whom she'd loved since high school. Her first love. Her only love. Good, sweet, thoughtful Owen, who would never betray her as she was betraying him now. Hadn't she always hated men who cheated on their wives? Think about Ron, she reminded herself. Think about the hell he'd put Barbara through. Is that what she wanted for her own marriage? Vicki was right. She'd hate herself in the morning. Hell, she hated herself already.

"No," she heard herself say. "No. Don't. Stop." Susan struggled to turn her face away from Peter's, but his lips clung stubbornly to hers, like Velcro. "Stop," she said again, spitting the words out of the side of her mouth, the only place where she had any room, but still he wouldn't stop. She grabbed his hands, tried pushing them aside, but he held tight. Was she going to have to scream to make him stop?

"Stop this," Susan pleaded, managing to break free, hold him at arm's length.

"What's wrong?" Confusion clouded his eyes, twisted his lips.

"I can't do this."

"Sure you can." Once again, his hands were everywhere, in her hair, on her breasts, tugging at her skirt. "Nobody's going to come in."

"That's not the point."

"What is?"

"I just can't do it." Susan pushed at him with such force Peter lost his balance, his hip slamming against the corner of the table.

He stared at her through eyes as hard as pebbles. "What the hell kind of game are you playing, lady?"

"I'm so sorry," Susan apologized, struggling to rearrange her clothing, tuck her blouse back inside her skirt. "I didn't mean for things to go this far. Can we just forget this whole thing happened?"

"Forget it? You've been leading me on for months, and suddenly you just want to forget it?"

"I'm sorry."

"Wiggling by my desk. Batting your eyelashes anytime you want some extra time off. Leaning over my desk . . ."

"I haven't . . ." Had she?

"Playing little Miss Helpless. Little Miss Depressed. So worried about her mother . . ."

"I *am* worried about my mother."

"Worry about your job."

"What?"

"I don't like being toyed with."

"I wasn't toying with you." How had this whole thing come to be her fault?

"I thought you liked me," he said, his voice a gentle plea. "I thought this was what you wanted."

Susan heard whispering outside the boardroom door. "I'm sorry," she said again.

Peter pulled himself together, adjusted his clothing, straightened his tie. He looked at the sheets of papers that had been knocked off the table during their scuffle and which now lay scattered across the floor. "Pick this shit up," he said, opening the door and exiting the room, leaving her alone to straighten up the mess.

* * *

Three weeks later, the phone in Susan's office rang.

"I need to see you in my office as soon as possible," Peter Bassett said. "Bring that article on hormone replacement therapy you've been working on."

Article? What article? Susan wondered, fumbling through the papers on her desk. He'd kept her so busy these last weeks, she hadn't had any time to work on the article at all. At best, she had a few preliminary notes. An outline maybe. Where were they?

The phone rang again.

"When I say as soon as possible," Peter Bassett said, "I don't mean whenever you damn well feel like it."

"I'm on my way." Susan coughed nervously into her hand.

"You're not getting sick again, are you?"

"Sick?" Sick *again?* When was the last time she'd been sick?

"Just bring the article."

Susan finally located the single sheet under a stack of other such sheets and read her notes over quickly before heading to Peter's office.

"Let's see what you've got," Peter said impatiently as she entered his office.

Susan reached across his desk, handed him the single sheet of paper, careful to avert her eyes. Every time she looked at him, she felt a wave of nausea. Had she been out of her mind?

"What the hell is this?" Peter asked, loud enough to be heard by those in the immediate vicinity.

Susan felt a warm flush scurry up her neck to her face, like an army of fire ants. "It's all I've got at the moment."

"You call this satisfactory work?"

"I call it an outline, a few preliminary notes . . ."

"Are you aware this article is due at the end of the week?"

"What? No, of course not. We never discussed any deadlines."

"Have the finished article on my desk by Friday morning."

"But that's impossible. You already have me editing three other pieces."

"Are you saying you can't do your job?"

"Of course I can do my job but . . ."

Peter Bassett smiled, leaned back in his chair. "Look, Susan, I've tried to be patient."

"What?" What was he talking about?

"I know you're having a hard time on the home front, what with your mother and your daughter and God knows what else. Maybe this job is just too much for you."

"What?"

"Chemotherapy takes its toll on everybody. Look at you. You don't look well at all. You're letting yourself go, putting on weight."

The words hit her like a slap on the face. "What?" How many times had she asked that?

"There are only so many chances I can give you."

"What are you talking about?"

"I know you love your job. Your enthusiasm is admirable. And I've tried hard to make allowances for your inexperience." He shook his head. "But I'm not sure I can keep covering for you."

"Covering for me?"

"Your work is simply not up to the standards of this magazine."

Susan could barely believe what she was hearing. Was he really saying these things? And did he actually expect her—or anyone else—to believe them?

The smile in his eyes provided her with the answer.

"Are you firing me?"

"No." He reached across his desk, lifted a black-and-white Mont Blanc pen into his hands, twisting it between his fingers. "I'm a nice guy, Susan. I'm going to give you one more chance."

"What does that mean?"

"It means I'm putting you on probation."

"Probation?"

"I think you need some time to think things through, decide just how much this job really means to you, whether you can give it your full attention, become more of a team player, as it were."

As it were, Susan repeated silently. "You can't do this," she said out loud.

"Ah, but I can," he said, a fresh chirp in his voice as he dismissed her. "That's all, Susan. Oh, remember to have that article on my desk first thing Friday morning. And close the door after you on your way out."

This isn't happening, Susan thought as she marched back down the hall toward her cubicle, muttering under her breath, "How dare you! You bastard! How dare you!"

What the hell was she supposed to do now? she wondered, looking neither left nor right as she strode past the long line of cubicles, ignoring the puzzled look on Carrie's face as she passed her desk. She plopped down hard into her chair, inadvertently dislodging the papers beside her computer, watching them jump into the air and dive toward the floor, as if looking for cover. "Damn you, Peter Bassett." What was she supposed to do now? There was nothing wrong with her work and they both knew it. Her work wasn't the point. Her work was beside the point. The actual point was that she'd rebuffed his advances. Rebuffed his advances! Who was she—a beautiful young heroine in some old-fashioned bodice ripper? No, she was a pathetic, overweight, middle-aged woman who'd let herself be so flattered by the attentions of the office lothario that she'd almost done something incredibly stupid, and now she was in danger of losing her job because of it.

God, what had ever possessed her?

Vicki had been so right. About everything.

Susan picked up the phone and punched in Vicki's number. "I need to speak to Mrs. Latimer," Susan told Vicki's secretary.

"She's in a meeting right now. Can I take a message?"

"This is urgent. Can you tell her that her friend Susan Norman needs to speak to her right away? I'll hold as long as I have to."

Thirty seconds later, Vicki was on the line. "Susan, where are you? What's wrong?"

"I'm at work. Remember what we talked about last month?"

"Goddamn," Vicki said slowly. "You've been shitting where you eat."

Twenty-One

Shit," Barbara said, feeling the sting of mascara as her nervous fingers accidentally jabbed the delicate makeup brush smack into her right eye. "Shit, shit, shit." She blinked rapidly, watching the errant mascara arrange itself mournfully around the bottom of her eye, as if someone had punched her. "Great. I look just great." She reached for a cotton ball, squeezed a drop of makeup remover across its soft surface, then delicately wiped the accidental artifice away while trying, unsuccessfully, not to take the rest of her makeup along with it. "Shit," she said again, understanding she'd have to start over despite her best efforts.

"What's the matter?" Tracey, wearing a blue chenille bathrobe identical to the one her mother had on, stood in the bathroom doorway.

"Look at me. I look like I just went ten rounds with Mike Tyson." Barbara reached for her bottle of cleanser, began rubbing the creamy, white lotion into her cheeks and across her forehead with deliberate, well-practiced strokes.

"I think you look nice."

"Thanks, sweetie, but nice isn't quite the adjective I was going for."

"What's the big deal? It's just you and me and Richard Gere."

Barbara stared at her daughter through their reflections in the bathroom mirror. What was Tracey talking about? What did Richard Gere have to do with anything? "What am I missing here?"

"*An Officer and a Gentleman*? Your favorite movie? The one you asked me to rent for tonight?"

"Oh, God."

"You forgot?"

"I'm sorry."

"You're going out?"

"I'm sorry," Barbara repeated.

"With that guy again?"

"With Howard, yes."

"You said we were going to watch a movie. You asked me to rent the tape. I bought popcorn."

"I'm so sorry, sweetie. Really, I forgot all about it."

"Can't you cancel?"

Barbara had been looking forward to tonight all day—dinner at The Maisonette, Cincinnati's finest restaurant, with Howard and several of his closest friends. No way she was canceling, especially at the last minute. Surely Tracey would understand. "I can't. I'm sorry, honey."

Tracey sighed audibly. "How about tomorrow?"

"How about Sunday?" Barbara asked instead.

"You're going out tomorrow night too?"

"Howard's firm is having their annual party. I'm sure I told you about that."

"No, you didn't." Tracey slumped against the doorway. "So, what's the story? You really like this guy?"

Barbara shrugged, tried to look more indifferent than she felt. There was no point in alarming her daughter unnecessarily. She and Howard had been dating for less than two months. There was no telling where it might lead. "I like him very much." She returned her attention to her face, wiping the cleanser off with a tissue, then rinsing with warm water and patting her skin dry. "Maybe you could invite one of your friends over to watch the movie," she suggested, realizing she'd be hard-pressed to name any of her daughter's friends.

Tracey shook her head, though not strongly enough to disturb the shoulder-length dark hair that flipped up at her shoulders. "No, I don't think so."

Was it possible her daughter didn't have any friends?

Barbara watched Tracey's eyes studying her as she expertly reapplied her makeup, starting with an assortment of moisturizers and eye creams, followed by a single stroke of concealer under each eye, foundation, blush, pale blue eye shadow, navy liquid eyeliner, then rich black mascara. She carefully outlined her mouth in cherry red, then filled in her lips with a burnt orange lipstick, blending one into the other. "How's that?" she asked her daughter when she was satisfied.

"Beautiful."

"Really?"

"What's the big deal?" Tracey followed her mother out of

the bathroom and into her closet. "I mean, how special is this guy? Are you two getting married or something?" She said it as a joke, but Barbara recognized the serious tone that lay beneath.

"No, of course not. He's just a guy." Barbara pulled a black cocktail dress from its hanger.

"Is that a new dress?"

"Not really," Barbara lied.

"Price tag's still on it."

Barbara felt instantly guilty, though she wasn't sure why. Why should she feel guilty about going out on a date? Why should she feel guilty about buying a new dress? Why had she lied about it to Tracey? "Well, I bought it last month, so technically it's not new," she qualified, wondering why she felt the need to justify herself to her daughter.

"It's pretty."

"It was on sale at the store. Fifty percent off plus my employee discount. How could I say no?"

"You don't have to explain." Tracey plopped down at the foot of Barbara's bed, watched her mother remove her robe and step carefully into her dress. "What shoes are you going to wear?"

"I haven't decided," Barbara lied again, mindful of the new pair of sequined, black, three-inch heels sitting in their box in the closet. "Maybe you could give Ariel a call."

"Ariel? Why would I call her?"

"I don't know. Maybe she'd like to come over and watch the movie with you."

"She's a freak. Have you seen her lately?"

Barbara nodded, wondering how Susan put up with it,

thankful that Tracey hadn't felt the need to hack off her hair or violate her body with ugly tattoos. Three by the last count, Susan had confided. An ersatz Japanese symbol on Ariel's right shoulder blade, something that looked like a squished pineapple on her left ankle, and the latest, a spiderweb on the back of her left thigh. Wait till she gets older and everything starts dropping. That spiderweb will look like varicose veins. Barbara checked the backs of her own legs for any sign of unsightly blue lines, mercifully finding none, although without her contact lenses, she couldn't really be sure. Probably the only good thing about getting older, she decided, is that it got harder to see your body disintegrating around you.

"What about Kirsten?" Barbara pictured Vicki's lovely flame-haired daughter, as popular as she was smart, and at fifteen, already decided on a career in law.

The look of disbelief on Tracey's face said it all. Just because you and her mother are friends, the look said, doesn't mean I'm going to be friends with her daughter.

I guess that's right, Barbara thought sadly, sinking down beside her daughter on the bed and putting her arm around her. Immediately Tracey's head burrowed into the side of her mother's neck. Barbara had always assumed that, like their mothers, their offspring would become fast friends. They'd known each other almost all their lives. And yet, none of the girls was even remotely close to any of the others, which maybe wasn't that surprising. They were all so different.

There was no point in even mentioning Chris's daughter, Montana. No one had seen the girl in more than a year. Poor Chris, Barbara thought, her heart breaking.

Had it really been eighteen months since Chris had shown

up on her doorstep on that bitter cold December night? Eighteen months since they'd sat together on this very bed? Eighteen months since they'd shared that wholly unexpected kiss?

Barbara brought her fingers to her lips, felt the ghost of Chris's gentle touch. She shook her head. This was no time to be thinking such thoughts. Howard would be here in less than ten minutes. She had to finish getting ready. "What earrings should I wear?"

Tracey shrugged her indifference, then shuffled from the room, clumping down the stairs to the kitchen. Hearing her rifle through the fridge, Barbara frowned. "Stay away from the ice cream," Barbara called out as she hurried into the bathroom to fluff out her hair and put in her lenses.

At exactly seven o'clock the doorbell rang, and Barbara floated down the stairs to greet the new man in her life. "I won't be late," she assured Tracey, kissing her daughter's forehead on her way out the door.

Tracey's eyes narrowed accusingly. "Are those new shoes?"

Barbara had met Howard six months ago when she'd signed up for a course in current affairs at the Mariemont Community Center, just down the street from the upscale boutique in which she'd been working for the better part of a year. The course was the last thing in the world she'd felt like taking—did she really care that Iraq had ignored the January 15 deadline for withdrawing from Kuwait, and that Allied forces, which included the United States, Canada, Britain,

France, Japan, Italy, and Pakistan, as well as members of the Arab League, had launched a retaliatory six-week air attack, or that the Soviets were suppressing independence movements in Baltic republics?—but it was a necessary part of her plan for getting on with her life. What choice had Ron left her?

Besides, if Chris could forge ahead despite Tony's repeated threats and constant harassment, so could she. Hell, it was the least she could do.

And surprisingly, after several sessions, Barbara had found she did care about what was going on in the Mideast and the Soviet Union, that she was genuinely interested in the plight of the people of Somalia and South Africa. She discovered she enjoyed knowing there was a world beyond Grand Avenue, enjoyed knowing what was going on in that world, enjoyed talking about it, discussing important issues of the day with Susan and Vicki and Chris.

She hadn't been looking for a man. In fact, she'd barely noticed Howard Kerble until the very last class of the term, when he'd accidentally dropped his heavily underlined newspaper to the floor, then spilled his coffee all over it while trying to retrieve it. "Problems?" Barbara had asked, helping him blot up the mess.

"Piles," he'd replied, then smiled sheepishly. "And that's only *one* of my problems."

Barbara had laughed out loud, laughed with her whole face, the first time she remembered having done that in years. And next thing she knew, she and Howard were having coffee together after class, then meeting for lunch the following week, then having dinner together the week after that.

Howard Kerble was a widower with two grown sons and a recent grandchild. I'm dating a grandfather, Barbara occasionally found herself thinking, relishing being cast in the unexpected role of the younger woman, although in truth, there were only eight years between them.

At first Barbara saw Howard Kerble only in relation to her ex-husband. Howard was tall, although not as tall as Ron, and more compact than Ron. His hair was sparser than Ron's and more peppered with gray. His eyes were blue as opposed to brown; his fingers were longer, his hands smaller. If Ron was admittedly the handsomer of the two, Howard was easily the more distinguished, although less fussy than Ron had been, more accessible. He was every bit as smart as Ron, but less intent on showing off. He never talked about his work—insurance—whereas Ron's conversation had always revolved around his teaching. Howard never made Barbara feel stupid, as Ron had. Howard made her feel valued. All Ron had ever made her feel was inadequate.

"Would you like to see my apartment?" Howard was asking her now. They were sitting in his black Lincoln Town Car in front of the modern, new condominium complex on Mehring Way.

"I'd like to, but . . ." But what? But it's almost eleven o'clock and I should be getting home? But it's been such a lovely evening, why ruin it? But I haven't been with a man since that awful marathon session with Kevin, and I haven't even kissed anyone since . . . ? My God, Barbara realized. Since Chris.

"You look beautiful," Chris had whispered that night. "I've missed you so much."

"I've missed *you*."

"I love you."

"I love you too."

And then the kiss, followed immediately by the noise that had pulled them apart, sent them scurrying in separate directions, brought an awkward silence between them.

"About what happened before . . . ," Chris had tried to explain later.

"I understand," Barbara had told her.

"Do you? Because I'm not sure I do."

"Can we talk about it in the morning?"

Except they never had. The kiss they'd shared had vanished much like a dream, fragments of it lingering, teasing, courting deeper meaning, then disappearing, returning, ultimately evaporating, neither woman quite able to make sense of it, both afraid to try. So what had happened between them was never discussed, never so much as alluded to again. Barbara and Chris had fallen back into their lives, into their roles as friends and confidantes. Barbara had ultimately decided the kiss had been an expression of two lonely, vulnerable women at a particularly lonely, vulnerable point in both their lives. Nothing more.

And the truth was that as much as she often wished she didn't, Barbara liked men—the sheer mass of them, their bodies, their bulk, their effortless strength, the roughness of their skin, their smell. It had been way too long, she decided now, throwing caution to the wind, smiling at Howard. "I'd love to see your apartment," she said.

The two-bedroom apartment was as beautiful as she'd known it would be. Simple but not overly macho. Floor-to-ceiling windows, hardwood floors, soft leather furniture, colorful area rugs, a spectacular view of the Ohio River.

"Would you like a drink?" Howard asked.

Barbara shook her head. "I'm not sure I can do this," she whispered.

He didn't ask what she meant. "Would you like me to take you home?" he asked instead.

"No. I don't want to go home."

"What do you want? I'll do whatever you want."

"That might be the nicest thing anybody's ever said to me," Barbara said, and they both laughed.

"How about I think I might be falling in love with you?" Howard asked.

Barbara felt her eyes fill with tears. "That's pretty nice too."

"So where do we go from here?"

"You haven't shown me your bedroom."

Moments later, they were standing beside his king-size bed and steady hands were unzipping her dress. "It's been a while," she warned him. "I'm not sure I'll even remember what to do. Are you going to tell me it's like riding a bicycle?"

"Hell, no," Howard said in genuine horror. "Every time I ride a bicycle, I fall off and break my wrist."

She felt her dress slip from her body and drop to the floor, raised protective hands in front of her black lace bra and panties. "These boobs aren't mine," she blurted out as Howard leaned forward to kiss the side of her neck.

He looked confused. "Whose are they?"

"I had them . . . what's the word? Augmented. Surgically enhanced."

"You paid for these?"

Barbara nodded, holding her breath. Why had she said such a stupid thing?

"If you paid for them, I'd say that makes them yours." Howard knelt down, kissing each one in turn.

"And I've had a tummy tuck," Barbara continued, unable to stop the unwanted stream of confessions, as Howard pushed her gently back on the billowy white comforter of the bed. "I'm only telling you this because you might see some scars."

"I had an appendectomy a few years ago." Howard pulled up his shirt to reveal a long, jagged scar of his own.

At that moment Barbara knew without a doubt she was falling in love.

He took his time, exploring her body with gentle fingers, although Barbara was too nervous to really enjoy herself, too eager to get the job done. Next time, she'd be more relaxed, she told herself. Next time she wouldn't be so concerned with mechanics, with making a good impression. Howard was a patient and caring lover, and it wasn't his fault she was incapable of experiencing orgasm, she decided. After about five minutes of resolute pumping away, she volunteered a few grunts and groans that had always worked with Ron but that didn't seem to fool Howard at all. Maybe they hadn't fooled Ron either. What was that awful joke she'd overheard one man tell another? "Why do women fake orgasms?" The answer: "Because they think we care."

Howard cared. "What are you doing?" he asked with a sly smile as she thrashed around energetically beneath him. "I know you're not ready."

How did he know? "It's not your fault," she assured him quickly. "I never have orgasms. It has nothing to do with you."

"Don't you think it should?" He slipped out of her gently.

"Lie back. Close your eyes. Don't think about a thing." And then his head disappeared between her legs.

"No, Howard, you don't have to do this."

"Have to?" he murmured, nuzzling the inside of her thigh. "Are you kidding me?"

His tongue was everywhere, weaving its way through all her secret folds. Gentle, strong, hard, soft. "Oh, my God," Barbara heard herself cry out. "Oh, my God. Oh, my God." And suddenly she was screaming out loud, actually screaming from the sheer pleasure of what she was experiencing. "Don't stop," she begged him. "Don't stop. Don't stop."

He didn't. And when he entered her again later, she was more than ready, and her body exploded with a series of violent spasms she'd never really believed were possible.

"What are you thinking?" he asked her, as they lay sweat-soaked in each other's arms.

Barbara was grinning so hard she could barely speak. "That I can't wait to tell my friends about this," she said, and they both laughed.

"Can you stay the night?"

Barbara suddenly pictured Tracey, who was probably waiting up for her, and shook her head. "Maybe next time." She kissed Howard on the lips, tasted herself on his tongue.

They got dressed. He drove her home, walked her to the door, made sure she was safely inside, kissed her again. "See you tomorrow," he said as she closed the door after him.

Barbara sighed deeply, threw her head back, and squealed with delight, throwing her hand over her mouth to stifle the sound. The house was in darkness. The TV was quiet. Maybe Tracey was asleep after all. Barbara slipped off her shoes, was about to carry them up the stairs, when she saw something move in front of her.

And suddenly the room was filled with the sounds of screaming, one scream echoing the other—first Barbara, then Tracey, then Barbara, then Tracey.

It was just the two of them, Barbara realized, her breath coming in ragged bursts as her terrified daughter emerged from the shadows, the golf club in her hands dropping from her open fingers and crashing to the floor, bouncing toward Barbara's stockinged feet. Tracey flew into her mother's arms, sobbing uncontrollably.

"My God," Barbara cried, hanging on to the girl for dear life. "What's going on? What happened? Are you all right?"

"I was so scared." Tracey was shaking so hard she could barely get the words out.

"Scared of what? What's going on?"

"I was in the kitchen getting something to eat and suddenly there was this noise, and I turned around and there was this face at the window."

Barbara raced to the kitchen window, squinted into the darkness, saw nothing. "A face? Whose face?"

"A man. I'm not sure. It happened so fast. I was so scared."

Tony! Barbara thought bitterly. It had to be him. Who else would it be? It wasn't enough that he continued to harass Chris, he had to terrorize defenseless teenage girls as well. "My poor baby." She should never have gone out. She should never have left Tracey alone. To think she'd been writhing around in ecstasy while her daughter was cowering in fear. Damn that Tony Malarek. Damn him straight to hell.

"I found one of Dad's old golf clubs at the back of the closet.

I thought I could use that, you know, to protect myself if I had to. I guess I should have called the police, but I didn't think of that. I was just so scared." Tracey was babbling now, her eyes moving rapidly, as if trying to keep pace with her words. "And then it got real quiet, so after a while I went back upstairs. I guess I must have fallen asleep. I don't know. Suddenly I heard the door, and I grabbed the club and started back down the stairs. I wasn't thinking clearly. I forgot it might be you coming home from your date."

"Oh, honey, I'm so sorry I went out."

"It's not your fault."

Had her daughter's imagination gotten the better of her, or had there really been someone lurking about outside? "I'll stay home tomorrow."

"No, don't be silly. I'll be fine."

"I'll stay home," Barbara said again, hugging Tracey tightly to her side and leading her up the stairs, "and we'll make popcorn and watch Richard Gere rescue Debra Winger from that dreary factory job. How does that sound?"

"Sounds wonderful," Tracey said with a grateful laugh.

They reached the top of the stairs. "You want to sleep with me tonight?" Barbara asked, as Tracey nodded vigorously. Lately Barbara had insisted that Tracey start sleeping in her own bed again.

"It'll be just like old times," Tracey said, pulling back the covers of her mother's bed and crawling inside.

Minutes later, Barbara climbed in beside her. She'd call the police in the morning, report a prowler. Howard would understand about tomorrow night. He'd have to. There was simply no way she could live with herself if anything were to happen to Tracey. "There was a little girl," Barbara began, her voice a soft singsong as she gathered Tracey into her arms and smoothed the hair away from her face, "who had a little curl, right in the middle of her forehead."

"And when she was good," Tracey continued, "she was very, very good."

"And when she was bad . . ."

"She was a really bad girl!" mother and daughter chimed in unison.

Twenty-Two

In the beginning I thought she was wonderful," Peter Bassett was telling the hushed boardroom. "Maybe her work wasn't up to professional standards, but she was bright and enthusiastic and full of ideas, and I thought she'd learn. Plus, it was so obvious she had a crush on me. I guess I was flattered. Look, I know it was stupid. I'm not proud of what I did—I *am* a married man. But Susan was the instigator here, not me."

Susan cleared her throat, stared into her lap, then cleared her throat again. Oh, God, she thought, looking to Vicki to rescue her. But Vicki merely smiled, the enigmatic little half-smile she'd had since the deposition hearing began, and said nothing.

Did she have to look so damn comfortable? Susan wondered. Although why wouldn't she look comfortable? She was in her element. Vicki loved that they were ensconced in the large boardroom of the largest law firm in Cincinnati, surrounded by expensive paintings and spectacular views, that the heavy oak table they were sitting at stretched almost the full forty feet of the room, that the sixteen high-backed, autumn-colored chairs arranged around it had probably cost more than what it had cost Susan to furnish her entire house, that Vicki's husband, an obviously bemused Jeremy Latimer, was flanked by a trio of high-priced, serious-faced, impeccably dressed attorneys, everybody waiting to see what she'd do next.

What were they doing here? How had she let it get this far?

"We'll sue the bastard!" Vicki had proclaimed when Susan had filled her in on the whole truth of what had taken place between herself and Peter Bassett.

"What!"

"It's called sexual harassment, and if this isn't a perfect example of it, I don't know what is."

"We can't sue him," Susan protested.

"Why not?"

"Well, for starters, you'd be suing your husband. It's his magazine."

"So?"

"So it's named after you. Isn't there a slight conflict of interest here?"

"Not if you trust me to represent your best interests."

"Aren't my best interests the opposite of yours?"

"Jeremy and I aren't joined at the hip. He's a big boy. He can take care of himself."

"Still, what's he going to say when you slap him with a lawsuit?"

"Are you kidding? He couldn't buy this kind of publicity. He'll love every minute of it."

"But . . ."

"But what?"

"But I'm not completely innocent here. I let Peter kiss me."

"Yes, and they'll brand a scarlet K on your forehead," Vicki deadpanned. "Come on, Susan. You didn't use that kiss to try to blackmail him into an affair. Peter Bassett as much as told you he'd fire you if you didn't sleep with him. I can't see he's left you any choice."

"You really think we have a chance?"

"Let's get one thing straight right off the top. There are never any guarantees when you go to court. And this isn't going to be an easy case to win."

"Then why risk it?"

"Because the next woman this creep harasses could be your daughter," Vicki told Susan simply.

After that there was no further discussion.

That was five months ago, before Anita Hill's accusations against Clarence Thomas made sexual harassment the hot topic of the day and elevated Susan's lawsuit to front-page news.

"Serendipity," Vicki pronounced. "We got lucky."

"Lucky?" Susan protested. "How can you say that? I don't have a job. My husband is barely speaking to me. I can't open the morning paper without seeing a picture of my big fat face. A jury is never going to believe I didn't come on to Peter."

"I think you photograph beautifully. Besides, trust me. This case never goes to court."

"Thank you, Mr. Bassett," his lawyer was saying now. "Mrs. Latimer, I'm sure you have some questions for my client."

Vicki's response was to reach into her briefcase and retrieve a small black object, which she deposited gently, but with flourish, in the middle of the long table. She pressed a button on the tiny tape recorder, then sank back in her chair and smiled over at Susan.

Susan held her breath, waiting for the sound of a distant door opening and closing.

"Well, well. What have we here?" the male voice asked.

Everyone in the room swiveled toward Peter Bassett.

"What the hell is this?" Peter Bassett demanded angrily.

"I finished the article on hormone replacement therapy," Susan mouthed along with her voice on the recording. "I know you're anxious to have a look at it."

"What kind of games are we playing here, Counselor?" the most senior of Jeremy Latimer's three attorneys asked, instantly on his feet.

"Sit down, Austin," Jeremy said firmly, and the portly older man promptly did as he was told.

"I object to this," the youngest lawyer said, his hands waving in several different directions simultaneously, as if he weren't quite sure exactly what he was objecting to.

"Save the histrionics, Tom," Jeremy said dryly. "We're not in court. Let's hear the damn thing."

All eyes quickly returned to the miniature tape recorder, staring at it as if it were a giant TV screen.

"What say we look this over in the boardroom," Peter Bassett's disembodied voice was saying, his lazy baritone filling the room, beckoning each listener forward. "You don't have a problem with that, do you?"

"You were wired?" Peter Bassett demanded dramatically, his voice bursting with indignation.

Susan refused to acknowledge him, looked toward Vicki instead.

Vicki smiled. My idea, the smile announced.

"Is this legal?" Peter Bassett asked.

"Shut up, Peter," Jeremy Latimer said.

Peter Bassett sank down in his seat and closed his eyes as, for a brief moment, a silence as heavy as black smoke filled the room.

Then: "I don't want any trouble, Peter. Please, can you just let me do my job?"

"Your job is very much at risk at the moment." The words spit through the tape recorder, spraying all those listening, like venom from a cobra's fangs. "I'd hoped you'd come to your senses. I like you, Susan. I like you very much. I thought you liked me. I thought you liked working here."

"I think you'll find the article more than satisfactory."

"I think I'll find it very *un*satisfactory."

"If you'll just have a look at it . . ."

"Convince me."

"What?"

"Convince me to have a look at it."

"Peter, please. Can't we just stop this now, before it's too late?"

"You think you can just waltz in here shaking that great ass at me and I'm not going to respond the same way any red-blooded American man would, the way you know you want me to?"

"I'm truly sorry if I've done anything to give you the wrong impression," Susan said, her voice full of tears.

"You'll be a lot sorrier in the unemployment line."

"You're serious?" Susan asked after a pause. "You'll really fire me if I don't sleep with you?"

"You make your bed," Peter Bassett said slyly, "you lie in it."

Susan watched him lift his hands into the air, as if he were surrendering, as if the next move were hers. "Please don't do this," she pleaded one last time.

"Consider it done. You're fired, Mrs. Norman. I'll call security to escort you out."

Vicki leaned forward and clicked off the recording. Silence seeped back into the room like a deadly gas, so intense it threatened to explode with the first spoken word.

"Does anyone want to hear the tape again?" Vicki asked sweetly, somehow managing not to sound smug.

"Thank you. I think we've heard quite enough." Defeat mingled with barely concealed pride as Jeremy Latimer tried not to smile at his wife. "My sincere apologies to you, Mrs. Norman," he began, nodding in Susan's direction, "for the pain and discomfort you've obviously suffered."

Susan nodded gratefully at her friend, her lips trembling as her eyes filled with tears.

"Why don't we take a little break," he suggested as Vicki returned the tape recorder to her briefcase. "Meet back here at, say, three o'clock?" He looked around the room. Everywhere around the table heads nodded up and down, like those toy animals people buy for the backs of their cars. "That should give my colleagues and me time to reach some sort of understanding, hopefully hammer out a deal we can all live with."

Vicki was instantly on her feet. "Sounds good to me."

Susan felt a tug at her elbow, and she pushed herself unsteadily to her feet, her head reeling with sudden dizziness.

Was this nightmare finally over? Could she go back to work and get on with her life? Was it really over? She grabbed hold of the table. Dear God, was she going to faint?

"I'm positively starving," Vicki said, ushering Susan into the hall, as the heavy oak door closed behind them.

"I'm feeling a bit light-headed," Susan whispered, collapsing against the nearest wall.

"A little champagne will take care of that." Vicki laughed, a short burst of energy, like a dog's bark.

"Champagne?"

"Champagne," Vicki repeated, then barked again, dragging Susan down the long corridor. "We won, darlin'. It's time to celebrate."

So, how many are coming?"

Susan temporarily stopped searching through the drawers of her dining room cabinet for candles that weren't at least two-thirds of the way burned down, and counted aloud the number of people coming for dinner. "Well, let's see. There's you, me, Ariel, Barbara and Tracey, Vicki and Kirsten, Chris . . ."

"Montana?"

"Montana had other plans." Apparently Montana had hung up the phone as soon as she'd heard Chris's voice.

"How come Daddy isn't eating with us?" Whitney asked.

"Too many women," Susan said, hoping the lie would satisfy her younger daughter, who was wise far beyond her almost thirteen years. Whitney was tall and willowy, and growing more beautiful every day. She has her grandmother's eyes,

Susan realized, her own eyes immediately filling with tears, so that she turned away, pretending to be absorbed in the hunt for unused candles.

"Did you and Daddy have a fight?"

"No. Of course not."

"Then why don't you talk to each other anymore?"

"We talk to each other," Susan protested weakly, although it seemed that not even the hefty settlement she'd won was enough to make up for Owen's hurt feelings and bruised ego. She shuddered, thinking back to that awful scene with Owen, when she'd finally confided in him the whole truth of her predicament.

"You kissed him?" Owen had asked, his face a mask of pain and confusion.

I let him kiss me, Susan had almost amended. *I didn't stop him.* But she'd said neither, since neither was the truth. "Yes," was all she'd said, watching the pain sink deeper into her husband's eyes. "It was stupid, I know. It didn't mean anything." Had she really said that?

"What's going on, Susan?" he'd asked simply in return. "Have the rules changed?"

"Of course not," Susan had assured him, pleading temporary insanity, swearing such a thing would never happen again, and telling him over and over again how much she loved him, how highly she valued their marriage. She'd begged his forgiveness. Ultimately, after much cajoling, after many tears, on both their parts, he'd said he understood, although Susan could see that he didn't.

Whitney was right, Susan realized now. Her conversations with her husband had become increasingly brief and impersonal these last few months, until they bordered on nonexistent. She could barely look in his eyes, so clear was the reflection of her betrayal.

Not that she blamed him. He had every right to feel hurt and embarrassed. The newspapers had had a field day with the news that Vicki was suing her own husband for sexual harassment. If they hadn't settled, if they'd actually gone to trial, if all the lurid details had come out . . . Susan shuddered. Owen might be understanding and supportive, but he was also very proud. And very disappointed.

She'd let him down.

Vicki said to give it time. Owen loved her; eventually he'd come around.

Of course, what did Vicki know? Hadn't she assured Susan she'd get her job back? "I'm sorry, Susan, but you didn't really expect them to hire you back after you sued them, did you? I mean, you're a bit of a troublemaker, you know," she'd added with a sly smile.

I guess I am, Susan realized, shaking her head in wonder, absorbing the room in one quick glance: the circular walnut table that sat beneath a modern brass-and-glass chandelier, and was surrounded by eight high-backed, wine-colored chairs; twin cabinets against two of the eggshell-colored walls; a fireplace that had never been used, despite Owen's best intentions and repeated assurances; billowy ivory curtains pulled open and secured with large bows at each side of the large window overlooking the street, as if providing a frame for the trees that had already lost much of their foliage, the remaining red, orange, and yellow leaves clinging perilously to life, most of their previous luster faded or trampled into the ground. Again,

Susan thought of her mother, lying pale and skeletal beneath harsh and graying hospital sheets, connected to life through a series of tubes and the sheer ferocity of her will to live.

She grabbed two dark red candles, no more than short stubs really, and stuck them into a pair of elegant glass candlesticks, then arranged her good crystal glasses around the table as Whitney laid down the cutlery. She didn't want to think about her mother or Owen or her problems finding another job. Thankfully, Peter Bassett was in an even worse predicament. Not only had he been summarily dismissed and publicly humiliated, but his wife had left him, along with their difficult teenagers and the family dog. "Should I change?" Susan asked her daughter.

"What for? You look nice."

"You're so sweet."

"Who's so sweet?" The voice was dark, vaguely menacing, much like the fifteen-year-old girl it belonged to. Ariel was dressed all in black, as had lately become her custom, her uncombed hair newly tinged with crimson streaks, her lips a deep purple gash. "Could it be the alien?"

"Don't start," Susan warned.

Ariel glared toward the freshly set dining room table as if it had deliberately been designed to upset her. "What's going on here?"

"A little hen party," Susan explained. "I told you about it last week. Chris, Vicki, Kirsten, Barbara, Tracey . . ."

"To celebrate your victory?" Ariel's voice trembled with irritation. Hadn't she complained to her mother repeatedly that Susan's lawsuit had made her the laughingstock of her class?

"Not really, no. It's just been a while since we all got together, and I thought—"

Ariel made a face, as if someone had just passed wind. "Count me out."

"What?"

"No way I'm having dinner with Tracey Azinger," Ariel scoffed.

"What's the matter with Tracey? She's a perfectly lovely girl."

"She's weird."

"She's not weird."

"She just sits there with this stupid smile on her face all the time."

"Since when is it weird to smile?"

"She looks like one of those wax dummies from Madame Trousseau's."

"Tussaud," Susan corrected.

"What?"

"*Tussaud,* not *trousseau.* A trousseau is something you have when you get married."

"I know what a trousseau is," Ariel shot back, pale cheeks burning angry red.

"Is Barbara still dating that guy?" Whitney interrupted.

"Howard Kerble," Susan said, grateful for her daughter's intentional diversion. "Yes, she is."

"Think they'll get married?"

"They might."

"Then she could have a Tussaud," Whitney deadpanned.

Susan laughed.

"Are you laughing at me?" Ariel accused.

"No, of course not," Susan said, weary before the evening had even begun. Increasingly, Ariel had that effect on her. "It was just a joke."

"Whitney's the joke."

"That's enough."

"She and Tracey should be sisters."

"I said *enough.*"

"Tracey *is* kind of weird, Mom." This time the voice, surprisingly, was Whitney's.

"What?"

Whitney shrugged.

"How come you don't yell at *her* for saying stuff like that?" Ariel demanded.

"I didn't yell at you."

"You're always yelling at me."

"I'm not always . . ." Don't bite. Don't bite. Don't bite. "Let's just drop it. Okay?"

"Good," Ariel said. "Because I'm going out."

Immediately Susan's jaws clamped down on the bait. "What do you mean you're going out?"

"I have plans."

"What kind of plans?"

"The none-of-your-business kind."

Susan took a series of deep breaths, silently counting to ten at least half a dozen times before responding. "You're not going anywhere, young lady. Now why don't you help us finish setting the table?"

Ariel's response was to march into the front hall, open the closet door, and start putting on her coat.

Susan was instantly at her side. "What do you think you're doing?"

"I told you I was going out."

"And I told you, you were staying put."

Ariel shook her head, stuffed her arms in the sleeves of the old black coat she'd gotten from Goodwill. "Then we have a problem."

Susan quickly decided on a different approach. "Look, Ariel, just do this for me tonight, okay? I've really been looking forward to all of us getting together. Surely you can tolerate Tracey for one night."

"No," Ariel said stubbornly.

"Come on, sweetheart. Is what I'm asking so unreasonable?"

"Yes." Ariel opened the front door. A jolt of cold night air pushed its way inside.

"Let her go," Whitney called from the dining room. "If she's not here, we might actually have a good time."

She has a point there, Susan realized, taking a step back. Why was she being so insistent that Ariel stay home? So that she could scowl her way through dinner? So that she could insult her sister and ignore her guests? So that she could spread her gloom and doom around the table like an infectious cough? Let her go, she repeated silently. Let her go. Susan backed out of the hall as Ariel stepped outside and pulled the door shut after her.

"It's better this way." Whitney smiled at her mother, motioned toward the dining room table. "Looks pretty good, huh?"

"Looks great. Thank you, sweetheart. I don't know what I'd do without you."

Suddenly the front door burst open and Ariel stormed back into the house, her face contorted with rage. "What do you mean, if I'm not here, you might actually have a good time!"

Susan would have laughed had it not been clear from the look on Ariel's face that she was deadly serious. Whitney rolled her eyes, said nothing.

"Don't roll your eyes at me, bitch!" Ariel shouted.

"Stop it, Ariel," Susan warned. "Stop it right now."

"Just ignore her, Mom." Whitney turned her back on Ariel's rage.

"Don't walk away from me, you moron!" Without any warning, Ariel lunged toward the dining room table and grabbed one of Susan's good crystal glasses, lifting it into the air above her head.

"Ariel, put that down this minute," Susan cautioned, but already the glass had left Ariel's hand and was flying toward Whitney. "Whitney, look out!" Susan screamed as the glass narrowly missed the side of Whitney's head and crashed against the wall, shattering into a million tiny fragments.

"I'm sorry," Ariel said immediately, her face reflecting the horror of what she'd just done. "I didn't mean to throw it. It was out of my hand before I could stop it."

"Get out of here," Susan growled, her voice so low she barely recognized it. How could things get so bad so fast? A minute ago, all had been calm. Now there was shattered glass all over the dining room floor. Whitney was already down on her knees, trying to gather the fragments together, and Susan could see the tears streaming down the child's cheeks even as she fought to hide them from view. "Get out of here," Susan said again.

"I thought you wanted me home tonight," Ariel protested.

"I changed my mind. Get out."

"Where'll I go?" she wailed.

"I don't care," Susan told her, and at that moment, it was the truth.

"This is all your fault," Ariel shouted at her sister.

"One more word out of that miserable mouth of yours," Susan said steadily, "and I'll call the police and have you arrested for assault."

Ariel stared at her mother in disbelief. "Why don't you make it sexual assault?" she sneered. "Isn't that your specialty?"

"Get the hell out of here. Now."

Ariel raced from the room into the front hall, shouting more angry words as she opened the door and slammed it shut after her. It took Susan a few seconds to decipher those words and play them back again after Ariel was gone. "You'll be sorry," her daughter had been saying over and over again. "You'll be sorry. You'll be sorry. You'll be sorry."

Twenty-Three

"I'm sorry, Mrs. Hallendale, what day next week did you say you'd like to bring Charlie back to see Dr. Marcus?"

Chris watched Emily Hallendale's shoulders rise and fall in obvious irritation. "I said Wednesday afternoons are generally a good time for me." She tucked Charlie, a tiny white teacup poodle, inside the lapels of her calf-length, black mink coat, her tone indicating her displeasure at having to repeat herself. At forty-plus, Emily Hallendale was a formidable presence, tall and buxom, with short, dark hair and an olive complexion, model-high cheekbones, and a low tolerance for incompetence.

She hates me, Chris thought, deciding the feeling was mutual as she entered Charlie's name in Dr. Marcus's appointment calendar. "Here we go. One o'clock, Thursday, March nineteenth, 1992." Chris shakily scribbled the information on an appointment card, trying to ignore the incessant ringing of the telephone beside her, and offered the card to Emily Hallendale, who was staring at Chris as if she were a complete idiot.

"Wednesday," Emily Hallendale corrected, her voice flat, as if Chris were no longer worth the effort inflection required.

"Sorry. Yes, you *did* say Wednesday, didn't you?"

"Three times."

"Yes, I'm very sorry about that."

The phone continued ringing. Chris stared at it, pushing errant strands of limp, shoulder-length hair behind her ears.

"Don't you think you should answer that?"

"No." Chris forced an uneasy smile onto her face and tried to keep from screaming. Who was this woman to tell her what to do?

"I'm not sure I appreciate your tone," Emily Hallendale said.

"I'm sorry," Chris apologized quickly.

"Maybe I should talk to the doctor about the people he has working for him."

"Maybe you should," Chris agreed, filling out another appointment card, slamming it down on the counter without looking up. "Wednesday. March eighteenth, 1992. One o'clock. Have a nice day."

Emily Hallendale remained motionless at the counter for several minutes, as if considering her options, before sliding the card into her large black alligator bag. "Don't forget to change the date on the doctor's schedule," she advised coolly before marching to the door, the small dog at her throat yapping his farewells.

"Isn't anybody going to answer that damn phone?" Dr.

Marcus's naturally gruff voice growled from one of the back rooms.

Chris nodded, thinking that the doctor was beginning to sound more like his patients every day, but she made no move to pick up the receiver. What for? She already knew who was on the other end.

"Answer the damn phone. Answer the damn phone," came the cry from the middle of the cramped waiting room.

"Be quiet, Lydia," Chris shushed the majestic white cockatoo who sat atop her large cage. Lydia was the office mascot, a cantankerous parrot who'd been brought in for a checkup six months earlier and then abandoned.

"Be quiet," the parrot repeated. "Be quiet, Lydia." The large bird began pacing back and forth across the top of her cage, her head bobbing up and down to an invisible beat.

"What's she doing?" a young girl asked from the row of black leather chairs against the wall. The girl, whose small, upturned nose was overrun with freckles, was maybe eight years old. She sat rocking a small gray kitten in her lap, a look of adult worry already settled into her child's face. Her mother sat beside her, her head resting against the pale pink wall, her eyes closed beneath a painting of a frolicking dolphin.

"Just getting some exercise," Chris told the red-haired little girl, trying not to picture Montana at that age.

The youngster was instantly on her feet and at the side of the cage.

"Careful, she could bite," Chris warned.

The girl took an instant step back, pale green eyes as big as saucers, protective arms automatically shielding her kitten from harm. "Will she bite Fluffy?"

She'd eat Fluffy for breakfast, Chris thought but didn't say, amazed at how early the protective impulse started, at how instinctive it was. Once again, she tried not to think of Montana, but as usual, her daughter was everywhere, her image filling each empty chair, her shadow covering the windows like heavy blinds, her eyes absorbing the light from the street, her mouth sucking the air from the room like water from a straw. Chris felt dizzy, faint, as if she couldn't breathe.

"The phone!" Dr. Marcus barked again.

"The phone," Lydia repeated, head bobbing for emphasis. "The phone. Answer the damn phone."

Chris closed her eyes, trying not to see her daughter behind them, and swallowed a deep breath of air, feeling it stab at her chest like a paring knife, as she lifted the receiver from its carriage, then dropped it back down without bringing it to her ear.

"How come you did that?" the little girl asked, green eyes growing wider, overtaking the rest of her face.

"It was a wrong number."

"How do you know?"

Chris smiled, said nothing. What was there to say?

"Is it going to be much longer?" the girl's mother asked, eyes still closed.

"Hopefully not." Once again the phone began its persistent ring. "The doctor had an emergency this morning," Chris continued loudly, trying to block out the sound. "A dog got hit by a car. That backed everything up. I'm sorry," she apologized to the other two people waiting, an elderly man holding a shaking German shepherd over his shoulder like a baby, and an old woman with white, curly hair singing softly to her overweight

Persian cat. Neither seemed unduly concerned. Probably they were used to waiting. Dr. Marcus ran a thriving practice. It was always busy. Probably the reason the boyish-looking veterinarian had hired her, despite her lack of experience.

Chris felt lucky to have gotten this job, wanted desperately to hold on to it. What had she been thinking of earlier? If she wasn't careful, she'd get herself fired. She'd have to call Emily Hallendale later and apologize for her rudeness. She couldn't allow herself to become so distracted. She couldn't jump every time the phone rang. Nor could she refuse to answer it. She reached for the phone, hesitated. Please don't let it be like the last time, she prayed, as she did every morning before leaving her small basement apartment to go to work. Please don't let Tony find me. Please let him leave me alone.

But of course he always found her. And she knew he'd never leave her alone. No matter how many times she moved—four times in the last six months. No matter how many times she changed her phone number—half a dozen times at least. Still, he found her, followed her, harassed her at home and at work, to the point where she couldn't sleep, couldn't concentrate, couldn't cope with even the most menial of tasks, so that her hapless employers ultimately had no choice but to let her go. "We're sorry," they told her, having reached the limits of their understanding, exhausted their patience. "We know it's not your fault. But we have a business to run."

Her first job had been as a waitress in a fifties-style diner. Tony found out where she was working and began following her to and from the restaurant, sitting quietly at a table in a corner during many of her shifts, watching her every move, looking at her with that eerie little smile on his face, that awful gargoyle grin that said he had big plans for her later on, until she could barely walk from one table to the next without tripping or spilling something.

She was fired after three months.

("We're sorry. We know it's not your fault . . .")

Barbara next suggested Chris try for a job in a high-rise building with a security guard. Chris finally found such a job, as a receptionist with an advertising agency on the twelfth floor of a fourteen-story building with round-the-clock security, but was let go four months later after Tony started bombarding the office with nuisance phone calls. (". . . but we have a business to run.")

Chris secured a restraining order against Tony. It had no effect. Nor did the second one she waved in Tony's face as he was trailing her home from work one evening. Restraining orders weren't worth the paper they were written on, he told her. Bullets were stronger than paper; fists carried more weight than judicial pronouncements. If anything, the restraining orders succeeded only in making Tony angrier and more determined than ever to make her life a living hell.

"You may have to shoot him," Vicki stated simply, as Chris searched Vicki's face for signs she was joking, finding none. "Don't worry," Vicki assured her. "I'll defend you. You won't serve a day in jail. That's a promise."

Was that the answer? Chris thought now, wondering whether she could do it. He's taken everything from me: my children, my home, my peace of mind. And even that wasn't enough. It was never going to be enough. *I'll dance on your grave,* he'd told her once. *I'll dance on your grave,* the phone was telling her now.

"Aren't you going to answer the phone?" the little girl was asking.

"Answer the phone," Lydia repeated loudly. "Answer the phone. Answer the damn phone."

"For God's sake, Chris. What's going on out here?" Dr. Marcus said, exiting the inner office and coming up behind her. He grabbed the phone from its carriage, took a deep breath. "Mariemont Veterinary Service," he purred.

"Thank goodness," Chris heard a woman exclaim. "I've been calling for the past half hour. I kept getting disconnected."

"We've been having problems with the phones," Dr. Marcus said quickly, small beagle eyes shooting Chris a puzzled glance. "What can I do for you?"

Chris sank back in her chair, looked blankly toward the window, listened to the doctor's calming voice as he removed the pencil from between her fingers, jotted down the woman's name in his appointment calendar. How long before she lost this job? she wondered.

"Yes, Mrs. Newman, I agree it sounds worrisome. Bring Snuggles in around four o'clock and we'll try to fit you in. And I'm sorry you had all that trouble with the phones." Again Dr. Marcus looked questioningly at Chris. "Is there a problem?" he asked softly.

"Problem?" Lydia screeched from the top of her cage.

"No, Doctor. I'm sorry. There's no problem," Chris answered.

"The phones are working okay?"

As if on cue, the phone started ringing.

"Answer the phone," Lydia instructed clearly. "Answer the damn phone."

Chris felt all eyes on her as she picked up the phone. "Mariemont Veterinary Service," she said crisply.

"Hello, bitch," the familiar voice said.

Chris paled, dropped the phone to the desk.

Dr. Marcus quickly retrieved it, lifted it to his ear. "Hello? This is Dr. Marcus. Can I help you?" There was a second's silence. "Certainly. We see all kinds of dogs here. When would you like to come in?" The doctor flipped impatiently through the pages of the appointment calendar. "Next Tuesday at ten o'clock would be fine. And your name please? . . . Smith? Well, that's easy enough."

Was it possible she'd heard wrong? Chris wondered. Was her imagination getting the better of her? Was she hearing things that simply weren't there?

"And the dog's name? . . . Montana?" Dr. Marcus repeated, as a sharp intake of breath pierced Chris's heart. "Interesting name. Don't think I've heard that one before." He hung up the phone, stared down at Chris, who was having renewed trouble breathing. "Can I talk to you for a minute please? Excuse us just a second," he apologized to those waiting. "Are you feeling well?" he asked, leading Chris into one of the examination rooms. For a minute, Chris thought he might use the stethoscope around his neck on her.

Chris leaned against the tall steel examining table in the middle of the small room, said nothing. What was there to say?

"Chris, what is it? Are you feeling sick?"

She saw the concern in Dr. Marcus's gold-flecked brown eyes and recognized it as the same look she'd seen on the faces of the men who'd fired her from her previous jobs. In another week or two, concern would give way to practicality. "I'm sorry. I wish I didn't have to do this," she could already hear him say, "but I have a business to run."

"Maybe you should take the rest of the afternoon off. Kathleen can take over the front desk." He motioned with his square jaw toward the back rooms where his nurses were tending their patients. "Go home, get a good night's sleep, and hopefully you'll feel better in the morning."

Chris shook her head. Tomorrow morning would only be worse. Today was just the beginning. The first new day of Tony's well-orchestrated campaign of terror. The first day of the rest of her life, she thought, and almost laughed. Tony was diabolical. He'd given her almost three months this time, three months to learn the ropes, relax, feel comfortable in her new environment. Two full weeks longer than the last time. Two weeks in which she'd gradually stopped jumping at the sight of her own shadow, two weeks in which she'd begun to feel like a human being again, to feel something approaching hope for a normal life.

And then the phone had started ringing as soon as she'd walked into the office at eight o'clock this morning. "Mariemont Veterinary Service," she'd said brightly. The sun was shining. Spring was a week away. It was a time of renewed optimism, new beginnings.

"Hello, bitch," came the shattering reply.

"I probably shouldn't come in tomorrow," Chris said now, pushing the reluctant words out of her mouth, her eyes filling with tears. She loved her job, adored the animals. She'd even been thinking of trying to save enough money to go back to school, become a veterinary assistant.

Who was she kidding? she thought bitterly. She was almost forty. It was too late for her to go back to school, too late to become anything other than what she was, which was nothing. Hadn't Tony been telling her that for years?

"You think you're coming down with something?" Dr. Marcus extended his hand, felt her forehead for signs of a fever.

"I'm not sick," she said, tears falling the length of her cheeks. "I'm sorry. I don't think I can work here anymore." She might as well be the one to say it, she thought. Spare the good doctor the discomfort. Save him the trouble. She was only hastening the inevitable.

"What's the matter, Chris? Is there something I can help you with?"

"Thank you, Dr. Marcus. No, there's nothing you can do." There's nothing anybody can do. "Please understand. It'll be better for everyone if I leave."

Chris watched indecision flicker across the doctor's quizzical face. Should he comfort her, try to find out what was wrong, or leave well enough alone, accept that she was trouble he didn't need, let her go before she caused him any further inconvenience?

"As you wish," he said after a lengthy pause.

Chris smiled sadly. It was better this way. She'd find another job, hopefully buy herself another month or two before Tony resurfaced. Maybe it was time to consider moving to another city, starting a new life.

A life without her children.

A life without her friends.

Except she didn't have any children. Not anymore. Rowdy had kicked her the last time she'd tried to take him in her arms. Wyatt refused to talk to her, to even look at her. She hadn't seen Montana in almost two years.

No, she had no children.

And her friends were busy with their own lives. Vicki's practice was thriving; she was growing more famous by the day; Susan had recently published several articles in the *Cincinnati Post,* and had been asked to be the keynote speaker at a symposium dealing with sex and the workplace; Barbara was busy making plans for a fall wedding.

Barbara, Chris thought, and smiled despite her tears. She wiped the tears away, the memory of the touch of Barbara's lips against her own still fresh despite the passage of time. Was it possible Tony had been right about her all along? That somewhere in his warped and twisted mind, he'd hit on a truth even she hadn't been aware of?

Chris shrugged. What difference did it make? Clearly, Barbara suffered from no such confusion. She was getting married in six months to a wonderful, caring man. Whatever awakening Chris had experienced that night in Barbara's bedroom, the epiphany was hers alone. The kiss she and Barbara had shared had been as brief as it was unexpected. But it was that kiss, more than anything, that had sealed Chris's fate. She'd crossed a line, she recognized; there was no turning back.

She'd surprised everyone, Tony especially, herself most of all. In the beginning, everyone had expected Chris to go back to Tony. Initially he'd acted contrite, sending truckloads of flowers, apologizing often and profusely. It was only a game, he'd tried to convince her. He was preparing to open the door when she'd disappeared. Surely she could see the humor in the situation. Surely she'd be able to laugh off the episode later. *Hey, remember the time I threw you out in the freezing cold in your Wonder Woman outfit?*

But Chris wasn't laughing, and she wasn't coming home. "You'll never see your kids again," he'd threatened, and he'd made good on that vow. Chris shuddered, remembering the look on Montana's face as she'd turned away in disgust from the mother who was standing almost naked in the snow, begging to be allowed back inside for even more abuse. Chris never wanted to see that look on anyone's face again.

She was so tired, she thought now, fighting off the urge to curl up in the middle of the steel examining table and fall asleep. Tired of being an object of scorn and derision, of pity and concern. Tired of the worried looks on the faces of her friends. Tired of reassuring them she was all right. Tired of moving from one horrible little apartment to another. Of learning the ropes for a job she knew she wouldn't be able to keep. Tired of always looking over her shoulder. Of living in fear. Of being disappointed. Of being alone. Tired of being tired.

What was she waiting for?

The answer was so simple.

"Damn," she whispered, the solution suddenly clear.

"Dr. Marcus," one of the nurses called out, as Chris became aware the doctor was still beside her.

"Be right there." Dr. Marcus hesitated, as if aware of Chris's thoughts.

"You better go," Chris told him. "Don't worry about me. I'll be fine."

"You're sure?"

"Thank you for everything."

Chris stood absolutely still in the center of the room for several long seconds after the doctor had left, then moved quickly to the cabinets along one wall, opening each one in turn, until she found the medication she was looking for. How much different could animal tranquilizers be from sedatives meant for human beings? Surely swallowing a bottle of one would prove as lethal as a bottle of the other. She pocketed one box of pills, then another. What the hell? Might as well be sure. Maybe in her next life, she'd come back as Emily Hallendale's tiny teacup toy poodle.

Chris returned to her desk to get her coat and purse and was startled to find Emily Hallendale standing there waiting for her.

"I want to apologize," Emily Hallendale began.

"Apologize?"

"For my rudeness, the things I said."

"Really, there's no need."

"I'm busy next Wednesday," Emily Hallendale stated sheepishly, Charlie's tiny white head peeking out from underneath her massive black mink coat. "After all that fuss I made about you mixing up the dates, I forgot all about this meeting I'm supposed to be chairing on Wednesday. I remembered it just as I got to my car."

Chris smiled. "Kathleen will take care of you," she said, slipping into her brown cloth coat as Kathleen replaced her behind the desk.

"Dr. Marcus said you quit?" Kathleen asked, as if she might have misunderstood.

"You quit?" Emily Hallendale repeated.

"You quit?" Lydia echoed loudly from the top of her cage.

"Not because of the anything I said, I hope!" Emily exclaimed in growing horror, bringing a gloved hand to her chest. Immediately the tiny white poodle began licking it.

"No," Chris said quickly. "Trust me. You had nothing to do with what happened."

"What happened?" Emily asked.

The phone started ringing. Kathleen answered it on the first ring. "Mariemont Veterinary Service."

Chris held her breath, felt her blood drain to her toes.

"Hello? Hello? Anybody there?" Kathleen shrugged, replaced the receiver. "Probably a wrong number."

Chris grabbed her purse. "I have to go."

She was halfway down the street when she felt the hand at her elbow. "What do you want from me? You win! I give up! Can't you just leave me alone?" She spun around, not sure what she would see first—Tony or his fist slamming toward her face.

Instead she saw Emily Hallendale.

"Oh, I'm sorry. I thought you were someone else."

"The same someone who's been phoning all afternoon?"

Chris said nothing, not trusting her voice.

"You dropped these on your way out," Emily told her, pulling a box of sedatives out of the pocket of her mink coat.

Chris's eyes widened in alarm.

"I think you could use a cup of coffee," Emily said.

Chris decided she was in the middle of a nervous breakdown, that Emily Hallendale and the tiny white poodle at her throat didn't exist, and that she might as well go along with whatever this apparition was suggesting.

"We'll go to my place," Emily said.

Twenty-Four

"Would you like a cup of coffee?"

"No, thanks." Susan smiled at Vicki, who sat erect beside her, her canary yellow pantsuit clashing with the too pink walls and burgundy vinyl furniture of the hospital waiting room. The August sun streamed in the windows through thin venetian blinds, casting dark shadows, like the stripes of a zebra, across the white linoleum floor. Stacks of surprisingly up-to-date magazines sat on various small tables scattered around the large room. Artificially cold air blew toward their faces from several nearby vents. Susan wondered how it was possible for a room to be too hot, too cold, and airless all at the same time. "I can't tell you how much your being here means to me. I know how busy you are."

"Slow day," Vicki said.

Susan knew Vicki was lying, that she'd probably canceled several appointments to be here.

"How's she doing?" Vicki asked.

"Not good."

"What do the doctors say?"

"That there's nothing more they can do, that she probably won't last the week." Susan glanced down the long hospital corridor toward the room in which her mother, barely recognizable beneath the ill-fitting blond wig Susan had bought her when she'd started losing her hair, lay sleeping. Years of surgery, chemotherapy, and radiation had reduced the poor woman to less than half her normal weight, robbed her of the strength she needed to fight the unmerciful progression of her cancer.

Vicki nodded understanding, clasped Susan's hand inside her own. "What can I do for you?"

"You're doing it."

"Do you need me to call anyone? Your brother and sister . . . ?"

"Kenny's flying in tonight. I'm still working up the nerve to call Diane."

Susan pictured her older brother and younger sister, the tortoise and the hare, her mother had once jokingly referred to them. Kenny was tall, stocky, sedentary, whereas Diane was gaunt, wiry, and never able to sit still for more than a few minutes at a time. While Kenny moved slowly and methodically through the various stages of his life, Diane, for all her excess energy, always seemed to be running around in circles. Running away, Susan decided now, remembering how her sister had fled when she'd emerged from the water with her legs covered in leeches. Not much had changed in the ensuing decades. Her sister was still running away from even the vaguest hint of unpleasantness.

"The last time I spoke to Diane, she said she'd love to come see Mom," Susan told Vicki now, "but it was a *real* bad time for her. I think the moon, or something, was in the wrong planet. I don't know."

"Why don't I try her for you now?" Vicki offered.

Susan scribbled her sister's Los Angeles phone number on a scrap piece of paper she found in her purse and handed it to Vicki, watching as her friend approached the pay phone on the far wall. Poor Vicki, Susan thought. She has no idea what she's in for.

Diane was one of those people who thought death was contagious. When her husband had died of a sudden heart attack in his sleep five years earlier, Diane had thrown out not only the sheets, but the bed as well. She'd immediately put their house in Westwood up for sale and moved into a small cottage in the Hollywood hills. There were no children because she'd always been convinced she'd die in childbirth; she refused to fly because she was absolutely certain the plane would crash; she even had a thing about driving over bridges.

"I don't think the doctors expect her to last that long," Susan heard Vicki say quietly into the phone. "No, I understand that. It's just that . . ."

Susan took a deep breath and forced herself out of her chair, her brown cotton pants sticking to the vinyl of the seat, making a rude sucking noise as she pulled away. "I better speak to her," she whispered, holding out her hand for the phone. Vicki might be a genius when it came to handling wily criminals and clever DAs, but she'd never run up against anyone quite like Diane.

"You know I really want to be there," Diane whined as soon as Susan said hello. "It's just that this is a real bad time for me."

The correct word is *really,* not *real.* It's an adverb, Susan wanted to shout. Instead she said, "There isn't much time left."

"Aren't you being a tad melodramatic?"

Susan had always hated the word *tad.* She had to bite down on her tongue to keep from screaming.

"She's been like this for months now," Diane insisted.

Susan heard the puff of her sister's ever-present cigarette. "This is different."

"How can you be so sure?"

"Because I'm here every day."

"And I'm not, is that it? Is that what this is really about?"

"It's about our mother," Susan said slowly, picturing the ashes of Diane's cigarette hanging precariously from their filter, then breaking off and falling toward the floor, scattering in the air like dust. "Who is dying."

"She'll get better."

"She'll get worse."

"You're being obstinate."

"You're being obtuse."

"Hang up," Vicki instructed impatiently from beside Susan. "Don't waste your breath."

"Who is that?" Diane demanded. "Did she just tell you to hang up on me?"

"Diane, I have to go."

"Look, I'll see what I can do," Diane said grudgingly, exhaling a long puff of smoke from her lungs into Susan's ear.

"That'd be great," Susan said, hanging up the phone.

"Isn't she a charmer," Vicki said.

Susan laughed, thinking of her older daughter. "I guess there's one in every family."

"Ariel still giving you a hard time?" Vicki asked, as if she had access to Susan's brain.

Susan shrugged, sinking back into a waiting chair. "I don't know how my mother did it. She was always so calm, so fair. I don't remember her ever raising her voice in anger." Susan shook her head in wonderment. "I try so hard to be like her."

"Just be yourself."

"I'm always yelling. I don't remember my mother ever yelling at me the way I yell at Ariel."

"That's because you aren't your mother, and Ariel isn't you. It's a whole different dynamic. Trust me, I bet your mother yelled plenty at Diane."

"You think?"

"You're a great mother, Susan. Stop being so hard on yourself."

"Ariel hates me."

"Of course she hates you. That's her job."

Susan smiled gratefully, collapsing against Vicki's side as the other woman wrapped her arms around her. "I'm so glad you're here."

"So am I." Vicki kissed the top of Susan's head.

The two women rocked gently together, the sound of their breathing filling the room. Gradually, Susan became aware of other voices, other people—a couple whispering in the far corner, a man flipping through the bathing suit issue of *Sports Illustrated,* a woman trying to read a book through eyes blinded by a steady stream of tears. "I'm not sure I'm going to be able to handle this."

"You'll handle it."

"I'm not ready to let her go."

"I don't think children are ever ready to let go of their parents," Vicki agreed, a sadness in her voice Susan hadn't heard before. "You know, I could really use a cup of coffee. How about you?"

"Okay," Susan said. "Double cream. No sugar."

"Be back in a few minutes."

"I'll be in with my mother."

Susan watched Vicki until she was out of sight, then she pushed herself off her chair and walked down the quiet hospital corridor. Her mind had long ago absorbed the steady flow of hospital sounds—bells ringing, carts being wheeled across the floor, announcements over the PA, patients moaning behind half-closed doors—so that she barely heard them now. They blew past her ears like a train whistle in the distance.

She reached the door to her mother's semiprivate room and pushed it open slowly, afraid of what she might see. "Hello, Mrs. Unger," she said to the sweet-faced, white-haired woman in the bed beside her mother, and the woman smiled her response, although her eyes shone with the blank stare of someone who had no idea who she was. "Hi, Mom." Susan sank into one of the two chairs pushed up against her mother's hospital bed, lifting her head to her mother only gradually, preparing herself for her matte gray pallor, for the skin stretched so tightly across her face it seemed in danger of splitting in half, for the eyes riddled with confusion and pain. But her mother's eyes were closed, her face relaxed. Susan's breath caught in her lungs as she listened for sounds of her mother's breathing, heard none.

Only when she saw a slight twitch beneath the hospital sheets did she know her mother was still alive. Susan stilled the trembling hand beneath the bedcovers with her own, although it too was trembling, and kissed her mother's chalky, dry forehead, dislodging the too blond wig that sat atop her head like a lopsided beret. Susan pictured her mother's natural hair, how each strand had always stayed exactly in place from one washing to the next, not requiring so much as a comb to touch it up. Her mother's hair had been one of the marvels of Susan's childhood, she recalled now, trying to adjust the wig without disturbing her mother. She sank back in her chair, straining for a comfortable position. "Kenny's flying in from New York tonight. And I spoke to Diane. She's going to get here as soon as she can. So you better perk up." Susan swallowed the threat of tears. "You know how Diane is around sick people."

"Diane's coming?" her mother asked without opening her eyes or moving her lips.

Was it possible Susan had imagined she'd said anything at all? "Yes, Mom, she's trying to make arrangements right now."

"I must be very sick," her mother said, lips twitching into a smile.

"No, in fact you're doing very well. The doctor said he saw a definite improvement."

"Susan." Her mother opened her eyes, said nothing further, as if Susan's name had exhausted all her strength.

"I don't want to hear any negative talk. You know how important they say it is for you to think positively."

"*They* aren't the ones in constant pain," her mother whispered slowly.

"Are you in pain now, Mom? Do you want me to get you something for it?"

Her mother nodded slowly. Immediately Susan buzzed for the nurse.

"We'll get you something, Mom."

Several long minutes later, a nurse appeared in the doorway. She was tall and angular. Small, wireless glasses balanced on the tip of her long, patrician nose.

"My mother's in pain," Susan said, trying to keep the sharpness out of her voice. What had taken the stupid woman so long to respond to her buzz? "She needs some medication."

"I'll check with the doctor," the nurse said, gone before Susan had a chance to say more.

"Would you like some water, Mom?" Susan realized she felt as helpless with her mother as she did with her older child. Mothers and daughters, she thought. Is there any relationship in the world more complicated, more *fraught?*

Susan filled a glass with water from the pitcher on the nightstand beside the bed and extended it toward her mother's cracked lips. She watched her mother sip dutifully at the clear liquid, although she doubted any reached her throat. "I love you, Mom."

"I love you too, darling."

"There's so much I want to say to you."

"You have a captive audience." Her mother tried to smile, winced instead.

Susan blinked back tears, stilled the quivering in her jaw. Could she say all that needed to be said, all that was in her heart, without breaking down? "I just want to thank you," she began slowly. "For everything you've done for me. For helping me with the kids. For always being there when I need you. For loving me. For taking such good care of me all my life."

Tears slowly trickled down her mother's cheeks.

She understands I'm saying good-bye, Susan realized. "I want you to know what a privilege it's been to know you," she said, crying openly now. "You've been the best mother a girl could ever hope to have. And I love you so much."

"It's been my pleasure, darling," her mother said, trying to smile, crying out in pain instead.

Susan was immediately on her feet. "Where does it hurt, Mom?"

"Everywhere."

Susan looked anxiously toward the door. "The nurse should be back in a minute with the medication." Where was that damn woman? What was taking her so long? If she didn't come back soon, if she didn't come back *right this second,* then Susan was going to write an angry letter to the hospital. No, forget that. She'd write an article for the *Cincinnati Post.* She'd make sure this issue got the attention it deserved, even if it meant suing the hospital. Patients shouldn't be forced to suffer needlessly. Her mother shouldn't have to spend her last days in excruciating pain.

As if on cue, the door swung open. "Thank God," Susan said. Only it wasn't the nurse. It was an orderly with the food cart. The orderly was short and black, and his head was as bald and shiny as a bowling ball. "Dinnertime," he announced.

Susan checked her watch. It was barely four o'clock in the afternoon.

"It's the early-bird special," the orderly said, answering the look in Susan's eyes as he lifted the covers from the plates. "Let's see what you ladies ordered. Roast beef in a yummy-looking beige sauce for Mrs. Unger, and chicken in a yummy-looking beige sauce for Mrs. Hill. Good choice, ladies," he said, depositing the food on the appropriate trays. "And let's not forget the lime Jell-O for Mrs. Unger, and the cherry Jell-O for Mrs. Hill. Personally, I prefer the cherry. *Bon appétit.*" He waved on his way out the door.

Susan stood for several seconds staring at the unappetizing display. "Well, doesn't this look . . . awful," she said, unable to lie. Just because the cancer had reached her mother's brain didn't make her an idiot. "What do you think, Mom? Think you're up for some cherry Jell-O?"

Her mother's answer was a sharp cry of pain.

"Okay, that's it. Where's that damn nurse?" Susan looked frantically toward the door as her mother's plaintive moans filled the room. "Try to hold on, Mom. I'm going to get a doctor. I'll be right back." She ran to the door. "I'll be right back."

Susan raced down the hall to the nurses' station. Three nurses sat chatting behind the counter. None looked up as Susan approached. "Excuse me," Susan said, banging on the countertop, securing their attention. "I asked a nurse for painkillers ten minutes ago. My mother is in agony."

"Could you lower your voice please?" one of the nurses said from her seat behind her computer.

"Could you get up off your ass and get my mother something for her pain?" Susan shot back.

The oldest of the nurses stood up, approached Susan slowly, cautiously. "Okay, can you just calm down now? We don't want to scare the other patients."

"*We* don't give a damn about the other patients," Susan told her. "*We* just want to get my mother some morphine."

"Please try to keep your voice down," the nurse, whose

black skin was topped by a short mop of curly, orange hair, advised. "Your mother is . . . ?"

"Roslyn Hill. In room four oh seven."

The nurse checked her chart. "Mrs. Hill had a shot of morphine at two o'clock this afternoon. She isn't due for another one until six."

"She's in pain right now."

"I'm sorry." The nurse lowered the chart to the desk.

"That's it? You're sorry?"

"There's nothing I can do."

"I want to speak to Dr. Wertman."

"Dr. Wertman isn't here right now."

"Then I want to speak to another doctor. Any doctor."

"I already spoke to Dr. Zarb," one of the other nurses piped up, the same sharp-featured nurse who'd responded to her mother's buzzer. She looks exhausted, Susan thought, refusing to feel sympathy. "He says he'd prefer to wait at least another hour."

"Really? And would he prefer to wait another hour if he were the one with cancer?"

"Please, Mrs. Hill . . ."

"It's Mrs. Norman. My *mother* is Mrs. Hill. *She's* the patient, and *she* has cancer. That cancer has spread from her breasts to her lymph nodes to her lungs and her spine and now her brain. She is terminal. And she is in horrendous pain. And you just sit here and do nothing." Susan looked helplessly down the long corridor, watched it blur with her tears as her voice echoed down the hall. "I don't understand you. My mother is dying. What would be the harm in giving her more painkillers? Are you afraid she'll become addicted? Is that it? Are you afraid she'll die a drug addict?"

"Susan?" Vicki was suddenly beside her. "Susan, what's the matter? Has something happened?"

"My mother's in horrible pain, and nobody will help her."

"I'll try to contact Dr. Wertman," the third nurse volunteered.

"Please try to calm down, Mrs. Norman," the second nurse advised. "Your hysteria won't help your mother."

"Fuck you!" Susan's arms flailed wildly at the air as she took off down the hall accidentally knocking the Styrofoam cups filled with hot coffee from Vicki's hands.

Vicki trailed after her. "Susan . . ."

"Please don't tell me to calm down."

"I don't want you to calm down. I want you to wait up."

Susan stopped, took a deep breath. "I'm sorry."

"For what?"

"I spilled coffee all over you."

"No. Mostly you got the floor."

"Think they'll call security?"

"Let them try," Vicki said as they reached room 407, and entered the room together.

Susan's mother was lying in bed, her neck and back arched in pain, her eyes tightly closed, bony hands clawing at the bedsheets.

"Oh, God, look at her," Susan whispered, her hand covering her mouth. "She's in such pain." She approached the bed, collapsed into the chair beside it, cried softly.

Her mother opened her eyes, used all her strength to raise her head from the pillow. "What's the matter, baby?" she asked Susan. And then another spasm ripped through her body and she cried out, a loud, piercing scream that brought the nurses running, and a young doctor scrambling for medication. Susan watched gratefully as the resident administered a shot of morphine, felt her mother's twisted body gradually begin to unravel and stretch out, the lines on her face uncreasing, like a crumpled piece of paper relaxing in an open fist.

"Maybe you should go home and get some rest," the young doctor advised.

Susan shook her head, clung tightly to Vicki's hand.

"Susan?"

"Yes, Mom?"

But her mother had already drifted off to sleep. Susan leaned forward, adjusted her mother's wig, brought the sheets up under her chin. Then she sank back down, Vicki's hand resting on her shoulder, and watched her mother breathe. "I'm here, Mom," she whispered. "I'm here."

Twenty-Five

Susan's mother died four days later.

Both Susan and her brother wanted to hold the funeral as soon as possible, but they had to delay it a week to give their sister time to drive in from California. Actually, she didn't drive. She took the train. "It was horrible," Diane told everyone who'd listen. "I didn't sleep for three days. I'm still completely nauseous. The thought of the return trip . . ." She broke off, as if the thought were just too much to bear.

She'd been complaining ever since Susan had picked her up at the station. She refused to visit the funeral home, dismissing such displays as barbaric and insensitive. Besides, she was too broken up, she said, taking to her bed in Susan's guest room. Of course the bed was too small, the mattress too soft, and Ariel played her music much too loud. "I knew there was a reason I didn't have children," Diane said more than once, although she thought nothing of asking Whitney to get her a drink, a sandwich, a magazine. "God, these magazines are so old," she said instead of thank you.

The funeral was more of the same. Diane wore black from head to toe, including heavy dark stockings and a floppy, feather-strewn hat whose translucent veil completely covered her face, despite the heat of the August day.

"Where'd your sister find that hat?" Barbara asked Susan at the chapel.

"I think she's been living in Hollywood too long," Chris said.

"You're sure she's not an Arab terrorist?" Vicki asked.

Somehow, even the funeral was all about Diane. While Susan and Kenny shared fond memories of their mother with the other mourners, and even Ariel, relatively cleaned up and soft-spoken, delivered a touching tribute to the grandmother she'd adored, Diane eulogized herself, discussing her various triumphs over adversity, of which her mother's death was only the latest in a long line of crosses to bear. "Would you like a copy of my speech?" she asked Susan at the conclusion of the service, and again at the cemetery.

"Would you like a copy of my speech?" Susan heard her asking Kenny's wife, Marilyn, back at the house. Susan had invited everyone over after the ceremony for coffee and cake, and as she scurried around making sure everything was running smoothly, Diane held court in the center of the living room. "The train ride was pure hell," Susan heard her expounding. "All that stopping and starting. And those damn whistles. I don't think I slept a total of two hours in three nights."

"She's so self-absorbed," Barbara commented.

"She's having trouble coping with her grief," Chris allowed.

"She's a cunt," Vicki said.

"Ssh!" Chris and Barbara squealed, almost in unison. "Don't let Susan hear you say things like that."

"Too late," Susan said, entering her kitchen, grateful beyond words to see her three best friends huddled together in front of the food-laden counter. Chris, Barbara, and Vicki had been over every day since her mother's death, keeping her company, holding her hand, listening when she wanted to talk, sitting quietly beside her when she needed to be still, crying with her, making her laugh. They sent food, made coffee, got the house ready for visitors. Diane, of course, did nothing. She was too upset. She was nauseated. She was useless, Susan decided. "Vicki's right," Susan said now. "She's a cunt."

Again Chris squealed, the sound a curious mix of outrage and admiration. She giggled. "You know I've never said that word out loud."

"Get out of here," Vicki said. "Say it now."

"I can't."

Vicki looked astonished. "After everything you've been through with that cocksucking, motherfucking, son-of-a-bitch ex-husband of yours, you're embarrassed to say the word *cunt?*"

Chris buried her face in her hands. "I don't believe you just said that."

"What? *Cocksucking, motherfucking, son-of-a-bitch,* or *cunt?*"

"Stop it!"

"Look at you." Vicki laughed. "You're blushing like a little kid. Say it."

"I can't."

"I've never said it either," Barbara admitted sheepishly.

"You've never said *cunt?* I don't believe you two. Come on, say it. It's very liberating. You'll see. Say it together if you can't say it alone."

"Susan, where are you?" The sound of Diane's voice assaulted Susan's ears from the other room.

"Say it," Susan told her friends. "I dare you."

"I double dare you," echoed Vicki.

Chris and Barbara grabbed hands, as if they were about to plunge off a high cliff. "Cunt!" they cried in unison, as the door to the kitchen swung open and Ariel appeared, stunned, in the doorway.

"Excuse me?" She was wearing a plaid skirt with a white blouse, and except for the spiky shock of pink-and-purple hair, looked astonishingly like a normal teenager, home from boarding school and waiting for her milk and cookies.

The four women collapsed in helpless laughter.

"Mom? Mom, are you all right?"

Susan couldn't remember the last time she'd seen Ariel so concerned about her well-being. It made her laugh even harder. "I'm fine, sweetheart. Is there something you need?"

"Diane wants another cup of coffee." Ariel moved warily toward the coffee machine on the counter.

"I thought your speech was wonderful," Chris said in the abnormally high-pitched voice of someone trying desperately not to laugh.

Ariel regarded the women suspiciously, as if they were about to pounce. "Thank you," she said, although she clearly wasn't sure.

"We weren't talking about you," Vicki said, as if to reassure her, and once again, the other women doubled over laughing.

"What's going on in here?" another voice demanded. The voice was so sharp it hurt the ear.

Susan watched her younger sister sweep into the room, like a deranged beekeeper mourning the loss of her hive. Her veil was pushed back to reveal a thin face framed by straight, yellow-blond hair. Bright red lips flamed out from an otherwise colorless complexion. Dark eyes radiated indignation. Immediately the laughter froze in Susan's throat.

"Really, Susan, we just buried our mother. How can you show her such disrespect? We could hear you laughing from the next room."

Susan felt the stinging rebuke like a slap to her face.

"Respect is something you show the living," Vicki said.

"Sometimes laughter eases the pain," Chris added.

"Aren't you awfully hot in that hat?" Barbara asked.

"Cunt," Ariel muttered under her breath.

"What?" Diane stammered. "What did you say?"

"I said 'cup.' As in cup or mug." Ariel held up the pot of freshly brewed coffee. "Which would you prefer?"

"Oh. Oh, yes. A mug will be fine. I'm feeling a little shaky. All these people to entertain." Diane adjusted her hat. The veil came loose and fell across her face. Diane impatiently whipped it back up.

"I don't think anyone expects to be entertained," Susan said.

"Well, one does what one can. Anyway, hopefully everyone will leave soon." Diane stared pointedly at Susan's three friends. "I can rest then."

"Yes, you're looking a little tired," Barbara said.

"I am?"

"Everyone was commenting," Vicki added.

"Must have been that awful train trip," Chris said.

Ariel approached her aunt, holding out the steaming mug of coffee. "Here's your coffee. Black, right?"

"Yes, that's right." Diane took the coffee without saying thanks. "Well, I guess I should get back to our guests." She didn't move. "I need a cigarette." With her free hand, she reached inside the small black purse dangling from her wrist.

Susan thought of objecting, but decided against it. Diane knew Susan's feelings about smoking. Diane knew Owen didn't allow smoking in the house. She obviously didn't care. What the hell, Susan decided. Her sister would be gone in a few days. It wasn't worth creating a scene.

"No smoking in the house," Ariel admonished.

Susan smiled at her older daughter, fighting the urge to smother the top of her purple-and-pink hair with kisses.

Diane impatiently waved Ariel's statement aside as she drew a cigarette out of its package and raised it to her lips.

"I'm sorry," Susan told her. "I'm afraid you'll have to smoke that outside."

"I'm surprised you smoke," Chris said.

"It's a filthy habit." Vicki shook her head disapprovingly.

"It causes wrinkles." Barbara motioned toward her own unlined face.

Diane looked at the ceiling as if hoping for divine intervention. When none was forthcoming, she tossed the cigarette back into her purse and headed for the door. "Fine. I'll go out front. You might think about seeing to our other guests." Purse in one hand, coffee in the other, she used her hip to push through the door into the living room.

The four friends watched her leave, then turned to one another. "Cunt," they mouthed in unison.

"I heard that," Ariel said with a laugh. "God, some example you guys are setting."

"Thanks, sweetie," Susan said.

"For what?"

For not giving me a hard time. For acting like a human being. For being young and alive and healthy. For being mine. "For the nice things you said about Grandma at the funeral."

Ariel nodded, swaying toward her mother, stopping as the kitchen door swung back open and Barbara's daughter, Tracey, poked her head inside the room.

"There you are," Tracey said, quickly at her mother's side, her arm snaking around her waist as Barbara kissed her forehead. "I wondered where you guys disappeared. Hi, Ariel."

Ariel grunted something unintelligible in reply.

Susan's eyes moved warily between the two girls, trying to squeeze them together in her mind, to borrow a little from one to give to the other, to mix and match the best qualities of each. To Ariel, she'd give Tracey's maturity and good manners. To Tracey, she'd lend Ariel's spirit and sense of adventure. She'd temper Ariel's rebelliousness with a helping of Tracey's respect for her elders; she'd enhance Tracey's quiet reserve with a dash of Ariel's outspoken fearlessness. Tracey was a big girl, the kind of girl Susan's mother would have described as big-boned. Pretty face, though she'd never be as beautiful as her mother.

Maybe if she cut her hair, punked it up a little, maybe added a few pink streaks. Susan almost laughed out loud. My God, what was she thinking?

"How's Kirsten?" Tracey asked Vicki.

"Great. She's a counselor at Camp Walkie-Talkie, or whatever they call the damn place. Loves it."

Tracey looked over at Chris, hesitated. "How are you, Mrs. Malarek?"

"Fine, thank you, Tracey." No one ever asked Chris about Montana anymore.

"Are you ready to go yet?" Tracey whispered to her mother.

"Not yet," Barbara said.

"Oh, no, please," Susan said quickly. "You guys don't have to stick around all afternoon. I know you have other things to do. Please. You've already done so much."

"You think we're going to leave you alone with Cunt Dracula?" Vicki asked, as the women once again collapsed in helpless laughter.

"You guys are really bad," Ariel said, shaking her head.

"I don't get it," Tracey said. "What's so funny?"

"That's what I'd like to know," Diane said, reentering the kitchen with a sharp push on the door, trailing an almost visible line of smoke in her wake.

"That was a fast cigarette," Vicki observed.

"I only smoke them half the way down. Besides, I met someone outside. Handsome man. Nicely dressed. He was coming up the front steps just as I was going out. Apparently nobody told him about the funeral." She glared accusingly at Susan, glanced back at the door. "He's very intent on paying his respects."

There was a slight commotion in the other room, the sound of voices. ("What are you doing here?" "I don't think this is a very good idea." "Now isn't the time or place.") And then the kitchen door swung open and Tony Malarek pushed his way inside.

"Oh, God," Chris moaned, backing into a corner, automatically grabbing the hair at the back of her neck.

Susan stared at Tony without speaking. If she didn't know him better, she might have described him exactly as her sister had. Handsome, in a rough-and-tumble sort of way, nicely dressed in black pants and black, short-sleeved shirt. His hair was close-cropped and salted with flecks of gray, his face and heavily muscled arms deeply tanned. He looked well-rested, confident. Even happy, Susan thought with a shudder, wondering what he was doing here, what his next move would be.

"Okay, Tony," Owen said, entering the kitchen, Jeremy Latimer at his side. "We don't want any trouble here."

"What's going on?" Diane asked, wary eyes darting from man to man.

"Relax," Tony said, his eyes coming to rest on his former wife. "I didn't come to make trouble."

"Who is this man?" Diane asked.

"I just came to pay my respects."

"That's not necessary."

"I think it is."

"Then why don't you say what you came to say and leave." Susan struggled to keep her voice steady.

"Ah, the voice of reason. As usual." Tony's voice dripped sarcasm as thick as melted toffee. "Sorry about your mother, Susan," he said, his eyes never leaving Chris.

Susan nodded, said nothing.

"I'm Tony Malarek, by the way," Tony answered Diane, as if suddenly remembering her question. "This pathetic little creature is my wife, Chris."

"Ex-wife," Chris said, her voice surprisingly strong.

"Ex-wife." Tony reached out his hand, his fingers folding into the shape of a gun aimed directly at his wife's head. "Guess she wasn't paying attention when the judge said, 'Till death do you part.'" His fingers pulled the imaginary trigger.

"Okay, that's enough," Jeremy Latimer exclaimed, knocking Tony's hand to his side as he and Owen pushed Tony toward the kitchen door.

"Asshole," Barbara muttered under her breath.

"Cocksucker," Vicki said out loud.

"Careful, girls," Tony called back. "This gun's got lots of bullets." His laugh echoed through the house. Seconds later, the front door opened and slammed shut.

For a minute, nobody seemed to breathe.

"My God, what kind of friends do you have?" Diane demanded.

Susan ignored her sister, moved quickly to Chris's side. "Are you all right?"

"I'm fine," Chris said. "I'm just so sorry. I never thought he'd come here."

"Is everything all right?" a voice asked from the doorway.

"Should we call the police?" another voice asked.

"Yes," Susan said.

"No," Chris countered.

"Why not?"

"They won't do anything."

"He threatened your life, for God's sake. We were all witnesses."

"I didn't see anything," Diane said quickly.

"The police won't help," Chris said with quiet resolve.

Susan's shoulders slumped. "At the very least, you'll stay here tonight," she insisted.

"Where will she sleep?" Diane asked.

"It's all right. I'll be fine."

"You can't ignore him, Chris. He's a ticking time bomb."

"I can't run from him forever. I'm through running."

"Not forever," Susan told her. "Just a few more nights. Till he calms down."

"It's all right," Barbara interjected. "I'm taking Chris home with me. No arguments."

Chris smiled her assent, as if she knew it was pointless to argue.

I can't run from him forever. I'm through running.

Susan replayed Chris's words over and over in her head after everyone had gone. She heard them twisting through Diane's voice as her sister finalized the arrangements for her return trip to California. She could still hear them bouncing around in her brain later that night, when she crawled into bed beside Owen and closed her eyes, drifting in and out of sleep. They were the voice behind her restless dreams. Dreams of naked women running in helpless circles, of lost children wandering through dense jungles. *I can't run from him forever. I'm through running.*

The phone rang.

Owen sat up in bed as Susan groped for the phone in the

dark. The clock on the bedside table said 4:42. The phone rang again. "Oh, God," Susan said instead of hello, crying even before she heard the voice on the other end of the line.

"Susan? Susan, is that you?"

"Yes, it's me." Who was she talking to? Susan struggled to recognize the voice. "What's the matter? What's wrong?"

"Help me. You have to help me."

"What happened? What's going on?"

"Oh God, oh God, oh God," the young girl wailed between anguished sobs, and only then did Susan recognize the familiar timbre of Tracey's voice.

"Tracey, what's the matter? Tell me!"

"I can't!"

"Tracey, please," Susan pleaded. "You have to calm down. You have to tell me what's going on!"

"Tony . . . !"

"Tony? Is Tony there?"

Owen flipped on the light, started climbing into his clothes.

"No." Susan could feel Tracey shaking her head. "He's gone. He . . . he . . ."

"He what? Tracey, what did Tony do? Did he hurt Chris?"

"Chris?" Tracey repeated the name as if she'd never heard the word before. "Chris isn't here."

"Tracey, what happened? Please tell me what happened." The breath suddenly froze in Susan's lungs. Why was she talking to Tracey? Where was Barbara?

Dear God, where was Barbara?

"Where's your mother?" Susan shouted into the phone. "Tracey, let me speak to your mother!"

Ariel and Whitney suddenly appeared in the bedroom

doorway. "Mom," Ariel said, holding tightly to Whitney's hand. "What's wrong?"

"Tracey, answer me," Susan directed. "Where's your mother?"

Tracey's response was a scream that shot through Susan's body like a bolt of lightning. A sound, Susan later remembered thinking, she would take with her to her grave.

Part Four

1992–1993

Vicki

Twenty-Six

At five-thirty in the morning, the phone rang in Vicki's bedroom. She reached for it on the first ring, heard Susan's trembling voice, absorbed the information quickly, hung up the phone, walked into her large en suite bathroom, and threw up all over the marble floor. Forty minutes later, she and Jeremy turned their new black Jaguar onto Grand Avenue and parked in front of their old house. The police were already there, the entire area cordoned off, Barbara's house surrounded by streams of yellow tape that identified it as a crime scene. "I'm Vicki Latimer," Vicki announced as she brushed by one of the officers.

"I'm sorry, Ma'am . . ."

"I'm Jeremy Latimer," her husband told the young officer, who immediately stood back to let them enter.

She saw Owen first. He was sitting on a chair by the fireplace, his head in his shaking hands, his skin ashen, as if he'd been dusted with a fine coating of chalk. Vicki was just about to ask where Susan was when she came out of the kitchen, her skin blotchy and pale. She was wearing a long, white T-shirt over a pair of baggy brown shorts, obviously the first thing she'd seen to throw on, Vicki thought, her eyes shifting uneasily to the young girl Susan had her arm around.

Tracey walked slowly, her large, round eyes open and blank, as if permanently imprinted with the horror of what they'd seen. Her face was swollen from crying and stained with tears. Her cotton pajamas were an unsettling combination of pink and red. It took Vicki only a few seconds to realize that the red was blood, and when she did, she almost threw up again. Likewise when she looked at Tracey's blood-streaked hands.

"Tracey?" Vicki asked, not really sure what she was asking.

Tracey lifted her head from Susan's shoulder, dropped it back without acknowledging Vicki's presence.

"Is she all right?" Vicki asked Susan.

Susan shook her head. "She's in shock." The look on Susan's face said they all were.

"Was she able to tell the police what happened?"

"Just bits and pieces." Susan directed Tracey to the old green sofa and sank down beside her, as Vicki grabbed a nearby chair and pulled it closer.

A policeman approached. He was tall and broad, with a football player's thick neck and biceps that cramped his light gray sports jacket. He was forty, maybe forty-five, with thinning blond hair and heavy lidded blue eyes. Vicki thought he looked vaguely familiar, but then all police officers looked vaguely familiar to her these days. "Mrs. Latimer," he said, as if he knew her.

"Officer . . ."

"Lieutenant Jacobek," he said. "I testified at the Keevil trial last year."

Vicki quickly recalled every word of the policeman's testimony. He'd been very good on the stand, she remembered. So good he'd almost sunk her case.

"I understand you're acquainted with the victim."

The word *victim* brought Vicki squarely back to the here and now. She swallowed hard to keep the bile from rising in her throat. "She was one of my closest friends." Vicki gasped at her easy use of the past tense. She noted a single tear running the length of Susan's face. "What exactly happened here?"

"We're hoping you might be able to get the girl to tell us," Lieutenant Jacobek stated, as several policemen raced past the living room and up the stairs.

Forensic officers, Vicki decided, leaving her chair to kneel in front of Tracey. Vicki could hear her husband talking to Owen. "Did you see her?" Jeremy was asking.

"Tracey, sweetheart," Vicki began, about to take Tracey's hands in her own when the blood on Tracey's fingers caused her to shrink back, leave her hands at her sides. "Tracey, can you hear me?"

Tracey nodded, although her eyes remained blank, unfocused.

"Tracey, can you tell us what happened, sweetheart?"

Tracey's body began rocking back and forth, a series of low moans escaping her throat. The moans filled the room, climbed the walls, dropped from the ceiling like rain.

"She's been like this since we got here," Susan said.

"She phoned you?" Vicki tried not to sound surprised that Tracey had called Susan and not herself.

"She was incoherent. We couldn't make out what happened. Owen called the police, and we rushed right over. The front door was wide open."

Vicki noticed at least one police officer taking notes. "And then what?"

"We rushed upstairs, found Barbara." It was the first time anyone had actually spoken her name, and the weight of it lingered in the air. Susan gestured helplessly toward the stairs. "Oh, God, it was so awful. She was lying on the floor beside her bed, covered with blood. At first I didn't even recognize her. Her face was all bashed in. Oh, God, after all that surgery . . ."

"Where was Tracey?" Vicki stared at Tracey, but Tracey was looking through her as if she weren't there.

"She was sitting on the floor beside her mother. Holding her hand. There was so much blood. We tried to get her to talk, but . . ."

"Tracey, talk to me," Vicki commanded now. Tracey looked away. Vicki's hand brought the young girl's chin around. "Tracey, you have to tell us what happened. Do you hear me? You have to help your mother."

"My mother . . ."

"She needs your help, Tracey. She needs you to tell us who hurt her."

"She's dead," Tracey said.

"Yes," Vicki agreed, although the word sounded strange, as if it were coming from someone else's mouth.

"He did it."

"Who?"

"Tony."

"He must have thought Chris was here," Susan said, as if

trying to explain. "The police are out looking for him now."

"Chris didn't sleep over," Tracey said, as everyone in the room leaned closer. "My mother wanted her to, but she said she was okay, that she'd be all right on her own."

"Where is Chris now?" Vicki asked.

Fresh tears fell across Susan's cheeks. "We don't know. She wasn't in her apartment."

Vicki didn't say what everyone was probably thinking—that Tony had Chris, that it was only a matter of time before yet another horrifying phone call. "Okay, Tracey," Vicki said again. "It's really important that you tell us exactly what happened here tonight."

Tracey looked around the room, blank eyes suddenly snapping into focus, like a shutter on a camera lens. "I was sleeping," she began, her voice surprisingly animated. "Suddenly there were these noises. At first I thought I was having a nightmare, but then I realized I was awake. I heard banging, footsteps, my mother screaming, more sounds . . ." Tracey lifted her hands into the air, dropped them again. "I was scared. I got out of bed. And then I saw him."

"You saw Tony?"

"Yes." Tracey looked from Vicki to Susan to Lieutenant Jacobek, then back to Vicki. "I'm sure it was him," she said, as if she weren't sure at all.

"Did you see his face?" Lieutenant Jacobek asked.

Tracey shook her head. "He was wearing a ski mask."

"A ski mask?" Vicki asked. In this heat? she could almost hear Barbara add.

"It was pulled down over his face. All you could see were his eyes."

"So, it's possible it wasn't Tony?"

"Who else would it have been?" Tracey asked in response. "Howard?"

"Howard?" Lieutenant Jacobek repeated.

"Howard Kerble, her fiancé," Owen offered.

"Impossible," Vicki said. "Howard worshiped the ground she walked on."

"Someone should call him," Susan said.

"We'll take care of that," Lieutenant Jacobek told her, with a nod to his partner.

"Howard adored my mother," Tracey interjected. "You should see the ring he bought her."

"Was she wearing the ring last night?" Lieutenant Jacobek asked.

"She always wore it," Tracey said.

"Ring's missing," a nearby policeman noted.

"Where were you when you first saw the man?" Lieutenant Jacobek asked Tracey.

"What?"

"Where were you?" Vicki repeated, wishing Lieutenant Jacobek would back off. If they weren't careful, Tracey would retreat back into near-catatonia.

"I don't know. In the hall, I guess."

"Did he see you?"

Tracey nodded. "He looked right at me."

"How tall was he?" Lieutenant Jacobek asked.

"I don't know. It happened so fast. He was all crouched over, running."

"He ran down the stairs?"

Tracey nodded vigorously.

"Was he carrying anything?"

"I don't understand."

"A baseball bat? A poker of some kind?"

"I don't know. I don't think so. I don't know." Tracey's voice was rising steadily.

Vicki sought to calm her. "It's okay, sweetheart. You're doing great. Tell us what happened next."

"I went into my mother's bedroom." Tracey's voice returned to normal. She spoke slowly, deliberately, as if retracing her steps one by one. "At first I didn't see her. I called out, but she didn't answer me. And then I heard moaning, and I came around the side of the bed, and that's when I saw her. She was lying on the floor. She was covered in blood. At first, I wasn't even sure it was her. Her face . . ."

Vicki looked to the floor, swallowed repeatedly before looking back up. Tracey had used almost the exact same words Susan had earlier.

"I ran to the phone," Tracey continued. "I called Susan."

"What about your father?" Vicki asked.

"What about him? It wasn't him."

"No, of course not."

"Just because they used to fight a lot doesn't mean . . ."

"Of course not," Vicki repeated, stealing a glance at Lieutenant Jacobek.

"Where can we contact your father, Tracey?" he asked.

"It wasn't him," Tracey insisted.

"Somebody has to tell him what happened here last night."

Tracey reluctantly provided the officers with her father's address. "My father's a very busy man. He has two little kids and Pam is pregnant again. I don't want to stay with them."

"You won't have to," Vicki assured her.

"You'll stay with us," Susan said, looking to Lieutenant Jacobek for his consent.

"That's fine. She can stay wherever she's most comfortable."

"I don't want to stay at my father's," Tracey repeated. "The bed creaks, and the kids get up so early. I'll never get any sleep."

For an instant Tracey reminded Vicki of Susan's sister, Diane. Vicki quickly pushed the ungenerous thought out of her head. We say all kinds of crazy things when we're under extreme stress, she thought, rising unsteadily to her feet.

Tracey giggled. "Your knees cracked."

There was a noise on the stairs and Vicki saw several uniformed policemen carrying a large green body bag toward the front door. "Oh, God," she whispered, looking away, knowing the body of her friend was inside.

"She was so beautiful," Tracey was saying to no one in particular. "She was a former Miss Cincinnati, you know."

Vicki nodded her confirmation.

"Her face was completely smashed in." Now that Tracey had been forced to talk, she was incapable of keeping quiet. "It was like she didn't have a face at all." She made a sound halfway between a laugh and a cry. "After everything she did to stay beautiful. Not to have a face." Her voice stopped as abruptly as a windup toy that's run out of steam.

Vicki closed her eyes, tried not to picture her friend lying across her bedroom floor, bludgeoned beyond all recognition.

"Can I take Tracey home now?" Susan asked, clearly exhausted by the events of the last week. First her mother's death. Now her friend's murder.

Lieutenant Jacobek nodded. "We'll drop by later, if that's okay." He handed his card to Owen. "If you or Tracey should think of anything else in the meantime. . . ."

"We'll let you know," Owen said.

"I'll go upstairs and pack some of your things," Susan offered.

"No," Tracey said. "I'll go. You won't know what I want."

Vicki watched the young officer who'd screened them at the door accompany Tracey up the stairs.

"I can't believe this is happening," Susan cried. "I keep thinking this is just a bad dream, and that any minute I'm going to wake up."

"You really think Tony is capable of this?" Vicki asked.

"I think Tony is capable of anything. Oh, God, poor Barbara."

"That's what doesn't make any sense," Vicki said. "Why Barbara?"

"What are you talking about?"

Vicki could sense Susan's growing annoyance. "It just doesn't make sense to me."

"Nothing about Tony ever made sense," Susan told her. "He's a vile, brutal man. You heard him at my house today. He threatened to kill Chris."

"Chris, yes. Not Barbara."

"He threatened all of us." Susan turned toward Lieutenant Jacobek, explained about the incident after her mother's funeral. "He made his fingers into the shape of a gun. He pointed it at Chris. He said there were plenty of bullets for the rest of us."

"I'll have police posted outside your house until he's apprehended," Lieutenant Jacobek said as he finished jotting down this latest information.

I don't think that will be necessary, Vicki thought, but didn't say. Even if Tony was responsible for Barbara's murder, she didn't think he'd come after Susan. It was Chris he'd been terrorizing for years, Chris he wanted to destroy.

So why kill Barbara?

Had he broken into Barbara's house on the assumption that Chris would be there? Had he been so enraged at not finding her, he'd struck out at Barbara instead? Had he killed her as a warning to Chris, as a sign of greater horror to come?

And then what?

Had he fled the scene covered in his victim's blood, confident no one would see him? Had he returned calmly to his house, to his children, changed his clothes, and destroyed the evidence, assumed he'd be neither suspected nor apprehended, despite the fact he'd left Tracey alive to identify him?

It didn't make sense.

Of course it didn't have to make sense, Vicki reminded herself. She'd tried enough criminal cases to know that murder seldom made sense, that people had their own elaborate systems of justification for everything they did, no matter how heinous. Nobody ever saw himself as the bad guy. There was always a reason, however convoluted, however insane. And murderers, like every other person who breaks the law, always assumed they were invulnerable. Despite all the clues they left behind, they never actually thought they'd be caught.

So it didn't have to make sense that Tony had killed Barbara and not Chris. What mattered was that Tony had been in a murderous rage and that Barbara was at the wrong place at the wrong time.

Except she was in her own home. In her own bed.

"There were no signs of a break-in," Vicki said to Jeremy on the long drive home. She brought her hands to her eyes, shielded them from the rising sun. Streaks of pink clouds, like long shreds of cotton candy, wafted across a brilliant powder-blue sky. *Red sky at night,* Vicki said silently, recalling the phrase from her childhood, hearing her mother recite the words along with her, *Sailor's delight. Red sky at morning, Sailor take warning.* Barbara would have loved this sky, Vicki thought, refusing to give in to the threat of tears, as she watched her husband rub his tired eyes. "Were you crying?" Vicki asked, not bothering to hide her astonishment.

"Weren't you?" he asked, equally astonished.

Vicki hadn't cried in almost forty years, since the morning she'd realized her mother had left her and was never coming back. That day she'd shed enough tears to last a lifetime, and where had it gotten her? Precisely nowhere. Her tears had fallen on the proverbial deaf ears. Her mother certainly hadn't noticed them. And had her heartfelt sobs made Vicki feel any better? No. If anything, they'd made her feel worse. Tears sapped your strength, blurred your vision, imprisoned you in a kind of free-falling grief, kept you from moving forward, from getting on with your life. There was no room in Vicki's life for wallowing in the past, in what was over and done with and could not be changed, no room in her life for tears. Not anymore.

"What do you mean, there were no signs of a break-in?" Jeremy asked, as if hearing her for the first time.

"I checked." Vicki fished in her purse for her sunglasses, pushed them across the bridge of her nose. "There were no broken windows. The front door hadn't been jimmied. The back door was locked."

"Maybe Barbara let Tony in."

"No way she'd let him in."

"Maybe he tricked her."

"No way Barbara let him in," Vicki repeated adamantly.

"So what are you saying?"

"I don't know."

"You think it was Howard or Ron? I guess either one of them could have a key."

"There was no blood on the stairs."

"What?"

"Whoever killed Barbara had to be covered in blood. There were no bloody footprints, no blood on the stairs, no blood anywhere except in the bedroom. And on Tracey," she added, feeling a chill run up and down her spine.

"Tracey? Well, of course, she was covered with blood. You heard Susan. Tracey was sitting beside her mother, holding her hand. Of course she'd be covered with blood. What are you getting at?"

"I don't know."

"You think Tracey's protecting someone?"

"I don't know."

"You think Tracey knows more than she's letting on?"

"I don't know." How many times could she say the same thing? "I don't know," she said again, and then again when she could think of nothing else. "I don't know."

"Did you mention any of this to the police?"

"Why would I do their job for them?"

Jeremy pulled the car into their driveway, turned off the engine, and faced his wife. "You're a strange and wondrous woman, Mrs. Latimer. Tell me, what happens next?"

"We go inside, shower, go to work, and wait for the phone to ring."

"And then what?"

"We hold our breath," Vicki said. "Pray I'm wrong."

Twenty-Seven

"How long are the police going to be here?" Ariel asked as she came into the kitchen and plopped herself down at the round, white table. She was wearing a relatively clean blue T-shirt that was tied in a knot beneath her breasts, and loose-fitting hip-hugger jeans. Susan tried not to notice the small gold ring piercing her daughter's navel.

"I guess until they find Tony," Susan said.

"I don't like them sitting out there all day. It gives me the creeps."

"It's for our own protection."

"I guess." Ariel looked around the room. "Is Tracey still sleeping?"

Susan looked up at the ceiling. "I thought I heard her moving around upstairs a little while ago."

"Did she sleep all day?"

"Pretty much."

"When did Diane leave?"

"Around noon." Susan collapsed against the kitchen counter. Her sister's suitcase had already been packed and was sitting by the front door when she and Owen had arrived home from Barbara's house with Tracey. Diane had mumbled a few hollow phrases about knowing what Tracey must be going through, having just lost her mother herself, then made herself as scarce as possible for the rest of the morning. She'd actually managed to look put out when Susan had declined to drive her to the station and she'd had to take a taxi.

Whitney, of course, had immediately offered to stay home from day camp and help out with Tracey, but Susan had insisted she follow her regular routine. Who knew how long Tracey would be staying with them? Who knew how long Whitney would be able to enjoy the luxury of a regular routine?

Ariel had emerged from her room long enough to take one look at her mother's face and decide she had to leave the house. Clearly, her mother's eyes contained more pain than she could bear. She was out the door before Susan had a chance to ask where she was going.

"Where've you been all day?" Susan asked now.

"Out." Ariel shrugged, ran tobacco-stained fingers through the pink and purple spikes of her hair.

Susan nodded, too exhausted to question her further. Ariel had gone out, and now she was home. She was safe. That's all Susan needed to know.

"I was over at Molly's," Ariel said.

Susan tried putting a face to the name, but failed, and quickly gave up. Friends moved in and out of Ariel's life regularly. No one seemed to stick around very long. It didn't really matter who Molly was.

"Molly's the girl I met at the tattoo parlor," Ariel elaborated, unasked.

"Hmm."

"She's a very nice girl," Ariel said defensively.

"I'm sure she is."

"She has this neat tattoo on her lower back. It's like this abstract flower kind of thing."

"I'm sure it's very nice."

Ariel looked puzzled, even alarmed. "Are you all right?"

Susan almost laughed. "Not really." Tears filled her eyes. God, did they never stop?

The look on Ariel's face said she wasn't sure whether to comfort her mother or bolt from the room. "I'm sorry," she said, reaching some sort of compromise. "I'm really sorry."

"I know, sweetheart."

"I didn't mean to be gone all day. But everything just seemed so overwhelming. First Grandma, and now Barbara. And poor Tracey. That horrible blank look in her eyes."

"I understand."

"Am I like Diane?" Ariel asked plaintively.

"What?" Again Susan almost laughed. "Dear God, no. You're nothing like Diane."

"You don't hate me?" Tears filled Ariel's eyes, and she looked away.

"Hate you? How could I ever hate you? You're my baby and I love you. I will always love you. Please know that."

Ariel nodded without speaking.

"Please," Susan asked, her heart filled with a tenderness for her daughter she hadn't felt in a long time. "Can I hold you?"

Ariel quickly collapsed inside her mother's arms. They remained this way for several minutes, swaying together, holding one another up. Ariel cried quietly on her mother's shoulders, wetting Susan's neck with her tears. "The radio said Barbara was bludgeoned to death."

Susan nodded, trying to block out the memory of her close friend lying on her bedroom floor, blood covering what was left of her once-beautiful face, knowing she would carry that image with her for the rest of her life. Whoever did that to Barbara had to have hated her very much.

"What's taking the police so long to find Tony?" Ariel asked, as if reading her mother's mind.

"I don't know."

"Have you heard from Chris?"

"No." Dear God, if Tony had done that to Barbara, what might he do to Chris? A fresh flood of tears burst from Susan's eyes.

"Oh, God, I'm sorry. I can't say anything right. I should have stayed at Molly's."

"No, sweetheart . . ." Susan patted her daughter's head, was amazed to find the spikes of her hair so soft.

"Who's Molly?" a voice interrupted.

Ariel immediately pulled out of her mother's arms. Susan turned to see Tracey standing in the kitchen doorway. She was neatly dressed in a white blouse and navy pleated skirt, and her dark hair was freshly washed and pulled into a ponytail. Susan tucked her own uncombed hair behind her ears and smoothed out the creases of the T-shirt and shorts she'd been wearing since early morning.

"Who's Molly?" Tracey asked again, sitting down at the kitchen table.

Ariel shrugged, joined Tracey at the table. "A girl I met at a tattoo parlor."

"I think tattoos are gross." Tracey glanced at Susan, as if waiting for her nod of approval. "Could I trouble you for a glass of milk?"

Susan pushed the tears away from her eyes, rubbing them into her cheeks as if she were applying blush. "What? Oh, sure." She poured Tracey a glass of milk and placed it on the table in front of her. "You must be hungry. Can I get you something to eat?" The very thought of food made Susan ill, and she imagined Tracey must feel the same way. But it was important that Tracey keep up her strength.

"I'd love some of those little sandwiches," Tracey said. "The kind you served after your mother's funeral. Do you have any more of those?"

Susan struggled to keep the surprise out of her face. Tracey was a teenager after all. She had a normal teenage appetite that obviously transcended tragedy. Besides, food might be Tracey's way of coping with the horror of what had happened. She had to be careful not to be judgmental. You could never know another person's pain. Susan returned to the fridge, withdrew the large platter of party sandwiches, and put them on the table in front of Tracey, beside her glass of milk.

"I like these the best." Tracey lifted one of the delicate sandwiches into her hands, studied the thick lines of tuna and egg layered between small slices of white and brown bread. She took one bite, then another. Only two bites and the sandwich was gone. Tracey licked her fingers, the same fingers that only this morning had been covered in her mother's blood. "These are so good," she said, taking another sandwich from the platter, raising it to her mouth.

Susan looked away, not sure she could effectively disguise her growing revulsion. You mustn't judge her, Susan reminded herself.

"How can you eat at a time like this?" Ariel asked, not bound by any such thoughts or constraints.

"What?" Tracey looked confused, stricken.

Ariel shook her head in disbelief. "I don't understand how you can be talking about sandwiches when your mother's been murdered."

"Ariel," Susan warned, not sure what else to say. She'd been thinking the same thing herself.

"Oh, God, my mother," Tracey wailed. She dropped the sandwich to the plate, grabbed her stomach, began rocking furiously back and forth. "My mother. My poor mother."

Ariel was on her feet. "Oh, God, I'm sorry, Tracey. Please forgive me. I'm sorry. Mom? I'm really so sorry."

"It's okay, sweetheart. Why don't you go outside and wait for Whitney's bus."

"Where's Whitney?" Tracey asked as Ariel bolted from the kitchen and raced to the front door.

When was the last time Ariel had been so anxious to see her sister? Susan wondered. "Day camp," she said, answering Tracey's question, finding it difficult to keep up with all the sudden transitions. "She's a C.I.T."

"What's that?"

"Counselor-in-training." Were they really having this conversation?

"I never went to camp."

"No?"

"I always wanted to, but my mom . . ."

"She liked having you around."

"She said I could go this summer, I guess because of Howard." Tracey made a face. "I haven't called him back yet. I guess that's awful of me, but I don't really want to talk to him. He'll just ask me about what happened, and I'm tired of talking about it. I don't want to talk about it anymore."

One sentence ran into the next. Susan was having trouble keeping up.

"My mom was all excited about the wedding, you should have seen her, she was even thinking of buying a white dress, did she tell you that?"

"She mentioned she thought ivory might be nice."

"Isn't that white?"

"More like off-white."

Tracey nodded, reached for another sandwich. "She wanted me to wear either mint green or lilac. I was going to be her maid of honor, you know."

"We were going to be her bridesmaids," Susan said, picturing herself walking down the aisle between Vicki and Chris.

Dear God, where was Chris?

"I remember my dad's wedding," Tracey was saying. "It was neat. Pam wore this beautiful white gown from Vera Wang. All the movie stars wear Vera Wang. Dad said it cost a fortune."

"I'm sure it was lovely," Susan said when she could think of nothing else to say.

"Yeah, well . . ." Tracey looked around absently. "Who's going to give me my allowance?"

"What?"

"My allowance. I get ten dollars every Friday."

"I'm sure your Dad . . . ," Susan started, then stopped.

"Have you spoken to him?"

"No. The police have been trying to locate him. Apparently he's out of town."

Tracey looked perplexed, her large brown eyes coming together at the bridge of her nose. "Oh, yeah, that's right. He and Pam were going to Atlantic City for a couple of days."

"Atlantic City?" Susan reached for the phone. "I should tell the police."

"I don't want to stay there."

The bed creaks and the kids get up too early, Susan repeated silently.

"Don't get me wrong. The kids are great. But they're babies. They make a lot of noise. Besides—" Tracey, lowered her voice, tears suddenly appearing in the corners of her eyes—"I don't think my mother would have wanted me to stay there, do you?"

"He's your father, Tracey."

"I guess." Tracey reached for another sandwich.

Ariel's right, Susan thought, watching the threat of tears evaporate with each bite. She's weird.

The phone rang. Susan reached for it, grateful for the interruption. "Hello?"

There was a moment's hesitation, then, "Mrs. Norman?" The voice was young, female, probably one of Ariel's friends. Maybe the mysterious Molly.

"Yes?"

"This is Montana Malarek, Chris's daughter."

"My God, Montana, how are you? Where are you? Is everything all right?" The words spilled from Susan's mouth like sand from a pail.

"The police just arrested my father." Montana's voice resonated with disbelief. "They say he murdered Mrs. Azinger."

"Are the police there now?"

"They're searching the house. They have a warrant. But he didn't do it, Mrs. Norman. I know he didn't do it. He was home all last night. He left early this morning because he had an appointment in Lexington. But the police don't believe that. They think he murdered Mrs. Azinger."

"Would you like me to come over?"

"No," Montana said quickly. "Dad said he'll be back as soon as he straightens this mess out. Mrs. Norman . . . ?"

"Yes, dear?"

Another moment of hesitation. "Have you heard from my mother?" A long pause. "Because the police said she's missing. And I was just wondering whether she'd contacted you . . ."

Susan heard the worry in Montana's voice, understood the love behind it, even if Montana didn't. "I don't know where she is," Susan admitted sadly. "Nobody's heard from her."

"You don't think anything's happened to her, do you? I mean, you don't think that whoever killed Mrs. Azinger would have—" Montana broke off.

"Why don't I drive over there and bring you and your brothers back to my house?" Susan offered, wondering how Tracey would react to being in the same room with the daughter of the man who'd murdered her mother.

"No. It's okay. My dad said he'd be back soon. He said not to go anywhere, he'd be home in time for supper."

"He might not be."

"Would you call me if you hear from my mother?"

"Of course."

"Don't let my dad know I called, okay? I mean, maybe Ariel could phone, pretend like she's my friend from school or something, in case he answers the phone."

"Montana, your father can't stop you from seeing your mother."

"I don't want to see her," Montana said quickly, although everything in her voice said otherwise. "I just want to know she's all right. So, like, could you have Ariel call?"

"Of course," Susan said again as Montana gave her her number, then hung up the phone. Susan stood absolutely still for several seconds, her head pressed tightly to the receiver as the dial tone buzzed impatiently in her ear.

"That was Chris's daughter?" Tracey asked.

"The police just arrested Tony." Susan wondered absently why she didn't feel more relieved.

"That's good. I hope he burns in hell. I'll never forget the way he looked at me. I thought he was going to kill me for sure."

"What?" Tracey hadn't mentioned this before.

"He looked at me, and then he took a few steps toward me."

He took steps toward her? "Did he say anything?"

"No. He just had this real funny look on his face, like he was wondering whether to kill me or not."

"How could you tell what kind of look he had on his face?"

"What do you mean?"

"You told the police he was wearing a mask."

"That's right. A ski mask. It was black."

"Then how could you tell what kind of look he had on his face?" Susan asked again.

Tracey shrugged. "I could see it in his eyes."

Susan nodded, deciding it was entirely possible Tracey had seen the murderous intent in Tony's eyes. Even if she hadn't, she could have imagined it. "And then what happened?"

"He just turned around and ran down the stairs."

"And you're sure it was Tony? Because Montana says he was home all night."

"Well, of course she says that."

"But you're sure it was Tony," Susan stated rather than asked.

Tracey shrugged.

"How tall was the man you saw?"

"I don't know. Average, I guess."

"Tony's pretty short."

"He was crouched over."

"Why?"

"What do you mean?"

"Why was he crouched over?"

"I don't know. He was running."

"But you said he stopped and looked at you, that he took a few steps toward you. Was he crouched over then?"

"I don't know. Why are you asking me these things? I was scared. I don't remember." Tears sprang to Tracey's eyes, as if she'd been slapped across the face.

"I'm sorry," Susan apologized quickly, grabbing a tissue from the counter and gently dabbing at Tracey's tears. "I didn't mean to upset you. I'm just trying to get what happened last night straight in my mind. I don't want to see Tony get off because of . . ." Because of any inconsistencies in your story, she'd been about to say.

"He won't get off," Tracey said with surprising certainty. "Is she coming over?"

"Who?"

"Montana. Is she coming over?"

"No."

"Too bad. I haven't seen her in a long time."

Susan nodded, almost afraid to speak. She was used to teenagers jumping from one topic of conversation to the next, but she'd never experienced anything quite like this. Maybe the shock of her mother's violent death had shaken loose several screws in Tracey's head. She obviously wasn't thinking clearly. Maybe Susan was expecting too much of the girl.

Except what was she expecting after all?

If anything, she'd assumed Tracey would be so overwhelmed with grief she'd have trouble getting out of bed. Instead, after a few hours of sleep, she was showered and dressed and ravenously hungry. She rarely cried. In fact, it was almost as if she had to be reminded to cry. And even then, her eyes dried with alarming speed. It was as if she weren't quite there, Susan thought, wondering if she'd always been that way. Certainly Ariel and Whitney thought so. Why had she never noticed it before?

"I think I'll go back upstairs now, if that's all right," Tracey said.

"Sure." She probably needs to crawl back into bed, Susan thought. She's only now beginning to realize what's happened. It's just starting to hit her.

"Is it all right if I watch TV?"

"What? Oh. Of course."

Tracey dutifully returned the platter of party sandwiches to the fridge and deposited her empty milk glass in the sink, then ambled from the room. Seconds later, Susan heard her footsteps on the stairs. She reached for the phone.

"Vicki," she said, as soon as she heard her friend's voice. "Could you come over? I think we might have a problem."

Twenty-Eight

It was almost six o'clock in the evening when Vicki arrived at Susan's house. She was somewhat dismayed to note that Susan was still wearing the same clothes she'd had on at Barbara's, and that her white T-shirt bore faint maroon smudges of what appeared to be dried blood.

"Sorry I couldn't get away earlier," Vicki apologized, accepting Susan's offer of a cup of coffee, settling easily into one of the kitchen chairs, looking around. "It's funny how we always end up in the kitchen, isn't it?"

"We could go into the living room . . ."

"No. I like it here. Where's Tracey?"

Susan lifted her eyes toward the ceiling.

"Asleep?"

"Watching television."

Vicki took a long sip of her coffee. "Strange girl."

"That she is."

"I take it she's part of the problem you mentioned on the phone."

Susan joined Vicki at the table, lowered her voice to a whisper. "I'm probably being paranoid . . ."

"But things just don't add up?"

"It's just that her reactions seem so out of whack. I keep telling myself she's in shock, but . . ."

"You think it's more than that?"

"Maybe once the police get a confession out of Tony . . ."

"The police let Tony go." Vicki watched the look of surprise that flooded Susan's face, washing all traces of residual color away, as if her head had been submerged in a basin of bleach.

"What!"

"They don't have enough evidence to hold him."

"I don't understand."

Vicki noted Susan's hands were trembling, covered them with her own. "Tony claims he was home all night. His kids back him up."

"Well, of course they'd back him up."

"Apparently, Rowdy has a bad cold and he kept everyone up all night with his coughing. Montana swears her father was giving Rowdy his cough medicine around the time Barbara was having her brains bashed in. Sorry to be so indelicate," Vicki apologized, seeing Susan wince.

"And that was enough to satisfy the police?"

"That and the fact there's no physical evidence linking Tony to the murder. No weapon, no ski mask . . ."

"He could have disposed of them."

"No blood. No traces of flesh or hair or bone on any of his clothes."

"Oh, God."

"Forensics went over his car with a fine-tooth comb. It was clean."

"Maybe he didn't take his car; maybe he took a shower; maybe . . ."

"Maybe he didn't do it."

"Oh, God," Susan said again.

Vicki finished the coffee in her mug, got up and poured herself another.

"So, who did? Ron?"

"Ron was in Atlantic City. The police finally got ahold of him. He's on his way home now."

"You don't think it could have been Howard, do you?"

"Well, he's still being investigated," Vicki answered. "He has no alibi for the time of Barbara's death."

"Then it could have been him."

"He also has no motive."

"So, what are you saying?"

"I think you know."

Susan shook her head. "I don't know."

"I think you do. I think that's why you called me earlier, said we had a problem, asked me to come over."

"I just meant we might have a problem because Tracey was having trouble keeping her story straight."

"People don't usually have problems keeping their stories straight when they're telling the truth."

"You think she's lying?"

As if on cue, a sudden burst of laughter funneled through the ceiling. "You think it's normal to be laughing at some dumb TV show twelve hours after your mother's skull has been pulverized?"

"Oh, God."

"Sorry. I keep forgetting that you actually saw her."

"It was so awful." Susan lowered her face into her hands, as if trying to block out the horror of what she'd witnessed, her shoulders shaking as she cried.

Vicki returned to the table, put one arm around her trembling friend as another sharp burst of laughter broke through the walls. "I'm really sorry. You know it's just my way of dealing with things I'd rather not be dealing with."

"Maybe it's the same way with Tracey. Maybe she's in denial," Susan persisted stubbornly. "Maybe her feelings are just so mixed up . . ."

"Maybe she doesn't have any feelings."

Susan lifted her head, stared directly into Vicki's eyes, as if pleading for mercy. "What are you saying? That you think Tracey could have murdered her mother?"

"Isn't that what you think?"

There was silence.

"But that would make her some kind of monster."

Vicki shrugged. The shrug said nothing would surprise her.

"It can't be," Susan protested. "I mean, why? Why would Tracey want to harm her mother? Barbara loved her more than anything in the world. Tracey was her life, for God's sake. She did everything for that girl. It doesn't make any sense."

Again Vicki shrugged. The shrug asked, What does? "I think we should get her down here. Try to talk to her before the police arrive."

"You called the police?"

Vicki rubbed her forehead. What was it about Susan? she wondered impatiently. How could a woman her age still be so damn naive? "Of course I didn't call the police. But how long do you think it's going to take them to start asking the same questions we've been asking? How long before they reach the same conclusions?"

"Oh, God."

"Do you think you could stop saying that?" Vicki asked, then immediately apologized. "Sorry. I guess my nerves are a little shot."

"It's okay. I understand."

More laughter from overhead.

"Perhaps you could explain *that,"* Vicki said.

Susan shook her head, took a deep breath, raised her chin to the ceiling. "Tracey!" she called out loudly. "Tracey, could you come down here a minute?"

Footsteps. The sound of the TV being turned off. More footsteps.

"Where's Owen?" Vicki asked, suddenly aware of his absence.

"Tracey asked if we could have Chinese food for supper," Susan said, the disbelief in her voice now clanging as loudly as a bell. "Owen went to pick it up. He took the girls with him."

"Is the food here?" Tracey asked, pushing open the kitchen door, her expression of happy anticipation disappearing when she saw Vicki. "Oh, hi, Mrs. Latimer. How are you?"

Under other circumstances, this might pass for a normal question, Vicki thought, studying the girl's placid face. "I'm fine, Tracey. How are you holding up?"

"Fine. . . . Well, you know."

"No. I don't. Tell me."

"I don't understand."

"Sit down, Tracey." Vicki pulled out the chair beside Susan, watched as Tracey plopped into it.

"Is everything all right?" Tracey asked.

Strange question, Vicki thought, understanding from the look on Susan's face that she was thinking the same thing. "Well, no, not really," Vicki said, occupying the third seat at the table. "The police questioned Tony all afternoon and then released him."

"They released him?" Tracey repeated incredulously. "Why?"

"Apparently, they don't have enough evidence to hold him."

"But that's ridiculous. Everyone knows Tony did it."

"They do?" Vicki asked. "How?"

"What do you mean?"

"Tell me about last night," Vicki said.

"I already told you about last night."

"Tell me again."

"I don't want to." Tracey fidgeted uncomfortably in her chair. "I don't want to go through it again." Tears appeared in the corners of Tracey's eyes, although Vicki noted none actually fell to her face.

"We know it's difficult, sweetheart," Susan said gently. "But you have to know how important this is or Vicki wouldn't be asking."

"Just go over things with me one more time," Vicki coaxed. "You were asleep when you heard a noise."

"I heard a noise," Tracey repeated.

"What kind of noise?"

"I don't know. A loud noise. Banging."

"What kind of banging?"

"I don't know."

"Banging on the floor, on the bed, on the wall?"

"I don't know."

"Because there were no marks on the floor or the walls."

"Maybe it was more of a scuffling noise," Tracey said, twisting between the two women.

"A scuffling noise loud enough to wake you up?"

"Yes."

"But you said before it was a banging noise. There's a big difference between a banging noise and a scuffling noise."

"I don't know what kind of noise it was. Just that it woke me up."

"And then what?"

"I heard my mother screaming."

"First you heard the banging, then your mother screaming?"

"Yes."

"Then what?"

"There were more noises. I called out for my mother but she didn't answer me."

"Go on."

"I was scared. I saw a man in a black ski mask. He was staring at me like he was going to kill me. I couldn't move."

"You were in your bed?"

"Yes."

"You told the police you were in the hall."

"What?"

"This morning. You told the police you went into the hall. That was when you saw the man."

"That's right."

"You just said you were in your bed."

"You're confusing me."

"When did you see the man, Tracey?"

"I was in the hall."

"You're sure?"

"Yes. I remember now. I heard the noises. I heard my mother screaming. I got out of bed. I walked into the hall."

"And that's when you saw the man in the ski mask?"

"Yes. He looked at me like he was going to kill me, and then he turned and ran down the steps."

"And out the front door?"

"I guess."

"How did he get in the house, Tracey?"

"What? I don't know. He broke in, I guess."

"There were no signs of forced entry."

"I might have left the front door unlocked." Tracey's eyes flickered nervously back and forth. "Sometimes I forget to lock it."

Vicki tried to hide her growing revulsion. Innocent people never speculated. Only the guilty provided you with unexpected explanations. "Was he carrying a weapon?"

"I don't know. It was dark. I couldn't see."

"It was light enough to see his eyes."

"I didn't see a weapon." Again the threat of tears.

"Tracey, I can't help you if I don't know what happened."

"I've told you what happened."

"You heard your mother screaming and you woke up," Vicki reiterated.

"Yes."

"You said before it was a loud noise that woke you up."

"I heard a loud noise. Then I heard my mother scream."

"And you rushed into the hall."

"Yes."

"And you saw the man."

"Yes."

"And you thought it was Tony."

"Yes. But I was scared, and he was all crouched over. It could have been anyone."

"Your father?"

"No. I don't know. Maybe."

"Wouldn't you have recognized your father?"

"He was wearing a ski mask."

"Even wearing a ski mask."

"I think it was Howard," Tracey said. "Howard Kerble. He and my mother had a big fight last night."

"You never said anything about a big fight before."

"I forgot."

"You forgot to tell the police that your mother had a big fight with her fiancé on the night of her murder?"

"I was confused. I was upset. I was afraid he'd come back and get me."

"You said you thought it was Tony."

"I was wrong!"

"Now you're saying it was Howard?"

"I don't know who it was!" Tracey bolted from her chair with such force, it fell backward, crashing to the floor.

Susan was instantly on her feet, righting the chair, trying to calm Tracey down. "Tracey, sweetheart, it's all right. Everything's going to be all right."

"Why is she doing this to me?" Tracey's eyes shot accusingly toward Vicki. "My mother is dead! Some lunatic killed her! I don't know who it was. What are you trying to make me say?"

They heard a key at the front door, heard the door open and close, followed by the sound of footsteps in the hall and the pungent smell of Chinese food as Ariel and Whitney appeared in the doorway holding large brown bags of food.

"Oh, great," Tracey said. "I'm starving."

Vicki shook her head in wonderment. One minute the girl was screaming that some lunatic had killed her mother, and in almost the same breath she was salivating over Chinese food.

"Where's your father?" a similarly shell-shocked-looking Susan asked the girls.

"He's talking to some guys outside," Whitney said, as she and her sister deposited the food on the counter, Tracey immediately at their side, peeking eagerly into the bags.

"Some guys? What guys?"

"Looked like cops to me," Ariel said.

Vicki rose to her feet as Owen marched into the kitchen, Lieutenant Jacobek at his left shoulder, a smartly dressed, if decidedly plain, woman following directly behind.

"Lieutenant Jacobek," Vicki said, assuming the role of hostess, greeting the police officer as if this were her home and not Susan's.

"Mrs. Latimer, Mrs. Norman." Lieutenant Jacobek nodded toward the woman, whose dark hair matched her dark complexion. "This is my partner, Lieutenant Gill."

"I understand you released Tony Malarek," Susan said.

"I'm afraid we had no choice."

"I think it was Howard Kerble," Tracey offered.

"Be quiet, Tracey," Vicki instructed without taking her eyes off the two police lieutenants. "Why exactly are you here, Officers?"

"We have a few more questions for Tracey," Lieutenant Jacobek answered warily. "Is there a problem with that? She obviously wants to cooperate."

"Can't this wait till after dinner?" Tracey asked.

Owen stepped forward, ushered his daughters from the room.

"Why do you think Howard Kerble killed your mother?" Lieutenant Jacobek asked Tracey as soon as they were gone.

"Because he and my mother had a big fight last night. I forgot to tell you about it."

"Tracey . . . ," Vicki interrupted.

"I was just telling Mrs. Latimer and Mrs. Norman about it," Tracey continued. "They had this huge fight because my mother told him she didn't want to marry him. She even gave him back his ring. That's why she wasn't wearing it."

"What time did this argument take place?" Lieutenant Gill asked, carefully noting down everything Tracey said.

"I don't know. Around seven o'clock, I guess."

"Howard Kerble was having dinner with his son at seven o'clock last night," Lieutenant Jacobek said.

"It was later," Tracey corrected immediately. "It must have been closer to nine."

"He didn't leave his son's house until almost ten."

"Then it was ten. What difference does it make what time it was?"

"Be quiet, Tracey," Vicki said again. "What are you getting at, Officers?"

"We're just trying to find out what happened," Lieutenant Jacobek stated, exactly as Vicki had known he would.

"Is my client under suspicion?" Vicki asked.

"Is she your client?"

"Is she under suspicion?"

"A bloody golf club was found hidden at the back of Tracey's closet. A diamond ring was found in her jewelry box."

"What were you doing going through my things?" Tracey protested. "Don't you need some kind of warrant?"

"Shut up, Tracey," Vicki said. She looked at Susan, saw her holding her breath. "I repeat, is my client under suspicion?"

"We'll go you one better, Counselor," Lieutenant Jacobek answered. "She's under arrest."

Susan gasped as the two officers approached Tracey.

"You have the right to remain silent," Lieutenant Gill began.

Tracey giggled. "This is just like on *Law & Order.*"

"Don't say another word," Vicki said over the lieutenant's continuing drone. "Call her father," she instructed Susan as the officers escorted a bemused-looking Tracey out the kitchen door, Vicki directly on their heels. "If he's not home yet, leave a message. Tell him to meet me at the police station as soon as possible."

"And then what?" Susan asked.

"Have your dinner. Get some sleep. Something tells me things are only going to get worse."

Twenty-Nine

Chris sat in the darkness of her apartment without moving. In front of her the television screen flickered without sound. Images of Barbara, of Tracey, of the house on Grand Avenue, took turns assaulting her dazed eyes until she almost didn't see them anymore: Barbara smiling her Mona Lisa smile, the smile that disturbed as few muscles as possible but still managed to convey the unrestrained joy in her heart; Barbara, her eyes radiating maternal pride, her arms wrapped tightly around Tracey, who stared impassively into the camera; Tracey as a pudgy infant, as a curly-haired moppet, as an awkward adolescent in a pink taffeta dress, a lone ringlet falling past her forehead toward the large, empty circles of her eyes. Why had she never noticed this emptiness before? Chris wondered. Or was it only in retrospect that Tracey's eyes seemed so void of emotion? *There was a little girl,* Chris could hear Barbara sing over the continuing barrage of photographs, *who had a little curl. . . .* Chris sat motionless, a sharp ache, like a knife wedged between her breasts, stilling the erratic beating of her heart, so that she had to remind herself to breathe.

How could this have happened? How could anything so horrible have happened to someone as wonderful as Barbara? How could Tracey be in any way responsible? No, it simply wasn't possible. Someone had made a mistake. Barbara wasn't dead; Tracey hadn't been charged with her murder. None of what Susan had told her was true. Susan was playing some sort of sick, practical joke. She was just angry at her for disappearing after the funeral, for not staying over at Barbara's house as she'd promised, for being gone all day and half the night.

"Where have you been?" she'd demanded as soon as Chris picked up the phone, before she'd even said hello. "I've been calling you all day."

"What's the matter?" Chris asked in return, knowing something was wrong, afraid to imagine what it was.

"You haven't heard? Where the hell have you been?"

"Heard what? What's going on?"

"Oh, God."

In that moment, Chris's stomach slid through her bowels to her knees. Her first thought was of her children. An accident involving Montana or one of the boys. Montana was old enough to drive now. Dear God, if anything had happened to her . . . "Tell me," she said, a strange gargle disrupting the normal cadence of her voice, as if her throat had been slashed from ear to ear, and each word was being forced to navigate its way through a violent rush of blood.

"It's Barbara," Susan's voice echoed even now. *Barbara. Barbara. Barbara.* "She's dead." *Dead. Dead. Dead.*

Chris couldn't remember what happened next. She vaguely remembered someone screaming, although she couldn't be sure now whether it was Susan or herself. Someone filled her in on all the horrible details. Maybe Susan. Maybe the TV. She didn't remember turning it on, but there it was, flashing at her like a strobe light, noisy and invasive even with the sound turned off. When had she turned it on?

Her purse lay on the floor beside her thin mauve sweater, where she must have dropped them in her rush to answer the phone. Somewhere there was the faint odor of vomit, although only the unpleasant taste in her mouth reminded Chris she'd been sick. "Who did it?" she recalled asking. "Do they know?"

"The police arrested Tracey."

It had to be a mistake. Or one of Tony's sick pranks. That was it—Tony. Of course. Why hadn't she thought of him earlier? It hadn't been Susan on the phone. It was Tony disguising his voice. Over the years, he'd perfected a pretty good imitation of all her friends. What was the matter with her that she hadn't recognized him right away?

Except, of course, how did that explain the images flashing across her TV screen, pushing themselves in her face, pressing against her nose and mouth like a deadly pillow, no matter how many times she changed the channel? How did that explain the curiously interchangeable announcers who recited the same grisly details of the crime with a bland indifference bordering on cruelty? Chris had pushed the mute button to silence their well-rehearsed nonchalance once and for all, although something stopped her from turning off the television altogether.

So it wasn't Tony.

And it wasn't a joke.

Barbara was dead. Tracey had been charged with her murder.

"Where is Tracey now?" Chris remembered asking Susan.

"At the Helen Marshall Correctional Institute for Women. Ron was going to post bail, but apparently his wife didn't want Tracey in the house."

There was probably more, but Chris was too tired to retrieve it from wherever her shocked brain had hidden it. Let it come to her in fits and starts, bits and bites, snips and snatches, Chris thought restlessly. Let it come and let it go.

Was this really happening?

Last night had been so wonderful. Everything was finally falling into place. And now this. . . .

Chris leaned her head back against the lurid blue-and-green checks of her couch. It was a hideous sofa, as uncomfortable to sit in as it was to look at, but what could you expect from a furnished apartment in one of the more modest sections of town? When she'd rented the one-bedroom unit, she hadn't expected to be here more than a few months. As soon as Tony discovered her address, he'd start harassing her again, bombarding her with phone calls at all hours of the day and night, standing for hours at a stretch outside her window, regaling her landlord with wild stories about her, leaving dog feces outside her door. It didn't matter how tight the security, Tony always found a way to breach it. It didn't matter what floor her apartment was on, it was never high enough. "Rise and shine," he'd sing through the phone wires at four o'clock in the morning. "And give God your glory, glory."

But now here it was the end of August, and until Tony's unexpected appearance at Susan's house the other day, she hadn't seen or heard from him in months. Part of his grand plan for keeping her off guard and on her toes? Or maybe he thought this apartment was torture enough. He had no way of knowing that Chris was happier here than she'd been anywhere since leaving Grand Avenue. That she'd finally found the peace that had eluded her all her life.

What would he say when he found out where she'd been last night?

What would any of them say?

What would Barbara have said? Chris wondered, a fresh scream building in the back of her throat. Barbara. Oh, God, Barbara. Why Barbara? What had Barbara ever done to deserve such a gruesome death? "It should have been me," Chris wailed out loud. Wasn't she the one they'd all feared for? Hadn't they all been holding their breath for years, waiting for that awful phone call in the middle of the night, the phone call that said their friend had been bludgeoned to death in her bed?

Except that when the call finally came, it hadn't been Chris's name whispered across the wires. It hadn't been her battered corpse lying, limbs akimbo, at the foot of her bed in a pool of her own blood.

And what had Chris been doing while her friend's head was being hammered to a bloody pulp? She'd been in a cozy double bed in a quaint little inn on the outskirts of town, listening to sweet phrases of love. As Barbara screamed in horror, Chris had been screaming with delight, brought to orgasm by the most delicate of touches, the gentlest flick of the tongue. Chris had drifted off to sleep as Barbara lay dying on the floor, waking up in the arms of her lover at the same time her best friend was being wrapped in a body bag and taken to the morgue.

She'd had breakfast in bed, gone for a long walk in the country, sucking the fresh air deep into her lungs, relishing the peace and quiet, careful not to let anything interrupt her newfound serenity. No newspapers, no television, no radio. Not even in the car on the drive back into town. A CD of Glenn Gould on the piano accompanied her home.

"Do you want me to come upstairs? Tuck you in?" her lover had asked.

"No, I'm fine," Chris had answered. And she was. For the first time in her life, she could honestly say she was fine and mean it. She was at peace. She knew who she was. She was no longer afraid.

She could hear the phone ringing as soon as she stepped off the elevator. Probably Tony, she thought, taking her time as she walked down the hall. He'd found her. Fine. So be it. She wasn't afraid anymore.

She opened the door, locked it behind her, debated whether to answer the phone or just let it ring. Who would be calling her at almost eleven o'clock at night besides Tony? She almost didn't answer it, but something propelled her toward it. What if it was important? She lifted the phone to her ears, the sound of Susan's voice assaulting her even before she said hello.

"Where have you been? I've been calling you all day."

Maybe it was a dream, Chris thought now, knowing it wasn't, but clinging to the pretense nonetheless. She closed her eyes, saw Barbara's face on the inside of her lids. Her sweet face, Chris thought, watching it change, grow perversely younger with the passage of time. Barbara hadn't needed the layers of makeup she'd insisted on wearing, or any of the plastic surgery she'd subjected herself to over the years. Indeed, Barbara had remained beautiful almost in spite of herself. Why had she never realized how beautiful she was?

"My sweet, beautiful Barbara," Chris cried into the hard pillow of the blue-and-green-checkered sofa. "I never even got to say good-bye."

The words unleashed a flood of angry, bitter tears, and Chris had to bite down on the pillow to keep from screaming out loud. "No!" she wailed, writhing on the sofa as if in physical pain, covering her face with the pillow, as if to block out all sight, all sound, all sensation. "No!" The word echoed against the cheap fabric, damp with her tears. "No, no, no, no, no!"

Chris almost didn't hear the timid knocking on the door, and even after she did, even after she understood that it was something other than the sound of her brain knocking against her skull, hammering for release, that there was actually someone in the hall, tapping to be let in, she wasn't sure she had the strength to get up off the couch and answer it. Probably it was Susan, come to see if she was all right. Or maybe one of the neighbors, having heard her muffled cries. Maybe Tony, come to deliver the good news personally. Or to put her out of her misery once and for all. "Who is it?" she asked from the sofa, forcing herself to her feet. But the only answer she received was more knocking on the door. Chris walked toward the sound, not bothering to wipe her face or dry her eyes, not bothering to ask again who it was, not bothering to look through the peephole, not caring who was on the other side. Fine, she thought. So be it. She took a deep breath and pulled open the door. Immediately, the breath caught in her lungs, the air froze around her. "My God," she whispered. "Oh, my God."

"Can I come in?"

Chris stepped back, her wet eyes wide with shock.

"Are you all right?"

Chris nodded, shook her head, fumbled for words that refused to come.

"I can't stay long. Dad thinks I'm at a friend's house. I can't stay long."

Chris wiped the tears from her eyes with an impatient hand. They got in her way, and she would allow nothing to hamper her view of the glorious young girl standing before her. "Montana," she whispered in a voice that could barely be heard, her eyes sucking her daughter in like liquid from a straw—the long blond hair, the pale skin, the apple cheeks, the wondrous navy blue eyes. She was a young woman now.

"Are you all right?" her daughter asked again.

"I'm all right," Chris heard herself answer.

Montana closed the door behind her, although she took only a few tentative steps into the room.

"It's a mess," Chris apologized, imagining the room through her daughter's eyes—the old-fashioned shag carpeting in the same garish tones as the sofa, the small glass-topped table hugged by two mismatched chairs, the tiny galley kitchen.

"It's fine."

"How did you know where to find me?"

"Susan told me. I called her this afternoon. She called me back after she spoke to you."

"You called her?"

"Barbara was dead. They thought Dad might have . . ." Montana stopped, swallowed, lowered her eyes to the floor, as if to escape the intensity of her mother's gaze. "Nobody knew where you were."

"You were worried about me?"

"Where were you?"

Chris tried, but couldn't take her eyes off her daughter, as if she were afraid that should she turn away, even for half a second, the girl would disappear. "Would you like to sit down?"

Montana shook her head, leaned back against the door.

"Can I get you anything to eat, something to drink? Water?"

"I'm okay," Montana said, then: "Would *you* like some water?"

Chris nodded, sinking to the sofa when she felt her legs about to give way, her eyes following her daughter into the galley kitchen, staying on her as Montana filled a glass with water and brought it back into the living room. Chris felt a bolt of electricity charge through her body as their fingers briefly touched. It took every ounce of strength she had to keep from throwing herself into her daughter's arms, smothering her sweet face with kisses.

"Where were you?" Montana repeated.

Chris shook her head, not sure what to say. "After Susan's mother's funeral, I went for a drive in the country. I stayed overnight at this little inn, spent the day walking around, visiting antique stores . . ."

"Alone?"

"No. A friend was with me." How much could she tell her? Chris wondered. Dear God, there was so *much* to tell her.

"So you didn't hear anything about what happened. . . . "

"Until maybe an hour ago." Chris sipped her water slowly, her eyes never leaving the beautiful young woman who shifted uneasily from one foot to the other before her. Montana wore white jeans and a pink, sleeveless sweater, and her arms were slim and toned. How she ached to feel those arms around her, Chris thought, watching as Montana pulled a chair away from the small, round, glass-topped table and sat down.

"At first they thought Dad did it."

"I know."

"But he was home last night, looking after Rowdy."

"Rowdy's sick?"

Montana shook her head with pronounced vigor. "He just has a cold. He coughs all the time. Keeps everybody up."

"Has he been to the doctor?"

"It's just a cold," Montana said, growing quickly defensive. "Dad's taking good care of him. He gets up every night to give him his medicine."

Chris said nothing. Her baby had a cold. Tony was giving him his medicine.

"He's a good father," Montana said. "He takes good care of us."

"I'm glad."

"You probably don't believe me."

"I believe you."

"I know you two had problems . . ."

You don't know, Chris wanted to say, said nothing.

"But ever since you left . . ."

"I've tried to see you so many times. You know how much—"

Montana jumped to her feet. "I should go."

Chris was instantly on her feet as well. "No, please. Please don't go. Please."

Montana's eyes moved nervously between her mother and the door, as if trying to figure out the time it would take to run the short distance, as if she were afraid that should she try, her mother might tackle her to the ground. She hesitated for what felt like an eternity before sitting back down. "He's been a good father," she repeated.

Chris nodded, afraid to say anything lest she say something that would send Montana catapulting out of her chair again. "How's Wyatt?" she ventured after a lengthy pause.

"He's okay."

"And you?"

Montana seemed surprised by the question. "Me? I'm fine."

"You look wonderful."

"Thank you."

"Enjoying school?"

"It's okay. One more year, then I'm off to college."

"Just one more year?"

"I'm thinking of applying to Duke. Or maybe Cornell."

Duke or maybe Cornell, Chris repeated silently, wondrously.

"I'm not sure yet what my major will be. Maybe political science. Maybe English literature. I haven't made up my mind."

Were they really sitting here making polite conversation? Was any of this really happening?

"Do you have a boyfriend?" Chris ventured, afraid to overstep, but so hungry for information, she could almost taste it on her tongue.

"I have a friend," Montana said, as Chris had said earlier. "I don't know if you'd call him a boyfriend exactly. We hang out."

"What's his name?"

"David."

"David," Chris repeated. "I always liked that name. What's he like?"

"He's tall, funny, really smart."

"Kind?"

"What?"

"Is he kind?"

Montana shrugged her growing impatience with the conversation. "I guess."

"That's the most important thing. To be kind."

A moment's silence as Chris willed Montana's eyes to hers. If you take nothing else away from this visit, Chris's eyes directed, understand that.

"So, where are you working these days?" Montana asked, shifting uneasily in her chair, crossing one leg over the other, returning both to the floor.

"I'm a receptionist at an advertising agency. Smith-Hallendale. Maybe you've heard of them. They're at the corner of Vine and Fourth."

Montana shook her head no.

"My boss is this really great woman. Emily Hallendale. I met her when I worked at the Mariemont Veterinary Service." Chris thought back to that awful day when she'd fled the doctor's office with her pockets full of sedatives and her thoughts full of suicide. She felt the hand on her elbow, watched herself spin around, saw the look of concern in Emily Hallendale's eyes. She'd reluctantly accepted Emily

Hallendale's offer of coffee, then gratefully accepted her offer of a job. At Smith-Hallendale, Chris had met the great love of her life. So funny how things work out, she remembered thinking at the time.

So funny how things work out, she thought now.

"Do you really think Tracey murdered her mother?" Montana was asking, her voice low, as if afraid someone might be eavesdropping on their conversation.

"I don't know what to think," Chris answered honestly.

"I never knew her very well."

"No," Chris agreed.

"But she always seemed nice."

"Yes, she did."

"I don't think she did it. I mean, how do you kill your own—" Montana broke off, looked uneasily around the room. "I really have to go." She pushed herself off the chair. "You won't tell Dad . . ."

"Of course not." Chris followed her daughter to the door, knowing it was pointless to protest. "Could we do this again sometime?" she asked, feeling like a nervous suitor.

Montana nodded slowly, her back to her mother. "I'll call you." She opened the door, about to walk through.

"Montana?"

Montana stopped, held tight to the doorknob.

"Can I hold you? Just for a minute? Would that be all right?"

Montana swiveled slowly toward her mother's open arms, hesitated, then stopped, drew back, shook her head.

Chris reluctantly dropped her arms to her sides. Clearly her daughter wasn't ready for such a momentous step. It had taken all her energy, all her courage, just to reestablish contact. Chris felt a slight tear in the muscles around her heart. "That's all right. I understand."

Montana turned back toward the door. "I'm glad you're okay. I'll call you."

And then she was gone, the door closing behind her.

Chris stretched out her arms to embrace the lingering aroma of baby powder mixed with a hint of lemon. She took a deep breath, wrapped her arms around the bittersweet scent, held it tight against her lungs. "I'll be waiting," she said to the empty room.

Thirty

Vicki pulled her black Jaguar into the crowded lot next to the Helen Marshall Correctional Institute for Women so that it deliberately straddled the dividing line between two parking spaces. Let them yell at her, she thought, climbing out of the car and making her way across the lot toward the depressingly modern eight-story structure that housed female offenders, the top two floors of which were reserved for those awaiting trial. At least she wasn't driving a Camry or LeSabre, or any of those other luxury wannabes with delusions of grandeur she occasionally saw overlapping two parking spaces, as if it mattered whether someone took a nick out of their sides.

She walked briskly up the front steps and into the spacious foyer of rose granite and black marble, sweeping through the metal detector as she handed her brown alligator purse and matching briefcase to the security guard for inspection. She retrieved both, signed her name to the registrar, and headed for the bank of elevators on the right side of the lobby, head judiciously down, a message to all who saw her that she had no time for casual distractions.

"Vicki," someone called out anyway, and Vicki looked up to see a lawyer whose name was either Grace or Joy or Hope or Faith, one of those inspiration-filled monikers that almost guaranteed disappointment, waving to her from beneath a predominantly orange-and-red tapestry that stretched across one wall. "Great picture of you in the paper the other day."

Vicki nodded her thanks, although she was more miffed than thankful. She hadn't thought the photo all that great. If anything, it made her look dour and even a little jowly. She'd have to be careful how she stood in the weeks ahead, to make sure she kept her chin up and her eyes down, confident but not cocky. Just a trace of the coquette. Enough to intrigue, not enough to alienate. It was tricky, but manageable. Tracey wasn't the only one about to go on trial.

And she'd do better to stick with darker colors. Thank God it was the end of September and fall colors were starting to reemerge. Aside from being naturally slimming, darker tones were more dramatic, especially in print. And Vicki expected to see a lot of herself in print over the coming months. She'd already been the subject of two articles, one in the *Cincinnati Enquirer,* the other in the rival *Post.* Of the two, the *Enquirer*'s profile was decidedly the more flattering. The *Post* continued to see her as merely an ambitious extension of her husband. A luxury wannabe, Vicki thought with a defiant shrug of her shoulders. The article had questioned her motives, her capabilities, even her judgment in agreeing to defend a young girl charged with the cold-blooded murder of one of her closest friends.

They weren't the only ones.

Susan, Chris, and even Jeremy had questioned the wisdom of her taking on this case.

"What if she's guilty?" Susan and Chris had asked almost in unison.

"What if she's not?" Vicki countered.

"What if you lose?" Jeremy asked.

"What difference would it make?" Vicki said, knowing that, down the road, the public would remember her name, not whether she won or lost.

Besides, she didn't intend to lose.

Vicki stepped into the elevator, staring resolutely at her brown Ombeline pumps as several bodies carelessly brushed up against the tan suede of her jacket. "Seven, please," she said to no one in particular, watching out of the corner of her eye to make sure the appropriate button was pressed, not looking up until she heard the elevator doors draw to a close. A slight bump and the elevator began its painfully slow ascent.

It stopped again almost immediately. Vicki looked to the panel above the doors. The second floor, for God's sake. She watched a heavyset woman amble out, clearly in no hurry to get where she was going. Would it have killed her to take the stairs? Vicki wondered, reaching over to press the door-close button, tapping an impatient foot when the door failed to respond quickly enough.

"Big date?" a familiar voice asked from behind her.

Vicki didn't have to turn around to know who it was. "Michael," she acknowledged, spinning around slowly, more to ascertain who else was in the elevator than because she was eager to see the assistant state's attorney who was her former lover. A woman in jeans and a sloppy yellow sweater stood near the back of the elevator seemingly absorbed in her newspaper, oblivious to the two attorneys. "How are you?"

"Great," he said.

In truth, he did look pretty terrific. Vicki noted that his hair was parted differently from the last time she'd been this close to him. She smelled his familiar aftershave, felt an unwelcome tingle between her legs. Yes, indeed, Michael Rose looked very dapper in his dark blue, pin-striped suit, pale blue shirt, and plain power-red tie. Every inch the successful prosecutor, she thought, fighting the urge to run her hand across the front of his trousers for old times' sake. Vicki shook the unwelcome thought from her head. She had no real interest in traveling down that path again, especially since she'd soon be seeing a great deal of Michael Rose in court.

"I understand *Time* magazine is doing a cover story on you," he said sarcastically.

"Not yet," Vicki said with a smile. In fact, she was considering an offer from *Vanity Fair* for an interview with regard to an article they were writing on the case, as well as a request for a photograph of her with her young client. A major law firm in New York had made polite inquiries about dispatching a representative to Cincinnati to meet with her over lunch when she had a free moment. A Hollywood agent had offered his guidance and expertise should she choose to spread her wings and fly west.

How long before she was chosen one of *People* magazine's Fifty Most Beautiful People? How long before *Time* actually did put her on its cover? Even if she lost this case, Vicki knew she'd already won.

The elevator stopped on the fourth floor, and the woman reading her newspaper flicked it closed and stepped out.

"Visiting your client?" Michael asked as the doors slowly came together again.

Vicki glanced at the keyboard, noted Michael was also going to the seventh floor. "You?"

"A sweet young lady who hired a hit man to kill her ex-boyfriend's new girlfriend says she's ready to talk a deal."

"I take it the hit man was an undercover cop?"

"Aren't they all?"

Vicki thought the girl should take her chances in court. Michael Rose, while a decent prosecutor, was as unimaginative in court as he was in bed. A good lawyer could run circles around him. And she was a very good lawyer, Vicki thought, a smile stretching across her narrow face.

"You might be smart to consider a plea bargain yourself, Counselor," Michael offered.

Vicki arched one eyebrow. Plea-bargain the biggest case of her career? Was he crazy? "What are you offering?"

"Man one. She serves the maximum."

"You're dreaming. Besides, she didn't do it. Why would I plead?"

"The evidence is pretty conclusive. Headlines are one thing. Substance is something else."

"A lot of people only read the headlines." God, how long did it take to get to the seventh floor?

"And that's all that matters to you? Headlines? I thought the murdered woman was a friend of yours."

"My motives—and my friendships—are hardly your concern, Michael."

"God, she speaks my name. Be still my heart."

Vicki took a deep breath, reached for her most conciliatory voice. "Let's not do this, okay?"

"My wife's suing me for divorce," he said, managing to sound as if it were somehow her fault. "Did you know that?"

"Yes, I think I heard something about it. I'm sorry."

"Are you?"

"Not really, no," Vicki snapped, her patience completely gone. "Look, I don't mean to sound—"

"Like a bitch?"

"I think this conversation is over."

"I'm dismissed?" Michael asked as the elevator doors opened.

Vicki brushed past him into the corridor without a word.

"You know, I'm really looking forward to beating your ass," he called after her.

Vicki threw her head back and laughed. "My ass is way out of your league," she said without looking back.

Am I ever glad to see you."

Vicki entered the small, windowless room at the end of the long hall. The walls were a sickly shade of green, like a too ripe melon, and not helped any by the recessed fluorescent lighting overhead. In the center of the room was a rectangular table of inferior walnut, heavily scarred with graffiti—*There is no gravity, the earth sucks! Martin loves Cindy, Cindy loves Joanne. Fuck you. Fuck the fuckers. Fuck the lawyers. Fuck. Fuck. Fuck. Fuck.* So many *fucks*, Vicki had lost count during her last visit.

She sat down in the straight-backed wooden chair across the table from Tracey. Aside from her obvious restlessness at having been confined for more than a month, Tracey looked remarkably well. Her color was good, despite the fluorescent lighting, her hair clean and brushed away from her face. There were no bags under her eyes, no sign she spent her nights crying herself to sleep. The pale blue of her prison uniform actually flattered her. Her arms looked newly toned, as if she'd been lifting weights, which was probably the case. Vicki shuddered as she realized that Tracey looked wonderful, that life inside the Helen Marshall Correctional Institute for Women actually seemed to agree with her.

"Is everything okay?"

"Oh, yeah," Tracey said easily. "Except for my roommate. That's why I called you. I need you to get her transferred."

Vicki dug her freshly manicured nails into the alligator briefcase that rested on the table in front of her. "That's what was so urgent you needed to see me right away?"

Tracey seemed genuinely puzzled by Vicki's surprise. "She just sits on her bed all day crying. It's kind of nerve-racking after a while."

"What's she crying about?"

Tracey shrugged, shaking loose several curls. She pushed them away from her forehead. One fell back. "She just keeps moaning. You know—she's sorry about what happened. She didn't mean to kick the kid so hard. She wants her mommy. Stuff like that."

"All that talk about her mother," Vicki offered generously. "I guess that upsets you."

"Yeah, well, like I said, it gets on your nerves."

"Do you miss your mother, Tracey?"

Tracey looked startled by the question. Her shoulders lifted toward her ears. "I guess."

"You guess?"

"Do you think you can get her transferred?"

Vicki nodded. "I'll see what I can do."

"Thanks." Tracey smiled.

"How's everything else?" Vicki opened her briefcase, drew out several files.

"Fine."

Vicki shook her head, afraid to lift her eyes to her client lest her eyes reveal what was going on inside her head. How many people would describe life behind bars as "fine" and sound as if they meant it? "How'd your meeting go with Nancy Joplin?"

Tracey looked blank.

"The staff psychiatrist," Vicki elaborated. "Weren't you scheduled to meet with her this morning?"

"Oh, yeah. She was nice."

"Nice," Vicki repeated, chewing on the word as if trying to digest it. "What sort of questions did she ask you?"

Tracey pushed the lone curl away from her forehead. "Things about my mother. You know."

"I don't know."

"Um, let's see. What kind of relationship we had, if we were close, how I felt about her engagement, stuff like that."

"What did you tell her?"

"The truth. Like you told me to. That we had a great relationship, that we were very close, that I liked Howard."

"What else did she ask you?"

"I don't want to talk about it."

"Tracey, time is running out. We go to court in January. I can't help you if you won't talk to me."

Tracey stretched her legs out in front of her, looked to the ceiling. "She asked me about the night my mother died."

"What did you tell her?" Vicki asked.

"You know." Tracey folded her arms across her chest, her lips gathering into a stubborn pout.

"I don't know," Vicki insisted, not bothering to hide her growing frustration. How many times did they have to go over the same territory? "You told her that a masked intruder killed your mother?"

"Yes."

"Then why is there no evidence such a person exists?"

"I don't know."

"Let me explain what we're up against here." Hadn't she explained this a hundred times already? "Aside from no signs of forced entry, no blood anywhere but in the bedroom and all over you, there's the little matter of the murder weapon the police found hidden in your closet and covered with your fingerprints, there's your mother's missing diamond ring that the police discovered in your jewelry box. . . ."

"I know all that."

"How did the murder weapon get into your closet?"

"I don't know," Tracey insisted. "Maybe he put it there."

"Who? The Lone Ranger?"

Tracey's response was a nervous giggle.

"*When* did he put it there?"

"I'm not sure."

"You said he didn't come into your room, that you confronted him in the hall."

"Then he must have come in later, when I was with my mother."

"But you said he ran down the stairs and out the door."

Tracey jumped to her feet, began pacing back and forth. "I don't know what he did. I'm confused. You're confusing me so much I can't remember what happened."

"That's not good enough."

"Why not?"

"Why not!" Vicki repeated in amazement. "Because you can't keep changing your story. You can't say one thing and then another. The district attorney is going to pounce on each and every little inconsistency. Michael Rose may not be the best prosecutor in the world, but he won't need to be. He's got a mass of forensic evidence; he's got opportunity; he's got motive."

"Motive? What motive?"

"He'll say you were jealous of your mother's relationship with Howard Kerble."

"That's not true. I like Howard."

"That you'd gotten used to having your mother all to yourself."

"So what?"

"That you killed your mother in a jealous rage."

"I didn't kill her in a jealous rage!"

"Why *did* you kill her?" Vicki shouted.

"Because!" Tracey shouted back, then gasped, as if trying to pull the word back into her mouth. She stood very still, stared at the wall.

Vicki held her breath, her whole body shaking. My God, had Tracey actually admitted killing her mother? Was she about to confess? Vicki felt her muscles turn to jelly. She grabbed the side of the table to keep from sliding off her chair to the floor.

"Because," Tracey repeated, as tears filled her eyes and rolled down her cheeks.

"Tell me what happened that night, Tracey."

Tracey shook her head. "I can't."

"Please." Vicki slowly pushed herself to her feet, her knees knocking together as she approached Tracey, who'd begun spinning around in increasingly frantic, tight little circles. Vicki reached out her arms, gathered Tracey inside them as a desperate wail escaped Tracey's throat.

"I can't tell you. I can't. Please don't make me. I can't. I can't."

Vicki guided Tracey to her chair, sat her down, knelt before her on unsteady knees as the door to the room opened and a muscular guard with a surprisingly feminine face peeked inside.

"Everything all right in here?" the guard asked.

"Yes, thank you," Vicki told the woman, although in truth the answer was no, nothing was all right. Nothing would ever be all right again. And it was about to get a whole lot worse. She was sure of that.

The guard nodded and left the room, closing the door after her.

"Tell me what happened, Tracey."

"You'll hate me."

"I won't hate you."

"I didn't mean to do it."

"I know you didn't."

"I didn't want to hurt her. I begged her to stop."

"Stop? Stop what?"

Tracey shook her head so hard, her hair whipped around her neck, catching Vicki in the face. Tears automatically sprang to Vicki's eyes. She pushed them aside, waited for Tracey's response.

"It was around nine o'clock," Tracey began. "Chris had already left. Mom said she was going to have a nice hot bath and crawl into bed." Tracey stopped, stared intently at the wall ahead, as if it were a movie screen. "She asked me to scrub her back, and I did. Then she asked me if I wanted to sleep in bed with her. I used to sleep in her bed a lot, but not lately. I didn't think it was such a good idea anymore."

Vicki shifted uncomfortably on the balls of her feet. Where was this going?

"I said okay, but I didn't want to. I didn't want her to . . ."

"You didn't want her to what?" Vicki repeated in a voice not her own.

"You know."

"I don't know." What was Tracey trying to say?

"I didn't want her to touch me."

"Touch you? What do you mean, touch you?" Vicki pushed herself to her feet, her arms twitching with growing agitation.

"You're angry," Tracey said immediately. "You hate me. I knew you were going to hate me."

Of course I hate you, you stupid, lying twit, Vicki raged inwardly. What she said was, "Of course I don't hate you. Go on. Please, Tracey, tell me what happened." Then go to hell, you lying little bitch!

"She was always touching me."

"She was your mother, Tracey. Mothers touch their daughters."

"Not like this. Not on their breasts. Not between their legs."

"Your mother touched you between . . ." Vicki couldn't bring herself to say the words. It took all her resolve to keep from slapping Tracey's face, from wringing her stupid, lying little neck.

"She called it our little game. We'd been playing it for years. I said I didn't want to play it anymore. She said I had no choice, that she was my mother, and she could do whatever she liked. I begged her to stop. I begged her to leave me alone. But she wouldn't. She took off her engagement ring, put it on my finger, said I was her one true love."

Vicki looked away. "And then what?"

"I don't remember exactly. I guess I kind of blanked it out. After it was over, she fell asleep. I just lay there, shaking. Sometime during the night, I went downstairs, got the golf club out of the hall closet. It was like I was in some kind of trance, like I was outside myself, like it wasn't me at all. I went back up to her bedroom. I remember standing over her. She opened her eyes, reached for me. And I remember thinking, I can't let you touch me anymore. I have to stop you. You're my mother and I love you, but I can't let you keep hurting me. I have to make you stop."

Vicki sank into the nearest chair, gritting her teeth tightly together to keep from throwing up. She knew everything Tracey had just said was a pack of filthy lies. Barbara was no more capable of sexually abusing her daughter than she was of shaving her head and wearing Birkenstock sandals. There wasn't the slightest chance anything Tracey had just told her was true. Was there?

Was there?

"My mother always said if I told anyone, no one would believe me, that everyone would hate me," Tracey cried. "And I can see it in your eyes. You don't believe me. You hate me."

Vicki said nothing. She felt as if Tracey had wielded her murderous weapon once again, this time squarely at her head. She rubbed her forehead with fingers as cold as the grave.

Dear God, what was she supposed to do now?

Thirty-One

"What the hell are you talking about!"

Vicki took a step back, sought refuge behind her massive new desk. "Susan, calm down."

"Don't tell me to calm down."

"Then please lower your voice."

"Tell me what the hell is going on here."

"I'd be happy to, if you'd give me half the chance."

"What is this nonsense I've been reading about?"

"It's not nonsense."

"Tracey killed Barbara in self-defense! You don't call that nonsense?"

"I call it a reasonable line of defense."

"It's an *indefensible* line of defense," Susan countered, taking several giant steps across the recently purchased Indian rug that graced the floor in front of Vicki's desk. The move caused Vicki to take another step back, raise her hands in warning.

"If you'd just sit down . . ."

Surprisingly, Susan plopped down into one of the two new bloodred leather wing chairs that sat like sentinels in front of Vicki's desk. She was wearing a smart black pantsuit and a white turtleneck sweater. Her light brown hair fell gently to her chin, framing cheeks flushed with righteous indignation. "Talk," she said as the phone began to ring.

Vicki ignored it, exhaled a deep breath of air, stayed on her feet. More power this way, she decided, although she was starting to wish she'd worn flatter shoes. Flats were easier to run in, easier if it became necessary to make a quick escape. "You know I wouldn't be doing this—"

"Why *are* you doing this?"

"—unless there was a good reason."

"I'm waiting."

The office door opened a sliver and Vicki's secretary's head popped into view. "It's Marina Russell from Global TV. She says you promised to get back to her by three o'clock and it's ten past."

"Tell her I'll have to call her first thing in the morning. And hold the rest of my calls." As if on cue, several other lines began ringing at once.

The secretary nodded, closed the door after her. The phones stopped ringing, only to start up again.

"Busy time," Susan observed.

Vicki shrugged, choosing to ignore the bitterness in her friend's voice, the accusations in her eyes. "I have to be very careful what I say," she told Susan after a lengthy pause. "You know about attorney-client privilege."

"No. I've been living on Mars for the last forty-four years."

"I can do without the sarcasm."

"I can do without the bullshit."

"Great." Vicki decided to sit down after all, collapsing into the enormous new swivel chair behind her desk, crossing one leg over the other beneath her beige Armani suit, leaning her head against the deep red leather, closing her eyes, wishing she'd kept her old office furniture. Her other chair had been much more comfortable. She hadn't felt so swamped, so overwhelmed, each time she sat down. Of course, she usually didn't have her closest friend raging at her, Vicki thought, trying not to feel wounded by the disdain in Susan's angry eyes. When this was all over, Susan would understand why she'd had to do this. "You know I can't betray my client."

"But you have no trouble betraying your friend."

"I'm not betraying my friend. I'm protecting the very thing that friend valued more than anything in the world."

"*Thing* is certainly the right word for her. How can you do this?"

"Tracey is entitled to the best defense under the law."

"And that would be you?"

"In this case, yes."

"Why?"

"Why?" Vicki repeated. What kind of question was that?

"Why does it have to be you?"

"Because Tracey trusts me. Because she needs me. Because I honestly believe it's what Barbara would have wanted."

"Barbara would have wanted you to defend the person who murdered her?"

"In this case, yes."

"She would have wanted her memory sullied, her reputation destroyed?"

"It's not my intention to do either of those things."

"Oh, really? You don't think her reputation might suffer just a bit once you label her a child molester?"

"I have to defend my client."

"And the best defense is a good offense?"

"Sometimes."

"This time?"

Vicki looked toward the window, watched the rain falling to the street below. "I was as shocked as you are by the things Tracey told me."

"Yes, the papers have been trumpeting your shock across the front pages every day. You wouldn't be trying to influence the potential jury pool, would you?"

"The public has a right to hear both sides of the story."

"The public has a right to the truth."

"Oh, please," Vicki said. Could Susan really be so naive?

"Are you telling me you actually believe the garbage Tracey is spouting?"

"It's irrelevant what I believe."

"Don't give me that crap," Susan said dismissively. "I may not be a lawyer, but I watch enough TV to know you can't put a witness on the stand knowing they're deliberately going to perjure themselves."

"Who says Tracey's going to perjure herself?"

"I do," Susan said adamantly. "And so do you, if you're being honest."

"Are you questioning my integrity?"

"I'm questioning your motives."

"What are you saying? That I'm in this for the money, the fame, the publicity?"

"I don't know. Are you? Whose attention are you really trying to get here, Vicki?"

Vicki felt her pulse quicken and her cheeks flush warm with anger. What the hell was Susan getting at? "I don't know what you're talking about."

"Don't you?"

"This isn't about me," Vicki snapped, in a voice that warned Susan she was on dangerous ground.

"Exactly," Susan countered, refusing to be intimidated. "Look," she continued in the next breath. "Barbara was sound asleep. Even if you accept the ridiculous things Tracey is saying, which I don't for one minute, how can you possibly argue that Tracey was afraid for her life at the time she killed her mother? What threat could Barbara possibly have been when she was sleeping?"

Vicki let go of the air trapped in her lungs, happy to be back on more comfortable terrain. "Tracey was convinced that when her mother woke up, the abuse would continue."

"And what? She couldn't run away? She couldn't tell her father? Murder was her only option?"

"She says the abuse had been going on since she was a little girl, that no one had ever done anything to help her."

"That's bullshit, and you know it."

"Do I? Do you?"

"What!"

"How can you be so sure that Barbara never molested Tracey?"

Susan shook her head. "This is absurd."

"The fact is, you can't be sure. None of us can be sure, no matter how good friends we all were."

"I'm sure," Susan insisted stubbornly.

Had Susan always been so damn confident about everything? "Would you categorize Barbara as a good mother?" Vicki asked suddenly.

"Of course."

"An involved mother?"

"Yes."

"Might you describe her relationship with Tracey as being a bit *overly* involved and enmeshed?"

"No, I *might* not. I *would* not."

"Think about it for a minute," Vicki instructed.

"*You* think about it. Just because you grew up without a mother . . ."

Vicki felt the word like a slap on the face. "Can we leave my mother out of this?"

"I don't know. Can we?"

Vicki held her breath, tried counting to ten, barely reached five before she exploded. "Okay, enough of this dime-store psychological shit! My mother is not the issue here. Contrary to what you might think, I am not using this case as a way of getting my mother's attention. Nor am I trying to destroy Barbara's reputation as a mother because I have a 'thing' against mothers in general, due to the fact that my mother deserted me when I was a child."

Susan looked genuinely startled by Vicki's unexpected outburst. "I didn't say that. I didn't even think it."

Vicki jumped to her feet, feeling a dangerous quiver in the muscles of her thighs. She grabbed the back of her chair for support. "You think you're so goddamn smart. You think you know everything. Did you know that Barbara used to make anonymous calls to Ron's house at all hours of the night?" Vicki asked, abruptly shifting gears, trying to regain control of the conversation.

"What? What are you talking about?"

"So, it appears there are some things about our friend you didn't know after all."

It was Susan's turn to look distinctly uncomfortable. She fidgeted in her chair. "All right, so, big deal. Even assuming Barbara made some ill-advised phone calls, which I don't necessarily believe . . ."

"Of course not."

"That's still a very long way from molesting your child."

"Why would Tracey lie?"

"Gee, I don't know. You think getting out of jail might have something to do with it?"

"You think she's making the whole story up?"

"I *know* she's making the whole story up."

"How do you know? You spent less than two days with her. How can you claim to know her so well?"

"I don't know her at all! But I knew Barbara. And so did you, dammit."

Vicki walked to the window, stared down at the street. Wait for me, she called silently after the pedestrians hurrying about below. "Okay, so what have we got here?" She turned back to Susan, noticed the tears in her eyes, pretended she didn't. "We've got a sixteen-year-old girl who's admitted to killing her mother."

"After lying repeatedly to the police. To me. To you."

"Yes, she lied."

"So what makes you think she isn't lying now? Do you have even one shred of evidence to support her allegations?"

Vicki bent her head back over the top of her shoulders and rubbed the muscles at the base of her neck. Susan was right. She had no evidence, nothing to back up Tracey's stunning accusations. A jury would need more than a few crocodile tears to return with a verdict of not guilty.

"You don't have any evidence, do you?" Susan demanded.

"There has to be a reason Tracey did what she did."

"Says who?"

"Girls don't just murder their mothers on a whim."

"Maybe Tracey didn't like not being the center of her mother's universe anymore. Maybe she didn't like that her mother was building a life of her own. Maybe she didn't like what Barbara served for dinner that night."

"Or maybe her mother was molesting her," Vicki stated flatly. "Tell me, Susan. Would you be so quick to discredit Tracey if she'd made these charges against her father? You can't dismiss Tracey's allegations just because Barbara was a woman."

"I don't dismiss them because she was a woman. I dismiss them because she was my friend."

"And if I were to call you as a witness . . ."

"I wouldn't do that if I were you."

Vicki shrugged. "You're not me."

Susan walked to the door, flung it open, stepped into the hall. "And I thank God for that every day." Then she slammed the door behind her.

* * *

"Goddamnit! Shit!" Vicki scooped a Mont Blanc pen from the top of her desk and hurled it at the door just as her secretary peeked through it. It missed the young woman's head by only a fraction of an inch. "Goddamnit, don't you ever knock?"

"I heard you yell," the secretary began, then burst into tears. "I'm sorry." She made a hasty retreat, closed the door after her.

"Goddamnit." Now she'd have to send the homely young woman flowers, Vicki thought. Worse than that, she'd have to apologize. Maybe she could just give her a raise. Goddamnit, why did everyone have to be so damn sensitive these days? Chris had been so distraught over Tracey's allegations, she'd refused to return Vicki's phone calls; Susan, suffering from no such timidity, had stormed into her office and openly challenged her motives and integrity. Those ridiculous inferences about her mother, for God's sake. Even Jeremy had questioned the wisdom of what she was doing.

"Maybe you should let someone else handle this case, darlin'," he'd advised.

"Maybe you should mind your own business," she'd snapped.

Why couldn't she listen to them? Was defending Tracey really worth the loss of her husband's respect? Was it worth losing her best friends? Did she really believe Tracey was anything other than a cold, calculating little psychopath not above using today's popular psychology to escape the consequences of her actions?

"I don't know," Vicki cried in frustration. What she did know, what she knew deep down in her bones, despite what Susan and

Chris and Jeremy thought, was that she was doing what Barbara would have wanted, that above all else, *irrespective* of everything else, Barbara would have wanted her daughter protected. If Tracey had killed her mother for no other reason than she damn well felt like it, Barbara would still have wanted Vicki to defend her, to do everything in her power to keep her daughter out of jail.

She was doing the right thing, Vicki told herself.

Even suspecting that Tracey was dangerously unbalanced and possibly a threat to others? a little voice whispered. Even at the expense of everything she held dear?

"This isn't about me," Vicki repeated. The offers from New York, the queries from Hollywood, the attention of the media, none of that mattered. What mattered was honoring her friend's memory the best way she knew how.

"What a crock," she heard Susan hoot derisively.

"A nice bit of sophistry," Jeremy concurred.

Chris turned away, refusing to speak.

"Great," Vicki said, turning her back on their judgmental images, as they had turned their backs on her.

On one point, however, they were all in agreement: she had no evidence. She could theorize all she wanted. In the end, she had nothing but Tracey's word.

"You know, I'm really looking forward to beating your ass," Michael Rose had said, his image winking at her from across the room.

"No way I'm going to let that happen," Vicki said out loud. She grabbed her purse and headed for the door. "Take the rest of the day off," she told her startled secretary before hurrying down the hall.

* * *

I don't understand," Tracey was saying. "What are you doing here?"

"I need more," Vicki repeated, amazed as she always was by the color in Tracey's cheeks, the way she seemed to be blossoming behind bars.

"I've told you everything."

"It's not enough."

"It's the truth."

Since when had the truth ever been enough? Vicki wondered, the harsh overhead fluorescent lighting hurting her eyes. "I need more," she said again.

"There isn't any more."

"Think hard, Tracey. Were there ever any witnesses?"

"Witnesses?"

"Someone who might have seen your mother touch you in an inappropriate way."

Tracey shook her head. "I don't think so. She only did it when we were alone."

"Did she ever make a suggestive comment in anyone's presence?"

"Suggestive, how?"

Vicki tried a different tack. "Is there anyone I can call to the stand to corroborate your story?"

Tracey shrugged, looked away.

"Tracey, is there anyone I can call?"

"No."

Vicki began circling the rectangular table. *Fuck. Fuck the fuckers. Fuck the lawyers,* she read, thinking this was already true. She was fucked all right. “I need something, Tracey. I can’t walk into court with nothing but your word for what happened that night.”

“You don’t think the jury will believe me?”

“Give them a reason to believe you, Tracey. Give *me* a reason.”

Tracey hunkered down in her chair, her long legs stretched out in front of her. She rubbed her palms on the pale blue cotton of her prison pants. “There’s something I could tell you.”

Vicki stopped circling, stood absolutely still, waited for Tracey to continue.

“Something that would convince you I’m telling the truth. Something that would convince a jury.”

“What is it?”

“Something about my mother. Something you don’t know. Something I’ve never told anyone.”

“You can tell me.”

Tracey pushed herself back up, so that she was sitting ramrod straight. She motioned with her chin to the chair across the table. “Maybe you better sit down.”

Thirty-Two

Opening arguments began on Thursday, January 14, 1993.

Vicki watched Michael Rose rise from his seat behind the prosecution's table and stride purposefully toward the jury. It had taken three days to select the panel, which consisted of seven women and five men. Eight members of the jury were white, two were black, and two were of Asian descent. Nine were married, two divorced, one single. They had a total of thirty-two children and grandchildren amongst them, of which twenty were girls. All swore they'd neither been influenced by the lurid pretrial publicity nor formed any preconceived opinions. Half looked nervous, their eyes shiny with anticipation as they leaned forward in their seats; the others looked bored, their eyes already half-closed as they leaned back, trying to get comfortable. The judge had already warned them that the trial could last anywhere from three weeks to three months.

"Ladies and gentlemen of the jury," Michael began, "good morning."

And let me thank you in advance, the familiar recitation echoed in Vicki's head.

"And let me thank you in advance," Michael continued, fastening the bottom button of his dark gray suit jacket, the one he always wore on the first day of an important trial. Kind of a good-luck talisman, he'd once explained to Vicki. Gray suit, yellow tie for opening arguments, blue suit, red tie for closing.

A man with a plan, Vicki thought as she covered her mouth with her hand and mouthed the words along with him. "The job ahead of you will not be an easy one."

"Did you say something?" Tracey whispered beside her.

Vicki took her hand away from her mouth, used it to reach beside her and pat Tracey's hand, knowing the movement would catch the eye of at least one of the jurors. Tracey's hands were nice and warm, Vicki noted, unlike her own, which felt as if they'd been locked in a meat freezer overnight.

"But I'm going to try and make it as easy for you as possible," Michael continued. Same damn speech every time, Vicki thought, glancing at Judge Fitzhenry, a deceptively kind-faced man of sixty-four. Judge Fitzhenry might look like everybody's favorite uncle, with his round face and wisps of white hair, but the friendly smile hid a tart tongue, and the forgiving blue of his eyes concealed a jaundiced soul.

"The facts of this case are really pretty simple," Michael continued. "Sometime between the hours of three and five o'clock on the morning of August eighteenth, 1992, a forty-six-year-old woman named Barbara Azinger was brutally beaten to death."

Vicki watched Tracey's face as Michael began his dramatic recital of the grisly facts. Tracey looked calm, even serene, in her pale pink sweater and pleated navy skirt, very much the well-behaved schoolgirl she was. Dark curls angelically circled a cherubic face devoid of makeup, save for the tiny kiss of mascara Tracey had insisted on applying seconds before the jury was led in. Her mother's daughter all right, Vicki thought, watching tears form in the corner of Tracey's eyes as Michael Rose detailed the nature and severity of Barbara's injuries. "Don't be afraid to cry," Vicki had instructed earlier. "Let the jury see how much you loved your mother."

Were the tears real or was Tracey simply following the advice of counsel?

None of my business, Vicki reminded herself, eyes restlessly scanning the high ceiling and dark wood of the comfortable old courtroom. I'm only the lawyer. Not the judge and jury. It is not my job to determine guilt or innocence, only to provide my client with the best possible defense.

How many times would she have to remind herself of that before she'd stop feeling so damn guilty? She had a job to do, and she was going to do it. That neither Susan nor Chris had spoken to her in months, that both had volunteered to be witnesses for the prosecution, only heightened her resolve, made her job that much easier.

"My esteemed colleague will try to convince you that Tracey Azinger killed her mother in self-defense," Michael continued, his voice an interesting combination of revulsion and disbelief. Now that he'd finished describing the prosecution's case, he was seeking to discredit the defense in advance, to blunt the effect of the arguments Vicki might put forward. "They will try to blur the simple, straight lines of this case by appealing to your need to believe that children don't just up and murder their parents for no good reason. And in order for them to do that, they will resort to that obscene old chestnut of blaming the victim."

Obscene old chestnut, Vicki repeated, picturing a gnarled brown chestnut rolling across the worn beige carpet of the courtroom. Vicki stopped the risible metaphor with the pointed toe of her black shoe and ground it into invisible dust with her heel. She shook her head in mock dismay for the jury's benefit, glanced at her watch. Michael had been speaking now for almost forty minutes.

"They will tell you that there was a side to the doting mother that no one but her daughter knew anything about, something she successfully hid from those closest to her for more than a decade. They will try to convince you that Barbara Azinger was a monster who regularly and repeatedly molested her daughter."

But what evidence do they have for these baseless accusations? Vicki heard Michael ask seconds before he actually spoke the words.

"None," Michael said, answering his own question. "They have absolutely no evidence whatsoever. Nothing but the word of the girl who killed her."

"Don't let them get away with this, ladies and gentlemen of the jury," Vicki whispered along with him, flicking a tiny piece of white fluff from her green straight skirt.

"The facts of this case are indisputable," Michael reminded the jurors, all of whom were listening intently. "Don't be swayed by the theatrics and verbal calisthenics of the defense counsel."

Verbal calisthenics, Vicki repeated silently. That was a new one.

"Don't let this girl"—Michael pointed at Tracey, who took a deep breath and looked him right in the eye—"who has already confessed to the killing, murder her mother all over again."

Vicki was on her feet and in front of the jury before Michael Rose was in his seat. "The prosecutor is right when he tells you the facts of this case are not in dispute, that in the early-morning hours of August eighteenth, 1992, Tracey Azinger took a five iron from her downstairs closet and bludgeoned her mother to death. He's right when he tells you she later lied about it to the police, that she made up a story about a masked intruder, that she even identified the intruder," Vicki said, eyes sweeping the spectator gallery, locating Tony Malarek, who acknowledged her with a knowing smirk. "He says she only changed her story when confronted with the mountain of evidence against her. This is true." Vicki paused long enough to let what she was saying sink in. "And it's not true." Her eyes moved steadily from one juror to the next, eventually making contact with each of them. "Yes, Tracey Azinger lied." Now Vicki turned abruptly to Tracey, confident all the jurors' eyes would follow. Tracey stared back through a heavy curtain of tears. "But she lied not to protect herself"—another pause, longer than the first—"but to protect her mother."

Vicki stood still, careful to keep the focus on her client. "She lied because she didn't want anyone to know the terrible, unnatural things her mother had been doing to her for years. If I may borrow the prosecutor's elegant phrase, she didn't want to 'murder her mother all over again.' But ultimately she had no choice. Just as she had no choice but to kill the mother she adored in order to protect herself from her mother's escalating abuse."

Out of the corner of her eye, Vicki saw Michael Rose shaking his head, as she had done earlier. "The assistant district attorney says we have no evidence to support our allegations. He's wrong. He says all you have is Tracey's word. He's wrong again. He's also wrong when he asks you to ignore that little voice in your head that keeps asking, 'Why? Why would a loving and much loved sixteen-year-old girl do such a terrible thing?' I'm asking you to listen to that voice. It's the voice of reason. It's the voice of reasonable doubt."

Vicki smiled sadly at the jury, then walked briskly past the prosecutor's table and resumed her seat.

The prosecution first called Lieutenants Jacobek and Gill to the stand. They gave similar accounts of the murder scene, Tracey's demeanor, her changing stories, her outright lies. Another officer reported having found the murder weapon stuffed into the back of Tracey's closet, and his subsequent discovery of Barbara's engagement ring, tiny flecks of bloody flesh still clinging to its thin platinum band, inside Tracey's jewelry box. Several forensic experts described in excruciating detail the number of savage blows Tracey had struck, the exact location of the injuries, the damage to the body, the deliberate obliteration of Barbara's face.

Vicki kept her questions short and direct. There was no point in trying to discredit the physical evidence. Prolonged questioning would only seal the horrific images in the jury's collective consciousness.

"How would you describe Tracey's behavior when you got to the house that morning?" Vicki asked each of the officers.

"She was very upset," Lieutenant Jacobek conceded.

"She was hysterical," Lieutenant Gill agreed.

"She seemed traumatized," the third officer read from his notes.

"No further questions," Vicki said.

On the fifth day of testimony, Michael Rose called Susan Norman to the stand.

"Raise your right hand," the county clerk instructed as Susan was sworn in. "Please state your name and spell it for this court."

Susan gave her name, spelled it slowly and carefully, then took her seat, refusing to acknowledge Vicki's smile.

Suit yourself, Vicki thought, noting that Susan's red turtleneck sweater brought out the natural blush in her cheeks.

"What is your connection to Barbara Azinger?" Michael Rose asked. He was wearing a brown, pin-striped suit whose double-breasted jacket was remarkably similar to the one Vicki had on. Vicki had frowned when she'd first noticed, wondered only half-facetiously if she should call him later to ask what color he'd be wearing the next day.

"Barbara was one of my closest friends."

"How long had you been friends?"

"For fourteen years."

"Can you tell this court what happened the morning Barbara was murdered?"

Susan took a deep breath, cleared her throat, looked

toward the jury, and slowly, carefully, described the details of that August early morning, hesitating only when her memory reached the door to Barbara's bedroom.

"What did you see in that room, Mrs. Norman?" Michael Rose asked.

"I saw Barbara." A violent tremble shook Susan's normally strong voice. "She was on the floor, covered in blood. She had no face."

"And where was Tracey?"

"She was on the floor beside Barbara, holding her hand."

"Did she say anything?"

"She said Tony Malarek had killed her mother."

"And then what happened?"

"The police arrived. And then the Latimers."

Michael Rose glanced accusingly at Vicki. "You mean the defense counsel?"

Susan nodded. "Yes. I called her. She and her husband were also Barbara's friends."

The rest of Susan's testimony concerned Tracey's odd behavior during her brief stay with the Normans, her changing stories.

"You were growing suspicious?"

"Yes. Tracey seemed almost indifferent to her mother's death. It was like she had to be reminded to grieve."

"Objection, Your Honor," Vicki said.

"Sustained."

"How would you describe Barbara's relationship with her daughter?"

"Barbara was a wonderful mother. She adored Tracey. She would have done anything for her."

"In all the years you knew Barbara, did you ever see her abuse her daughter in any way?"

"No. That's ridiculous. Barbara would never have done anything to hurt Tracey."

"No further questions," Michael Rose concluded.

Vicki pushed herself to her feet. "Mrs. Norman, you stated that when Tracey phoned you that morning, she was crying so hard you couldn't make out what she was saying."

Susan pulled her shoulders back, glared at Vicki with undisguised contempt. "That's right."

"So she was hysterical?"

"She gave the impression of being hysterical."

"Did she or did she not sound hysterical?"

"Yes."

"She was so hysterical that you rushed right over. So hysterical you called the police. Isn't that right?"

"Yes."

"And when you found Tracey, she was on the floor beside her mother's body, is that also correct?"

"Yes."

"Holding her mother's hand, I believe you testified."

"Yes."

"Odd behavior for a cold-blooded murderer, wouldn't you say?"

"Objection." Michael Rose made a halfhearted attempt at rising to his feet.

"Sustained."

"What did you do when you saw Tracey sitting in her mother's blood, holding her hand?"

Susan gave the question a moment's thought. "I think I put

my arm around her, helped her to her feet, took her out of the room."

"So you were concerned about her well-being?"

"Yes."

"And was there any doubt in your mind that Tracey was genuinely upset?"

"Not then."

"Not then," Vicki repeated. "And after the police questioned her, you took Tracey back to your house. Is that correct?"

"Yes."

"Why was that?"

"Her father was out of town. I couldn't very well leave her alone."

"Because she was so upset?"

"Because her mother was dead."

"And you had no reason to suspect Tracey of any wrongdoing," Vicki stated rather than asked.

"Not then, no."

"But then you started having suspicions."

"Yes."

"And what did you do?"

"I'm not sure I understand the question."

"Did you call the police?"

"I called you. I asked you to come over."

Vicki nodded toward the jury. "And when I got there, what did you tell me?"

"I don't remember exactly."

"To the best of your recollection."

"I believe I expressed concern over Tracey's behavior, that

she seemed to be having a hard time keeping her story straight."

"Do you remember my response?"

For the first time since she'd taken the witness stand, Susan smiled. "You said that people don't have a hard time keeping their stories straight if they're telling the truth."

Vicki also smiled. It was exactly the response she'd been hoping for. "So I was the first one to suggest that Tracey might be lying."

"Yes."

"And you argued with me, didn't you?"

The smile disappeared abruptly from Susan's lips. "Yes."

"Didn't you ask me what possible reason Tracey would have for killing her mother?"

Susan squirmed in her seat. "I might have."

"So it seemed inconceivable to you that Tracey could have done such a thing?"

"At first, yes."

"And now? Don't you still ask yourself why?"

"Objection, Your Honor."

"I'll rephrase the question," Vicki said quickly. "The prosecution has suggested that Tracey killed her mother because she was jealous of her mother's new relationship with Howard Kerble. Had Tracey ever said or done anything to give you that impression?"

"Objection, Your Honor," Michael Rose said again. "The witness isn't a psychiatrist."

"Overruled," the judge said. "The witness is perfectly qualified to answer the question."

"No," Susan admitted.

"Had Tracey ever said anything that made you think she was unhappy with her mother's engagement?"

"No."

"In fact, she seemed happy for her mother, did she not?"

"She *seemed* happy."

"Wasn't she excited about being the maid of honor at her mother's wedding?"

"I guess."

"You had no reason to suspect otherwise, did you?"

"No."

"Had Barbara ever expressed any concern that Tracey might be jealous or unhappy?"

"No."

Vicki turned a puzzled face toward the jury. "You testified that you'd known Barbara Azinger for fourteen years. How often did the two of you get together?"

"It varied."

"Were you together twenty-four hours a day?"

"Of course not."

"What then? A few hours every day?"

"We tried to get together at least once a week."

"I see. A few hours once a week. And yet you're able to swear with absolute certainty that Barbara never molested her daughter."

"Yes," Susan said stubbornly.

"Did Barbara ever discuss her sex life with you?"

Susan glanced at the assistant state's attorney as if appealing for help. He dutifully rose to his feet, made his objection.

"I'll allow it," the judge said.

"Occasionally."

"Had she ever told you she found her sex life with her former husband unsatisfactory?"

"Yes."

"And that during her marriage, she regularly faked her orgasms?"

"Yes, but so what? Millions of women fake orgasms. It doesn't make them child molesters. Barbara was a normal woman. She liked normal sex."

"Barbara liked sex with men; therefore she had no reason to molest her daughter. Is that what you're saying?"

"Yes," Susan said warily, her voice wobbling, her eyes flitting skittishly from side to side, as if she might have stepped into a trap.

"Thank you, Mrs. Norman," Vicki said with a smile. "I have no further questions."

Thirty-Three

The following Monday, the prosecutor called Ron Azinger to the stand.

Ron, who'd grown less dashing and more beefy-looking in the last several years, testified that, despite their divorce, Barbara had always been an exemplary mother, that she and Tracey were exceptionally close, and that Tracey had never said anything to him about her mother abusing her in any way.

"She never complained about her mother?" Vicki asked on cross-examination.

"No, never."

"A teenage girl who doesn't complain about her mother? Didn't that strike you as odd?"

The jury laughed. The prosecutor objected to the question.

"Get to the point, Counselor," Judge Fitzhenry instructed.

"Mr. Azinger, how often did you see Tracey after the divorce?"

"Every Wednesday evening and every other weekend."

"What sort of things did you talk about when you were together?"

Ron cleared his throat, crossed one arm over the other, lifted one palm into the air. "I'm not sure. The usual, I guess."

"Did Tracey talk about school?"

"Yes," Ron said, though he looked far from certain.

"Her friends?"

"I guess."

"Does Tracey have a lot of friends, Mr. Azinger?"

"I'm sure she does."

"Name three."

"What?"

"Can you name three of your daughter's friends?"

"Well . . ."

"How about *one?* Can you tell me the name of one of your daughter's friends?"

Ron looked to the ceiling. "I think there's a Lisa."

"Ah, yes," Vicki said with a smile. "There's always a Lisa."

Laughter broke out among the spectators, as well as in the jury box.

"The truth is that your daughter doesn't have many friends, isn't that right?"

"Tracey never seemed to need a lot of people around her."

"Because she had her mother?"

Vicki saw Michael Rose hesitate in his chair, not sure whether to object. Such questions might actually help his case, Vicki could hear him thinking.

"Isn't it true, Mr. Azinger, that you used to complain that Barbara was too wrapped up in her daughter's life? That during your marriage you often felt excluded and shut out?"

"Tracey and her mother were very close."

"Unnaturally close?"

"Objection."

"Sustained."

"Didn't you urge your former wife to see a psychiatrist?" Vicki asked.

"I may have."

"Specifically, didn't you once tell her she was a sick woman who needed her head examined?"

How did you know that? Ron's eyes questioned.

Have you forgotten she was my friend? Vicki's eyes asked in return.

Have *you?* the ensuing silence demanded.

"I was very angry when I said that," Ron said.

"Did you or did you not tell your wife she was a sick woman who should have her head examined?"

"Yes."

Vicki swallowed, took a deep breath, debated whether to do the unthinkable, to ask a question to which she wasn't 100 percent certain of the answer. She looked at Ron looking at his daughter, knew he'd rather be anywhere but where he was. He loved his daughter. He had no loyalty to his ex-wife. He was a sociology professor, for God's sake, she could almost hear him thinking. A proud, upstanding member of his community. No way could he have produced a cold-blooded sociopath.

Vicki felt a smile tugging at the corners of her lips. Who said she didn't know the answer? "Mr. Azinger," she said with confidence, "do you think it's possible Tracey was being molested by her mother?"

There was a long pause. "It's possible," Ron said.

* * *

Howard Kerble made a much better witness for the prosecution. A less imposing figure than Barbara's former husband, he nonetheless radiated quiet authority. He spoke movingly of meeting Barbara, of falling in love, of their plans for a future together. Their sex life was wonderful, he said when asked. Barbara was a normal woman with normal sexual desires. She wasn't into anything remotely kinky. The assertion that Barbara had molested her daughter was beneath contempt. Barbara was a devoted mother. Tracey always came first.

"So Tracey had no reason to be jealous of your relationship with her mother," Vicki stated when her turn came to cross-examine the witness.

"You'd have to ask Tracey."

"I intend to," Vicki said, allowing the witness to step down.

The state calls Christine Malarek."

It was the beginning of the third week of the trial when the rear doors of the large courtroom opened and Chris walked briskly up the center aisle, looking neither to her left nor right. She was wearing a mauve sweater and gray slacks, and her blond hair fell to her shoulders in soft layers.

She looks more beautiful than ever, Vicki thought, catching sight of Tony in the same seat he'd been occupying every day since the trial began, directly behind the two rows of seats reserved for the press. Would he make a scene? Vicki wondered. Would he whip out a gun and start spraying the courtroom with bullets? Thank God for metal detectors, she thought, noticing Susan in the back row as Chris was sworn in. Michael Rose asked Chris some perfunctory questions regarding her age and occupation before getting to the heart of the matter.

"Could you describe your relationship with Barbara Azinger?" he asked.

"We were friends for fourteen years. Best friends," Chris clarified.

"And are you also acquainted with her daughter, Tracey?"

"I've known Tracey since she was two years old." Chris looked toward Tracey, her eyes connecting briefly with Vicki's before turning away.

"Would you describe Barbara Azinger as a good mother?"

"She was a wonderful mother."

"Did you ever see her strike her daughter?"

"Barbara didn't believe in corporal punishment."

"She never lashed out in anger?"

"Never. Barbara was a very loving mother. She adored Tracey."

"Did you ever, in all the years you were friends, see Barbara touch her daughter in an inappropriate manner?"

"Of course not."

"Did she ever confide in you an unnatural interest in her daughter?"

"No. That's absurd."

"Thank you," Michael Rose concluded, nodding in Vicki's direction. "Your witness."

My witness indeed, Vicki thought, rising slowly to her feet. Could she really do this? she wondered, tossing such concerns aside with a shake of her head. Did she have a choice?

"In what way was she loving?" Vicki asked.

Chris hesitated. "I'm not sure I understand."

"Did you ever see her stroke her daughter's hair?"

"Yes."

"Did you ever see her kiss her daughter?"

"Of course."

"Hug her?"

"Yes."

"And how did Tracey respond to her mother's caresses?"

Chris tried to remember the many times she'd seen Barbara and Tracey together. "There was never any problem, if that's what you're getting at."

"You never heard Tracey object?"

"No."

"Were you shocked when you heard that Tracey had been arrested for her mother's murder?" Vicki waited for Michael Rose to object, almost smiled when he didn't.

"I thought there must be some mistake."

"Were you shocked to learn that Tracey had confessed?"

"Yes."

"Why?"

"Why?" Chris repeated.

"Why were you shocked?"

"I'm not sure how to answer that."

"Were you shocked because you couldn't imagine Tracey doing such a horrible thing?" Surely the prosecutor would object to that one, Vicki thought, waiting.

"Objection," Michael Rose dutifully called from his seat. "The witness's opinions in this matter are irrelevant."

"Sustained."

"Had Tracey ever said or done anything to indicate she was unhappy with her mother or her mother's recent engagement?"

"No."

"So, as far as you knew, everything between Barbara and her daughter was fine."

"Yes."

"And yet Tracey killed her mother. How can that be?"

"Objection."

"Sustained."

"Wouldn't you agree there has to be a damn good reason for a daughter to kill her mother?"

"Objection."

"Sustained. And watch your language, Counselor."

"Did Tracey have a bad temper, Mrs. Malarek?" Vicki asked, ignoring both the prosecutor's objection and the judge's warning.

"Not to my knowledge."

"And to your knowledge, had she ever struck her mother before that fatal night?"

"Not to my knowledge, no."

"And yet, this young girl who was, by all accounts, a model daughter suddenly rose up in the middle of the night and killed her mother. Does that make sense to you?"

"No," Chris admitted before the prosecutor had a chance to object. "Nothing about what happened that night makes any sense."

Vicki took a long, deep breath. It's now or never, she thought. She took another breath, then pushed the next question from her mouth. "Were you and Barbara Azinger ever lovers?" she asked, listening as a series of hushed whispers somersaulted across the courtroom floor.

"What!" Chris's face had turned a ghostly white.

Michael Rose was on his feet, storming toward the judge's bench. "Objection, Your Honor!"

"Your Honor," Vicki countered, already at Michael's side, "we've heard testimony that the victim was a normal woman with normal sexual appetites. The district attorney didn't object then. I think I should be allowed to show proof that Barbara Azinger was not always what she led others to believe, and that included the range of her sexual proclivities."

"She's right, Counselor," the judge told a dejected Michael Rose. "I'm going to allow the question."

"Were you and Barbara Azinger ever lovers?" Vicki repeated immediately.

"No!" Chris said.

"I remind you, Mrs. Malarek, that you're under oath."

"I don't need to be reminded."

"Objection, Your Honor. The witness has answered the question."

"Sustained."

"Are you married, Mrs. Malarek?" Vicki asked, quickly shifting gears.

Chris looked as if she were about to tumble from the witness stand, her eyes darting around the courtroom, stopping on her ex-husband. "Divorced," she whispered as Tony smiled, leaned forward in his seat.

"Sorry," Vicki said. "I didn't hear you."

"I'm divorced."

"You left your husband when exactly?"

"A little over two years ago."

"Could you describe for this court what happened the night you left your husband?"

"Objection, Your Honor," Michael Rose sneered. "Relevance?"

"I believe I can show relevance in due course," Vicki stated.

"Hurry up," the judge instructed.

"On the night you left your husband, you went to Barbara Azinger's house, is that correct?"

"Yes."

"In fact, you showed up in your underwear, isn't that right?"

"Yes, but that was because Tony had locked me out of the house."

"So you went back to Grand Avenue, to see Barbara Azinger."

"I didn't know where else to go."

"What time was this? Nine o'clock? Ten?"

"It was around midnight."

"So you showed up at Barbara's house around midnight in your underwear," Vicki recited. "What happened then?"

Chris shook her head, as if reluctant to recall the details of that night. "I don't remember exactly."

"You don't remember?" Vicki asked incredulously.

"I think Tracey made me some tea."

"And Barbara poured you a bath?"

"I was freezing cold. She was trying to make me warm."

"Is that why she invited you into her bed? To make you warm?"

"Objection!"

"Where did you sleep that night?" Vicki asked instead.

"In Barbara's bed."

"Alone?"

"No."

"Barbara slept there too?"

"Yes. But nothing happened."

"You didn't kiss?"

"What?"

"Did you and Mrs. Azinger share a kiss?"

Chris looked helplessly around the room, as if she couldn't believe the words coming out of her friend's mouth. "Why are you doing this?"

"Could Your Honor direct the witness to answer the question?" Vicki turned away from her friend. She already knew the answer. Tracey had seen the two women together, then run back to her bed and pretended to be asleep when her mother had come to check on her moments later. What would she do if Chris denied it?

"We kissed, but . . ."

"On the lips?"

"Yes."

"Was it the kind of kiss you normally exchange with a friend?"

Chris said nothing. Tears filled her eyes, ran down her cheeks.

"Mrs. Malarek, was it the kind of kiss one normally exchanges with a friend?"

"No."

"What kind of kiss was it?"

"I don't know."

"A lover's kiss?"

"Yes," Chris said softly, as Michael Rose buried his head in his hands. "But nothing happened. We kissed. That was all."

"Are you gay, Mrs. Malarek?"

"Objection, Your Honor. What possible relevance could this have? The witness is not on trial."

"Your Honor, it is our assertion that Barbara Azinger and Chris Malarek were engaged in a lesbian affair," Vicki countered, "which would prove that Tracey's mother was not averse to having sex with a woman. The witness's sexuality is very much an issue."

"I'll allow it," the judge ruled after obvious thought.

"I have three children," Chris whispered.

"Are you gay?" Vicki repeated, hating the sound of her own voice.

"Please don't do this."

"A young woman's life is on the line."

"So is mine," Chris said softly.

Judge Fitzhenry leaned forward, directed the witness to answer the question.

Chris closed her eyes, released a delicate trickle of air from her lungs. She sat this way for several long seconds as Vicki wondered again what she would do should Chris deny the allegation. Could she actually confront her with the findings of the private detective she'd had shadowing Chris for weeks, the photographic proof of her ongoing affair with a woman in her office? Please don't make me do that to you, Vicki urged silently, feeling Susan's fiery contempt burning a hole into the back of her dark blue cashmere jacket, hearing Tony's malignant chuckle metastasizing its way through the courtroom.

"Are you gay, Mrs. Malarek? Yes or no?"

Chris opened her eyes, a look of calm settling across her heart-shaped face, as if she'd finally made peace with who she was, as if she were through running scared. "Yes," she admitted, her voice steady and strong. "Yes, I am."

Thirty-Four

"Vicki," her secretary informed her over the intercom. "That was the courthouse. The jury's back."

"What? That's impossible." Vicki checked her watch. "It's been less than three hours!"

It was too soon. It was *way* too soon, Vicki thought, grabbing her coat and rushing for the parking lot. After a trial lasting the better part of five weeks, it was inconceivable the jury could have reached a verdict in less than three hours. What did it mean?

"Is it good they're back this fast?" Tracey asked as they resumed their seats in the courtroom.

Vicki lifted her hands into the air. Your guess is as good as mine, the gesture said. Jury trials were always a crapshoot. You could never predict what a jury was going to do, no matter how many experts you hired, no matter how carefully you researched the jury pool. Juries created their own dynamic, their own logic, their own rules. It was impossible to second-guess them. It was useless to try.

Just as it was useless trying to predict a verdict by the length of time the jury took to reach it. Some juries were slow and methodical, reviewing each piece of evidence before casting their votes; others were quick and decisive. Some were so impatient, they voted as soon as they reached the jury room. Why waste time reviewing the evidence when everyone was already in agreement? Five weeks was long enough. Let's get this show on the road and get the hell out of here.

"Ladies and gentlemen of the jury, have you reached your verdict?" Judge Fitzhenry inquired, sounding surprised by the question, as if he too hadn't expected to be back in court so soon after his final instructions.

"We have, Your Honor," the middle-aged man who was the jury foreman answered.

Vicki held her breath as she and Tracey rose to face the jury. This was it. Another few seconds and it would all be over. Ditto her friendship with the two women whose love and support had sustained her for fourteen years.

Perhaps in time Susan and Chris might have forgiven her for defending Tracey. They might have come to understand that she'd done it as much for Barbara as for herself. But her cross-examination of Chris had gone too far. She'd stepped over the line, used the shared intimacies of their friendship as a weapon, inflicted more damage in an hour than Tony had managed in a decade. Hell, Tony was an amateur compared to her.

No, Susan and Chris would never forgive her. Whether

she'd ever forgive herself would depend largely on the verdict.

The jury foreman looked directly at the judge. "We find the defendant . . ."

He looks so serious, Vicki thought. And he's not looking at Tracey. None of the jurors were looking at Tracey, which wasn't a good sign. I'm sorry, Tracey, she apologized silently. I'm sorry, Barbara. Please forgive me.

" . . . not guilty."

"Oh, my God," whispered Vicki, her knees buckling.

"Oh, my God," Tracey squealed as the courtroom erupted. "Oh, my God. Oh, my God." She threw herself into Vicki's disbelieving arms. "Thank you. Thank you so much."

And suddenly lights were exploding in Vicki's eyes as cameras clicked and reporters thrust microphones at her mouth, waved notepads and pencils in her face. Spectators were shouting their congratulations at her from all directions as Michael Rose pushed angrily past her into the corridor, the word *bitch* dropping from his tongue like acid, searing her soul. *Sore loser,* Vicki almost shouted after him, but laughed instead, knowing the sound of her laughter would be far more corrosive. She watched Ron approach his daughter, carefully wrap Tracey in his arms, although his young wife hung back, a look of discomfort haunting her unlined face. Tracey thanked each member of the jury. "Good luck to you, dear," Vicki heard several of the jurors murmur.

"Thank you," Tracey repeated again and again, as convincing in victory as she'd been on the witness stand. "Thank you so much."

It took over an hour for Vicki to pull herself away from the assorted members of the media and get back to her office, where she received an impromptu round of applause from her partners and colleagues.

"Bravo!" her secretary chirped, leaving her desk to offer a congratulatory hug.

Vicki found the display unsettling. Maybe she was just tired. Definitely grumpy. Which was strange because she normally felt so elated after a victory. Especially a victory of this magnitude, unquestionably the biggest of her career. A muted "Thanks" was all she was able to muster for the excited throng gathered outside her office door.

"Your husband called to congratulate you," her secretary said after everyone had left. "He said to tell you he's tied up in a meeting, but he'll see you later."

Vicki nodded, pretending to brush some hairs away from her forehead in an effort to mask the disappointment she felt creeping into her eyes. Surely she wasn't about to cry! Good God, she *must* be tired! Still, it would have been nice to share her triumph with somebody other than the hired help. If not Jeremy, then with Susan or Chris. Or Barbara, Vicki thought, entering her office and collapsing into the massive chair behind her desk, for the first time in months fleshing out the person behind the name, allowing thoughts of her murdered friend to fill her mind. Images of Barbara marched before her eyes. Still wearing those damn three-inch heels, Vicki thought with a smile. "I know you understand," she whispered into her hands as tears rolled down her cheeks and into the corners of her mouth. And then, suddenly, all the phones were ringing at once.

"Are you here?" her secretary called out.

"No," Vicki called back, impatiently wiping the tears from her cheeks. "Take messages."

"What's the matter?" a voice asked from the doorway. "Not in the mood to celebrate?"

Vicki didn't have to look up to know whose voice it was. "Susan," she acknowledged, her voice as flat as a deflated tire. "To what do I owe the pleasure?"

"I heard the news on the radio. Thought I'd take a chance you'd be here."

"I take it you didn't come to congratulate me."

"On the contrary. You were brilliant, as usual. It's not everyone who can pander to a jury's basest prejudices and make it sound so noble."

"You think that's what I was doing?"

"What would you call it?"

"The truth," Vicki said simply.

"The truth?" Susan shook her head in wonderment. "The truth is that nothing happened that night between Chris and Barbara and you know it. The truth is that even if something *did* happen, it was completely irrelevant. The truth is that being gay doesn't make you a child molester. In fact, most adults who molest children are straight. Twisted as hell," she continued, her voice lowering, as it always did when she was very upset, "but straight." Susan walked to the window, her eyes focused on the light snow falling to the street below.

"I know you don't understand."

"What is it I don't understand, Vicki? The jury's decision? You're wrong. I understand that jurors are human. I understand that no one wants to believe a nice, middle-class teenager would up and murder her mother for no good reason. It's much easier, much more comforting, to demonize the mother. And why not? We hate mothers in this country almost as much as we hate homosexuals." Susan stepped back from the window, focused her strong gaze on Vicki. "I think I even understand why you took this case."

"And why is that?" Vicki braced herself for the accusations she was sure would follow.

"Believe it or not, I *don't* think it was all about fortune and fame. I think you were doing what you honestly felt Barbara would have wanted. And the *really* funny thing is that I agree with you. I think Barbara *would* have wanted you to protect Tracey, in spite of everything."

Vicki realized from the burning sensation in the middle of her breasts that she was holding her breath. "Then you understand why I had to do the things I did."

"No," Susan said quickly. "I'll never understand the things you did."

"You're talking about Chris," Vicki acknowledged, rubbing a budding headache away from her forehead. "Is she all right?"

"Well, let's see. She lost her job because of all the negative publicity, and she had to move out of her apartment. Plus her relationship with Montana is back at square one, and she can forget about ever seeing her kids again. But, hey, let's look at the bright side—a cold-blooded sociopath got off scot-free. So, why wouldn't she be all right?"

Vicki said nothing. What could she say?

"The extraordinary thing is that I think Chris really *is* all right. She'll find another apartment. She'll get another job. I think in time she might even find it in her heart to forgive you. You know Chris. She's very loyal to her friends."

Vicki felt the words stab at her heart. "And you? Can you forgive me? We've been through so much together."

"Yes, we have."

"I love you," Vicki said, tears returning to her eyes.

"I love you too."

"Will you ever forgive me?"

Susan walked to the office door. "Not a chance in hell."

Vicki was on her fourth glass of red wine when the doorbell rang. "Rosa," she called out before realizing her housekeeper had left at least an hour ago. What time was it anyway? She checked her watch, but the two hands were dancing back and forth across the diamond-circled dial, and she couldn't make out whether it was closer to eight o'clock or nine. Who would be dropping by without calling, no matter what time it was? She pushed herself off her dining room chair and stumbled toward the front door. Probably Jeremy or one of the kids. How many times did they have to be reminded to take their keys? Where was everyone anyway?

"Tracey!" Vicki said, opening her front door to the rosy-cheeked young woman, stepping back to allow her entry. What was she doing here?

"I probably should have called." Tracey shook the fine dusting of snow from the bottoms of her black boots, although she made no move to take off her heavy lambskin jacket.

"Is everything all right?"

"Great," Tracey replied easily, looking around. "Am I interrupting anything?"

Vicki waved away her concern with a tipsy hand. "Not a thing. Actually, I'm all alone. Jeremy's tied up in a meeting, and the kids are . . . somewhere." She laughed. She vaguely remembered Josh muttering something about hockey practice, and Kirsten was probably at the library. "You want a glass of wine?" Hell, Vicki thought, weaving her way back to the dining room, if the kid's old enough to kill her mother, she's old enough to have a drink.

Tracey followed after her. "Better not. I'm driving."

"Your father let you drive his precious Mercedes?" Vicki poured what little wine remained in the bottle into her glass.

"Actually, I'm driving my mother's car." Tracey giggled. "I guess it's mine now."

Vicki gulped at her wine.

"You have such a beautiful home."

"What brings you all the way out here?" Vicki plopped back into her chair, almost missing the burnt orange leather of its seat.

Tracey remained on her feet on the other side of the long, narrow table. She shrugged, as if she weren't quite sure what had brought her to Indian Hill. "I needed some air. It's so chaotic at my dad's house. The kids are always screaming. I think I might have to get a place of my own."

Vicki downed the rest of her wine.

"What happens to the house?" Tracey asked.

"The house?"

"My mother's house. Is it mine or my dad's? I know he still pays the mortgage and everything."

"I don't have a clue," Vicki told her impatiently, eager now to get the young girl out of her house. "You'd have to ask a lawyer."

"I *am* asking a lawyer."

"Sorry. Not my area of expertise." Vicki covered her nose with the now empty wineglass, inhaling its heavy musky scent. She debated going downstairs to the wine cellar and opening another bottle. Or maybe she'd just hit herself over the head with it. Knock herself unconscious. Hell, whatever gets you through the night.

"I guess I should go." Tracey smiled, went nowhere. "Are you gonna be okay?"

"Me? I'm fine. Thank you for asking."

" 'Cause you seem sort of . . ."

"Drunk?"

Again Tracey giggled.

God, what an annoying sound. "Tracey, do you mind if I ask you something?" Vicki heard herself ask.

"Shoot."

An unfortunate choice of words, Vicki thought, before plunging ahead, the room tilting slightly to the right. "Why did you kill your mother?"

Tracey swayed from one foot to the other. Or maybe it was Vicki's head that was swaying. She couldn't be sure. "You know."

"I know the case we presented to the jury."

"Then you know everything."

"I also knew your mother."

A look somewhere between boredom and consternation settled across Tracey's normally placid face. "What are you saying?"

"I'm saying that the jury's not here right now. The trial is over. The defendant has been exonerated."

"And I can't be tried again, isn't that right? No matter what?"

A feeling of queasiness curled around Vicki's stomach, like a cat in a basket. "That's right."

Tracey shrugged, studied the brass and crystal chandelier hanging above the dark, antique oak table. "Then you're right," she said easily. "My mother never molested me."

The room tilted violently on its side. Vicki gripped the sides of her antique chair, fought to stay upright, to keep from screaming. "You made the whole thing up?"

Again Tracey shrugged. "Well, not all of it. I mean, she *was* always touching me. You know how she was."

"I know your mother loved you more than anything else on earth."

"I loved her too."

Vicki closed her eyes, saw Barbara, Susan, Chris. Dear God, what had she done? "You loved her but you killed her for no reason."

"There was a reason."

"What was it?" Did this conversation make any sense? "Because you were jealous of her relationship with Howard?"

Tracey was already shaking her head. "It wasn't that."

"What was it?"

"You won't understand."

"No, I probably won't. But tell me anyway."

"I'm not sure I can explain." Tracey undid the top button of her winter jacket, fanned her face with her fingers, as if trying to get air into her lungs. "We were so close, it was almost like we were the same person sometimes. Like I didn't really exist when she wasn't around. Do you know what I mean?"

Vicki nodded, but in truth she had no idea what Tracey was talking about.

"It was so great after my dad left and it was just the two of us. We were always together. But then she met Howard, and everything changed. Suddenly she had this whole other life, and I was just . . . I don't know . . . I was nothing. It was like I didn't exist anymore. Like she'd stolen my breath away. And the only way I could get it back, the only way I could get my life back, was to kill her. Do you understand? I didn't want to hurt her. I just wanted my own life back."

Vicki's head was swimming. Had anything Tracey just said made any sense? "And now?" she asked, the words banging against the side of her skull. Like the club Tracey had wielded at her mother's head, Vicki thought, closing her eyes. "You feel nothing? No guilt? No remorse?"

There was a long pause. "I feel relief."

Oh, God.

A key twisted in the front-door lock. "Hello," Jeremy called out seconds later. "Anybody home?"

"In here." Vicki made no move to stand up, knowing she'd never make it to her feet.

Tracey smiled. "I should go. My dad'll start to worry. I can show myself out. Thanks again," she called back when she reached the hallway, then: "Hi there, Mr. Latimer. How are you?"

Ever the polite young woman, Vicki thought, as behind her the grandfather clock ticked away the minutes. Vicki pictured her father sitting in his bed, staring at the nursing-home walls. Was this how he spent his nights? she wondered. Counting the minutes till morning, praying for unconsciousness to overtake him?

"Vicki?" she heard her husband say. His voice was coming

from a far distance, although he appeared to be standing right in front of her. "Are you all right? Vicki?"

Vicki blinked, slowly nodded her head, thinking, He looks so old.

"Tracey seems like a very happy girl."

"Well, we certainly wouldn't want Tracey to be unhappy." Vicki held up the empty bottle of wine. "I've been celebrating. Why don't you get another bottle from downstairs and join me?"

Jeremy smiled sadly. "I'm not sure I'm up to celebrating tonight, darlin'."

Oh, God, him too, Vicki thought. What was *his* problem?

"I had an interesting meeting earlier this evening."

Vicki regarded him quizzically. Why was he talking about meetings?

"With Michael Rose."

Oh, God. Vicki felt her stomach drop to the floor. "You had a meeting with Michael? Why?"

"Trust me, it wasn't my idea. He showed up at my office, ambushed me as I was about to leave, gave me quite an earful."

"Well, I certainly hope you didn't take anything he had to say seriously. He's just angry and jealous and probably drunk."

"Probably. Still, he was pretty convincing."

Vicki stared into her husband's hurt and knowing eyes. Could she really insult him further by lying about her affair to his face? Hadn't she done enough damage already to the people she loved? "It didn't mean anything," she admitted, sobering up much faster than she would have liked.

"What does?" Jeremy asked simply.

"What?"

"I'm just starting to wonder, darlin', that's all."

Was he going to walk out on her? Vicki wondered, thinking that all her life people had been walking out on her. She could get their attention, she thought, but despite all the theatrics, she couldn't make them stay.

"Anyway, darlin', it's been a long day, and I'm tired. I'm goin' to bed." Jeremy paused. "You comin'?"

"Soon," Vicki said gratefully. "I'll be there soon."

Then she sank back against the stiff back of the antique dining-room chair, drifting in and out of consciousness, and listening to the grandfather clock behind her tick away the minutes till morning.

Epilogue

Almost nine years have passed since Barbara's death, eight years since the trial that sealed our fate once and for all. We have entered a new century, a new millennium. The years have passed quicker than I ever thought possible. So much has changed, although Grand Avenue remains essentially the same, at least on the outside. I still live here. I'm the only one left.

The film ends. Automatically, I press the rewind button, listen as the tape whirs quietly past my ears, like the hum of a dying fluorescent light. How many times have I watched this tape already today? Five? Six? Maybe more. I try not to think how many times I've watched it over the years. Must be hundreds. Birthdays, anniversaries, too many days in between. Still, I'm not ready to say good-bye to these young women I love and will love until the day I die. The Grand Dames, I say silently, almost like a prayer, as once again their faces fill the giant TV screen, and their laughter melts my heart. Can twenty-three years really have passed since that first afternoon? Is it possible? Why can't I let go?

The doorbell rings.

"Mom, the door!" a voice calls from upstairs.

"Can you get it, sweetie?" I ask. "It's probably for you."

Footsteps on the stairs. They sound like a herd of elephants, although it's only a twenty-one-year-old girl.

"Check who it is before you open the door," I call out, but it's already too late. I hear the door open. Soft voices wind through the small foyer toward the newly constructed "media room" to the left of the front hall. "Who is it, sweetie?" I ask as my daughter appears in the doorway.

"Someone for you." Delicate shoulders shrug. "She says she knows you."

I stop the film, watching the women freeze on the screen. I've become very adept at manipulating the VCR, which amazes me as much as it does the rest of my family. In fact, I'm the only one who knows how to program it so that it will tape something while we're away or asleep. I even know how to tape a show on one channel while watching something on another, and I am curiously, even alarmingly, proud of this accomplishment. "Did she give her name?" I ask, reluctant to push myself off the sofa.

Another shrug. I get to my feet, follow my daughter toward the front of the house.

Sitting all afternoon in my air-conditioned den, the drapes pulled, the room dark save for the light coming from the TV screen, I've forgotten how bright the day is, how warm the July sun, how fresh the outside air. It almost knocks me over in its rush to embrace me as I approach the door.

She is standing in the doorway, her face partially obscured by the shadow of a nearby weeping willow tree. She brings with her the scent of freshly cut flowers. I see a bouquet, like a baby, resting in her trembling arms. "Hi," she says simply, as my heart stops.

I open my mouth to speak, but no words come. What cruel trick of the imagination is this? I wonder. Have I been sitting in the darkness for so long that I'm starting to see ghosts, that I'm no longer able to differentiate between what is real and what is impossible?

"Mrs. Norman?" she asks, bringing me back to myself.

"Mom?" Whitney touches my arm. I feel the concern in her fingers.

"I guess you don't remember me. I'm Montana," she says, almost as if she isn't sure. Her voice has a nervous, breathy quality, quite unlike her mother's, but aside from that, the two women are almost identical. It is as if Chris has stepped out of my VCR, assumed solid form, run around to the front of the house, and now stands in front of me. It is as if I have pressed the wrong button and miraculously erased the last twenty-three years. "Can I come in?" she asks.

I step back to allow her entry. "Montana," I murmur, unable to say more.

She smiles, tucks her long blond hair behind her ears in a gesture remarkably similar to her mother's. "Actually, I prefer Ana. One *n*."

"Ana," I repeat, savoring the simple sound.

"I was never very comfortable with Montana." She looks at the flowers in her hands, as if noticing them for the first time, pushes them toward me. "These are for you."

"For me? Thank you."

"I'll put them in water," Whitney volunteers, sensing my inability to function at normal speed. "Why don't you guys go into the living room and sit down?" She points the way, as if I might have forgotten. Dutifully, I lead Montana—Ana, as she now prefers to be called—into the sun-filled room at the back of the house. From the kitchen, I hear water running in the sink.

"You have a lovely home," Ana says, sitting at the edge of one of two floral-print wingback chairs on either side of the never-used black marble fireplace.

Neither Owen nor I have the slightest interest in fireplaces, which suddenly strikes me as odd. We *look* like the kind of people who would like nothing better than throwing a few logs on the fire and sitting back to bask in its warm glow. The image is, admittedly, lovely. The reality is too much work. Neither of us can be bothered. It's easier to simply turn up the heat.

How often, I wonder, hesitating between a wing chair and the rose-colored sofa at right angles to it, are things what they seem?

Ultimately, I select the sofa. It takes several seconds to get comfortable. "Would you like something to drink? Water? Lemonade?"

"Nothing, thank you."

Seconds later, Whitney appears with the flowers neatly arranged in a deep crystal vase, deposits them on the glass coffee table in front of the sofa. "If you don't mind, I'm going to go back upstairs." She looks to the ceiling, as if this is explanation enough.

"It was nice seeing you again," Ana says as Whitney makes her exit. Then, lowering her voice: "I can't believe how grown-up she is."

I nod. I can't believe it either. Actually, I'm surprised Montana even remembers my younger daughter. It's been so long since she's seen her. "She'll be a senior this year."

Ana shakes her head with the kind of dulled amazement usually reserved for women decades her senior. She is only twenty-five, too young to be so aware of the passage of time. "What university?"

"Duke."

"Is that where Ariel went?"

"Ariel chose not to go to university," I say, trying to hold on to the smile in my voice. It still bothers me that my older daughter decided against a higher education, that she chose instead to marry a modern-day cowboy and move with him to a ranch outside Casper, Wyoming, where she is expecting my first grandchild in December. "It's so strange," I hear myself confiding. "I spent half my life working for a degree. I'm considered something of an authority on women's issues. I give speeches all over the country. I'm even writing a book . . ." I stop. What does this young girl care about an aging woman's résumé? "And I have this daughter," I continue, despite my best efforts, "this throwback to another era, who thinks it's romantic to be barefoot and pregnant."

"She might go back to school later."

"Easier said than done."

"You did it."

"You're right." I smile, feel better. "Anyway, what can you do? It's her life. Gotta let her live it."

"She'll be fine," Ana says with such certainty I find myself believing her. Then: "I hear Vicki's become quite the star."

My smile vanishes. "No surprise there."

"Do you ever watch her show?"

I shake my head. Four years ago, Vicki and her family took up residence in Los Angeles. Lately, she's become a fixture on Court TV and was recently anointed one of the fifty most beautiful people in the world by *People* magazine. The accompanying article said she'd recently been reunited with her mother. There was a photograph of the two of them together, and even though the picture was very small, the family resemblance was unmistakable. They each have the same thin face, the same ferocious intensity around the eyes. Vicki's hand was draped casually across her mother's shoulder, but I couldn't help but wonder if Vicki wasn't subconsciously trying to keep her mother from running away from her again. Owen said I was reading too much into the picture, and he's probably right. At any rate, I hope their reunion was everything Vicki wanted and needed, that her mother was everything she'd hoped her to be. I thought of calling her, wishing her well, decided against it. Some wounds are just too stubborn to heal.

"What about Tracey?" Ana asks. "Do you ever hear from her?"

"No, thank God. Last I heard she was acting in some off-Broadway play." I pause, momentarily overwhelmed by one of life's little ironies. "What about you? What brings you back to Cincinnati? Don't tell me you got tired of French cooking."

Chris's smile radiates from her daughter's heart-shaped face. "No, Paris is great. I can't imagine living anywhere else. And there's this guy I met . . ." The sentence stops, the words lingering like smoke from a cigarette. She rolls her eyes, laughs her mother's laugh.

"Have you seen your father?"

A frown creases Ana's forehead. "It's my brothers I came back to see."

"How are they?"

"They're doing okay. It's hard to tell. You know boys—they don't say much."

"I haven't seen Tony in years," I remark, speaking more to myself than the girl I once knew as Montana.

"He hasn't changed. He was in this car accident last year. It slowed him down a bit. He walks with a bit of a limp, but other than that . . ." She stops, takes a long, deep breath. "Tell me about my mother," she says softly.

I close my eyes, open them again, see Chris where her daughter sits. What can I say? "What do you want to know?"

Ana tilts her chin toward the ceiling, as if to prevent the tears growing in her eyes from releasing down her cheeks. "Everything."

I shake my head, still angry at yet another of life's bitter ironies. "About three years ago, I found a lump in my breast," I begin, feeling its shadow still. "My mother died of breast cancer some years back. I don't know if you remember that."

Ana nods respectfully.

"Anyway, the doctor scheduled a mammogram. I was terrified. Your mother volunteered to keep me company, then decided she might as well schedule a mammogram for herself. My lump turned out to be a harmless cyst. . . . "

"My mother wasn't so lucky," Ana whispers.

"Everything happened very fast after that. In less than two years, she was gone."

Ana stifles a small cry in the back of her throat. "I had no idea she was sick."

"We tried to contact you, but your father gave us the wrong address. Our letters all came back."

"Bastard," Ana says clearly under her breath. "All I got was a phone call after she died." She jumps to her feet, although once there, she doesn't move. "Although I really can't put all the blame on him, can I? It was *my* decision to cut her out of my life, *my* decision to take off for Europe."

"You were a confused young girl."

"I was a self-absorbed brat!"

"No," I tell her, longing to take her in my arms, afraid to overstep the invisible boundary between us. "You mustn't feel guilty. Your mother loved you. She was so proud of you."

"Why? What did I ever do to deserve her pride?"

"You were her daughter."

"Is that enough?"

Ariel's face, in all its assorted transformations, appears before me, growing from jealous toddler to rebellious teen to expectant mother in a fraction of an instant. "Yes," I say softly. "It's enough."

Ana wipes a tear from her cheek, sits back down. "Tell me about those two years. Did she suffer? Was she alone?"

"She didn't suffer," I tell Ana honestly. "She had wonderful doctors. They made sure her pain was minimal. And no, she wasn't alone. Her friend, Donna, was with her."

"Donna was the woman she lived with?"

"She met her when she worked for Emily Hallendale. Donna's a lovely woman. I think you'd like her."

"Do you have her phone number?"

I nod. "It's in the kitchen. I'll get it for you."

"Thank you."

It takes a while to locate Donna's number. My kitchen drawer is a mess of loose scraps of paper and old newspaper clippings. Of course there's an address book, but it's hopelessly out-of-date. I haven't written anything in it in years. So I'm forced to examine every torn envelope, every change-of-address card, until I find Donna's current address and phone number. Amazingly, it's right near the top of the pile, but I missed it the first time around. I close my fist around it, carry it back to the living room.

Ana isn't there.

A moment of panic ensues as I run to the front door. Has she left? Maybe I can still catch her. . . .

And then I hear her crying softly. I walk toward the sound, knowing exactly where I will find her.

She is standing in the doorway of my renovated den, now a full-fledged media room, with its impressive array of computers, stereo equipment, CD players, assorted speakers, and giant television screen. She is staring at her mother, only a few years older than Ana is now. I tiptoe into the room behind her, press the start button of the VCR, stand back and watch the women come to life. The camera pans jerkily from Chris to Barbara to Vicki. Barbara's face fills the screen as she grabs the camera, waves it in my direction, then returns to Chris's struggles trying to keep Montana on her lap.

Ana watches the child Montana kick angrily at her mother's ankles before sliding off her lap, the toddler's face awash with tears, as Ana's is now. Chris extends her arms, waits patiently for her daughter to come back. But Montana refuses her entreaties, remains stubbornly on the edge of the frame. "Come on, baby," Chris coos. "Be a good girl. Come to Mommy."

"Oh," Ana cries now, the word escaping her lips like a lover's sigh. Her arms lift from her sides, as if she is being pulled by gentle strings. She sways, floats toward the screen. Instinctively, I reach over, press the pause button, watch as Montana folds into her mother's waiting arms.

She's been waiting so long, I think, approaching quietly,

assuming Chris's place, drawing her daughter close. I feel Ana's legs give way, her body collapse into mine. We cry together, both of us embracing a memory, taking unexpected comfort in one another.

If life is the choices we make, as my mother once told me, then too much of life is spent bemoaning those choices. Too much time is wasted on regret. We can do nothing with the past but acknowledge and accept it. It is over. Done with. It is gone.

But if I am no longer the young woman I see laughing with her friends on my giant TV, I know she hasn't disappeared altogether, that she is still a part of me. Sometimes I see her winking at me through tired eyes when I look into the mirror. Sometimes I feel her pulling my shoulders back when I'd rather slouch. She pushes my fingers when I write, selects the words I speak. She is the voice of my youth, of all I hold dear and close to my heart, and she is still whispering in my ear.

She is my friend.

Who says life has to make sense? That it owes us any explanations? Perhaps there is no such thing as justice. Perhaps there will never be peace. Or resolution.

But there is hope, I think, hugging Ana to me, embracing all that was and all that will be.

And there is love.